To Be Determined

By the Authors

Mardi Alexander & Laurie Eichler:

To Be Determined

Mardi Alexander:

Twice Lucky

Spirit of the Dance

Laurie Eichler:

Written as Laurie Salzler:

A Kiss Before Dawn

Right Out of Nowhere

Positive Lightning

In the Stillness of Dawn

To Be Determined

by

Mardi Alexander & Laurie Eichler

2017

TO BE DETERMINED

ISBN 13: 978-1-62639-946-4

This Trade Paperback Original Is Published By
Bold Strokes Books, Inc.
P.O. Box 249
Valley Falls, NY 12185

First Edition: August 2017

Credits
Editor: Ruth Sternglantz
Production Design: Susan Ramundo
Cover Design By Sheri (graphicartist2020@hotmail.com)

Acknowledgments

Mardi Alexander:

What an adventure and what a fun ride this story has been writing with my friend Laurie. I don't have adequate enough words to thank you for taking an enormous leap of faith and collaborating on this story. It hasn't felt like work, not once. It's been a bucket load of enormous, amazing, weirdly coincidental moments, exciting spontaneity, and fun. It's been a real gift and for that I will be forever grateful. xx

A big thank you to Renee and Hayley—your enthusiasm, help, advice, and inspiration guided this story from day one. You girls rock. xx

To all the crew at BSB, to Rad for giving us the nod, for Sandy and Ruth who both pushed to make us, and the story, better—thank you.

To my gorgeous Flamingoes—you are just the best kind of crazy wonderful. To Karen for being our sounding board, our proof-reader extraordinaire, and for dragging us off to fish and clear our heads. Love you guys to bits.

And finally, to Michelle, who helps me be all the things I need to be. Cheers to you, babe. xxx

Laurie Eichler:

Who knew? I'd never considered writing a book with someone else, let alone someone from a different country. But somehow, over several glasses of fine whiskey, wine, and bottles of beer (not necessarily during one get-together, but we never ruled that out), and many hours of conversation that rarely had anything to do with writing, Mardi & I decided to have a go at it. What we ultimately discovered, and frankly, what surprised the heck out of both of us, was that not only could we write together, but we also fell in love with the characters, storyline, and had a helluva lot of fun doing it.

We created such a seamless story that by the final read before submitting it, who wrote what was often questioned.

I can't even express the fun and enjoyment I have when collaborating with you, Mardi. You have put the fun back into writing lesfic for me. And for that, and so many other things, I thank you from the bottom of my heart. xx

To Rad, Sandy, Ruth, and numerous other members of BSB, thank you for accepting me into your clan. I believe Mardi & I will have several more stories for you.

To the readers who follow me as Laurie Salzler, thank you for wanting more from me. I hope you enjoy the new direction.

There are a few close friends who know what they mean to me. You all keep me going and give me the hope and confidence to do what I do.

Dedication

To all the animals that enter our lives, past, present, and future—to know, love, and care for you is both a gift and a great honor. We look forward to carrying your legacies forward for many, many years to come. This one's for you, Roothie and EmmyRoo.

Chapter One

"Ladies and gentlemen, please ensure your seat belts are secure, your tray tables locked in the correct position, and your seats upright. The captain has indicated we'll be landing shortly."

Charlie Dickerson opened her eyes and squinted against the glaring morning sun streaming through her window. The white reflection of open water over which they were still flying beat against her tired brain. She barely noticed the monotony of the plane's engine any more.

She'd slept somewhat fitfully during the fourteen-hour flight from Los Angeles. Excitement and nerves kept her awake, while exhaustion and boredom allowed her to sleep intermittently. Her neck and back were stiff and achy. She longed to stretch her legs and get the blood pumping with a nice long walk. Soon, she reminded herself. She'd have to call on all of her patience, which was something she had very little of these days.

The seat next to her was empty so she hadn't been forced to make nice with anybody, except the cute flight attendant who brought her a cup of tea and a package of miniscule chocolate cookies every couple of hours.

She couldn't believe it. After years of suppressing a childhood dream, she was finally going to Australia. She exhaled a deep breath. Although the opportunity had arisen out of the blue, she still battled the apprehension of doing it on her own. The burning tingling began over her scalp and flowed down her body right on cue. Sweat oozed from her brow and suddenly the plane felt too closed-in. She pulled her shirt away from her chest and fanned herself until she felt cool again. *Fucking anxiety attack.*

At first she had suspected they were the dreaded hot flashes that came with middle age. But her shrink said differently. After a few sessions of analysing them, they'd discovered that they happened every time she thought about the demise of her fifteen-year relationship. She was suddenly on her own, had to make her own decisions, had to make a new life.

She shook her head, determined to focus on what lay ahead. She certainly didn't want to meet the director of WREN reeking of stale body odour. Gooseflesh peppered her skin. Blowing out a heavy breath, she reached up and redirected the flow of air from the panel above. She hated the temperature fluctuations of her body. And Australia was going into their summer. Which meant heat. Lots of it. *Great. Just great.*

The portfolio she'd been sent was tucked into the seat pocket in front of her. She'd read it so many times she could nearly recite the entire thing word for word. WREN stood for Wildlife Rescue and Environmental Network. Based in Sydney, there were branches all over New South Wales and the organization was devoted to rescuing, rehabilitating, and releasing native wildlife. While most of the rescuers were volunteers, they had a couple one-year work-study positions available, one of which she had been accepted for.

On a whim, she'd applied online when she'd discovered the internal posting for the employee foreign exchange opportunity. Her counterpart from Australia was on his way to her home office at the Wildlife Rehabilitation Service in Cody, Wyoming. She didn't know where in New South Wales she'd be going though. Terese Skeel, WREN's director, would inform her of the destination and her assignment in—she checked her watch—three hours.

Forward focus, Charlie. Forward focus.

❖

Pip Atkins balanced precariously in the verandah doorway on one leg, trying to pull her boot off the other. At the same time she juggled three feeding bottles, a bag of soiled linen, and a cotton rucksack in her arms, whose contents were wriggling determinedly.

The phone rang.

"Hang on!" She hopped about, flicked off the boot, and finally caught her balance. But only fleetingly. She lost her footing when her socks hit the kitchen lino surface and she clumsily skidded across the floor.

"Shit."

As she reached for the phone and activated the speaker, one of the bottles toppled free of her grip to hit the floor where the top popped off, spilling its contents. A wriggling grey velvet head poked its nose out of the bag as her foot slid into the spilled milk. Her feet flew out from under her.

"Oh, for fuck's sake!"

"Hello? Pip? Is that you?"

She landed unceremoniously on her arse with a grunt as her teeth clacked together. She grimaced as she felt the milk soaking into the seat of her trousers. "Bloody hell."

The kangaroo joey, fully emerged from the bag, blinked its long black eyelashes at her. When it shook its head, its long soft ears slapped awkwardly against the sides of its face. It stretched up to nuzzle and suck her chin.

"Pip? You okay?"

Looking into the joey's big, soft brown eyes, she couldn't stay mad for long, even if she *was* sitting in a puddle of milk and surrounded by soiled and smelly linen. "Hello, Terese. This had better be good."

"And good morning to you too. What happened just then?"

Disengaging herself from the joey's soft lips, she gently guided the tiny marsupial back into the dark recesses of the bag and tucked the folds of cloth over to block out the light. She absent-mindedly rubbed the underside of the makeshift pouch in a mutually soothing motion. A wry half grin pulled at her lips ever so briefly. "Gravity and I had a quick get together."

"You okay?"

"Yup, all good. To what do I owe the pleasure of this early morning call?"

"I need a favour."

Pip squinted with suspicion. "Why do I get the impression I'm not going to like it?"

"Look, normally I wouldn't ask, but plans this end have fallen through with Jerry breaking a hip. You've got the ideal set up, and with the silly season upon us, you're the best person to hook up with."

"A hook up with what?"

"An American exchange partner for the program."

"*What?*"

"You'll be great—you're a natural."

Through clenched teeth she tried to manage a calm voice. "How long for?"

"Just remember, you owe me."

A growl started low in her throat. "How. Long."

"A year."

"You have *got* to be joking."

"Nope, sorry."

"And what if I don't want to babysit a Yank?"

"Then you'll need to get over it. You know I wouldn't ask if I wasn't desperate."

She and Terese had known each other for many years, so she recognized the unspoken stress easily enough in her voice to know she spoke the truth. And dammit if she wasn't right. She owed her good friend big time and payback was on the other end of the line.

"I know." She sighed. Her shoulders sagged slightly with the effort. "Doesn't mean I have to like it though."

"Well, you'll just have to get over it."

"And why's that?"

"Because we'll see you tomorrow. Bye."

Pip stared open-mouthed at the phone as the buzzing dial tone mocked her.

❖

Charlie righted her overstuffed bag on wheels and shook her hand to regain blood flow to her fingers. She shifted her weight from one foot to the other, getting more impatient by the minute. There were people lined up everywhere waiting to be admitted through customs and border control. *Freakin' hell. Did all the planes land in Sydney at once?*

The family in front of her had eight suitcases and four children, who all seemed to talk at once. The parents apparently were used to the constant chatter, which seemed more noise to Charlie than anything.

There was a time when she'd thought about having kids. Well, one anyway. But it never seemed to fit into her lifestyle. She'd regretted it several times when she saw the fun her brother had with his two kids and then later when she thought they'd be good slave labour when there was work to do in the garden and the house needed cleaning. She was always able to justify her decision when she was able to go home to her dogs. They could be left alone for a few hours, were happy to eat dry kibble out of a bowl on the floor, and for the most part, they were quiet. She could toss them a bone and they'd entertain themselves without television, video games, and endless piles of toys.

There was obvious commotion as the family moved their heap of belongings forward when a customs officer directed them to a different line.

"Do you have an e-passport, miss?" The official's voice brought her to attention.

"Yes." Thankfully she'd renewed her passport a few months prior and when it was returned, there was a little gold camera on the front. A little research on her end had confirmed it.

The officer rerouted her and several others to a different line. She merely had to insert her passport into a machine and answer a few questions. Thinking she was free and clear she walked around a corner only to find she was in another line. She peered around the people in front of her and watched as the contents of a suitcase were dumped onto a table. An Asian man complained as his belongings were sifted through. *Good grief.* She mentally went through her baggage to make sure she was carrying nothing illegal. *I wonder how they'll feel about my knife.* Her dad had given her the Buck knife when she graduated from college. It'd been her grandfather's and she carried it everywhere.

The knife had come in handy over the years from cutting fishing line, to freeing a tortoise, to prying porcupine quills out of her boots. Then there was the time she had to whittle a spear to ward off a wolverine when he tried to claim the dead moose she was collecting data on. Or the time when—

"Miss, you can go on through."

Charlie looked up in surprise. She'd been so engrossed in her thoughts she'd barely noticed the line had moved more efficiently than the last. She nodded her thanks and breathed a huge sigh of relief, glad that was over with.

There were several well-dressed stewards waiting just outside the gate. They held boldly lettered name-cards. Some had already collected their passengers. Of course Charlie didn't recognize a single soul. She paused to see if any of the signs had her name written on them. *Nope. Okay. Now what?*

"Charlene! Over here. Charlene Dickerson." A white card rose briefly from the back and disappeared. It popped into view again and Charlie realized whoever held it had to be jumping up and down. She wove her way through the crowd and nearly ran over the woman who'd been beckoning to her.

"Oh, geez. I'm sorry." Charlie took a step back and considered her.

She had a robust frame but was by no means fat, although because of her height one could mistakenly assume it. Laugh wrinkles complemented her slate-coloured eyes set in a lovely tanned face. The thin blouse and shorts that reached just past her knees matched her feathered cut grey hair.

"I'm so glad you're finally here, Charlene. I saw your plane had arrived and got here as soon as I could. Bloody Sydney traffic. Then I'd forgotten what a drama customs could be. Anyway, welcome to

Australia. I'm Terese Skeel, but you've probably already figured that out." She extended a hand, which Charlie took and shook.

Charlie grimaced. "Trust me. I thought I'd never get out of those lines. I'm so pleased to meet you, and please, call me Charlie. I've been called Charlie for so long, I don't recognize myself when someone calls me Charlene."

"Charlie it is then. Let's get you out of here so you can put your feet onto some real Australian soil."

The heat and humidity soaked through her clothes as soon as she stepped outside the terminal. She instantly regretted wearing jeans and not the zip-off pants she'd originally planned, but that would've made for a cold flight. She unzipped her sweatshirt and wiggled her way out of it as they walked.

"Plans have changed slightly," Terese said after paying the parking fee. "I was originally going to partner you up with Jerry, but he broke a hip. Bit of a shame, as it would've been quite convenient, given he's only half an hour away, in Paramatta. But anyway, Pip'll actually be better because she has a lot more varied hands-on contact than Jerry. When it comes to native animals, there's not much Pip doesn't know. So we'll be heading up there first thing in the morning."

"Okay. Whatever works. I'm easy." She was already fascinated with Terese's Australian accent.

Terese cocked her head and smiled. "Don't tell Pip that. Anyway, are you okay with going straight to your hotel and having a rest? I'd like to get an early start, to get you up there and settled before I drive back to Sydney."

Charlie noted the fast change in subject. "Sure. How far of a drive is it?"

"Oh, not far. 'Bout eight hours north."

"Wow."

"Australia's a lot bigger than most people realize. If you like wide-open spaces, then you'll love it here."

❖

A couple of days she could do, a week she wouldn't mind too much, and a month would be tough but tolerable, but a whole year? What was Terese thinking? Okay, granted, she owed Terese for saving her bacon, but being tied to someone for a whole year, let alone a bloody American, was really pushing the envelope of friendship. Surely after this they had to be even.

While cleaning out the cockatoo cage, the birds sensed her mood and screeched noisily. Her favourite, Old Bill, who had seen one too many TV reruns, looked at her with his head cocked sideward. "How *you* doin'?"

"Crap. How you doin', Bill?"

"*Goood.*" He jigged up and down on the makeshift branch.

Pip grumbled, "Nice to know one of us is." She pushed the broom in short, sharp movements around the pen.

Old Bill was reportedly forty-three. He had come into her care after his original owner had died. He had an undershot jaw and palsy in one of his wings, meaning he could never fend for himself in the wild. Under normal circumstances Pip didn't keep pets, much preferring to release native creatures back into their natural habitats, whenever possible. But Old Bill had been hand raised and had never learned to fend for himself. He was also a natural show-off so he was not only easy to care for, but a good assistant on the rare occasions when she would help out at community educational training sessions offered by WREN.

Pip wasn't so much a hermit as an individual who preferred animal company over human any day of the week. Unlike her experience with people, she'd never met an animal she didn't like. She had a small circle of friends, including Terese, but preferred the simplicity and quiet of her own company. Being on her own was safer with no one to influence, coerce, manipulate, or use her.

Home was a large two hundred and fifty acre bush block that bordered a national park and was twenty minutes drive from the nearest town, nestled between a large freshwater creek and timbered hillsides. Her nearest neighbour was a good five-minute walk down the road. There were several homes along her stretch of road, and all of the residents were well acquainted with each other, with seasonal get-togethers at Christmas and the onset of spring. Mostly they kept each to themselves, all of them enjoying the peace and serenity that the rural lifestyle afforded them. Pip could go days without seeing and talking to anyone and that was exactly how she liked it.

She screwed her nose up briefly as she laid out fresh bedding in the wallaby pen, not relishing the thought of being stuck with someone chattering away in her face, getting in the road, following her around like a shadow. Her mood darkened and a hint of suffocation wafted close in the air. Closing her eyes she took a deep breath. She took another, and willed herself to relax. She was out of the habit of dealing with people full-time. Still, they weren't here. No point wasting any more time fretting over what wasn't here yet.

She opened her eyes and glanced at her watch. She figured she could be finished with chores by ten. Time would afford a drive into town to pick up some fresh supplies and spend the afternoon at the beach, sitting on the headland, the wind and water guaranteed to calm her ruffled feathers. It had been a while since she and Chilli, her faithful Labrador, had dipped their toes into the salty water. She sniffed, then figured it might be a while before they got another chance to do so. Stretching her shoulders to relieve the build-up of tension, she smiled at Chilli.

"Wanna go for a drive later on?" The dog's tail wagged. "Fancy sharing fish and chips on the beach?"

Chilli barked in seeming agreement.

"Righto then, let's get this lot sorted so we can head on out." Cleaning up the last of the pens, she put the equipment away, humming in anticipation of the day's plan as she and Chilli headed back to the house to get changed.

❖

Charlie breathed a sigh of relief when Terese finally navigated the small truck off the chaotic streets of Sydney. They'd encountered bumper-to-bumper traffic at every turn. It did her head in with the busyness. Having lived in the foothills of the Rocky Mountains for the past umpteen years, she'd never seen such congestion. Unless, she thought, you counted the annual elk migration through town.

"I can't even imagine putting up with traffic like this every day." She rubbed the stiffness out of her neck. "I think I'd go nuts, or at the very least be part of some road-rage incident."

Terese laughed. "You get used to it. But I will admit there are days I'd love to leave it all behind and go walkabout."

Terese didn't elaborate further and Charlie didn't ask. It seemed this Pip was some kind of character. Whether or not she could get along with such a person was yet to be determined.

Although she was an introvert by nature, she found most people navigated in her direction. Fortunately that usually only occurred on a professional level when she was involved with some sort of wildlife project. On a personal level, she would much rather be left alone with her dogs. When she and Kim had first gotten together, Kim had accepted her need to periodically have big space around her. But as the years went by, Kim eventually grew tired of being alone while Charlie was off in her head, or deep in the mountains.

Charlie's dad had been the biggest influence in her youth. He'd instilled in her his love of the outdoors by taking her hiking nearly every weekend. She fondly recalled accompanying him into the wilds of Montana in pursuit of the elusive wolverine.

"Are you originally from Wyoming?" Terese said, interrupting her thoughts.

"I was born in New Hampshire. Once my mother and I were discharged from the hospital we left for Montana. My dad had to start school at the university in Helena the following week."

"Right. What was his major?"

Charlie chuckled. "My mother used to ask him that all the time. By the time he finished his doctorate in wildlife management, he also had degrees in botany, Latin, and ornithology. She never knew which one he was working on from one year to the next."

"Sounds like your father is a very smart man."

"Brilliant, actually. And was." Charlie paused for a moment. "He died when I was fourteen, doing what he loved. He was up in

Saskatchewan assisting a study of the impact snow geese have on the tundra."

"Where is that?"

"Oh, sorry. Canada."

"No worries. You may find that most Australians are more familiar with Indonesia and the UK than with the US and Canada."

"Mm, I get that. Other than Canada, Australia is the only foreign country I've been to. There's a lot of North America to explore and I guess I've been content to stay within those boundaries."

"I'm sorry about the loss of your father by the way."

"Thanks." Charlie was grateful she hadn't been asked to describe the circumstances of his death.

She gazed out the window and watched a variety of landscapes rush by hour by hour. As they travelled north of Sydney she watched, fascinated, as the landscape changed. Coastal communities morphed into pastoral and dairy cattle farms, only to change the further north they went into banana plantations that slid up the hillsides. As they continued the land flattened, and herds of beef cattle grazed within miles of barbed-wire fencing. Every once in a while she'd get glimpses of the Pacific Ocean to the east. The amount of state forest land they drove through impressed her. But her biggest amusement was trying to mentally pronounce some of the names on the road signs. Charlie assumed places like Boolambayte, Coolongolook, and Nymboida had Aboriginal roots. She wasn't brave enough to try to say them out loud.

"Wow, is that all sugar cane?" Charlie stared out at the thick expanse of tall green stalks that lined both sides of the road for as far as she could see ahead.

"Yes. This is about the furthest south you'll see it growing. There's a lot more of it the further north we go."

Charlie laughed. "I have to get my head around the fact that weather from the south will be cool, and hot from the north."

"Ah, it's the other way around where you're from, isn't it?"

"It sure is. I stay as far north of the equator as possible."

Terese threw her a sideways look. "How do you think you'll handle the heat? The temperatures might not get as high as some of the places inland, like Lightning Ridge or Broken Hill, because you'll be close to the ocean. But the heat and humidity can still ramp up and knock you for six during summer."

Charlie shrugged and smiled. "I guess I'll deal with it when it comes then."

She wasn't a stranger to harsh climates. However the extreme temperatures in her experience had always been in the minus-degrees Fahrenheit.

"Take my advice. Whatever you do and wherever you go, make sure you always have plenty of water with you. And don't let Pip argue with you about eating. You both have to keep your energy up when it's hot, even when you don't feel like putting anything in your mouth except a cold drink. So always have some food within reach. Have I made myself clear?"

"Yes, ma'am." Charlie glanced over at Terese. Her words, although light, seemed to have been chosen deliberately and delivered in a serious tone. She wondered if there was something about Pip she wasn't telling her.

In an effort to lighten the mood, Charlie decided to try to get Terese to talk about herself. She'd noticed the engagement and wedding rings on her left hand.

"Is your husband involved in wildlife rescue as well?"

Terese loosened her grip on the steering wheel and twirled the rings around her finger with her thumb. "Only when he had to be. That is, whenever I brought something home with me. Derek's involvement went as far as cleaning cages and doing laundry. He liked seeing the animals more than handling them."

Terese looked at Charlie and must have seen the confused look on her face as she'd spoken of him in past tense.

"The big goof was a thrill seeker. His biggest love was skydiving and that's what killed him. The lines on his chute ripped off and he free fell for the last hundred metres."

"Oh God." Charlie covered her gaping mouth with her hand. "I'm so sorry. That had to have been terrifying for him."

Terese surprised her by laughing. "I would've screamed until the ground shut me up. But according to witnesses on the ground, he started yelling, *It's not a bird, it's not a plane, look out everybody, it's...*"

"It's...?"

"Well he hit the ground right then, so nobody knows what he was going to say."

Charlie couldn't help herself. Despite being horrified by the story, she barked out a laugh. "I'm sorry." She tried to keep from dropping into complete hilarity by pushing her fist tightly against her mouth, but it was difficult.

Terese threw her head back and laughed. "No worries. I'm sure Derek knew he wasn't going to walk or even crawl out of that tight spot. It was just like him to keep everyone wondering. He was always the prankster. When I received the phone call, I was sure it was one of his jokes. Even after his death he couldn't keep from pulling tricks."

"Oh?" Charlie raised her eyebrows and bit her lip in anticipation.

"Per his wishes, he wanted to be cremated and have his ashes spread from a plane. So up I went, with him in his little box. The pilot was a friend of his, so he offered to help carry out his last wish. After the crew harnessed me in so I wouldn't meet the same fate as my husband, they opened the hatch and, despite my terror, I leaned out and opened the box with all the romantic intentions of letting him blow away. But of course Derek had to have the last laugh. Instead of being swept away, his ashes blew back in my face."

"Oh no."

"Oh yes. And right into my mouth. I told the bastard that was the last time he was going to come in my mouth and tossed the box out and made them close the door."

Charlie completely lost it at that point. All the laughter she'd tried so hard to hold back came pouring out. When Terese cleared her throat and pretended to spit, it made it all the more funny.

The remainder of the trip was much the same. Terese relayed stories of her late husband's pranks. By the time Terese signalled to exit the highway, Charlie's face and stomach burned and ached from laughing.

Terese called Pip from the car and when she answered, Charlie heard her voice for the first time.

"Hello."

"Pip, darling, we're about twenty minutes out. I wanted to give you fair warning to make sure you were home."

"I'm in the middle of feeding."

"Okay. I'll let you go then. See you soon."

There was silence on the other end. Charlie assumed Pip had hung up. Her palms suddenly grew sweaty. This Pip person sounded like a...well, like a bitch. She hoped she was wrong.

Chapter Two

Chilli heard the car before Pip did and offered up a cheerful series of barks. Despite her nervousness, she couldn't help but chuckle at Chilli's enthusiasm. "Go on. Go and say hello to your Aunt Terese."

The dog bounded off, tail rotating helicopter fashion in excitement towards the sound of tyres crunching on the gravel driveway.

With a garden hose trailing behind her, Pip leaned over to turn off the tap and wrap the plastic length around a stump. Neat and tidy, an important philosophy she lived by. She just hoped this newcomer wasn't a slob. Caring for and raising wildlife centred around good housekeeping principles to reduce opportunities for infection to arise. She was a stickler for cleanliness—cleanliness was healthy, safe, ordered, and something she could control.

She stood still and took a quick deep breath for courage as she heard the squeak of the side gate opening. Approaching footsteps morphed into bodies coming around the corner of the house: Terese smiling, Chilli dancing with excitement beside her, and a tall, dark curly-haired woman who stopped slightly behind.

Terese opened her arms and enveloped Pip, holding her tight against her before relinquishing her grip. She held her at arm's-length before turning her around for a full scrutiny. "You need a haircut and you're too skinny."

"And you look revoltingly unruffled and fresh, considering your long drive, and I've missed you too."

Terese chuckled and gave her a last quick hug before letting her be. She turned and extended her arm to the woman standing behind her. "Charlie, this is Pip Atkins, one of our busiest and most experienced members. Pip, this is Charlene"—Terese held a hand up in apology—"sorry, *Charlie* Dickerson, on exchange from the Wildlife Rehabilitation Service in Wyoming, America."

"Hello." Pip held a hand out and was pleased to be greeted with a solid handshake. *Huh, one tick in your favour for a good grip.*

"Nice to meet you. Thank you for taking me under your wing while I'm here. It's a big ask and I am most grateful. In return, I promise to try and not get in your way, but to learn as much as I can, to help out as much as I can, and hopefully get lots of hands-on experience."

Pip regarded her with one slightly raised eyebrow. *She's sharp, this one. She might have some potential. Two ticks in your favour.*

Chilli nudged her thigh, sat in front of her, and looked up. Her hand drifted down habitually to caress the big square blonde head.

"I was going to show you around first up, but I think maybe some afternoon tea might be in order, considering your long drive."

Knowing that Terese was staring at her, Pip did her best to ignore her and turned to her guest. "If you'll all follow me."

Pip led them up the back step and into the cool house, stopping briefly to leave her gumboots at the back door.

Once inside she put the kettle on to boil on an old but serviceable slow-combustion stove. She waved to a small round dining table set with plates and mugs. "I just need to wash up. Terese, you know where the fridge is—can you grab out the fruit plate and milk please? I'll be back in a jiff." Chilli followed attentively behind her.

The pair returned several minutes later just as the kettle signalled it had come to the boil. With an economy of movement Pip produced both a plunger of fresh coffee and a pot of tea to the table. "I have some cool water and juice if you'd prefer."

Charlie shook her head. She closed her eyes and sniffed appreciatively at the coffee steam. "This will be perfect, thank you."

Pip retrieved a covered plate from the cupboard and placed a plate of cupcakes onto the table. "Don't think I didn't see your nose scrunch up at the fruit, Terese."

Terese dived on a cupcake and tore into it, humming with delight. "And that, Charlie, is why I keep Pip as one of my oldest and dearest friends—because she knows too much." A comfortable chuckle went around the table.

Pip rested her elbows on the edge of the table and cradled a mug of tea between her hands in front of her face. She studied Charlie as she tasted some of the local fruits. The American had big square hands with long tapered fingers that spoke of both strength and eloquence in their fine motor movements, supported by strong wrists and corded forearms that didn't appear shy to hard work, and long arms that swept up to join her lean frame. As her eyes rose to study the face, hazel eyes caught her scrutiny and held hers, steady in a wordless challenge before Pip looked away and sipped her tea.

"You can have your choice of either the spare room here at the house, or the cabin by the creek. If you're anything like me, you'll enjoy the cabin. It's only a short walk away, close as to be handy, but away enough to be private and to have your own space."

"Okay," Charlie said over the top of her mug.

Terese picked the crumbs of cake off her plate with a damp fingertip and stuck them in her mouth. "I can personally vouch for the cabin. I came and stayed up here with Pip for a few months, after Derek died. It's a truly beautiful and peaceful place and if you want to get to know the Australian bush, well, you'll be surrounded by it."

"It sounds perfect, thank you."

Pip tilted her head to one side. "Righto then, I'll take you down directly and leave you to settle in. Dinner will be back here at seven. I've taken the liberty of buying you in a few groceries to kick-start you. There's a writing pen and pad on the table—feel free to make a list of the things you want, and we'll take a run into town and go shopping in the next day or two."

"That's very kind, thank you."

"No problems. All part of the service."

"So what sort of creatures do you have in your care at the minute?"

Pip did a quick mental check. "I've got three eastern grey joeys, two wallabies, four possums, sixteen various birds, and two koalas."

"Oh, geez. That sounds busy."

Pip huffed softly. "The silly season hasn't started yet. I expect things'll pick up in a couple of weeks. You'll have your hands full soon enough. Can you drive?"

"Yes."

"Manual or automatic?"

"If by manual you mean stick shift, then yes, I can do either."

"How about motorbikes?"

"It's been a while, but yes."

"Good, good. We'll go out on rescues initially together, but before the year is up I expect you to be doing solo runs."

Charlie agreed with a wave of acknowledgement.

"Well, if we're finished up here then, let's go and pick up your gear and get you settled in."

❖

Charlie reached into the truck bed to retrieve the two suitcases. She mentally cringed. An entire year with this woman. She wasn't sure what to make of Pip, although the fact that she appeared to be in her late forties might help them find some common ground, aside from the animals. She'd already witnessed the flash of Pip's blue eyes beneath her sun-bleached shaggy brown hair.

"Nah, just leave them in there. It's too far to drag them." Terese opened the truck door on the right side and got in, which momentarily confused Charlie again, until she remembered the Australian vehicles were opposite those in the US. That was going to take some getting used to.

Pip offered a half wave. "I'll meet you down there."

"Okay." Charlie watched as Pip and her dog disappeared into the woods, and then took her seat in the truck.

"Pip'll warm up to you. She's just used to being on her own." Terese turned the ignition.

"And doing things her way no doubt."

"Look, don't we all?"

Charlie pondered Terese's reply. She was right. In so many respects, it came naturally. She'd spent a lot of years studying and working with wildlife. Professionally she had developed her own discipline of behaviour. God forbid anybody tried to make her deviate from what she knew to be correct.

Terese started the truck and pointed it down a barely visible narrow dirt path. High grass in the middle of the tyre path scraped the undercarriage, while low-hanging leaved branches and ferns scraped the roof and sides.

After several minutes, the front of the truck finally broke through the vegetation and the cabin came into view. It looked to Charlie like they'd just driven into a different world. Large smooth-barked trees with high canopies took over as far as she could see. Their bark was mottled and ribbons of dead bark hung from various parts. The newly exposed bark was smooth and brightly coloured with orange and yellow. On some, it seemed the colours had weathered to a mottled grey.

"Wow."

Terese chuckled. "That's what I say every time I rock through here. The colour schemes and bark textures are always changing."

"What species are these trees?"

"They're eucalypts, but you'd probably know them better as gum trees."

"They're beautiful. No wonder the kookaburras like to sit in them." Charlie winked at Terese as she made a play on the childhood song.

"That's exactly right." Terese parked next to the cabin. "Here we are. Your humble abode for the next year. It doesn't look like much from the outside. Pip built it so it would blend in with its surroundings. But the inside is divine."

Charlie got out and studied the building. It was built on a hillside and completely supported on stilts. Wide slabs of nearly black wood comprised the siding. Moss coated the eaves, contrasting nicely against the portion of the dark-toned tin roof that she could see. A magnificent staghorn fern clung to a large tree, level with the window. A ramp with a barely discernable incline over a lot of air led to the front door. Charlie figured the drop to be about twenty feet. Fortunately a sturdy railing was attached on both sides. A window looked out on either side and an overhang protected the entrance.

Charlie marvelled at the quiet, but for the rustle of the leaves overhead, disturbed by a soft breeze. Cicadas buzzed in the background reminding her of late summers in Wyoming.

"We'll just wait for Pip and Chilli to get here. I'm actually surprised they're taking this long."

As if on cue, the front door opened and Chilli bounded out to greet them. Pip stood in the doorway. Charlie thought she looked less than enthused.

"There you are! You should have left the door open to let us know you were in there." Terese reached into the back of the truck and lifted out one of Charlie's suitcases.

"I had to turn the pump on for the water tank and make sure the solar panels were charging over here."

Charlie nodded her approval. "You're really off the grid here. I'm impressed."

"Don't be. It's more a state of necessity. I'm too far out to be connected to town water or have the electricity put on. So I rely on solar and, when we have a streak of cloudy days, a generator."

"Oh. Okay." Charlie lowered the larger suitcase to the ground and extended the handle so she could wheel it behind her. She followed Terese across the ramp and through the front door.

When Charlie walked in, her mouth dropped. The interior looked nothing like the exterior. In fact, the inside of the cabin looked more like a suburban home.

Although the interior was painted white, it was very stylishly decorated. The main feature however was the trunk of a gum tree growing through the floor and extending through the highest part of the cabin. The ceiling was painted to look like a canopy of leaves with glimpses of branches.

"Wow," Charlie whispered. "Is that a living tree?"

Terese laughed. "Sure is. Put your suitcase down and have a gander. I need to work out a few things with Pip."

Charlie needed no further encouragement. The door on the far end drew her forward. She opened it and walked onto a wide porch that extended out and wrapped around the left corner. She looked beyond the immediate trees and realized she was overlooking what seemed to be miles of canopy. A flock of white parrots screeched and carried on as they darted in and out. She made a mental note to ask Pip what they were.

She turned around and looked inside from the doorway. The tree impressed her again. A thick circle of what looked like rubber surrounded it where it rose out of the floor, probably to give it room to grow. The ceiling was adapted identically.

A small kitchen area was to her left. The granite benches were wide and there was plenty of storage space. The stove and refrigerator sat at opposite ends of the benches, which were divided by a spacious sink. Next to that was a very generously sized bathroom with a huge glassed-in shower.

A glass-topped wooden table, with a map beneath the glass, served as the eating area as near as she could tell. Charlie examined it closely. It was a topographical map of the Northern Rivers area of New South Wales. That would come in handy, she thought.

A desk sat looking out another window with a stylish two-shelf bookcase on top. Various field identification guides for Australian mammals, insects, birds, reptiles, trees, and flowers crowded the lower shelf. The top shelf contained more folded maps than she thought she'd ever seen in one place, her office at home included.

On the right and across from the kitchen area was a queen-sized bed. The mattress sat upon a foundation of drawers. It was situated beneath a skylight that opened and closed. A small screen maintained a barrier against insects.

A half wall divided the bedroom from the sitting area where she'd entered the cabin.

"Like it?" Terese asked from the couch. Pip sat next to her but something outside held her attention.

"I love it." Charlie blinked. "It's so beautiful I could hang out here all day."

"Don't plan on it. There's a lot of work to do." Pip stood up and without looking back said, "Don't forget about dinner at seven. Unless you'd rather stay here." She walked out, called for Chilli, and disappeared back into the woods.

Charlie grunted softly in frustration. "Terese, are you sure there isn't someone else that might rather work with me? Pip doesn't seem like she wants me around."

Terese flipped her hand as if she were swatting at a bug. "You couldn't ask for a more knowledgeable or bush-smart person to train with. It'll be fine. Now get yourself settled and if you want to score points with Pip, show up at her place in an hour and help her with the feeding. It'll be a good start for you anyway."

"Okay."

"I have to get going if I want to get back home before midnight." Terese opened her arms and Charlie stepped into them for a hug. "I'm going to keep tabs on you to see how you're progressing. Who knows? You may fall in love with Australia and want to stay permanently."

"Thanks, but I kind of doubt it."

Throwing her a quick wink, Terese smiled at her. "Never say never, Charlie. Just see how it plays out."

Charlie waved back as Terese stuck her arm out the window just before the truck disappeared into the thick foliage. She suddenly felt alone and questioned any sane rationalization she'd had for coming to Australia.

❖

Pip scowled and couldn't care less how it marred the planes of her face as she and Chilli made their way back up the wooded path to the main house. She supposed if she were a child, one would say she was stomping her way back, but she preferred to think of it as producing a sufficiently loud series of footsteps to warn any snakes and lizards who might be basking in the last warmth of the afternoon sun along the path.

Terese hadn't given her much lead-up time to prepare anything for the newcomer. Not the house, lists of instructions, a plan for learning and caring for everything...She nibbled at her bottom lip. They would both have to wing it on the fly for a week or two until she had things sorted.

"We just need to get her fed and settled for the night, Chilli. We can work on a better plan tomorrow." The Labrador trotted amiably beside her, looking relaxed, and stopping to sniff occasionally or listen to nearby sounds in the grass.

Leaning down to ruffle the scruff of the dog's neck, Pip couldn't help but smile back at the grinning canine. "Speaking of food, let's get things started for dinner before we come back outside and feed the hungry horde." Chilli barked as if in agreement with the plan.

After preparing the vegetables and putting the casserole on low to simmer on the stove, Pip moved outside to her greatest achievement, the prep room. She had lovingly restored the weatherboard house over a long period of time. But the prep room she had designed from the ground up. It adjoined the house and looked over the enclosures in the backyard.

It was light and spacious with a combination of cupboards and bench space running around the perimeter of the room. Behind the door, against the far corner, were a washing machine and dryer strictly for the animal pouches, linings, blankets, and towels. The other long walls housed a bench space with cupboards above and below, all beautifully labelled and sorted by species. One side was dedicated to macropods—food, teats, and bottles in the top cupboards, with bedding, towels, and pouches in the cupboards below. The wall directly opposite the doorway was framed with a large double-glazed window overlooking the garden. The cupboards underneath the window housed food and bedding for koalas and wombats on the left, with possums and gliders on the right. The right-hand wall had a comparatively smaller section for birds, with the remaining space reserved for a sink, hot water urn, fridge, small chest freezer, a digital set of scales on the bench top, and a large free-standing medicine cabinet with a smoky-glassed front that stood near on six feet tall. A computer sat sentinel on the bench top, with folders and books in an overhead bookshelf standing guard, similarly organized by species.

To the left of the door was another cupboard. This storage space shouldered up against four stacked square stainless-steel animal cages and a stainless-steel examination table. Hiding in the corner was an old comfortable low-slung chair and matching lounge, whose sweeping wooden armrests were curved and ran down the front face of the chair, past faded and thinning heavy cotton upholstery.

This was the working hub of her home—in essence its beating heart. Everything had its place, its order. The room was easy to move around in, to clean, and ultimately to store most everything she needed. It was the personification of efficiency and effectiveness for the care of a multitude of species in one small, contained, single area.

She walked along the wall shelves containing her books and raised her hand to brush her fingertips in reverence along the spines of knowledge and resourcefulness. She continued to the far wall and braced her pelvis and hips against the sink edge, her arms folded across her chest, and stared out across the grassy expanse and the pens of animals in her care.

How much did Charlie know? Maybe she was a world expert in something or other, or on the other hand, maybe she knew stuff-all. Had she come to Australia to learn, or had she been sent to the colonies as punishment, penance for not performing? How on earth was she expected to work with this woman when she didn't even know a thing about her, let alone where to start? Pip briefly closed her eyes and rubbed at her temples in an attempt to stave off a pressing headache. She felt sure it was largely due to the tension and the stress of having a stranger living on her property. She took a series of slow breaths in an attempt to calm herself.

Terese's words echoed in her head. *Just relax, Pip. The more uptight you are, the more uptight she will be, and then the more nervous you get. Trust me, Charlie's a beaut swap. We're lucky to have her. I have a feeling you'll make a dynamite team together. But you* have *to learn to* relax, *girl.*

Relax. Yeah right. Pip screwed up her nose in disgust with herself and the situation she found herself in. With a quick shake of her head she pushed the thoughts aside to examine later. It was time to start getting things ready for evening feed. Moving smoothly to the relevant cupboards she mentally ran through what she needed for the night feeds and began pulling out the needed ingredients and feeding devices in preparation.

A soft clearing of the throat stopped Pip in her tracks. Turning slowly, she saw the tall American standing in the doorway. Charlie's hazel eyes looked tired, and almost as nervous and uncomfortable as Pip felt. She seemed to be trying to sport a shy but brave smile, appearing a bit apprehensive as she tucked a shoulder-length strand of dark, curly hair behind her ear.

"I thought…I mean, I'm a bit early, but I wondered if, perhaps, I could help or observe while you did the evening meal." Charlie bit her bottom lip after finishing her stuttered question.

Pip mentally approved the woman's bravery. *I reckon that might be three ticks in the Yank's favour.*

Pip still had no idea how she was going to make this arrangement work. But she admired Charlie's courage for turning up early and tipping her hand to help. The cynical voice inside Pip wondered if she was just trying to impress, or if she was truly genuine, but she pushed the question aside and decided to accept it on face value for the time being.

Taking a steadying breath, Pip made an effort to relax her face and offered a smile in return. She gestured for her visitor to come on through. "We can go into more detail tomorrow, but for tonight, how about you take a look around the prep room while I get things together. I imagine you've had a long couple of days, so I won't bombard you with too much first up. I'll introduce you briefly to some of the mob in care as we feed them, and if you have any questions I'll do my best to answer them."

Pip held her breath, waiting to see what Charlie would do, and was relieved when she finally got a smile.

"That sounds like a good place to begin."

Pip felt satisfied that they had found a small, if tentative, place with which to make a start. Charlie walked around the perimeter of the room, pausing to read the labels and look into some of the cupboards.

Pip quickly ran through her head what was second nature to her, attempting to sort out a plan to start Charlie with. Adopting honesty as the best place to start, Pip cleared her throat. "I have a confession to make." She pulled several laminated sheets from a folder near the computer and laid them out on the counter nearest the sink. She turned to face Charlie, who looked at her with her head slightly cocked to the side, a questioning look on her face.

"Your arrival"—she licked her lips, feeling oddly a touch nervous—"has caught me a bit by surprise. So I might be a bit scattered until we can get things sorted. I'll write up a rough schedule tomorrow and we can run through it in more detail. But tonight, if you're okay with it, I might get you to help me with a couple of meals. For the most part a lot of the food and equipment is in here. There's some stuff outside, but this is where a lot of the action happens."

Pip paused as Charlie gazed around the room.

"I don't know what you're used to where you come from, but this room'll cater to most of the situations that we'll encounter over the next year. So the sooner you get to know where everything is, the easier your life will be."

As their gazes met, Charlie nodded once in acknowledgement of the plan.

"First up, we'll wash our hands. The antibacterial soap mix is on the wall next to the sink." Pip rinsed the soap and water off and stood back, wiping her hands on some towelling to allow Charlie to step in and do hers. "Hygiene is everything. For you and for the animals in care. They're in a stressful, unnatural environment because they're injured, orphaned, or unwell. As a result, their immune systems are compromised by the stress or illness, and infections are a very real threat. This stress can have an immediate or longer term impact, all of which have the potential to lead to death."

Charlie finished wiping her hands and turned her attention to Pip.

Satisfied she had Charlie's full focus now, Pip continued. "Righto." She picked up the first of the laminated sheets and waved Charlie to move closer. "Tomorrow I'll talk you through mixing up the meals using this sheet and the animal's weight and age as a guide. Tonight though we'll use a mix I made up this morning. If you could go to the fridge and pull out the three medium sized glass bottles, second shelf on the door."

Pip pulled a mixing bowl from the drying rack on the sink and filled it with hot water from the urn and handed over three blue teats. She saw Charlie's look of surprise at their shape and chuckled quietly. "Bit weird, huh? Don't worry, tomorrow I'll show you why they're shaped this way and it'll make more sense."

Charlie raised an eyebrow, but much to Pip's relief it was accompanied by a tentative smile. She handed over the teats. "Slide them over the lips of the bottles and then place the bottles in the water to warm the milk. It won't take long."

Pip walked over to the hanging rack at the back of the door and pulled down an apron. She held it out to Charlie. "Put this on. It smells like me, so when you feed the joeys it'll help relax the babies a little, until they get used to you."

"Makes sense." Charlie slipped the loop over her head and tied off the strings at the back.

"The milk should be good to go." Pip tested the milk of each bottle against her wrist and encouraged Charlie to do the same. "Follow me."

Pip led the way outside, down a path and to an enclosure, approximately one acre in size, with a shed tucked neatly in one corner. Pip unlocked the gate, ushered Charlie inside, and indicated for her to take a seat on an upturned milk crate just inside the door. A grassy pen dotted with trees, shrubs, and native garden pockets was surrounded by a fence, five metres high with the bottom two metres screened off in forest-green shade cloth. Pip called the joeys, who immediately bounded out to her, reaching her midthigh. They were in high spirits and Pip knew they were keen for their evening drink.

She crouched and held the three bottles in her hands. Pip smiled as she watched over her charges who, with only a quick cursory glance at the stranger, hungrily latched on to the teats and suckled voraciously.

Pip saw Charlie staring wide-eyed in fascination. She grinned and motioned for Charlie to take hold of the bottles. "I'll leave you to finish off here while I go and sort the others out, and then I'll come back and collect you."

With only a brief fumble, Charlie quickly adapted her fingers and hands to accommodate the bottles. "Okay, thanks."

Charlie was sporting a huge grin when Pip left her. She was confident the joeys would keep her busy for the minute. She paused at the gate and turned back to see the woman beaming and obviously enthralled. Turning on her heel, she shut the gate behind her and strode off purposefully to feed her other charges.

❖

Charlie's face hurt from the constant smile she wore as she experienced her first interaction with a kangaroo. The suckling noises they made while feeding were just adorable. Their eyes, framed by long dark lashes, became heavy lidded as they filled their bellies. She had an intense desire to touch them, but refrained because she wasn't sure if Pip would approve or even allow it.

The joeys held on to the teats for a while longer after the milk was gone. Then one by one they released them from their cute little lips. Using their tails to form a tripod with their front limbs, they raised their hind feet forward and crawl-walked a short distance away. They each found one of the few remaining spots in the sun and plopped down onto their sides.

"And such is the life of a kangaroo."

Charlie tilted her head up and met Pip's eyes. "How on earth do you ever get anything done?"

A soft smile crossed Pip's face. "Oh, trust me, they're good time wasters. Sometimes it's only the hungry squeaks and carryings on from the other animals that make me move on."

Charlie exhaled in appreciation. Back in the States, the otters she'd worked with elicited a similar response. But somehow it seemed more acute with the joeys. Maybe because they were so new, she reasoned.

"Tea's ready after we clean up."

"Tea?" Charlie rose to her feet and with a last look at the joeys, gathered the bottles, and followed Pip.

"What you'd call dinner, I think."

"So the word is used in a different context then." Charlie took the teats off the bottles and dropped them into the sink.

"There's breakfast, morning tea, lunch, afternoon tea, and tea or dinner as you'd call it, and supper."

Charlie stared at Pip in amazement. "Holy crap. Is that all you Australians do, eat?"

Pip chuckled. "Hardly." She finished washing the bottles and teats in the hot water and set them on a drying mat. "The term *tea* can mean a few different things. Yes, like the hot drink you referred to. Afternoon tea is normally a snack or light meal. I think you'd recognize biscuits—no, hang on, I think you call them cookies—and maybe small sandwiches or scones. There's also high tea, which is a hangover from our British influence and is basically dinner and eaten in the early evening."

Charlie rolled her eyes in exasperation. "I'll take your word for it. Just let me know when it's time to eat."

"It's time to eat." Pip laughed softly. "Come on into the house."

As they walked back, it suddenly occurred to Charlie that the house resembled what she remembered as an old schoolhouse. The roof peaked sharply over sides of clapboard. A huge porch wrapped around three of its sides. The windows had obviously been replaced by rectangular six-sectioned library glass. It had an older appeal to it, but not something that could be replicated.

"Was this house here when you bought the property?" Charlie followed Pip up the three steps to the back door.

"No." Pip opened the door and let Chilli walk in.

"I wondered." Charlie followed Chilli.

"You wondered what?" Pip closed the door behind her and walked past Charlie and into the kitchen.

"Oh, that's an American saying. But I had a hard time imagining a school being this far back in the woods."

"Woods?"

"Yeah, the woods. What do you call this?"

"The bush. Or the trees."

"Oh." Charlie shook her head. "I can see the language in itself is going to be interesting." After washing her hands, she pulled a chair out from the kitchen table and sat down while Pip busied herself at the oven. When she'd sat here earlier, she'd been so distracted about meeting Pip and talking to Terese that she hadn't paid any attention to what the interior of the house looked like.

Charlie noticed Chilli, who was lying on one of the mats. The dog's gaze never shifted from her owner. At one point she got up and nudged Pip, earning her a smile and pat.

"Be right back." Pip and Chilli disappeared briefly into another room before returning.

Charlie used the time to look around the room. White was definitely the main colour. But it contrasted nicely with the mottled-grey granite benches. The wood slatted floor was a deep red and accessorized with earthy coloured mats. Linoleum covered the kitchen floor. A strip of grey striped wood covered the seams between the two starkly different floorings. It wasn't anything she was familiar with. But so far nothing about Australia seemed similar to the States.

While Pip moved between a wood-burning stove and a granite-covered kitchen island that looked identical to the cupboards, Charlie's gaze roamed around the rest of the room. The furniture was definitely old but, from what she could tell, well made to stand the test of time.

Curiosity got the better of Charlie when she realized Pip hadn't elaborated on where the house came from, nor when it got here.

"Terese said you built the cabin."

"Uh-huh. It took me a while, but I eventually got it done." Pip placed a casserole dish on the island.

"Don't you want to live in it? It's such a beautiful place." Charlie ignored the rumbles in her stomach, but the aromas made her mouth water.

"I did for a while. But when I saw the schoolhouse in Chatsworth with a *For Sale* sign on it, I knew I had to have it. So I arranged for it to be moved here. It took me a couple of years to fix it up to how I wanted. When I finished, I decided I wanted to live here instead of the cabin. With the animals coming in, I designed the prep room and added it on. I knew I'd made the right decision."

"Well, the cabin makes a wonderful guest house."

"It stays empty most of the time." Pip scooped dinner out onto two plates and delivered Charlie's with a fork, spoon and knife.

"This smells wonderful."

"It's just chicken and veggies, with a bit of rice." Pip shrugged. "Simple, but it does the job."

"Job?"

"It fills your belly."

Charlie picked her fork up and speared a piece of chicken. She was about to put it into her mouth when she saw Pip turn her fork upside down and push food onto the back of it with her knife. She continued to eat in this fashion. *Weird. To each their own I guess.*

"Why don't you tell me what you did back in the States? That'll give me an idea of where we can make a start and how to approach things with our native wildlife."

Charlie finished chewing and swallowed. "Sure. This is delicious by the way."

"It's not much, but I'm pleased you like it."

"To answer your question, I'm in charge of all raptor rescues and rehabilitation in the tri-state area. But, like you I'm sure, I have to be prepared to deal with any species."

"From what I know about the States, that's a huge area."

"Yeah. I wasn't home a lot." Charlie reflected on the implications her frequent absence had on her relationship with Kim. A pang of sadness hit her in the chest.

"Wasn't there some kind of chemical that impacted your birds years ago?"

Charlie welcomed the diversion. She'd already spent way too much time thinking about Kim. She had no doubt it was the source of the panic and anxiety attacks that frequented her all too often.

"Yes, back in the fifties. Nasty stuff called dichlorodiphenyltrichloroethane, or better known as DDT."

"Ah, that's right. I remember now from my uni wildlife courses. Your raptor populations would've suffered a lot, I guess."

"All bird populations suffered. It was first discovered in Michigan when they sprayed DDT to control the beetles responsible for Dutch elm disease. It literally slaughtered uncountable numbers of robins. But eventually it worked up to the highest in the food chain, the raptors. There were many uncertain years, but I think we're over the hump now, especially with the eagles and condors."

"That's good to hear. Do you get many eagles in care?"

Charlie squinted. "Way more than we should. I don't see too many golden eagles. Loss of habitat being the main reason. Most of my bald eagles come in because some idiot has taken a shot at it."

"Target shooting?"

Charlie felt her heart race as her irritation level rose. "No. Unfortunately they think the eagles are preying on their sheep. They have no clue that baldies are mainly fish or carrion eaters."

"So they're a sea eagle?"

Charlie nodded. "Yes, genus *Haliaeetus*."

"Well, you just may come into contact with our sea eagles here. Same genus. Or if you're lucky maybe a wedge-tail, but you never know. But we certainly have a good number of different raptors about the place."

Charlie smiled. "The eagles are my favourite. I love all the raptors, but the eagles are just...magnificent." She scraped the remains of her dinner and scooped it up. "Thank you again for dinner. This was great." She slid her chair back and rose to her feet. "Can I help you clean up?"

"Don't worry about it tonight. You must be exhausted."

Charlie stifled a yawn. "I am. I think I'll just head back to the cabin and make it an early night."

"Good idea."

Charlie opened the back door to total blackness.

"Did you bring a torch with you?"

"A torch?" All Charlie could imagine was a stick with a burning cloth at the end of it.

Pip scowled, went to a drawer, pulled out a flashlight, and handed it to Charlie.

This is a torch? Why the hell couldn't she have just said flashlight? Charlie felt a little disillusioned at that moment. They seemed to be having such a nice evening and then Pip reverted to her earlier attitude. Charlie couldn't figure her out.

"Okay. Thanks. I'll see you in the morning."

Charlie trudged back to the cabin. The bright flashlight lit the way, sending shadows fleeing in every direction. She thought about the last few minutes. If Pip had just *said* flashlight, she would've been able to tell her that no, she hadn't brought one with her. Of course Charlie wasn't about to tell Pip that it hadn't even occurred to her to bring one when it was broad daylight out when she'd made the trek up to Pip's house. It suddenly dawned on her that Pip could've given her a ride back. God, the woman had a rude streak. The only time she'd smiled the entire evening was when Chilli demanded her attention, or when she was interacting with the animals in her care.

Along with the flashlight, Pip had also given her a two-way radio. She'd told her that they could get called out on a rescue at any hour, so she'd need to get in touch with Charlie quickly. *I suppose I'll have to run up to her house then. God forbid Pip comes to pick me up.*

The night woods were alive with different sounds. Crickets rubbed their wings together, making the classic chirping sound, things scurried in the branches overhead, and everyplace the light grazed there was suspicious rustling. She should have asked if there was cause to be cautious of any dangerous animals in the dark. At least snakes didn't move at night. They'd most certainly be holed up somewhere taking advantage of the residual heat from the day, she reasoned.

Charlie saw a light in the near distance where she estimated the porch entrance to the cabin would be. She knew she'd not left a light on. Why would she, when she hadn't thought to bring a *torch*? She stomped in exaggeration and frustration. So the light must be run by solar power, which she thought was pretty cool.

A few minutes later she swiped the switch up inside the cabin. The resulting light bathed everything in white and she was once again amazed at the interior. She just couldn't get over the tree growing in the middle of the room.

While the kettle heated water for tea, Charlie shed her clothes and took a quick shower. She forced herself out of the decadent bathroom when she heard the whistling. She dried herself quickly and wrapped the oversized towel around her torso, ran her fingers through her hair, and then focused on pouring the tea.

She sat down at the desk and pulled out a few of the maps. Having no idea what or where she was looking at, she quickly became bored and decided to put it all away. She had no desire to watch television. In fact, she really didn't want to do anything.

The excitement she'd felt as an adrenaline rush in her chest earlier had waned and pretty much disappeared. Charlie knew Pip was a large part of it. Christ, and she had signed up for a year of it. What in the world had possessed her to come to Australia anyway? To leave her beloved dogs behind and come to a country where she didn't know anybody, a place where she couldn't just hop in a car and drive home for a weekend visit.

Charlie swallowed against the thickness that had built up in her throat. Hot tears stung behind her eyelids. She rubbed her arm absently, searching for some soothing contact. A longing so intense rose into her chest and manifested into a painful homesickness for something familiar.

She couldn't let herself slip into a depressive slump. *I have to think of it as a job. It's the only way I'm going to survive.* Charlie pulled her laptop out of its case. While she waited for it to boot up, she sipped her tea and flipped through a bird field guide. She decided to start a list of the birds she'd seen. As an afterthought, she programmed a calendar to cross off the days until she could go back home. As it was a warm evening, she opened all the windows and enjoyed the cross breeze.

By the time she was done, it was nearly ten o'clock and a lovely breeze wafted through the cabin from the open windows. Although physically tired, her mind wouldn't shut off as she lay in bed. She stared up at the stars through the skylight that she'd opened wide as well. The Milky Way painted a silver streak through a black abyss dotted with bright stars. The static sound of the wind soothed her and she finally closed her eyes.

Charlie had just started to doze off when she heard something else. subtle scraping on the roof. She kept her eyes closed and tried to identify the sound. She was sure it was coming from outside. Maybe a branch moving against the tin roof?

The noise shifted until it was directly above her. She finally looked up. Something blocked her view of the sky. The screen squeaked and seemed to complain about whatever weight was on it.

What the hell? Charlie sat up and reached over to turn on the bed stand light. The screen strained and popped. A dark bulge with even darker stripes oozed over the edge. Charlie's heart nearly stopped. She didn't need any field guide to know what was hovering directly above her.

"Holy shit!" Charlie pumped her legs to push the sheet off, but only succeeded in getting tangled up in them. More pops came from the screen as it slowly gave way. She rolled to the left and fell off the bed.

With a last final pop a snake fell in a heap onto the bed.

Charlie crab crawled backward and hit the tree. "Oh my God."

The snake remained motionless but for the flicking of its tongue as it tasted the air.

Small beads of perspiration formed on Charlie's upper lip. Waves of heat and cold swept over her like a fever vying for control of her body. Loud thumping seemed to drown out all other sounds as her heart pounded against her ribs. Her lungs struggled to take in sufficient air.

She suddenly remembered the radio. Surely Pip would come and help her. But the radio was on the nightstand next to the light. And that was next to the bed. Where the fricking huge snake was.

Charlie kept her eyes on the snake as she slowly crawled closer until she finally was able to grasp the radio.

She swallowed hard and pushed the transmit button.

"Pip!" Charlie whispered. "Pip, are you there? Oh *please* answer I need your help there's a snake in here and I don't know what to do *please* Pip answer me or better yet just get your ass over here!" As she waited for Pip to answer, her panic rose. How was she supposed to deal with this twenty-foot monster? She realized she was still holding the transmit button down. She released it and heard Pip's voice.

"—is it?"

"What?" Charlie licked her lips and tasted salt.

"What *kind* is it?"

"Fuck, I don't know! It's a *snake* for God's sake. In the cabin. On my bed. Get your ass over here and get it out!"

"Is the head triangular and distinct from its body? That will tell me if it's poisonous or not."

"I have no idea. I sure as hell wasn't about to sit there with the damned thing in my lap."

Charlie realized she was crouched down, and in her current position it was impossible to see anything but the floor. She straightened up and checked the top of the bed. It was empty.

"Oh shit, oh shit, oh shit." She looked wildly around the room only to realize she was probably on the same level as the snake. In a movement that would make Superman proud, she sprang to her feet and jumped onto the bed.

"What's wrong now?" Pip sounded like she was mildly amused.

"It's gone!"

"Well, you have to find it."

"What do you mean *I* have to find it? Please, Pip, I'm begging you."

"All right, all right. I'm on my way. I'll keep my radio with me."

Charlie mumbled into the air. "Big of you."

"Sorry? Charlie?"

"Just hurry, will you? Please?"

Charlie felt only slightly more secure on the bed. With Pip now on her way she didn't feel like she was going to pee her pants any more. She leaned forward as far as she dared without falling off the bed and craned her neck in both directions. The snake was nowhere to be seen. *Shit, shit, shit.*

She caught movement to her left, level to her knees. The snake had curled itself around the tree. It extended the front part of its body and got a grip with its ventral scales. It then pulled the rest of its body upward in a very slow ascent.

"Pip, it's climbing the tree. Can it get out through the roof?" Charlie shuddered. If it could get out that way, the damned thing could get back in.

"Bugger."

"What? At least it's not on the floor, right?"

"Uh-uh. There's a gap between the ceiling and the roof. If it gets in there we'll *never* get it out."

Charlie only heard the *we* and was about to make a comment when Pip broke her train of thought.

"You have to stop it."

"What? How? What am I supposed to do? Call it over nicely, like *Here, snakey snakey*?"

"Grab it by its tail, and hold on." Pip's voice was flat and calm.

"You have got to be kidding me. No way. No. Fucking. Way."

"Charlie, you have to. I won't get there in time."

Charlie threw the radio down, swallowed hard, and tried to summon every ounce of courage in her body. *I'd rather grab a wolf by the tail, thank you very much.*

The snake's tail was now chest high to her. It was now or never. She reached up, shuddered, grabbed the tail, and held on.

The snake stopped its forward movement but was tugging hard against her hold. She couldn't believe how strong it was. She tightened her grip and prayed for Pip to come through the door.

Something wet and slimy oozed onto her hand and down her wrist. She looked up and gagged. The damned thing was shitting on her. The foul musky smell seeped into her sinuses, its assault so strong, she was convinced she could taste it. Charlie nearly let go. She'd pack her things, call Terese, apologize, and catch the next flight home. This was ridiculous. At home, skunks smelled bad, but she wasn't afraid of them.

The door was flung open. Much to her relief, Pip walked in and closed the door behind her. She glanced at Charlie, then at the snake, and sniffed.

A wry half smile slid across Pip's face. "Got pooped on by a python, huh?"

"Just get your ass over here and do what you need to do. I'm not holding onto this thing for one second longer."

Pip worked the muscles in her jaw. She rubbed her hands on her pants and grabbed the snake above Charlie's hand. "It's going to eventually give up, and when it does, it'll fall on the floor. I'll need you to open the door so I can guide it out."

"You didn't think to leave the door open when you came in?" Charlie was back on the bed again.

"I could've, if you wanted to be carried away by the mozzies."

Pip and the snake tugged against each other for another ten minutes in a silent stand-off of wills. In a blink, Charlie got off the bed, sidled over to the couch, and took a stance on top of it. She held her hand away from her body as if she had touched nuclear waste.

"You're going to have to get off that lounge in order to open the door."

"Yeah, well, I'll do what I need to do when I have to."

Pip's efforts began to win over against the snake as the snake's head lost traction against the pole, its body swaying at the sudden loss of leverage. Pip growled, "Now would be a good time."

Charlie looked over at Pip with questioning eyes.

"The door, Charlie. Get the bloody door."

Charlie nodded as she jumped off the couch and scrambled to the door. "Yep, yep, onto it." She swung the door open and held it safely against the length of her body. She peeked nervously around the edge.

Still holding it by the tail, Pip guided the python in the direction of the door, ushering it out to the porch where it slithered swiftly to the edge to drop over the side with a resounding thump.

Pip stood in the now empty doorway and wiped her hands down the length of her thighs. With a sigh, she turned to face Charlie, who still hid behind the door. “Was there anything else you wanted? No? Good-oh. See you in the morning then.”

Charlie watched as the slight Australian turned on her heel and left, leaving her feeling stranded behind the door. In a rush of adrenaline she slammed the door and ran to the bedroom to feverishly crank the skylight closed. Catching a whiff of what the snake had painted on her arm, she bolted for the bathroom and scrubbed the effluent off. With nothing now left to do, she sank onto the far corner of the bed, hugged a pillow tightly against her body, and curled into a fetal position. She rocked herself for comfort, in the now overly quiet cabin in the middle of seemingly nowhere. Sleep was going to be virtually nonexistent as she was sure she’d be reaching for the light switch with each and every scrape or creak she heard.

Chapter Three

Pip gathered the last of the now empty feeding bottles together as Charlie walked into the prep room. "Ah, I see you've survived the rest of the night then. Did you get much sleep after your visitor left?" Pip bit the inside of her lip to keep from smirking.

"Not a lot."

"I was almost expecting to see you curled up asleep in the ute this morning."

Charlie huffed. "I probably would have if I knew where you kept your keys."

Pip laughed. "Remind me to show you where they are later."

"I'll hold you to that," Charlie said and chuckled.

"Do you like the beach?" Pip washed the last of the kangaroo feeding bottles and left it upside down on a rack to drain.

"I do." Charlie sipped from her second cup of coffee that morning. "It's been a very long time since I've been to one. You don't find many in the middle of the mountains."

"I thought we could venture down and check out one of my favourite places later after we do a bit of grocery shopping. It's a lovely place called Brooms Head."

"That sounds great."

"Excellent. Chilli likes the beach too, don't you, girl." Pip ruffled the canine's thick coat, the dog's tail slapping against her leg.

She barked when Pip said the word *beach*, which brought a chuckle to Pip's lips. "The beach it is."

Pip took Charlie through the routine of feeding the birds and explained the different sorts she had in care. A tawny frogmouth from the nightjar family, whose colouring provided the ultimate camouflage as it resembled a piece of dead timber, sat stock-still midbranch, leaning slightly to one side, not unlike a tree limb. Pip stood back, giving Charlie some space to locate it in the large aviary, and then showed her how to feed it. She noted the smooth way Charlie moved: no sharp or swift movements, always mindful of the birds in the pens, and avoiding looking at them directly. Pip was impressed by Charlie's questions. She had a natural understanding, which she applied and adapted to the varied species even though she was unfamiliar with them.

Pip talked Charlie through feeding the four juvenile rosellas that she'd hand raised as hatchlings. They'd come into her care when they'd been thrown from the nest after a big storm. She held her breath as one of her renowned cranky residents, a rainbow lorikeet, bit down hard on Charlie's finger, drawing blood, when she was placing some mashed up banana and some oats drizzled with honeyed lorikeet mix into the cage. Pip grimaced, waiting for a negative reaction, but was pleasantly surprised when laughter bubbled forth along with murmurings of, "Sassy thing."

Pip introduced Charlie to one of the feeding charts for the eastern grey kangaroo joeys. She explained how the coat of each animal was assessed and measurements taken to help determine the kangaroo's age bracket and what type of milk mix was appropriate for the joey. Pip held each of the joeys, showing Charlie how to safely capture and hold them, before taking her through weighing and measuring the hind feet and tail of each animal.

Having matched the weight up with categories on the chart, Pip showed Charlie how to make the mix, adding the special formula, boiled water, and a colostrum mix to stave off infection. Together they made up enough to do a full day's feed for all of them.

"How often do you weigh and measure them?"

"In the early stages, every week. As they get a bit older, every couple of weeks. Every animal has a file and their details are recorded on the computer. Here, I'll show you and let you write up today's notes."

Pip pulled the chair out and indicated that Charlie should sit. Leaning over Charlie's shoulder, Pip pointed out the different folders on the computer screens, encouraging her to open up each folder and find the joey's files. As Charlie's fingers danced across the keyboard entering data, Pip couldn't help but notice the sweet spicy perfume radiating subtly from Charlie. Her curls shone in the morning light streaming through the window. They looked so soft.

Pip blinked hard, stood up straight, and shook her head to clear it. "Huh."

Charlie turned in the seat and looked up at her expectantly.

"Sorry. Come again?"

"Do you want me to put some notes in for the birds too?"

"Um, okay. Sure. Just open up the files and you'll see the sort of notes that I've been keeping."

Chilli whined softly from her bed in the corner of the prep room.

Charlie looked from the dog to Pip. "You okay?"

"What?"

"Pip, are you okay?"

Pip ran a shaky hand through her hair before shoving her hands into the pockets of her jeans. "Yep. Fine. You keep going there and I'll be back in a minute." Not stopping to wait for Charlie's reply, Pip turned on her heel and made her way back to the house and straight for the bathroom. She shut the door and sat down on the closed toilet seat and rested her head in her hands, elbows braced on her knees, and concentrated on taking some deep breaths to stave off the slight dizziness that was creeping over her. After a short moment she rose and splashed some cold water onto her face, wondering what the unexpected sensations were all about. *I just hope I'm not coming down with the flu or some sort of bug. Now is* definitely *not the time to be sick.*

With a shrug, she straightened her shoulders and went back out to the prep room, just as Charlie had hit save on the last file.

"Happy?"

Charlie nodded. "I think so."

"Good. How do you feel about keeping the records for the next month? I'll help you for the first week or so with the measurements, but after that, I'll leave it up to you if you'd like. That way you can gauge their progress and observe and record their development."

"That would be fine. Thank you."

"Good-oh. What say we pack up and head into town? Do you need anything from the cabin?"

"My wallet and maybe some sunglasses. Oh, and I've started a shopping list."

"Well, if you want to head on down and pick them up, I'll just get my things together and I'll meet you down there. Bring your camera if you brought one. See you in, say, fifteen?"

Charlie checked her watch. "Okay, fifteen."

Pip stood in the now empty room, a strange tingling sensation fluttering in her stomach. She checked her watch. It was a bit early for a snack, but maybe some food would settle the odd sensations. Another flutter skittered inside. Yes, food should do the trick.

❖

Charlie nearly skipped back to the cabin, the python episode a distant memory. The morning had been so fulfilling, what with interacting with the animals and Pip. She'd already learned so much and was flattered that Pip trusted her enough with the records. It had taken months before she'd trusted her assistants enough to enter data. Even though her finger throbbed from the lorikeet's sharp bite, it was spellbinding being so close to these exotic animals, all of whom she'd only previously observed in videos or zoos.

The sun streaming through the canopies was already growing in intensity. She decided to quickly change into shorts and a T-shirt before Pip arrived. Birds chirped from the high branches as she walked. When she had some time she'd have to get her binoculars out and try to identify them.

When she got to the cabin, she traded her jeans and long-sleeved shirt for cooler gear. As she sat on the bed, a stream of sunlight poured through the skylight. A brief flash of the previous night's reptilian misadventure caused a shudder to briefly ripple across her consciousness. She quickly shrugged it off, rummaged around in her toiletries, and stuffed a small tube of sunblock and her wallet into the cargo pockets. Before she walked out the door, she grabbed her camera, donned sunglasses, and slipped on her sandals—and just in time because Pip had pulled up in a truck identical to the one Terese drove. Only Pip's had a cab over the tray bed. Chilli sat in the passenger seat with bright delight in her eyes.

Charlie opened the door and Chilli jumped into the back. "You're going to give me the front seat, are you, girl?" Charlie slid in and received a lick on her ear from Chilli. "Silly girl."

"All set?" Pip put the truck into reverse and managed to turn it around in the small area.

"Yep." Charlie studied Pip. She seemed a little pale. Pip's eyes were hidden behind sunglasses so it was hard to determine if she was really okay. It sure hadn't seemed so back in the prep room. But whatever it'd been, Pip looked like she had recovered. The muscles in Pip's forearms flexed as she gripped the steering wheel. Charlie let her gaze slide over Pip's well-muscled legs before moving her attention to fastening her seat belt.

When Pip pushed the gear stick into reverse, Charlie said, "Boy, Toyota sure has the market on white trucks. I don't think I've ever seen so many of them in my life, except on a factory parking lot."

Pip chuckled. "A white ute is definitely a necessity."

"Ute. That's what you call them here?"

"It's easier to say than *utility vehicle*, which is what it originally stood for. Nowadays it means any vehicle with a tray bed in it." Pip turned out of the long driveway and headed in the opposite direction from which Charlie had come yesterday.

They crossed two bridges before turning again and followed a river on the right.

"That's the Clarence River. It used to be a working river to haul cane and logs. Now it's about the most underutilized river in Australia."

"It's beautiful. I didn't realize we were so close to a river."

The road imitated the winding river. Cords of soft light speared down from above, bathing the water's surface with glinting sparkles, like thousands of diamonds blessed with an inner fire.

"Can you swim in it?"

"You can, but there are sharks that breed in the channels."

Suddenly the river lost a bit of its charm. "This is a salt water river?"

"Tidal as well. She has attitude. You'll be here long enough to see."

The road veered slightly inland on the south side of Maclean. As Pip signalled for a left turn, Charlie gasped.

"Holy hell! Are those bats?" She craned her head around trying to get a good look. Trees on both sides of the road were covered with perching upside-down flying foxes. Their screeching could be heard over the diesel motor.

"Sure are. They're the bane of Maclean. They've been trying to get rid of them for years."

"Why? They're beautiful."

"Uh-huh," Pip said as she pulled over. "Go ahead and roll down your window a bit."

Charlie pressed the button to lower the window. The raucous screeches and squeaks got louder. Her nose was immediately assaulted by what smelled like a thousand dirty hamster cages left in a hot room. "Shit!" She closed the window quickly and took the liberty of turning the air conditioning on higher.

"Pee, actually. The residents around the colony have it bad. The bat droppings get on everything and they carry diseases, one of which can be transferred to humans."

"Oh. Have they tried—"

"Nearly everything imaginable," Pip finished for her. She checked her rear view mirror and pulled out onto the road.

They rode in silence for the next several miles. Charlie wasn't surprised at all. They barely knew each other and needed common ground on which to converse. So far they hadn't ventured outside of a safe zone. As with her ride north, Charlie was completely transfixed by the countryside. When they left Townsend, pasture traded places with cane and back again. Cattle and kangaroos dotted the grasslands and the cane grew in varying heights.

"Keep your eye out. Sometimes you can see emus around here."

Charlie sat up straighter and strained to spot one. She gave up when forest enveloped them and the road took them through Yuraygir National Park. But soon the landscape changed yet again, this time into a flowering bushland.

"God, that's beautiful." Charlie reached for her camera, hoping to capture the yellow, purple, white, and green colours.

"The low vegetation is heath and the trees are gum and bottlebrush. Beyond that you can see the ocean."

Sure enough, the blue of the ocean painted the horizon with yet another colour.

"I pity those who have desk jobs," Charlie muttered.

A few minutes later, Pip parked the truck on a grassy strip just up from the beach. Chilli nudged Pip's shoulder and yipped.

Charlie chuckled. "She knows where she is."

Pip gave her a sideways glance before opening her door and allowing Chilli to jump over her. Chilli didn't act the way Charlie would've expected, which was to race down to the water. Instead, she stood by the truck waiting for Pip to get out.

"I'll be back in a minute. I have to go to the toilet." Pip slapped her thigh and Chilli followed her across the street to the public bathrooms.

There was something about Pip that Charlie just couldn't put her finger on. She tilted her head, pursed her lips, and stared after her until the sound of the waves hitting the shore drew her attention.

The sand was incredibly white and clean. A short reef, about a hundred feet out, followed the length of the beach. A natural break wall of enormous rocks jutted out into the water. Huge waves crashed over them, spraying the flocks of terns and gulls with seawater. It was impossible to not be mesmerized by the ebb and flow of the water.

She shed her sandals, shoved them under the truck, and walked onto the sand. "Holy crap, that's hot!" She quick-stepped down to the water's edge. As she ran, she heard a weird squeaking. She didn't dare stop for fear of burning three layers of skin off the bottom of her feet, until she was standing in the water. The waves gently washed in and afforded her much needed relief.

Charlie heard squeaking again and realized it was coming from Pip and Chilli as they approached.

"Is that the sand that's making that noise?"

"Sure is. Cool, isn't it? Depending on which beach you go to, the sound is a little different."

"Really?" Charlie walked onto the loose sand and scuffed her foot, repeating the noise, much to her delight. "What makes it do that?" She shoved her sunglasses up and bent over to peer at it more closely.

"Apparently it has something to do with the sand being round, a certain diameter, humidity, and it has to contain quartz."

Chilli sniffed near Charlie's moving foot. Every time it squeaked, she cocked her head to the side and then to the other.

"It is just the coolest thing."

Pip laughed. "You two are quite the sight."

"But, Pip, this is just the coolest thing." Charlie offered a bemused smile. "You have to admit."

Suddenly a different kind of noise erupted from Charlie's pocket. A chorus of frogs notified her of an incoming message. Without taking her eyes from Chilli and the sand, she pulled her phone from her pocket. Her smile melted from her face when she saw the sender's name: Kim. Her ex. What the hell was she messaging her for? She felt the hair stiffen at the nape of her neck and at the same time an ache formed in her chest.

Pip must have seen her smile turn into a frown. "Something wrong?"

Charlie sighed. "No. Just, I wasn't expecting to hear from..." She forced a smile to her face. "It's not important. Now, are you and Chilli going to give me a tour of this gorgeous beach or not?"

Pip studied her for a moment longer. "Sure."

They wandered down the beach in silence. Chilli seemed to be the only one having fun. With her mouth open in complete glee, she raced to the water and back again. She seemed to love to challenge the waves to see if they could get her belly wet.

Charlie was lost in her own thoughts. She couldn't figure out why Kim would be making contact. After all, she was the one who ended the relationship. She was the one who wanted a change. And she was the one who left. Part of Charlie was curious to read what the email said. The other part didn't want to give a damn.

"We should probably head back. By the time we get home, it'll be feeding time."

Charlie turned around. She hadn't realized Pip had stopped and she'd kept on going.

"Oh. Sure. We better then."

❖

As they settled into the vehicle, Pip pulled her seat belt across her chest and turned to look at Charlie who stared out the passenger door window. Charlie was suddenly very quiet. And she looked lost, concerned somehow. Had Pip done something wrong? Was it the phone message? Did she not like the beach? Pip pulled her sunglasses off the top of her head, down onto her nose, and stared ahead as she mindlessly fingered the keys in the ignition. She clenched her teeth in frustration. Animals she had a connection with, but this people stuff was so confusing. *Just drive. Figure the rest out later.*

They made a quick stop off at the local supermarket to top up on groceries, with Charlie managing to get most of the items on her list. She watched in quiet amusement as Charlie studied and compared all the different foodstuffs. Despite her protests, Pip paid for them, and waved her off when she tried to argue. "Tell you what, while I duck into the chemist, how about you shout us a sandwich from the café two doors down? A roadie."

Charlie looked back at her, confusion evident in her eyes.

Pip scratched her head. "Which bit didn't you get?"

Charlie winced slightly. "Chemist—is that a drugstore?"

Pip nodded. "Uh-huh."

"And a roadie?" Charlie raised upturned hands with a shrug. "Sorry. You lost me there."

Pip expelled what she hoped didn't sound like an exasperated sigh. She was getting hungry and that always made her tetchy and short-tempered. "A roadie is one for the road—a takeaway. A meal that you can order and they'll package it up for you to take away."

Charlie chuckled. "Ah, okay. A roadie. What would you like on your sandwich?"

"I'm good for anything, except red meat. Surprise me."

Pip turned on her heel and headed towards the chemist. She placed her order at the counter and waited for it to be dispensed. She drummed her fingers in thought. *Being on your own is so much simpler. Have I rushed things? Maybe going to the beach and shopping was too ambitious a trip. After all, we've got all bloody year. Still, she has to learn her way around sooner or later.*

It wasn't until a young assistant came up and tapped her on the shoulder, causing her to jump, that Pip understood she'd been so engrossed in her own musings she'd missed them calling her name. Checking her watch, she realized that time had started to get away on her. She could eat her sandwich on the way home.

Charlie waved a sandwich bag triumphantly in the air as she approached the ute and climbed in. "I hope turkey, cranberry, and avocado is okay?"

As Pip turned the vehicle onto the main road she held out her hand for the bag. "Perfect."

"What? You want to eat it now?"

Pip unwrapped a half slice and shoved it unceremoniously into her mouth, nodding as she chewed.

"I guess you were hungry then." Charlie half mumbled under her breath as she unwrapped her own meal, calmly taking a more dignified approach.

Pip waved the second half in the air. "Worms."

A cough and splutter cut the air, as Charlie half choked on a mouthful of bread. "What?"

Pip glanced across at Charlie, affording her a half smile, and accompanied it with a cheeky wink, as the second half of the sandwich went the same way as the first.

Charlie didn't reply and continued to eat in silence.

Pip blew out a short breath. *So much for that.* She fingered the grip on the wheel at a loss as to what to do next, the silence in the vehicle only broken by Charlie folding her wrapper into a neat square and placing it back into the original bag. When Pip thought it couldn't get more uncomfortable, thankfully her phone rang. She pulled off the road.

"Hello, Pip speaking." Pip listened to the person on the other end of the line and reached beside her seat to retrieve a clipboard.

"One moment please." Pip transferred the call to speakerphone and placed the phone on the console so Charlie could hear.

"Can you tell me the address again, please?" She filled in the details on the sheet, including the name of the caller and their contact details, her hand circling or ticking parts of the prepopulated form in her lap as the conversation continued. "Thank you so much, Jenny. We're on the road now and can be there within twenty minutes." Pip signed off from the conversation and filled in a few more details on the form before handing over the clipboard to Charlie.

Charlie scanned the sheet and looked up expectantly at her. "A wallaby. We're going to rescue a wallaby?" Pip watched as her widened hazel eyes shone with the excitement of the upcoming prospect.

Pip pulled out into the traffic. "A woman just rang to say she saw a wallaby get hit by a car in front of her. She's not sure, but she thinks it might have a joey. So we're going to go and check it out." Charlie studied the sheet. "And so it begins—day one, Charlie. You ready for this?"

Charlie raised her eyes and beamed back at her. "Never readier."

Pip smiled back and nodded, happy with the response.

❖

Once they located the downed animal, Pip pulled over behind it and turned the hazard lights on. She walked to the back of the ute and opened up the cabin door. Inside the canopy were several carriers of various sizes and two large plastic tubs with lids. She pulled two fluorescent yellow vests from a hook on the side wall. "Here, put this on. It identifies you as a member of the organization."

Charlie donned the vest "And makes it easier to see us too, huh?"

Pip opened up one of the tubs. "Yup. Gives the traffic something to aim for."

She looked up to see a shocked look on Charlie's face. "Sorry. Old joke." Pip dragged over the tub she had opened and pointed out each item as she pulled them out. "Gloves, a pair of scissors, pillowcase, knitted pouch, and a bag."

Pip handed a pair of latex gloves over and donned a pair. Charlie copied her actions. "Remember what I said the other day about the importance of hygiene?" Charlie nodded. "Well, it starts now." Pip held up her gloved hands and wiggled her fingers. "Tuck the pillowcase and scissors into one of your pockets and the woollen pouch in another and let's go take a look-see."

Bright red rivulets of blood ran from the downed animal's nose, its sightless eyes staring blindly off into the distance. It had been a clean hit, with massive head injuries. The wallaby hadn't stood a chance. A piece of broken blue plastic lay off to one side. A part of the car's panel. Pip went through the routine of looking for signs of life. She didn't linger. She was confident she wouldn't find any.

"Macropods, like this little wallaby here, might look cute, but always be mindful and respectful of their hind legs, feet, and tail. That's their powerhouse. A badly hurt roo or wallaby can lash out with his hind legs and do plenty of damage. So if the animal is still conscious, cover its head with a towel or blanket to reduce its stress."

"The same as a lot of animals, I imagine." Charlie stood by her side as if waiting for Pip's next move. When Pip squatted, she followed suit.

"This is where the gloves come in handy. Check Mumma's pouch." Pip rocked back on her heels to give Charlie more room and watched as Charlie tentatively pulled back the pouch opening. "Don't be shy, it's very elastic. Open it wider. That's it. What do you see?"

A grin spread over Charlie's face. "Oh my God. A head. A tiny dark head."

Pip smiled at Charlie's reaction. She could remember her first joey all those years ago and knew that this would be a significant bookmark moment for Charlie too.

"Uh-huh. Now slide your hand in. Can you feel it moving?"

"It is! It is."

"All right, with your other hand, pull the pouch down far enough to see if the joey is still attached to the teat. If it is you'll have to cut it off."

"No, no, it's not."

"Okay, gently lift it out. I'm going to rub the pillowcase around the inside of Mum's pouch, to get the scent on it so bub here has something familiar, and then I'll hold it out for you to pop the joey in."

Charlie followed Pip's instructions and finished with sliding the pillowcase, complete with joey, into the woollen pouch.

"We need to get bub warm, but I'll just show you something quickly, while we still have Mum here. Remember about the rubber teat's funny shape?"

"I do. Oh, look at Mum's teat—it's long and tubular. Ah, like the teats we use. Clever. Makes total sense."

"If you go back to the car, you'll find a heat mat on top of the tub we got the gear out of. Wrap it around the woolly pouch and then pop it into the bag."

While Charlie undertook the next set of instructions, Pip dragged the mother's body off the road into the undergrowth. She gently slid her hand down the sightless eyes to close the lids. "We'll take good care of your baby, Mumma." She headed back to the car and got in. After stripping off her gloves and vest she leaned over and plugged the heat mat cord into the cigarette lighter. "Let's get this little one home."

"Should we give it something to drink?"

"No. First rule of thumb is to get the baby warm. Never feed any marsupial until you first warm it up."

"What sort is it?"

Pip grinned at her. "I could tell you, but when we get home I'll show you how we identify them."

"So what are you going to call it?"

"Me? Nothing. This one's yours. This is your first baby."

Pip raised her eyes from the bag and met Charlie's. She had no doubt her own grin matched her new colleague's.

Chapter Four

When Pip thought the joey was warm enough, she showed Charlie how to identify the species by the markings, the shape of its feet and head, and by the photograph Pip had taken of the mother after she had dragged it off the road. They also gave the joey the once-over and determined that it had incurred no obvious injuries from the car that killed her mother.

"So she'll be all right?"

"Well, that really depends. We might see some bruising come out in the next day or so. She could have a small internal bleed." Pip shrugged lightly. "You just never know. The biggest risk is stress. Too much immediate stress can kill them pretty quickly, or prolonged stress can build up and leave them open to infections, or can kill them later, even as an adult. Basically their system overloads and they eventually have heart failure."

"So what you're telling me is not to get my hopes up?"

Pip handed the joey to Charlie and retrieved the scale and tape measure.

"Not really. With a bit of good luck, good management, and a bucketload of hard work and determination, you'll give this little one every chance." Pip looked up at her and held her with a steady gaze. "But determination is the key. For both of you. To give this the best shot possible, both of you will need to be determined."

They took measurements of the joey's back leg, tail, and foot, and weighed it to determine her age. What Charlie now held wrapped protectively in her arms was a small female swamp wallaby, seven hundred grams in weight with a hint of toffee-brown colouring coming through in the form of a fine velvety covering.

"How old do you think she is?"

Sitting across from the kitchen table, Pip referred to the book she'd brought out to help Charlie identify and to categorize the joey. "See here, according to the chart, she's probably around about one hundred and seventy-five days old."

"Almost six months old? She's awfully tiny for that age."

"They're definitely slow growers."

Charlie traced across the grid with her finger. "That means we have to feed her a total of sixty-five mils a day." She tapped the growth and feed chart. "This is really handy."

"Yep, it's my bible. Or at least one of them."

Charlie wordlessly paged through the book with her free hand.

"Once she's warm enough we'll give her a hydrating drink first up. Then after that we can start her on the milk mix. She needs to keep warm and quiet to minimize her stress. You'll need to keep records of mealtimes, how much, toilet habits, colour, weight, et cetera. I'll help you along the way, but it's all up to you. You're her mum now."

❖

You're her mum now. Pip's words echoed in Charlie's mind. She looked down at the multi-layered bundle that held the precious joey. She pushed her hair away from her face and bit her lower lip. The joey was so fragile. According to Pip, it might still die. She wasn't a stranger to death. Far from it. It was the nature of the game whenever wildlife was involved. So why did she feel so uncertain? Again. When Kim left, her world was filled with uncertainty. And that bled into other decisions and situations.

Her breath caught in her chest. Kim's message. She hadn't read it yet. Did she want to? Oh no. What if something had happened to her dogs and the vet contacted Kim?

Charlie wiggled her phone out of her pants pockets beneath the apron she still wore. And there it was. Her stomach tensed. She took a deep breath and selected the message from Kim Carlton. Charlie closed her eyes for a moment, mentally preparing herself for the worst.

Hi, babe.

(Babe? You gave up the right to call me that, Kim.)

I went to the house to see you and somebody strange answered the door. A renter. I had no idea where you were, so I contacted your secretary.

(Crap. Alice has such a big mouth.)

She was surprised I didn't know where you were and even more surprised when she found out I didn't have the dogs.

(Because it wasn't any of her damned business.)

I don't think she wanted to tell me where you are, but I put on my charm and she finally gave in. Australia? WTF made you decide to leave?

(Duh. Maybe to help me get over you.)

Anyway, I need to talk to you about something. I guess since you're there, and I'm here, well, I may as well say it. I miss you. I want to come home.

Charlie read that last line over and over in complete shock. "I can't believe this. Are you kidding me?" She tossed the phone onto the cushion next to her, then carved through her hair with her hand. She felt lightheaded and a pain grew in the back of her throat. Just as quickly, her shock and anguish grew to anger. She gritted her teeth and willed herself to not pick up her phone and hurl it against the wall.

"After putting me through all that, now you're telling me you've changed your mind? Fuck."

The joey squirmed inside the sack and squeaked. Charlie listened closer and realized it was also making little sucking noises. She peeked inside the bag and smiled as a long leg and foot stretched out and then disappeared back into the depths of the pouch. The joey wiggled around and suddenly two black eyes stared up at her.

Charlie's heart melted at the sight. "Hello, little squeak. Are you hungry?" She put her cheek against the top of the pouch and felt the warmth emanating from it. The heat mat was keeping the bag warm at a nice steady temperature. The joey squirmed and shook its head. Its little ears flapped against its head. "I can tell you're going to be a big time waster for me."

"Told you." Pip stood in the doorway.

Charlie grinned at Pip. "Yes, you did. I think she's hungry. She's been moving around and making noises."

"Good. That means she's warm enough and we can hydrate her with an electrolyte mix. Rule one, get warm. Rule two is hydrate. If they're stressed, they're also dehydrated. If she does okay with that, we can make her second meal the milk, but we can mix both solutions up at the same time in readiness."

After they'd washed their hands and while Pip measured out the appropriate amounts of both items into bottles, Charlie took the initiative and retrieved two nipples. She then put the kettle on.

"Thanks." Pip added water to the bottles and waited for the kettle to come to a boil.

"I figured I might as well get my feet wet."

Pip looked down at Charlie's feet. "An American expression."

"Ha. Yep." Charlie cocked her head and looked at the kettle. "That turns off when the water boils? The one I have in the States whistles."

"It's the only kind of jug I've ever owned."

"Jug. God, that's what my ex used to call women's breasts." Charlie rolled her eyes.

"Sounds like something a man would say." Pip poured hot water into a mug. She slid one of the nipples onto the bottle containing the clear mix and placed it into the hot water.

"Actually, my ex is a woman." Charlie bit her lip, waiting for Pip's reaction.

Pip didn't seem to skip a beat. "Huh. So's mine." She pulled the bottle from the mug and tested the temperature on her wrist. "Always check the temp before you offer it to an animal. Too hot, and it'll scald their throat. Too cold, and it'll set their body temp way back."

Charlie shook her head. She couldn't believe how blasé Pip was about her sexuality. Australians were an interesting breed. Charlie started to hand the bundle over to Pip.

"Nope. You're her mum. She has to get used to you."

"Okay." She set the bundle on the counter but wasn't sure what to do next.

"Relax. I'll coach you through it. Pull the woollen pouch the joey is in out."

Charlie did as told and held it up with two fingers.

"Okay. Now cradle her in the crook of your arm. That's it. Notice how she's lying on her back, with her hind feet higher than her head? When joeys are in the pouch, they feed like that, kind of upside down."

"No kidding. I had no idea." Charlie positioned the joey so that her legs stuck up out of the pouch.

Pip handed her the bottle with the long nipple. Charlie put a few drops of the liquid on her wrist then held the nipple in front of the joey's mouth. Unfortunately nothing happened. She tickled its mouth with the tip of it, but still nothing.

"Why aren't you taking it, you silly squeak?" Charlie looked at Pip imploringly.

"The texture and smell are very different from Mum's. You have to teach her to take it." Pip placed her hand over Charlie's. "Let me help."

Charlie's only thought was how soft and strong Pip's hand felt. She'd nearly forgotten what it felt like to be touched by someone else—not necessarily sexually, but just the sense of it made her feel content. And maybe even a bit closer to Pip.

Pip wiggled her finger alongside Charlie's, bringing her focus back on the task at hand. "Put the tip of your finger at the end of the nipple and with just a little pressure, prise her mouth slightly from the sides—careful." The joey's mouth opened a crack under the pressure. "Now push it into her mouth. She'll suck the whole thing in once she gets a taste."

Charlie fumbled a little, but with Pip's guidance, they managed to get the nipple into the joey's mouth. Charlie sighed contentedly when the joey started to suckle.

Pip let her hold the bottle herself, and Charlie missed the warmth of Pip's confident hand.

The joey spat the teat out.

"Okay. See if you can get her to suckle by yourself this time."

Charlie was sorely tempted to feign a struggle, but was delighted when she succeeded in getting the nipple in the joey's mouth by herself.

"Have you thought of a name for her yet?"

Charlie sighed. "No. Actually, I haven't."

"Every animal we get has a call number attributed to it, but I always give out names of some sort or other. It just makes it a bit more personal, but you feel comfortable doing whatever works for you."

As if on cue, the joey gave a little squeak as she finished sucking down the contents of the bottle and spat out the nipple.

"Squeak. That's what we'll name her." Charlie looked at Pip for approval.

"Squeak it is then. But I'll have you know, they all do it. She's calling for her mother. You'll have to work out a sound that is special to both of you."

"What do you do?"

"I make a sort of clicking or ticking noise with my tongue against the roof of my mouth." Pip chuckled and opened a drawer from which she withdrew a wad of cotton balls. "That was the fun part. This is the not-so-fun part."

"What's that?"

"The toileting. You have to encourage joeys to toilet. Just like very young puppies and kittens. I'll show you."

Charlie raised an eyebrow in question. "She's this old and she can't do it herself?"

"Nope." Pip dipped a cotton ball into the now tepid water in the mug and handed it to Charlie.

"Just like a puppy?"

"Just like a puppy."

Once Squeak had relieved herself and was tucked back into the rest of her layers, Pip pulled a stand made of PVC from under the counter. Two clamps mounted on the top bar held a knapsack a few inches above the floor.

"What's that for?"

"It's to simulate a kangaroo pouch. Knapsacks work really well because they have a flap to keep the light out, with warmth and the joey securely inside."

"We're putting her in that now?"

"Yep. You can't hold her for the next couple of months or so. We have other things to do. Here, she'll be safe, warm, and quiet."

"Oh. Okay. I guess you're right."

"I'll set you up with enough stuff to take back to the cabin with you, along with her food and extra pouches."

"It's warm enough. Won't she be good to stay here at night?"

"She could. Except for the first little while, when you'll have to feed her every four hours."

Pip must have seen the surprise on her face because she laughed out loud. "As I said, welcome to the party."

"Would it be all right if I go eat dinner first and then come back for her?"

"Sure. You go. I'll put together a bag for you." Pip checked her watch. "If you come back at eight o'clock and feed her here, you'll only have to take two bottles back with you."

Charlie surrendered Squeak to Pip so she could show her how to deposit the bundle into the main pouch, with the heat mat, and fold the flap over the top. She was surprised to see her actually latch the knapsack buckles.

"Keeps her in. You'll be thankful for them in a month or so."

"Okay."

"If you want a hand with the next feed, just holler—the door's always unlocked. I'm only a walkway away. But if you're right, then I guess I'll see you tomorrow morning. If you need anything or you're concerned that Squeak isn't doing so well, call me on the radio." Pip slapped her hip for Chilli and disappeared out the door.

Charlie breathed a weighted breath. Pip had left her alone to deal with this strange and very helpless animal. She hoped she didn't end up killing Squeak with her ignorance.

❖

Sitting at the kitchen bench, Pip finished off the last of her steamed veggies. She frowned as she tried to work her way through an instruction booklet that had come with the packet she had collected from the chemist earlier in the day.

Since Charlie had left, taking her groceries back to the cabin, Pip had fed all the other animals. After that she made up a box ready for Charlie to take back with her when she came back to give the joey another feed. She'd included a spare frame for the joey's bag to save Charlie dragging one back and forth with her each day. It wasn't like she didn't have plenty of spares. She had chuckled to herself when she packed it in the back of the ute, along with the box, anticipating that Charlie would need more than one hanging frame before her time was up on the exchange program.

She had left a note on the bench in the prep room telling Charlie that her vehicle was packed and enough milk for several meals was made up in the fridge. Beneath the note she'd put a book for Charlie to keep her notes in and the keys to the ute. It was silly to expect her to carry the joey and all the gear back to the cabin at night. She hoped she'd be okay driving back in the dark. And if not, well, it was insured. She grimaced slightly at the thought of the risk, then had to make a deliberate effort to relax her shoulders and walk away, leaving the keys with the note.

Pip continued to flip through the pages of the booklet through several yawns, noting the pertinent details through teary eyes. She rubbed them and rolled her neck around to dispel some of the day's tension. She was tired. It had been a long day and she hadn't eaten enough. She'd just decided to chop up some fruit when the phone rang. She hit the speaker button and rinsed her sticky hands under running water.

"Hello."

"Hello, darling, it's me. Just ringing to check to see how things are."

"Hey, Terese."

"So how are things?"

"By things, if you mean your American friend, then I suggest you call her and ask."

The sound of Terese's gentle chortling laughter burbled across the phone line. "Then I take it things are going well, otherwise you'd be midstream giving me a gobful by now."

Before Pip could reply another yawn escaped her.

"You sound tired."

Pip scrunched up her nose briefly. "Mm. Big day."

"Everything okay?" Terese's voice had gentled.

Pip sighed. "Yes. Everything's fine." Well, as fine as things could be when you were stuck with a person you knew very little about. "We went shopping, to the beach, and picked up a wallaby on the way home. Charlie's keen, sharp, and interested in everything around her. So it's all positive."

"And how are you going?"

It was early days, and as much as Pip hated having someone thrust unexpectedly on her, Charlie was proving to be quite reasonable. It was, so far, bearable. Pip raised an eyebrow in mild surprise at the realization. "It's fine. I'm fine."

A beep sounded from the package she had unwrapped.

Pip turned her head towards it.

"What's that?" Terese had obviously picked up on the sound.

Pip grunted in mild self-annoyance at the timing.

"Pip?"

"My new pump arrived today. I was just working out some of the settings when you rang."

"Is it much different?"

"Doesn't look like it, but then, I've only just opened it."

"Have you told Charlie about—"

"No." Pip's voice came out sharper than intended. She took a breath and softened her tone. "No. And no, before you ask."

"What would it hurt to tell her?"

"I'm fine. It's none of her business and she doesn't need to know."

"There's no harm in letting her know. In fact, it might be good to have a backup."

"Is that why you sent her?"

"No. Of course not. I told you why and how Charlie came to be with you. Pip, you know I wouldn't lie to you."

Pip rubbed at the headache that was starting to build behind her temple. Her friend didn't deserve her cranky retorts when all she had were her best interests at heart. "I know. Sorry."

"All right, I'll leave it for now, but promise me you'll give it some thought."

"Mm."

Terese laughed. "I'll take that as a small win."

Pip couldn't help herself and joined in along with her friend. Terese caught Pip up on some of the organization's latest news before signing off, promising to ring later in the week to check up on how both of them were going.

Pip looked at the fruit in front of her and pushed it aside, her appetite having deserted her. All she really wanted was a hot shower and to hop into bed. She put the fruit into a container and shoved it haphazardly into the fridge. She could always have it later. She wrote up a few brief notes on the day's undertakings before gathering her instruction booklet and the package and putting them on her bedside table, fully intending to read them after she had had a shower.

❖

"Crap, I forgot my phone." Charlie knew exactly where it was: on the couch where she'd tossed it. She gave it little thought as she walked the final hundred feet to the cabin. If she wanted to check her email, she'd only have to log on to her computer. Which she didn't at the moment. Kim's message lurked in the far back of her mind, but she wasn't going to dwell on it. Yet. She knew she'd have to address it at some point, but she was still enjoying today's high.

The entertaining laugh of at least three kookaburras filtered through the canopies as she stepped onto the deck. She leaned against the doorway, her two bags of groceries hanging low enough to touch the floor, and closed her eyes and smiled.

The day, sans Kim's message, had been wonderful. The beach was lovely. And watching Chilli play in the surf made it even more magical. She licked the back of her hand and tasted ocean salt and vowed to ask Pip to take her back there again. Or at the very least to another beach.

And Pip. She had seemed much more relaxed and less judgemental, although admittedly, she hadn't made any drastic mistakes. Pip as a tour guide seemed more likeable than Pip as a coworker. But the jury was still out on that, she guessed. Early days.

Then there was her new charge, Squeak. Charlie puffed out her cheeks and blew the air out. She hadn't realized how much intensive care a macropod needed. But she was sure if she needed a break or extra help, Pip would help her. Wouldn't she? *God, how does she manage all by herself?*

After unpacking her groceries, Charlie set about making some instant soup. She really wasn't all that hungry from lunch. She'd barely been able to finish the huge sandwich. But if she was going to be up a couple times in the night, she figured she'd better eat a little something.

She filled the kettle and pushed the lever down to start it. As she stood waiting for the water to boil, she chuckled. "*Jug*. I'll have to remember that." How interesting that Pip was a lesbian. She wouldn't have guessed, but then her gaydar was crap. Kim had to just about tattoo *lesbian* on her forehead to make Charlie notice her.

Dammit, Kim.

Charlie shook her head. "Give me a break." She just wanted to take some time to get used to the fact that Kim had contacted her before she gave it any deep thought.

She let her mind wander back to Pip. So she had an ex. Interesting. Curiosity always arose about break-ups. People just didn't understand there were two sides to every story. More like they just picked sides, like they did with her and Kim. She'd lost some good friends because of their ignorance.

Why did it always come back around to *her*? Charlie forcefully slid the mug closer to the jug and added water. She stirred it quickly and went outside onto the back porch where the sun was sinking below the treeline. Lorikeets squawked from the high branches and the distinct call of a whipbird reached her from the forest floor. Charlie took a deep breath and consciously relaxed the muscles in her shoulders and neck. She'd been on edge for the most part ever since she got here. Well, ever since she'd met Pip. Kim just added fuel to the fire with her damned message.

Charlie swallowed the last of her soup, washed up, and decided to take a shower. The ocean salt and wallaby smells clung to her sweaty skin and clothing. And according to Pip, she needed to take advantage of any free time offered.

❖

Her hair was still wet when she began the trek back to the prep room. She'd dried off quickly and ran her fingers through her hair in her haste to get back to Squeak and her needs.

Although the sun had long since disappeared, light from the rising full moon lit the path in front of her. Even though she remembered to bring a flashlight, she found she didn't need it except for where the canopy was thick overhead.

It didn't appear there were any lights on in the house. But she guessed it was possible Pip might be somewhere in the back. The spotlight on the back porch came on when she neared the prep room entrance. Chilli barked once from the depths of the cottage, but other than that, all was quiet.

Charlie saw the note on the table as soon as she flipped the light switch.

"Wow. She's letting me borrow the truck? That's awfully nice of her." Charlie glanced at the wall clock. She had about an hour before Squeak's next feed. It was as good a time as any to update the records. But that only took a few minutes as she and Pip had done the majority earlier in the day.

Charlie drew a deep breath and released it. She might as well get it over with. She settled herself on the couch and scraped a hand over her face before picking up the phone. She didn't want to deal with Kim, but knew she had to. But what would she say? You had your chance? You made your bed, now sleep in it?

She dropped her head back and closed her eyes. A ticker tape of good memories streamed past her closed eyelids. Like the summer

Kim had accompanied her on an otter release project. They'd spent nearly a week next to a river introducing the kits to the wild. Kim's face had seemed permanently etched with a smile. Her laughter at the otters' antics had been infectious. Their lovemaking under a million stars and the Milky Way was most magical.

Their relationship had been solid, she thought. Kim had known what she was getting into. Knew Charlie spent loads of time in the field. What had changed? Had she not spent enough time with Kim when she had been home? Had she been too sidetracked thinking about her work duties? Maybe not told her she loved her often enough? Or how much she appreciated her holding down the fort when she was away? Kim had been her rock. She'd known she could depend on her to pay the bills on time, organize their social life, and be there to hold her when an animal she'd spent hours of time and energy on, died for no reason.

Those questions were just repeats among many others she'd spent days pondering since Kim had broken her heart by telling her she wanted out. When she left, so did Charlie's confidence and self-esteem. Kim's departure had torn a huge hole right out of Charlie's heart and she'd taken that piece with her. And now she wanted to give it back?

Charlie's emotions wavered back and forth. One side of her brain urged her to tell Kim to go to hell. But the other side, the side that kept those good memories to the forefront, was still in love with the old Kim Carlton. Both sides swung her back and forth like a pendulum.

Movement from the pouch caught Charlie's eye. She checked the time. Squeak had to be fed in ten minutes. It would take her that long to boil the water and gather everything she needed. She washed her hands and hung the apron over her neck, securing it around her waist with the strings.

Once she had the bottles settled into the hot water, she set the mugs on the table in front of the couch. It was time to get Squeak out. She unbuckled the bag and lifted the inner pouch containing the joey, and settled it into the crook of her arm.

The joey squeaked and wiggled forcefully.

"Hungry, little girl?"

Charlie spread the pouch open and gasped as a rank smell rose up to assault her. "Oh, pew! You're not going to eat until I get you cleaned up." She set the joey into a new, clean pouch before the feeding, and pulled the sides up and over her. Squeak wriggled around until she was finally on her back with her legs stretched up, her feet sticking out of the pouch.

Charlie tested the milk on her wrist and tucked the bundle in the crook of her arm. "Please take this nipple for me." She touched the side of Squeak's mouth with the tip. A few small drops came out the end and rolled down the joey's jaw and neck. Charlie pressed the side of Squeak's mouth with her finger, and to her relief, the joey quickly grabbed onto the nipple and sucked. "That's a good girl."

When she finished feeding, Charlie toileted Squeak and began cleaning up. She didn't really want to put the joey back in the hanger as she wanted to bond with her a bit more. So she carried her around as she cleaned. It made things a bit awkward, but Charlie managed with one hand.

When she finally sat back down on the couch, an unexpected release of tension came over her as the day's activities finally took their toll.

Charlie closed her eyes and listened to the little squeaks coming from the pouch. On a whim, she pulled the apron off and shoved the pouch under her shirt. She could still hear Squeak making her little noises and now she felt every movement against her chest. *This must be what a new mother experiences.* Charlie closed her eyes once again, fully intending to get up and take everything over to the cabin in a few minutes.

Chapter Five

Pip looked at her watch. It was now seven fifty in the morning. By her calculations, Charlie should've been making up a new batch of milk formula ready for an eight a.m. feed. She'd been waiting, wondering whether or not to call her on the radio or walk down to the cabin and make sure that everything was okay. Maybe…maybe the joey hadn't survived the night and Charlie needed some time alone. She could appreciate that. Or maybe she was having trouble feeding and could use some support.

Pip chewed her lip, momentarily unsure of what she should do next. After a few minutes of internal arguments, Pip grunted as she pushed herself upright from the kitchen chair and headed out the back door, only to come to a halt as she spied the ute exactly where she'd left it. She could still see the silhouette of the frame she had packed the night before through the canopy's side window. She did a mental double take, knowing she had left the keys and instructions for Charlie to take it. Had she miscalculated? Was Charlie too tired to drive? Or not confident enough yet to drive a vehicle with the steering wheel on the right-hand side? Pip's mind leapt and swerved over several possibilities as her body automatically carried her towards the prep room.

That was where she found her, laid out, asleep on the couch. She stood for a moment, transfixed in the doorway. Charlie looked so peaceful, her eyes closed, framed by long dark lashes. Her clothes from the previous day were crumpled and twisted around her slumbering body. Pip closed her eyes and breathed slowly, trying to steel herself for what needed to come next.

Her first concern was not for Charlie, but for the joey. The bag lay on the floor beside the lounge, empty. It didn't take long for Pip to realize that an unusual bulge under Charlie's shirt equalled a joey in a pouch. Charlie's notebook was on the table. The last recorded feed was just prior to midnight. The page was blank after that. Either Charlie hadn't entered in the feed details or…Pip's jaw set. The joey had missed a feed and was in grave danger of missing a second one if she didn't take charge.

Opening the fridge door, Pip spied the milk made up from the previous evening, confirming her suspicions. The joey hadn't been fed since midnight. She put the jug on to boil, plugged the heat mat in, and started to warm a fresh pouch and bag. As she readied the milk in a mug of heated water she deliberately refrained from disguising any noises. Pip opened and shut cupboards without care. She placed mugs loudly onto bench tops. With a sense of grim satisfaction, she heard Charlie stir after a drawer was noisily shoved back into its housing framework with a sharp flick of her hip.

"Ugh. What time is it?" Charlie struggled to sit up. She swiped at an errant curl that had fallen into her eyes as she yawned and stretched. A brief startled look crossed her face as she appeared to remember the parcel currently swaddled in her cotton T-shirt. She pulled the woollen pouch from under her shirt and stuck her fingers inside. A brief look of horror crossed her face at the realization of what she had done.

Wordlessly, Pip handed her a pre-warmed lining and woollen pouch in the heavy-duty bag containing the heat mat. Her eyes sought and captured Charlie's.

"Rule one."

Pip noted Charlie at least had the good grace to look mortified knowing she had let the joey's temperature drop. Charlie had no choice but to wait until after the baby was warm enough before she could feed it. Pip silently went about preparing the food for her other charges.

Charlie sat up straight, pale-faced. "Pip, I—"

Pip held out a hand and shook her head. She pointed to the pouch with a jerk of her head and chin, her voice quiet but firm. "See to your joey. We'll talk later."

Not bothering to look back, Pip gathered the food, turned, and continued outside, silently chewing over the seeming flippancy of the American.

She fed the older joeys and the birds. She raked up the dung in the koala pen and restocked the containers with fresh leaves and water. By the time she had returned, Charlie was standing by the sink washing up the bottles and hanging them up on the drying rack. Pip added her bottles to the wash mix.

Charlie turned and looked at her, a stricken look on her face. Pip looked past her out the window.

"Write up your notes and join me in the main house kitchen in ten minutes." It wasn't an invitation. She had just enough time to see Charlie open and shut her mouth before swallowing and nodding once, complying with the directive.

❖

Alone but for Chilli, Pip leaned on the kitchen bench and waited for the tin kettle on the old wood-fired stove to boil. As she put more wood on the fire, she noticed her hands trembled in anticipation of the upcoming showdown. Damn Charlie! Did she think this was a holiday? She'd had such high hopes. She'd thought she'd found someone who got what she did. Opening up a jar she kept on the bench near the window she tossed down a few chewy fruit-flavoured animal-shaped lollies. As she chewed, she tried to figure out who she was more angry with—Charlie, or herself, for misreading the American's competency and drive. Chilli whined, evidently picking up her mood. "Sorry, bub, not your fault. It's mine. You'd think I'd know by now not to be so trusting."

A clearing of the throat from the doorway alerted her to Charlie's presence. She felt a hot flush cross her face as she hoped that Charlie hadn't overheard her last privately intended remark. But by the scowl on the American's face she suspected she had. She poured the coffee into two mugs and set them on the kitchen table.

"Milk?"

Charlie nodded and took a seat at the table.

"Sugar?"

Charlie shook her head.

Both sat with their hands wrapped around their respective mugs. The air was heavy in anticipation of what was to unfold. Pip set her mug carefully on a coaster and steepled her hands together under her chin. She looked directly at Charlie. "Talk me through what happened last night." She had a thousand thoughts and words rolling around her head but wanted to give Charlie the first course of recall of events. If she was wrong, then Charlie would fill in the blanks and they could work out a plan. If she was right, then her guest was in for a pasting.

Charlie explained about arriving back at the house, writing up the notes, getting some research in, and putting the joey inside her shirt as she waited for the midnight feed, hoping that it would help them to bond. She looked down into the milky depths of her mug. "I'm sorry. I guess I was more tired than I thought. I just…I just fell asleep. I'm really sorry."

The waves of remorse coming off Charlie were almost palpable. It could have been worse. Still, the stress of being cold and not fed…the result of the extra stress on the joey's little body wouldn't be fully realized for another day or so.

Pip swallowed the last mouthful of coffee, but opted to cling to the sides of her mug, if only to keep her trembling hands still. "It's not me you have to apologize to. I wasn't the one who was cold and hungry for most of the night."

Charlie avoided her gaze and stared at her mug.

Pip slid a macropod care guidebook across the table. A bookmark stuck out from the top. Pip nodded to Charlie who looked at her with questions in her eyes. "Open it up."

Charlie carefully opened the book to reveal a page of information on joey care. A single line was highlighted. Pip knew it by heart: *When a velvet or just furred joey first comes into care it will require heating from twenty-eight to thirty degrees Celsius (depending on its length of fur) for the first twenty-four hours in order to assist in the reduction of further shock.*

Pip's voice remained low and calm. "We talked about shock. We talked about the importance of keeping the joey warm, didn't we?"

"Yes, but—"

"I'm not finished."

Charlie's mouth opened and then clamped shut.

"I am not going to insult your intelligence by pretending caring for wildlife is easy. I have read your rap sheet. You know how hard a job it can be sometimes. Bonding is important, but it's something that occurs over time. What you did last night was foolish and selfish. You didn't put that baby under your shirt to make the baby feel better. You did it to make *you* feel better. If you were in the middle of nowhere, with no facilities, no resources, then yes, putting the joey next to your skin and under your clothing would be the best you could do. But you had pouches, heat mats, food, and access to alarms on your phone or the computer in the prep room to wake you."

"I know. I'm sorry."

Although Pip didn't raise her voice, her next words sat heavy in the quiet of the room. "Sorry's not good enough."

Charlie's head snapped up and Pip could see the anger radiating from her with the flush of her cheeks and the stiffening of her spine as she sat rigidly upright. "Well maybe *you* should take over her care then."

"You committed to a year, Charlie. During this year you will have good times, bad times, and a few weird and wonderful moments in between. You came here to learn. Not for a holiday. If you want to bail out now, then by all means, I can't stop you. But if you balk at the first tough hurdle, then you may as well pack your bags and go home—this job is not for you." Pip paused to let the words sink in. She sighed and rubbed a hand over her tired eyes. "It's my fault."

"What? No."

"It was. I gave you too much, too soon. Your body is probably still adjusting to our time difference and, even after a night's sleep, I can see how tired you are. I should have stayed up and helped you."

"I—"

"However, you need to use today to really think over what it is you want to do and what it is you want to get out of the program and your time here. Take the joey back to your cabin, catch a few more hours of sleep, and think about it. Your choices are simple. If you stay, then I will continue to help you to look after the joey and whatever else comes in as the year progresses."

Charlie's eyes narrowed. "You said I had choices. What's my other choice?"

Pip sat back and folded her arms across her chest. "You can opt out. I will take the joey back, call Terese, and arrange for your transport out of here. If you don't want to put in the hard yards and make an effort, then you may as well leave. There's no point in wasting both our time."

Pip stood and gathered the mugs up. "Stay or go, Charlie. Only you can decide. Take this guidebook and your joey and go and get some sleep. Dinner will be at half six tonight. You can let me know what you've decided then."

Not knowing what else to say, Pip retrieved the keys to the quad runner and made her way outside. The koalas needed a fresh batch of leaves for the next few days and now seemed like the perfect opportunity to escape and go and get them.

She made every effort to control her posture and her walk, to appear calm and in control. It was only after she rounded the corner of the shed, out of sight of the house, where the bike was garaged that she bent over and vomited into the dirt, finally releasing the nerves and tension.

❖

Deflated. Charlie felt completely deflated as she sat alone in Pip's house. And defeated. This put her on the verge of an anxiety attack. Her first real one since she'd left the States. Her heart palpitated in her tight chest. She blew out a series of short breaths to gain control.

Her body felt heavy as she lifted it out of the chair. She sagged against the table and reached out to steady herself. She hadn't felt this worthless since Kim left her.

The rumbling of the motorcycle started up from out back, increased in volume as Pip drove past the house and was gone. Charlie felt the prickly burn of tears behind her eyes. *I should've known better. I'm such an idiot.* She knew it was all common sense, and yes, Pip had pointed out the things that she'd inevitably done wrong. She was well versed in shock and body temperature regulation. There wasn't much difference between a macropod and any animal she was familiar with. Except for the fact that the effects might not show up for a while.

Charlie rubbed her eyes. Her mind replayed Pip's words over and over in agonizing detail. She'd seen the disappointment and anger in Pip's eyes. There'd also been a *Why me?* in one of Pip's heavy sighs.

She washed both mugs and set them aside to dry. Like Pip said, she had some thinking to do and choices to make. But at the moment she needed to heed her responsibility, which was Squeak. She'd be damned if the little thing was going to get sick on her watch, for however short a time she might be in her care.

The truck keys were still on the table on top of Pip's note in the prep room. Charlie picked them up and marched outside. There was no birdsong, as if Pip had taken all of it with her and left a vacuum when she'd gone. Charlie looked around, wondering where Chilli was, as there was no sign of her either. Surely she wouldn't have taken the dog on the bike with her. Would she?

"Not my problem." Charlie peeked inside the truck and looked at the bundle of stuff Pip had put in the back for Squeak's care.

"Holy crap," she mumbled. "Looks like she packed enough for the entire year I'm supposed to be here."

There were two bundles of towels held together by bungee straps, another frame, and a box with extra milk mix, bottles, pouches, and other miscellaneous things. "No wonder she left me the keys." She closed her eyes and rubbed her temples with her fingertips. "Christ, I don't know if I can do this." She hated letting Pip down. In just the short time they'd been partnered, Charlie had felt the beginnings of a strong camaraderie. But in one fell swoop, one stupid mistake by her, it'd been annihilated. She had also let herself down.

Pip was right. The choices were simple: remain here, try to recover what she'd lost with Pip, and succeed in accomplishing the objectives in coming to Australia, or go home a failure. She'd have to deal with peer questions and disillusionment. She could do that and just jump back into the work she loved and was so familiar with. But could she cope with the truth that she'd have to keep bottled up inside?

Her life in the States was already under the microscope because of the break-up. Being the only lesbian couple in the area had been fodder for locals and colleagues alike. The break-up had caused a gossip party.

A mournful howl sounded from the back of the house.

Charlie snapped out of her self-imposed pity party and jogged in the direction she thought it came from.

Another howl made Charlie change direction towards the shed. It was there she found a very despondent Chilli lying between two ruts in the dirt, obviously where the bike was normally parked. When she saw Charlie approach, Chilli got up slowly and, with her head hanging low and tail wagging from the tip only, nearly crawled to her.

"Aw, poor baby." Charlie dropped to her knees and hugged Chilli around her furry neck. "She'll be back soon. In the meantime you can hang with me."

Charlie got to her feet and patted her thigh. "Come on, sweet thing."

Chilli brightened slightly and followed Charlie to the prep room, but she stopped at the door and refused to go any further. Charlie left the door open in case Chilli changed her mind.

She took a few minutes to update Squeak's records, making sure she noted her missed feeding in a red font. Why, she wasn't sure. Maybe to beat herself over the head and have a stark reminder of her asinine mistake every time she opened it. Or very likely to make Pip feel guilty for the way she made her feel. Either way, it was there and now saved.

Charlie picked up Squeak's frame with the joey securely inside and walked outside. "Come on, Chilli. Get in the truck."

Chilli paced between the prep room and the open truck door.

"Come on. Get in."

Chilli hesitated, looked towards the shed, and, with a single leap, jumped in.

Charlie set the frame onto the back seat and got in. She pulled the keys out of her pocket and only then realized there wasn't a steering wheel in front of her. She blew a raspberry, got out, and walked around to the other side. The side with the steering wheel and everything else she needed to drive the truck. She inserted the key and brought the diesel engine to life.

Chilli howled again. In the closed space of the truck it was nearly deafening.

"Jesus, Chilli! What's wrong? You damned near scared the hell out of me."

Chilli had turned in the seat and was looking behind them. She whined a few times before another howl escaped her.

"Damn you, Pip." She turned the truck off and rested a hand on Chilli's back. "I can't very well leave you here all by yourself." Her thoughts jumped to her own dogs, whom she'd left behind. She wondered if they missed her as much as she missed them.

Chilli was obviously distressed, uncertain whether to go with Charlie or stay near the house waiting for Pip to come home.

Charlie opened the door and slid out, followed closely by Chilli. She threw her hands up. "I give up. I'll stay here until your mom decides to come home."

A few minutes later, Charlie was sitting on the couch back in the prep room. Chilli nestled against her leg and Squeak remained in the pouch, hanging from the frame. The battery in her cell phone was dead, rendering it completely useless, and the charger was back at the cabin.

Charlie leaned her head back and closed her eyes. She suddenly opened them, got up, and set the timer on the microwave for Squeak's next feeding. When she took her place on the couch, she rested her arm on Chilli's back and burrowed her fingers into the long coat. The sound of the dog breathing and the warmth she exuded lulled her to sleep.

❖

Charlie had no idea how long she'd been asleep when the motorcycle roused her. Chilli jumped down and yipped excitedly. When she opened the door, the dog took off like a shot and disappeared around the corner, no doubt heading straight for the shed. "About time." She closed the door behind her and checked the time. The clock showed ten minutes before she had to feed the joey, so she busied herself warming up the milk in preparation.

Watching through the window, she saw Pip offload several buckets full of branches and leaves from a trailer connected to the motorbike and place the buckets under a shaded lean-to by the fence before heading up the path to the prep room entrance.

"You look a bit more rested. How're you going?" Pip walked past Charlie with a basketful of leaves and flowered branches, which she shoved into a bucket of fresh water in the corner of the room.

"Fine." It wasn't until now that Charlie realized how angry she was that Pip had left Chilli. She turned and put her hands on her hips. "Actually, no. I'm not fine. Poor Chilli was so stressed that you left without her. The poor thing howled and paced the entire time you were gone." She knew she was stretching the truth somewhat, but didn't give a damn.

Pip froze in place. Her face went slack and her eyes widened.

"You forgot about her, didn't you? In your haste to get away from me, you forgot all about that dear little dog who looks like she'd follow you to the ends of the earth and back." Charlie rolled her eyes and spun around. "Nice," she mumbled to herself.

Pip groaned softly behind her. "You're right. I'm sorry."

"It shouldn't be me you're apologizing to. Except maybe you should. I had no idea where you were. What if we'd gotten a call-out? What if I'd had an emergency? Or…or what if I'd left a note telling you to shove this assignment up your ass and left?"

"You wouldn't have gotten far." Pip tottered slightly, sat down, and scrubbed her face with her hands. Chilli came to her, nudged Pip's elbow with her nose, and whined.

"I could've called a taxi." Charlie crossed her arms over her chest and narrowed her eyes.

Pip shook her head and closed her eyes. "Look around. Taxis don't come out this far."

"Well then, you're lucky I'm not leaving. Yet." Charlie noticed Pip had a sheen of sweat on her brow and upper lip. "Hey, are you okay?"

Pip nodded but didn't meet Charlie's eyes.

"Pip?"

"I just need something to eat."

Chilli whined again and scratched Pip's arm with her paw.

"Can I get you anything?" Charlie was beginning to worry. Pip was awfully pale.

"In the house, there's a popper in the fridge. Could you please bring me one?"

Charlie crossed the walkway to the kitchen and opened the refrigerator door and stared at the contents. She raised her voice. "What the hell is a popper?"

"A small carton of juice."

"Oh, yeah. Right." She took one out and was about to shut the door when she noticed some small vials of clear liquid on the top shelf of the door and what appeared to be tubes of some sort of glucose mix. Closing the door, she shoved the straw out of the plastic casing and made her way back to Pip.

"Thanks."

Charlie couldn't help but notice how Pip's hands shook when she took the proffered drink. "You sure you're okay?"

❖

The stress of the morning, losing her breakfast out behind the shed, missing morning tea, on top of a good workout getting all the different types of leaves for the koalas, had thrown her body out of whack and she needed to right it. Pip glanced at the clock: almost lunchtime. Pip drained the last of the juice from the container.

"I'm fine. And thank you for looking after Chilli. But you have the afternoon to yourself. Go on, choof off. Think, sleep, explore, study…do whatever you need or want to do. I'll see you back here for dinner."

"You're sure? I mean, you still—"

Pip stood up and made shooing motions with her hands. "Go." A soft chuckle escaped her lips. "Take the free time while you have it. It's a rare and fickle beast at best."

Charlie looked down at the car keys. "Is it still okay to take the truck?"

Pip tossed them to her. "Sure. I know where you are if I need it."

Charlie hesitated in the doorway and looked back. Pip shooed her away again and watched as she made her way to the ute. A wry half smile crossed her face as she watched Charlie open the passenger door and lift a leg to get in, only to step back out and walk to the right side, the driver's side. Charlie looked up at the window just then and caught Pip watching her and smiled, raising her hands in the air and shrugging at her own bemusement. With a last wave Pip turned and made her way into the house.

She didn't need to test to know her levels were low after the morning she'd had.

She needed to get back on track and the best way to do that was to have some lunch. A nasty headache was brewing as she knew it would. Perhaps after lunch she could sneak in a nap herself. With the new pump she was supposed to test every two hours, even in the middle of the night, ideally for the next week, to make sure she had the levels and the settings right. She grabbed her mobile phone and set it to vibrate every two hours. It was lucky that the new pump wasn't too different from her original one but it was imperative to be careful and to monitor it closely so that she could get it right. She'd deliberately ordered her new pump for this time of the year as it was typically quieter, and she thought she would've had the time to get used to it. That was before Charlie arrived. The timing couldn't have been more awkward.

As she sipped her tea, Pip wondered what Charlie would choose. She hadn't meant to leave Chilli behind when she left to get the leaves. But if the charm and power of a cute defenceless joey and Chilli couldn't get Charlie over the line, well, there was probably nothing she could do to convince her to stay.

Pips hands stilled midway to raising the mug to her mouth as she studied her reflection. Only a handful of days ago the thought of having someone sharing her day-to-day life was abhorrent, and yet, here she was, wondering—okay, hoping—that Charlie would still choose to stay.

Pip's stomach rumbled. She did the math. She could afford another piece of fruit before snagging a brief doze.

It wasn't that she enjoyed Charlie's company or anything, but she knew how fascinated Charlie'd be with the Australian wildlife if she just gave herself this chance. She knew deep down in her heart the American's connection and fascination for all things wild. Pip could feel it in her, and saw it in her movements and her care. She knew that if Charlie stayed, she'd tap into a richness that couldn't be paralleled. And a part of her really wanted Charlie to find that magic. To taste it. To become one with it.

But if Charlie left, well, Pip was used to being on her own. God knew it would be simpler and it wouldn't be for a lack of her trying to accommodate her guest. But as Pip lay down, the thought of Charlie leaving left a strange dull empty heaviness deep in the pit of her stomach.

❖

Movement from the bush path caught Pip's attention as she stacked the bone-white striped bare branches from the kangaroo pens into the box trailer. Chilli, resting in the shade under the trailer, thumped her tail. As Charlie walked out from under the thick growth of trees, Pip saw that she had the joey's backpack across her chest, accompanied by a colourful bag slung across her shoulders. A tentative smile crossed Charlie's face as she waved.

Pip straightened, stretched, and offered a smile in return. It was going on four in the afternoon. She squinted into the sinking sun as Charlie drew nearer. "I wasn't expecting you until a bit later."

Charlie shrugged. "I came up to see if you wanted a hand with anything before dinner."

Pip couldn't tell from Charlie's face or body language whether or not that meant she'd decided to stay, or if this was her last hurrah. She had one card left to play.

"Well, I'm glad you came. There's someone I want you to meet."

"Oh?" Charlie's raised eyebrows spoke of her curiosity.

Barely managing to hold back a smile, Pip crooked her finger for Charlie to follow. "I suspect you'll get on like a house on fire."

Silently, Charlie followed in Pip's wake as they moved to a high-fenced area, where Pip slid a padlock and bolt off the door and stepped inside, closing the door behind Charlie. In the middle of a screened-off pen was an open-sided structure with a pitched roof. Two Y beams at either side and several poles made out of stringy barked branches traversed the space. Sitting on top of one of the Y segments was a koala. As Pip drew near, the koala yawned and stretched her arms out, not unlike a small child asking to be picked up. Pip stepped up to the marsupial and allowed it to claw its way across to her body to rest just up from her hip and along her side, supported by Pip's arm wrapped around its waist.

"Charlie, I'd like you to meet Lucille. Lucille here is one of two permanent residents. She helps me with orphaned babies and rehabilitating older koalas. For her efforts she gets a milk treat every morning, fresh leaves every day, and cuddles whenever she asks." Pip moved in front of Charlie. "Lucille, this is Charlie."

Lucille looked from Pip to Charlie and back again before stretching out her arms and prepared to walk across to Charlie. Pip saw Charlie stiffen, one hand raised protectively against her joey bag.

"It's okay. Just relax."

And Charlie did, allowing the koala to cross their bodies until she was settled on Charlie's hip. A wide grin split her face. "Oh my God. Look at that."

Pip couldn't help but mirror a similar look at Charlie's obvious wonder and delight. "I think you've just been confirmed an honorary member of the team." Charlie looked up at her but said nothing. Not wanting to push things Pip indicated an upturned plastic milk crate off to one side. "Why don't you take a load off over there on the seat while I do a quick clean-up and freshen her leaves."

As she raked the pellets up and replaced the branches whose leaves had been stripped, Pip took the odd occasional sideways glance, pleased to see Charlie thoroughly absorbed in Lucille's company.

Pip moved to the pen next to Lucille's to clean and feed the other koala in residence. When she returned, she found Charlie walking around with Lucille still on her hip, murmuring softly to her. Her noises stopped as Pip re-entered the pen.

Charlie glanced at Pip. "Do you want her back?"

"No. If you just walk over to the beam, she'll climb off." As if on cue, Lucille smoothly left Charlie's embrace to sit in the fork of the branch with a fistful of fresh leaves and started munching contentedly.

Pip held the pen door open. "What say we head back and wash up? I'll get dinner together while you feed Squeak. You can feed her in the house and tell me about your afternoon while I get the veggies ready."

"Okay."

Chilli joined them as they walked back to the house. Pip chewed her bottom lip. She was trying to be open and calm, and not put any inflection or pressure on Charlie or her pending decision, but damn if it wouldn't be helpful to know which way the woman was going to swing.

Pip's phone vibrated as they walked through the back door of the house.

"Make yourself comfortable, I'll be back in a minute."

By the time Pip returned, the joey's dinner had already been prepared. Charlie look stressed and she frowned, trying to get the marsupial to take the bottle. Pip moved the food and utensils out of the way and laid them on the bench to give Charlie space to work through feeding the restless joey.

Milk spattered everywhere as the joey spat the teat out.

"Come on, Squeak. Why won't you take it, little one? Come on now. Try harder."

For several minutes Charlie appeared to wrestle with the infant animal. Squeak finally got the upper hand when she struck out with one of her back legs and kicked the bottle out of Charlie's fingers and onto the floor. "Goddammit."

Pip put the knife down and wiped her hands. Walking around the bench she picked the bottle off the floor. "Clean your girl up and I'll make you a fresh bottle."

When Pip returned she could see the high colour on Charlie's face. She wasn't sure, but there may even have been a hint of moisture on her cheeks. But she made a point of paying it no mind. She handed the bottle over to Charlie who took it with a shaking hand. Charlie tried again, only to have the joey shake its head in refusal of the offered teat. Pip could see Charlie's breath was starting to become short and shallow. Her chin quivered. Pip wrapped her fingers around Charlie's and removed the bottle from her grasp, placing it on the bench top. With quiet steps she stood behind Charlie and placed her hands on top of her shoulders.

"Charlie, I want you to close your eyes for me." Charlie's shoulders tensed under Pip's hands. She kept her hands soft and light. "Come on, Charlie. Close your eyes. That's it. Now slow your breathing. Slow. Slow. That's it. Keep your eyes closed, and with your free hand, stretch your fingers out and rub Squeak's tummy." Pip watched as the fur trickled over and under Charlie's light stroking touch. "Slow breathing. That's the way. Nice and slow. Feel how soft she is. Feel how her breathing is starting to settle too. That's it. Keep going."

Pip followed Charlie's long fingers back and forth as they eased across the joey's short coat. When she felt it was time, she held out the fresh warm bottle. "Okay, good job. Now try again to see if she'll take it." Pip stayed behind her, her hands still feather-light upon her shoulders. When she saw the joey take the teat and suckle hungrily she gently squeezed Charlie's shoulders. "There you go. Good job."

She walked back around to the other side of the island and resumed chopping the vegetables. As Charlie looked up at her through moist eyes, Pip smiled and winked at her before turning back to put a pot on the stove.

Chapter Six

Given Charlie's distress at dinner, Pip decided not to push her for a decision. Instead they bantered back and forth, comparing years at university studying and funny stories about growing up and moving away from home. Pip nearly inhaled her mug of tea laughing as Charlie regaled her with stories of her first hosted dinner party with friends. She admitted to serving up a still-frozen-in-the-middle roast chicken, beautifully garnished with lava-like chunky gravy that did little to disguise the cremated vegetable offerings that had been cut into prehistoric dinosaur shapes hiding underneath the savoury sludge.

Charlie yawned as she nursed the joey through its last feed. Pip put the last of the washing-up away. "You need to go to bed."

A sleepy half smile slid across Charlie's face. "Mm. It just hit me all of a sudden. It's your fault."

Stunned, Pip came to a halt. "Huh?" What had she done wrong?

Charlie's smile grew into a state of fullness. "Good food, good company, and loads of things to take in today. I can honestly say I'm beat."

"Oh. Good." Pip relaxed from her stiff, defensive stance. "I've made you up a fresh bottle for tonight. Why don't you head on home and hit the hay. Tomorrow's another big day."

Charlie packed Squeak back into her bag, and then looked directly at Pip. "Why do I get the feeling most days are big days around here?"

Laughter bubbled forth as Pip walked Charlie to the door. "Probably because they are. You right to get home on your own?"

Charlie hoisted Squeak's bag up onto her back. "I think we'll be okay." She clicked the torch on and walked out the door, only to pause along the pathway. She turned back to face Pip who was still standing in the doorway. "Thank you for today…and tonight. I…" Charlie looked down at her feet "Thank you."

Pip didn't need Charlie's words. She could read enough by Charlie's expression. "You're welcome. Sleep well, Charlie, and I'll see you in the morning. Shout yourself a sleep in and just come on up when you're ready." With a brief wave, Charlie was gone.

Pip stepped back into the quiet house. She stood for a moment wondering what to do next. The phone vibrated on her hip. With a mental shrug, she figured writing up her sugar level was as good a place to start as any.

❖

Squeak had fed well through the night, and both the joey and Charlie had managed a total of eight hours of much needed sleep. Over a leisurely breakfast she studied the birds through the big floor-to-ceiling window and sipped her coffee. She managed to identify at least seven different birds with confidence and a possible ID on two others that she hoped to run past Pip when she got up to the main house.

Pip. What a difference it was proving to be in getting to know her a bit better. Rather, Pip allowing it. Maybe Terese was right and under Pip's ice maiden act lived an actual nice person. She snorted softly to herself. Looks could be deceiving. Look at her ex, Kim. She'd thought they were happy. The shift in their relationship was so slow, she never saw the changes until it was too late.

Charlie stood up and pushed the chair away forcefully. No. She was not going to think about Kim and Kim was *not* going to ruin her morning. After a quick wash, she grabbed her bird book, Squeak, and the keys to the truck and drove back to the main house.

She lowered the windows and eased down the short track while listening to the birdcalls. When she rolled up and turned the engine off, she noticed how quiet the place seemed. She hung Squeak up on a frame in the prep room and was about to knock on the back door of the house when she heard a gasp, followed by a series of expletives that would make a sailor proud.

"Pip?"

Apart from the sound of running water, there was no response.

"Pip? You okay?"

Not bothering to wait for an answer. Charlie strode in and found Pip in the kitchen leaning over the sink, her head resting on a forearm, and her other hand outstretched under a stream of water. A knife and a quartered half-frozen block of fruit and ice sat on the bench top. A trail of blood led from there to the sink and Pip.

"Hell. Pip, what did you cut?"

Charlie strained to hear Pip's tense hissing whisper through clenched teeth and over the sound of the water.

"Finger." Pip swayed slightly.

Charlie reached behind her and snagged a bar stool. She shoved it under Pip's behind. "Sit. Where's your first-aid kit?"

"Bathroom."

"All right. Don't move. I'll be back in a minute."

She followed the corridor down to the bathroom. She opened the mirrored unit above the sink but didn't find anything useful. She tried the vanity drawers. There was nothing of use in the bottom or middle drawers. The top one though was quite a different matter. A box of small white strips was set inside, similar to the bloodied ones she noticed in the cane wastepaper basket, and a mobile phone sized unit of some kind sat next to it and a second smaller device. Charlie pulled it out of the drawer and turned it over in her hands. Her fingers slid over the moving parts and she jumped in surprise as something sharp jabbed her finger and drew blood. "Ow!" Charlie sucked her finger and dropped the offensive device back into the drawer and shoved it closed. She looked at the discarded white strips in the bin and pulled her finger out of her mouth. A deep red bubble blossomed on its surface.

Charlie took half a step back as she put the pieces together. "Huh." She blew a breath out and focused on what she'd come into the bathroom for. She turned and opened the linen cupboard. On the bottom shelf, below the towels, was a first-aid kit. She grabbed it and hurried back to the kitchen to find Pip had turned the water off, and now clutched a kitchen towel wrapped around her hand. She sat upright on the stool, but her face was pale.

Charlie opened up the kit and pulled out some dressings, tape, and a bandage.

Pip swallowed audibly. "It's not that bad."

"Uh-huh. After I wash my hands, I'm going to take a look at it."

The fact that Pip didn't say anything further made Charlie suspect that things might not be as okay as Pip professed them to be. After drying her hands, Charlie carefully peeled the towel away from Pip's hand, wincing in empathy at the oozing, jagged tear running across Pip's first and second fingers. "These'll need stitches."

Pip shook her head. "It's fine."

"It's not, and you know it. Here's a clean towel. Wrap your hand up in that while I go and get the truck keys. You're going to get them stitched. No arguments."

Charlie fully expected a litany of excuses to spew forth from Pip, but they never came which only made her feel more secure in her bold decision to seek medical help.

For once, she remembered to get in on the right side of the vehicle, and the trip into town was largely silent. As they approached the outskirts she heard Pip's phone vibrate. Charlie automatically reached into the middle console, pulled out a muesli bar, and handed it over to Pip, who stared at the outstretched offering.

"Go on, take it. You need to keep your energy up." Pip hesitated. Charlie wiggled the bar mid-air in emphasis. "Eat." Stealing sideways glances, Charlie noted Pip's wordless acceptance as she chewed slowly, staring out the window.

As they sat in the waiting room, Charlie filled in the medical form as Pip dictated, despite feeling a bit uncomfortable learning such personal information. Pip listed Terese as her next of kin, which tweaked her curiosity.

Charlie didn't hesitate to circle *yes* to diabetes on the medical section. After finishing the form, she handed it over for Pip to check and sign. Pip scanned the document, then looked up at Charlie. Her gaze was hard, sharp, penetrating Charlie's very core, making her sit up and move slightly back in defence as if waiting for a verbal onslaught. She was saved by the appearance of a nurse who informed them that the doctor was ready to see Pip.

Charlie stood up with her and followed her in. Pip scowled at her.

"Don't look at me like that. I'm just making sure you don't chicken out at the last minute." In an attempt to take the edge off her words and Pip's glare she put a gentle hand on the lower curve of Pip's back and helped guide her in. "Come on now, the sooner we get this done, the sooner we can head on back home. Besides, I need your help later today. I was hoping you might come on a walk with me and help me identify a couple of your birds down near the creek."

The nurse read over Pip's medical history sheet. "When was your last tetanus needle?"

Pip stared at her lap and mumbled, "About ten years ago."

The nurse scribbled some notes down on the form. "Well, while you're here, we may as well give you a booster shot."

Pip suddenly looked up at Charlie with an accusing glare. "When did you last get a tetanus shot?"

Squinting slightly as if to help her see back through time, Charlie finally shook her head. "I'm not real sure exactly. Maybe somewhere around ten years ago too."

A fleeting smirk crossed Pip's face. "You better make that two shots please, Nurse. If I'm going down, then so's my friend here."

Charlie put her hands up in a defensive gesture. "Now hang on a minute. This is not about me, it's about you."

Pip shook her head. "If we're gonna be a team, then it's all in, or all out. Besides, misery loves company. Whaddya say, Yank—arm or bum?"

Charlie narrowed her eyes at Pip but couldn't hide her smile. She rolled up her sleeve and presented her arm to the nurse.

Pip snorted off to the side. "Wuss."

❖

The ride home was quiet. Pip dozed with her head against the window. Charlie's left arm ached from the damned injection Pip had challenged her to get, so she concentrated on driving on the left side of the road while stealing glances at the mighty Clarence River. She pondered the fact that the water flowing through it was never the same. It was never still, despite the glassy texture. It reflected the sky above, and the pelicans, grebes, ducks, and cormorants that skimmed its surface. It mirrored and, at the same time, gave life to the fig trees and mangroves that lined its banks.

Chilli greeted them at the door with lots of yips, whines, and licks to their hands.

"She really doesn't like being separated from you." Charlie watched Pip squat down for a face-to-face onslaught from Chilli, but after a few moments, Chilli stopped abruptly to sniff Pip's hand and mouth.

It suddenly dawned on Charlie what she was doing. "She lets you know when your sugar is getting low, doesn't she?"

Pip nodded. She braced her hands on her knees and pushed herself upright. "Terese got her for me. She knew someone who knew someone who trained dogs especially for this type of thing. Chilli helps keep me on track, don't you, girl?" Pip ruffled the fur around Chilli's neck.

Charlie rubbed her hands on her legs and then clasped them in front of her. "I think between the two of us, we can keep you healthy."

Pip's posture stiffened, and a blush of colour suffused her cheeks. "Chilli does her job just fine. I don't need anyone's help. All you need to worry about is the animals, okay?"

"Oh." Charlie cleared her throat and nodded. "I guess. Sure." A tingle swept up the back of her neck and across her face. "Sorry. I didn't mean to be overbearing."

"Just forget about it. How about some lunch and then that walk you mentioned?"

Charlie felt a bit claustrophobic after Pip's gentle reprimand. She needed to get some air. "Yeah. I have to feed Squeak. How about when you're done, you come by the cabin and we'll go from there. I have to put my boots on and get my binoculars anyway."

"Sure. Say in an hour?"

"Yep." Charlie avoided Pip's eyes and walked out. She retrieved Squeak from the prep room and headed down the trail towards the cabin. Squeak wiggled against her back and made little grunting noises. "I know, little one. You'll get your milk in a few minutes." She felt a little guilty because the joey should've been fed half an hour ago. But it couldn't be helped. Pip had needed her. She stopped short. No, Pip hadn't really needed any help other than in making a decision to get her hand tended to. It was obvious she was self-conscious about her diabetes. "Well, I won't make that mistake again."

Charlie multitasked to prepare both Squeak's lunch and her own. While she waited for her own cup of soup to cool enough for her to eat, she fed and toileted Squeak. She'd just finished washing up when she heard a knock on the door.

"Come on in. I'm just about ready." Charlie wiped her hands on a dish towel.

"Everything good?" Pip walked through the door with Chilli on her heel.

"Yep. Squeak ate great and is back in her pouch with a full tummy." Charlie sat down and traded her sneakers for leather boots.

"Good-oh."

"How's your hand?" Charlie refrained from asking Pip how she felt. She wasn't about to set herself up for another rebuke from her regarding her diabetes.

"Not bad. My bum hurts worse." The taunting gleam in her eye made Charlie chuckle.

"A pain in the butt overrides pretty much everything." Charlie draped the binoculars strap over her neck and pulled a baseball cap onto her head. "All set. Lead on, Macduff."

"Bugger me. That's a blast from the past." Pip held the door open for Chilli and Charlie.

"Ah, Shakespeare. The universal school text."

"Yep, here too." Pip looked past her and pointed with her chin. "Let's head out this way. I want to show you something."

Charlie tried to keep up with Pip and at the same time watch for birds in the trees. "Oh! Hey. Hold on. See that little bird?"

Pip turned around and walked to Charlie's side. "The little one flitting around?"

"Yeah. There was one outside my window this morning, but it wouldn't stay still long enough for me to figure out what it was." Charlie raised the binoculars to her eyes and focused on the olive-brown coloured bird.

"It's a brown thornbill. I'm actually pleased to see one in here. I had a hazard reduction burn done last year and hadn't seen any since. I guess now the undergrowth is growing back, the thornbills are returning."

"A hazard burn? There's not enough to burn here, is there?"

"That's the point. To reduce the fuel load in case of a bush fire. Summers are notorious for bush fires. Look at this tree trunk. See the scorch marks?" Pip traced the patterns with her fingers.

"Huh. I actually thought that was the normal colour of the bark. But now that I look closer, I see the marks. But wouldn't the trees be sufficient fuel to cause a hell of a wildfire?"

"By reducing the undergrowth and dry grass, as well as leaf and bark litter on the forest floor, if a fire should come through, then it'll travel slower and have a lower flame height. It'll be much less intense and a whole heap less damaging."

"You seem to know a lot about fire."

"As a landowner and someone who lives in the middle of a high fire risk area, it's my responsibility to know about fire. Aside from my home, the animals in my care depend on me to keep them safe."

"True." Movement on the ground to Charlie's left caught her eye.

A kookaburra cocked its head and swiftly grabbed something wiggly in its beak.

"Whoa! Did he just catch a snake?" Charlie shook out her hands knowing full well her voice had raised three or four octaves.

"Looks like it." Pip cleared her throat. "Looks like a juvenile red belly."

"Aren't those poisonous?" Charlie fidgeted. She really wanted to get moving.

"Eh, not so much. They're pretty shy though. You'd just about have to step on one to get bit." Pip was silent for a moment as the kookaburra flew to a nearby limb. "Watch. He'll bash it against the limb to kill it, and then swallow it whole."

Charlie wrinkled her nose. "Lovely. Can we keep going?"

"Sure," Pip answered without hesitation.

The woods were quiet as they walked, except for the high-pitched squawks of four king parrots that flew over on fast wings. They stepped down into a wide-banked creek with a trickle of water moving lazily down the middle.

"Not a lot of water moving through, is there?" Charlie widened her step over the tiny rivulet.

Pip paused while Chilli wandered a short distance upstream and drank her fill. "Don't let it fool you. It can turn into a raging river if we get good rain up in the catchments. A decent enough fall and this entire area can flood. You wouldn't recognize it then. It's quite something."

The damp coolness disappeared as the canopy opened up and the trees were more intermittently dispersed.

"You must come out here often. There seems to be trails everywhere."

"Only when I need to start a roo on soft release." Pip pointed to the right. "See the pens over there?"

"Yeah."

"That's where I move the joeys to after they're weaned, but still need the comfort and safety of a night enclosure. They can come and go, and when they want, eventually, they leave for good."

Charlie raised her eyebrows and looked around. "These are all kangaroo trails?"

"Pretty much."

A bird began singing in the bush in front of them. Its nasal sneezing *kneep* ended with a melodiously rising *peer-peer-peepee*.

"Oh! What's that?" Charlie raised the binoculars to her eyes and tried to locate the singer.

"See if you can find it first."

Charlie scanned the low vegetation for a few minutes. "Ah, there you are," she said when it finally changed branches. The bird was pale brown with a whitish throat. A white line separated a tawny crown from its black mask. "He's got some good camouflage. Hmm. Based on the bill, I'd guess it's a honeyeater of some sort." She looked at Pip for confirmation.

Pip smiled. "It's a tawny-crowned honeyeater. They're one of the only sedentary birds living in the coastal heathlands."

Charlie looked at her feet and realized that most of the ground cover was heather. "I always thought heather only grew in the UK."

"She does. This is a distant relative."

Charlie smirked at Pip's tongue-in-cheek reference.

Pip plucked a small segment of the plant and handed it to her. "We have a couple of different sorts—this particular one is an arid type, so it's perfect for our Australian environment. Just wait until the bush goes into full bloom. It'll take your breath away."

"Can't wait to see it." She admired the mixture of greens, brown, and whites, interrupted by splashes of tiny blue and yellow flowers.

"I love this area. It's where I come when I need to slow down and settle. It soothes my soul. Close your eyes for a minute. Listen. Feel the sun touch your skin and let the quiet embrace you."

Charlie closed her eyes and lifted her face to the sun. A constant wind blew, tousling her hair and rustling the heath. The only other sound at the moment was a lone cricket.

"Oh, bugger."

Charlie opened her eyes and looked at Pip. "What? Did you see something else?"

"Mm."

They were surrounded on all sides by a large mob of kangaroos. All stood erect on their hind legs, ears pricked high and watching them intently.

"Cool!"

"Not."

"But you said—"

"Most of these roos I know. I raised them."

"Then they would know you." Charlie smiled. "That's great."

Pip shook her head. "Except for the big buck to our right." Pip grasped Charlie's upper arm and pulled her closer.

"Ow! Dammit. That's where I had my shot."

"Shh. You should've gotten it in your bum. Stay close to me and don't move. We need to stay still, no sudden movements. We need to see what he's gonna do. Chilli, stay by me."

"Jesus! He's got man boobs." Charlie stared in amazement at the huge kangaroo that stood at least six feet tall. His forearms and shoulders were massive, his chest a solid block of bulging muscle.

The buck bent over and scratched at the ground vigorously and threw dirt around his large frame.

"Bloody hell. He's not happy."

"You think?" Charlie moved as close as possible to Pip without crawling into her arms. "What do we do?"

The kangaroo stood up tall on its hind legs and stared at them. He growled and snorted before taking a hop towards them.

"We need to back away, slowly. But keep eye contact with him," Pip whispered.

Charlie swallowed hard. She held her breath, gulping it down to stay quiet. Images of what those long sharp claws could do flashed through her mind. She'd heard stories of how a kangaroo could disembowel a person, but thought they were only that—stories. Her mind jarred at how the cute, furry, doe-eyed, little joeys in the pen back at the house could grow into monsters like this.

Pip's and Charlie's movements were stiff on shaky limbs as they retreated. They held onto each other for confidence as well as for support.

After several minutes, the kangaroo either lost interest in them, or didn't feel threatened any more. Charlie figured both. When they reached the trees once again, Charlie maintained her hold on Pip. She was exhausted from the walk and the tension. From the beads of sweat on Pip's lip and forehead, and the way she'd stumbled and weaved on the path, Charlie guessed that Pip's body was also reacting to the stress.

Charlie took Pip by the elbow and guided her to sit on a downed tree trunk. Without a word, she unzipped Pip's backpack and handed her a Snickers bar and a fruit juice.

Pip looked at her blankly.

"Eat. And I don't want to hear a word about it." She stared at her until Pip took the first bite, and then crouched down next to Chilli.

"Poor girl. That frightened you just as much as it did us, didn't it?" Charlie rubbed Chilli's head between both hands until her shaking stopped. She finally got a tail wag. "Good girl."

By then Pip had finished eating the chocolate and was sipping the juice. "Good *girls*." Charlie winked at her and smiled. Her heart beat a little faster when Pip smiled shyly back.

❖

They spent a leisurely afternoon feeding animals and undertaking some running repairs to the pens, replacing a panel here, a railing there, or reattaching some screening that had come loose in the last set of storms. As a thank you for the day Pip offered to make dinner.

"Here, let me do that." Pip looked up to see Charlie crooking a finger at her and pointing at the knife.

Pip was attempting to pull on a latex glove to cover her wounded fingers so she could chop the vegetables for tea. "I can do it."

Smiling, Charlie deftly moved around the kitchen island and retrieved the knife and the nearest vegetable. "I know." Pip recognized the compassion in her voice.

Pip stood her ground for a few seconds before stepping away. Charlie was offering to help, no more, no less. With a blink and soft sigh, Pip backed away and allowed Charlie to assume command of the chopping board. She sorted the ingredients in order, her back to Charlie, as she began to heat the curry paste on the stove. The rhythmic sound of the knife against the board as Charlie worked through the vegetables was comfortable.

"Your idea of nirvana this afternoon was rather interesting."

Pip chuckled softly. "Ah, yes. That was a bit...unexpected."

"Why's that?"

"I haven't seen that big buck before. He must be the new boy in town. I'm guessing that poor old Felix's use-by date got cashed in and he's now on the outer. He was the mob's alpha male the last couple of years."

"Ah, so that would explain New Boy's show then. He didn't know you."

"Mm. Something like that. I reckon we surprised him almost as much as he surprised us."

Charlie huffed softly. "I think maybe he surprised us more."

Pip chuckled. "You could be right there." She shivered involuntarily, fully aware of what damage an adult male kangaroo of his size could inflict and happy to have everybody walk away, safe and able to tell the tale.

"So, were you going to tell me you were a diabetic?" The knife continued its rhythmic chopping.

Pip's hand stilled momentarily as she absorbed Charlie's question before resuming the steady pull and push motion of the spoon through the curry paste. "No."

"And why not?" Charlie's voice was soft, and suddenly very close. Pip jumped. Charlie had stopped chopping and was now standing directly behind her, a board laden with vegetables in her hand. Charlie's breath was warm on her neck as she asked the simple, yet complex question.

Pip's throat closed over, making her voice come out with an edge of huskiness to it. "It's nobody else's business."

Pip felt Charlie's body heat against her side and back as Charlie leaned over her to place the chopped vegetables onto the bench beside her. She shivered as she felt Charlie's breath against her ear.

"You said, back in the hospital, we were a team. All in, or all out."

"I..." Pip struggled. Charlie's proximity was confronting enough without the unanswered question hanging in the air over her head.

Just when she thought she would suffocate with Charlie's nearness, a cold rush of air replaced her body heat as Charlie moved back to sit on the bar stool at the cooking island.

Pip closed her eyes. She heard Terese's voice in her head. What would it *hurt* to tell her?

Her jaw clenched tight now as it did then. Internally she railed. It felt like all her life had been defined by type 1 diabetes since her childhood diagnosis, which required strict monitoring and insulin injections. Her mother's sing-song voice reprimanding her at family gatherings in front of everyone sounded in her head. *Don't eat that, darling. Check your blood sugar, darling. Are you counting your calories, dear?* And her father reprimanding her mother, telling her to stop fussing, leave her alone, frequently to the point where it escalated out into a familiar pattern of arguments. Years later, after she'd left home, her mother used to text her every two hours reminding her to test herself or asking for an update on her condition. Smothered. Suffocated by other's concerns, when all she wanted was to be left alone and treated like a normal person.

Charlie poured her a glass of white wine and left it on the bench. Pip snatched at it, took a big gulp, and swallowed. She took a breath and attempted to gather in some small measure of control. Her second mouthful was sipped with more restraint.

"I wasn't going to tell you because there's nothing to tell. Yes, I have diabetes, but I manage it, and I get on with my life. End of story. There's nothing to see, nothing to do." Pip stopped to sip another mouthful of wine. She would have felt more convincing in her statement if it weren't for the flush of heat she felt creeping from her neck up to her cheeks. She turned and stirred the pot again.

"Having a dog is a bit unusual, isn't it? For your diabetes, I mean."

Pip sighed. She should have known that hoping to change the subject was being optimistic. Not telling people hadn't worked so well for her in the past, so she might as well take Terese's advice and tell Charlie. Besides, if Terese was wrong, she could always kill her later. Pip turned the stove down to simmer, picked up her wine glass, and sat down at the island, opposite Charlie. "Yes. It is. Sometimes my diabetes is hard to control, no matter what I do. Growing up, the condition was occasionally referred to as brittle diabetes. Brittle be buggered. It's a pain in the arse trying to balance everything out. Terese was worried about me being all the way out here on my own, so she got me Chilli. But I'm better than I used to be, thanks to Chilli and my pump."

At the mention of her name, the dog sauntered over and sat next to Pip's chair. Pip dropped her hand and stroked her head affectionately. "In the past, I've found that people get…weird sometimes, about the condition." Pip stopped to take a sip of wine, using the time to push away the memories and gather her thoughts. "I don't make a big deal out of it. It is what it is. Together"—she gave Chilli's head a last pat—"we manage just fine."

Charlie regarded her intently. "What do you mean, weird?"

For some strange reason, Pip felt okay with Charlie's question. She seemed genuinely interested, not freaked-out, nosey, or pushy.

Pip played with her wine glass, spinning the stem between her fingers. "It was a bone of contention between my parents. My mother…she developed a sort of a cross between a neurosis and OCD about my condition. I couldn't go anywhere, do anything without her measuring, analysing, and fussing. My father tried to be more relaxed and not make a big deal out of it. They fought about it constantly. Eventually their differences caused too much tension and they spilt." Pip sipped her wine. Her mind travelled back. "Later, when I left home, all I wanted was to be like everyone else—normal. I never told my ex. We met at uni. When I finished studying I found work while she stayed on and studied for her doctorate. I got sick and eventually was laid off. After that, I had to take on several odd jobs to keep the money rolling in. With the stress and odd hours, I ended up in hospital a couple of times. When my nan died, I went home for a week to help sort out some family stuff and came back to find she'd emptied out the apartment, sold up, and left to teach in South Africa." Pip shrugged. "After that, well, what with one thing and another, I ended up here." Pip looked up and smiled shyly. "Apart from Terese and my doctor, you're the only other one here that knows."

Charlie's warm hand encircled hers and gave her a gentle squeeze. Charlie never said a word. She didn't have to. Pip felt her genuineness through her touch. A sense of peace, with a hint of relief, washed over her. She didn't have to protect or hide her condition any more. It felt strangely wonderful to be able to relax in the newly shared knowledge. Through Charlie's gentle acceptance she had unexpectedly found a sense of what it might be like to be normal.

She got up and served dinner, opting to stay at the comfortable setting at the kitchen bench.

"Panic attacks," Charlie uttered between mouthfuls.

Genuinely confused, Pip's spoon stopped halfway to her mouth. "Sorry?"

"Panic attacks. Since my ex left me. Damnedest thing. I turn to jelly. Drives me insane. I was hoping, coming to Australia, that things might improve."

"And have they?"

Charlie looked up at her. A half-smile crossed her face. "Early days yet, but I'm feeling hopeful."

Pip blinked, not sure if she was reading more than one meaning into Charlie's statement.

"Charlie, can I ask a personal question?"

Charlie put her fork down, folded her hands into her lap, and sat back on her stool. "Sure."

"Why did you come here? To Australia, I mean."

Charlie pushed her now empty plate away. "Lots of reasons. I've always wanted to come to Australia. The animals, the climate… it's called to me for a long time." Pip topped up Charlie's wine glass but chose to leave her own empty. "To get away. To escape." She took a sip. "I needed a fresh start. I live in a small town. After Kim left—that's my ex—well, let's just say I felt a cross between suffocating from everyone's over-interest in my love life, and feeling shattered at having my whole world come crumbling down. Running away somehow sounded far more appealing by comparison. I saw the ad, applied, and now, voila, here I am."

As Pip cleared the dishes away, she considered that each of them had merely skimmed over their histories to each other, but that in the telling, a new level of trust had been brokered between them. She turned to find Charlie had stood up and was stretching.

"I don't know about you," Charlie said, "but I'm beat. I'll just wash up the dishes and be on my way, out of your hair so you can get some rest."

"No, really, it's okay. I'm going to be lazy and chuck them in the dishwasher tonight."

Pip walked Charlie to the door and watched as she retrieved Squeak from the prep room and slung her over her shoulder.

"Thank you for a lovely dinner."

Pip leaned against the door frame. "You're welcome."

Neither seemed keen to move. Pip held out her good hand, and Charlie met and easily entwined her fingers into Pip's. "Thank you. For today. The driving and hospital, and…listening." Pip opened and shut her mouth a few times, the words never quite coming. "Thank you."

Pip felt Charlie's fingers return the pressure. "You too."

Their eyes met and held. Two hands linked. Neither seemed ready to break the spell.

Chilli moved between them. A soft whine emerged from her velvet canine lips, provoking a soft chuckle from them both.

"Goodnight, Charlie."

"'Night, Pip. Sleep well."

Their fingers slipped away from each other, but the warmth lingered against Pip's palm as she watched the shape of Charlie's back grow dimmer. The night shadows finally closed around Charlie as she traversed the path back to the cottage.

Chapter Seven

Charlie woke the next morning at eight am, barely remembering having fed Squeak at two. In between that feeding and the six o'clock one, she'd slept soundly for the first time since arriving in Australia. Well, since the break-up, really.

She clenched her fist and pounded the table lightly. "Dang, I need to send Kim a note." Determined not to let Kim drag her down again, she'd purposely ignored her latest email. She hadn't been in the mood to put up with Kim's pleading and rationalizations.

But something had happened between her and Pip last night. They'd become friends. And based on that came the recognition that, like Pip, she didn't have a lot of them. She'd always thought her co-workers were friends, but in truth, they were only friendly acquaintances. She'd felt incredibly alone when not one of them had asked how she was doing after Kim left. Now she understood why. And to be honest, they had no place in her personal life. Not then, not now.

Oddly, this awakening made her feel stronger. This new-found strength satisfied her—she'd survived one of the worst times of her life. She knew the anxiety and panic attacks would probably still plague her off and on. Hopefully they would diminish with time. But she might just be able to work out of them faster rather than letting them take control and leave her in a pile of sweaty exhaustion.

Charlie took a deep cleansing breath and powered up the laptop. She felt good. A quick note to Kim and it'd be done. She could go on with her life without any more interruptions and accomplish a new goal. Instead of merely surviving, which was what she now realized she'd been doing, she could develop goals and work to achieve them. This was how she'd always conducted her professional life, but this was something entirely new to her on the personal level.

She drummed her fingers, deciding where to start. She bit her lip and tilted her head to the side. Finally, she raised her hands above the keyboard, wiggled her fingers, and began to type.

Dear Kim,
Sorry

She deleted that. She wasn't sorry.

I know you sent your note a few days ago and probably expected a quicker reply. Not only have I been busy, it's taken me a while to digest your proposition. I've also had to do some thinking about how to answer you.

You're probably going to be surprised at my response.

Kim, there was a reason you made the decision to leave. At this point in time, I can finally understand why. I was hurt, yes. Probably more than you could ever imagine. But you were, in effect, living alone and managing quite well, I might add. I will own up to being the cause of that situation. Since you left, I've had to learn to do that too. Thank you for that.

You see, being single, I've had to learn to manage and to crawl out of my own hole. I've had to learn to make decisions on my own, one of them being the choice to travel to Australia and expand my knowledge of wildlife, albeit foreign. New South Wales is beautiful, by the way. Anyone would be crazy not to fall in love with this area.

Charlie reread what she'd written. She sounded more confident than she felt. But she wasn't going to let Kim in on that bit of information.

I've also learned to take care of myself. I know that sounds funny, a woman in her forties with a college education having to work to become comfortably independent.

She glanced at the time in the upper right hand corner of the screen. It was getting late. She needed to get a move on to see what Pip had in store for them today.

So to be perfectly honest with you, I think we need to continue living separate lives. I'm not averse to being friends. After all, we were friends before we were lovers. I hope you understand, and even more, I hope you find happiness.

Charlie

Her hand hovered above the send button. If Kim had wanted them to get back together three weeks ago, Charlie would've done it in a heartbeat. But things had changed. She needed to recover and find the person her dad would once again be proud of.

Charlie hit send and pulled the laptop lid down. There. It was done. Kim could go her own way. Again. And she would go hers. She would finish out the year here and when she returned to the States, she'd be in a much healthier frame of mind than when she'd left.

❖

Pip and Chilli were coming out of the house when Charlie strolled up.

Pip juggled the keys in her hand. "Good, you're here. I have to go into Yamba to the vet's office and pick up a joey. Want to ride along?"

"Sure. Let me put Squeak in the prep room. I'll be right back." Charlie hung the pouch bag on the frame, and ensured everything was secure. "I'll feed you when I get back, little one." She chuckled. "It's not like you even hear me. All you do is eat, sleep, and poop."

She strode out and checked her stride to keep from going to the wrong side of the truck…again. She mentally shook her head.

"All good?" Pip said when Charlie slid into the passenger seat.

"Yep. Sorry I didn't get down here sooner. I had a few emails to take care of." Charlie drew the seat belt across her chest and clicked it in.

"No dramas."

"So tell me about where we're going." Charlie settled herself into the seat.

"Yamba. It's mainly a holiday resort town because of the beaches. It was built at the mouth of the Clarence River and is one of the best fishing areas around. If you're into beach, rock, estuary, or deep-sea fishing, well, it's the town for you. If you can put up with all the terrorists."

"Terrorists?" Charlie jerked her head in Pip's direction. "Is that something we have to worry about?"

Pip laughed. "No. It's a nickname we give to the tourists. They can be a right pain in the arse over the holidays."

"I'd say that's the case for a lot of the really nice places. Wouldn't you?"

Pip nodded. "Yes. But sometimes us locals would rather keep things to ourselves."

"Don't I know it?" Charlie said and chuckled.

"Yeah, yeah."

The rest of the ride was quiet. Charlie was enthralled with the countryside and spent most of the time looking back and forth on both sides of the road.

"I'll bring you back here another day. I want to see what's up with this joey."

"No problem. It's why we came in, right?"

Pip grinned. "You got it."

❖

Pip rolled her eyes as she pushed the door of the vet surgery open, anticipating the obnoxious electronic mooing sound that announced their arrival. She turned to Charlie. "Lucky I don't work here. I'd have the batteries pulled out of that door chime box in ten seconds flat."

"And I'd stand over the top of you and put them straight back in, just because I can." Laughter bubbled forth from a tall brunette who came from behind the counter to enfold Pip in a hug. "How've you been, stranger? And don't think I've forgotten our bet. You still owe me a beer."

"I'm fine, and no, I haven't forgotten, even though you earned it on false pretences."

The brunette held a hand to her heart. "Are you implying I cheated? Me? You must have me confused with someone else."

Pip snorted. "Hardly. Jodi Bowman, I'd like you to meet Charlie Dickerson. Charlie's come over from America to live and to study our native animals for a year."

The women exchanged handshakes. "Nice to meet you, Charlie."

"Likewise."

Jodi indicated over her shoulder with her thumb. "If Pipsqueak here gives you any drama, you just holler."

"I can assure you that Pip has been terrific, but I'll keep your offer in mind."

Pip watched the playful banter at her expense and blew out a mock exasperated sigh. "Great. Now I'm getting double-teamed by the Tall Twins. Give me a break. Come on Jodes, where's this little one you phoned me about?"

"She's out back. While you're here, I'd love it if you could take a look at a possum that came in about an hour ago."

Pip looked at Charlie and waved her forward, giving her the lead. She was rewarded with a huge grin. "We'd love to."

She put her hand briefly on the small of Charlie's back and pointed down the corridor. "You go with Jodes and start the assessment on the joey and I'll collect some carriers from the car." Charlie looked at her with uncertainty in her eyes. Pip rested her hand on Charlie's forearm and gave it a light squeeze. "I trust you, Charlie. I wouldn't ask you if I didn't. Just do what we did with Squeak. I'll be back in a minute and you can give me a rundown on what you think."

Pip took her time outside. She knew Jodi would answer any questions Charlie had. She also knew the opportunity would afford both of them some valuable time to begin building a working rapport so that Charlie would feel comfortable coming to the surgery with or without her.

❖

On the way home, Pip nursed a canvas bag in her lap. "Hey, Chilli, you let me know if Miss Possie has a hissy fit on the way home."

Chilli, who was dozing on the back seat next to a strapped in carrier box, raised her head briefly and grunted in apparent acknowledgement, before resting her muzzle back down into her snooze position.

Pip had thrown Charlie the keys when they'd come out of the surgery. She enjoyed sitting back, allowing someone else to drive home as she nursed the canvas bag containing the kangaroo joey. "I feel like Miss Daisy."

Charlie glanced in her direction. "Excuse me?"

"Miss Daisy. Y'know, *Driving Miss Daisy*. That's what I feel like."

Charlie shook her head and smiled.

"So what did you and Dr. Bowman discover, Ms. Dickerson?"

Pip delighted in seeing Charlie's face relax. She grinned and played along.

"Well, the possums are Common Brushtails. Mom has what looks like a concussion. Jodi thinks maybe a couple of quiet days under observation. The baby—weird that you call them joeys too, but I suppose it makes things simpler. Anyway, the young male joey appears to be fine at this stage, but we still need to keep an eye on them."

"Okay. We've got plenty of empty cages at the minute. When we get back we can look up what they like to eat and set one up in readiness."

"But I'm guessing you know already what they like to eat."

"Mm. But it's more fun doing it together, don't you think?"

"Indeed."

"And the eastern grey kangaroo joey?"

"Contused, dehydrated, cold on arrival, slowly warmed. Was found on dead mother's teat. Victim of hit and run. I have the address details in my pocket."

Pip nodded.

"Hasn't yet been hydrated, but probably pretty close to warm enough to try by the time we get home. Not sure how long Mom had been dead for, so we should probably keep an eye out for infection given that she was still attached to the teat when they found her."

Pip rearranged the heat mat she had plugged into the car's power supply, which was currently wrapped around the joey's bedding inside the bag she held on her lap. She stuck her fingers into the bag and rested them against the joey's skin. At home, she used a temperature gauge, but she had raised enough joeys over the years to be able to estimate on the fly, within a degree or two, the range of heat in an infant marsupial's bag.

"And what should we give her when we get home?" Satisfied with the joey's warmth, she folded the bag closed again.

"An electrolyte mix for the first feed at least, and see how she goes to determine if the next feed is milk or a follow-up electrolyte mix."

"And if we give her milk, what sort should it be?"

"Oh." Charlie's brow furrowed in concentration. "We need to weigh and measure her first, but I think, just looking at her, no hair, probably under eight hundred grams, that a 0.4 mixture is best."

Pip grinned. "Spot on." She stretched out in the passenger seat. "Nice work, Charlie."

As soon as they got home, Pip gave the kangaroo joey some hydrating fluid while Charlie drew up a feeding plan and opened up a new record for the joey's details. She would need to be hydrated every couple of hours and then fed every four hours. Pip read over the plan. It was a solid one even though she knew she would be tired over the next couple of days. It meant more sleep deprivation, on top of testing her levels every two hours to try and track and measure the right sequence for her new insulin pump. She rubbed her eyes. Oh well, she could always catnap if she needed to.

They spent the next couple of hours out on the quad runner collecting fresh leaves for the koalas and some flowering native foliage to go inside the possum cage. As they progressed their way through the bush, Pip explained what sort of leaves to pick, and marked several trees in readiness for their next trip when she would let Charlie do the selecting. She would get her to use the marked trees as her examples and then go off and find other trees matching the tagged ones. Her whole aim was to provide Charlie with enough skills to be able to operate independently.

Once home Pip fed the joey and watched on while Charlie created a safe and sheltered environment for the possums within the cage. The mother possum wouldn't want too much to eat just yet, but needed access to plenty of fluid and to be kept quiet and in the dark. The hairless joey was tucked safely inside the mother's pouch and fed on, seemingly oblivious of the alien environment. Much to Pip's delight, Charlie didn't need much guidance until it came to asking the best way to handle the possum. Pip pulled out a stuffed toy from one of the cupboards and demonstrated, using a towel, how best to grip and hold it on the transfer from the box to the cage.

She sat back and gave Charlie some space. After a couple of false grabs and hissing from the cage, Charlie's grasp finally gained purchase. Pip observed the set to Charlie's jaw as she strong-armed the towel-covered lump into the cage and the triumphant arm raise to the invisible crowd upon her success.

Pip grinned at her enjoyment. "Nice one, Slick. But you might wanna close the cage door before she runs out and you have to chase her."

"Oh, crap. Yeah." With a nervous giggle, Charlie swung around with lightning speed and secured the door. "Shall I put them next door?"

"Good idea."

A sense of satisfaction suffused her as Pip noted how Charlie smoothly and quietly gathered the cage into her arms and carried the possums next door. The closed-in annex was warm and dry, and had blinds on the windows to block out the light. More importantly it was close and provided easy access for assessment.

Pip settled her joey back into the heated pouch as Charlie walked in, her mobile phone in one hand, her brow furrowed as she read the screen. Pip cocked her head. She was no psychologist, but she knew enough to know Charlie didn't look happy. "Everything all right?"

"Yes. No? I don't know." Charlie's fingers curled into a fist. "It's my ex. Kim." She glanced down again at the phone screen again.

"How about I put the kettle on. You can vent to me."

Charlie looked up at her, but still seemed lost in the message. Taking a chance, Pip linked her arm through Charlie's, led her into the house, and sat her at the kitchen island. She set a steaming mug in front of Charlie, her fingers lightly brushing against Charlie's longer ones, her voice soft and neutral. "Floor's all yours, if you want it. Or if you want space, that's okay too."

Charlie sipped her tea. "Thank you. I…"

She imagined she saw several expressions cross Charlie's face over the course of a handful of seconds before Charlie released a long exhale. She straightened her shoulders and looked up, offering a soft smile to Pip. "Can I take a rain check? I'd love to talk to you about it. But first, I think I need to get my own head around a few things."

She nodded and smiled back. "No worries. The door's always open."

"Thank you."

Pip's phone rang. She pulled it from her hip and saw that it was the Yamba vet's surgery again. She handed the phone over to Charlie.

"Hello?"

Pip slid a pen and paper across the countertop and watched as Charlie simultaneously took notes and listened to the conversation.

"Uh-huh. I can be there in…?" Charlie pulled the phone away from her mouth, held it against her breast, and whispered, "How long?"

Pip whispered back. "Half an hour."

Charlie put the phone back to her mouth. "A bit over half an hour." She hastily scribbled a few more notes down before she hung up, a grin on her face a mile wide. "We got a tawny frogmouth."

"Uh-uh. *You* got a tawny frogmouth. Think you can remember your way back to the vet's?" Pip scribbled on Charlie's piece of paper. "Here's the address if you need to plug it into the GPS."

Pip pulled the keys from her back pocket and tossed them lightly to Charlie who was dancing excitedly from one foot to another. She caught the keys effortlessly. She was halfway out the door before stopping to turn back to Pip, who was still sitting at the kitchen island sipping her tea, smiling.

"You're not coming?"

"Nah. I reckon you got it covered. If you're not back by tea, I'll send Jodes out to find you." She snickered.

Charlie all but skipped out to the ute on her first solo run.

❖

Charlie couldn't get to the truck fast enough. Although it wasn't a field rescue and the frogmouth had already been examined, it was a new experience for her. It suddenly occurred to her she needed a rescue basket, so she retraced her steps and got one out of the prep room. On her way back, she could've sworn she heard a chuckle come from inside the house.

She smiled. Things with Pip were so easy now. She knew the turning point was when Pip finally admitted her condition. That had to have been hard, Charlie thought. Especially since she'd had such a difficult time of it with her family and past relationships. Sad, because once you got to know her, Pip was a genuinely nice person. Charlie snorted and shook her head. Her opinion of Pip had sure changed, and apparently so had Pip's of her.

She was back in Yamba before she knew it. Once again the mooing chime announced her entrance into the vet office.

"I thought that might be you guys," Jodi said as she came out to the patient area. She looked past Charlie and frowned. "Pip decide to let you do all the work this time, did she?" Jodi crossed her arms over her chest. "You can tell her she owes me two beers just for that."

Charlie laughed. "It's okay. She thought it would be good practice for me to go solo. I don't mind."

"Just so long as Pipsqueak isn't trying to get out of work." Jodi flashed a mischievous grin. "Come on, the bird is back here."

Charlie followed Jodi into the kennelling area and into a darkened room. When Jodi flipped a switch, a red light illuminated four cages of various sizes against the back wall.

"This used to be a storage room until Pip convinced us it would be a good place to house the wildlife that came in."

"Good idea. The darker the room, the less the stress."

"Exactly." Jodi pointed to a large cage at the end. "The frogmouth is in there. A woman on her way to work saw it sitting on the side of the road. She managed to catch it by throwing a blanket over it, and then brought it here. It's a bit concussed, as most that come in are. I think it has a sprained wing. The X-ray was inconclusive."

Charlie looked into the cage. The bird sat on the floor with its eyes closed. One wing drooped noticeably lower than the other. "Poor thing."

"Unfortunately, this is one of the lucky ones. A lot of them get hit and lie helpless in the road until someone either picks it up or, the most likely scenario, runs over it."

"Why do you think they're so susceptible to getting hit?"

"Well, if you think about it, they're nocturnal insect eaters. Bugs are attracted to the lights of the cars, and frogmouths are attracted to the bugs. When they swoop in to get the bugs, that's when they collide with the windshield or grille."

"That makes sense. I have to keep reminding myself that these guys aren't owls." Charlie set the basket down and pulled gloves over her hands.

"What brought you to Australia?"

"Well, the opportunity was there and the getting good. The timing was right."

"You like it so far?"

"Love it. Pip's teaching me loads."

"She's a good one. I just wish she wasn't out there by herself all the time. You're here a year, right?"

"Yep."

"Well at least I won't have to worry about her for the next twelve months. She looks to be in your good hands."

Charlie shook her head slightly. "More the other way around. I suppose I should get going. I want to get her all settled before dark."

"Righto."

Charlie opened the door, reached in, and gently lifted the frogmouth out. Despite the bird's hissing and beak clapping, she was able to calmly place it into the basket and secure the lid without incident.

On their way out, Jodi was pulled aside by one of the technicians. Charlie returned her wave, disappointed that she didn't get to ask what the bet with Pip was all about. Oh well. Another day. She was sure it wouldn't be the last time she'd have to pick up an animal from here.

Charlie secured the basket in the passenger seat and was soon on the road home. She hadn't had time to dwell on the latest note from Kim. She'd only read it once, as she'd been otherwise occupied, but something Kim said implied she wanted to revisit the circumstances of their relationship face-to-face. Since Charlie still had the better part of a year overseas, it'd have to be via Skype. Charlie rubbed the bridge of her nose. Did Kim really expect seeing her and hearing her voice would change anything? *I don't think so.*

There was no sign of Pip when Charlie arrived home, so she took it upon herself to mirror a cage set-up like the other frogmouth they had in care. After she'd gently placed the bird in its new dwelling, she had enough time for lunch before Squeak's next feed.

Charlie retrieved the joey and went to the cabin. The sun was high overhead, which accentuated the eucalypts' light turquoise hue. Lorikeets and blue-faced honeyeaters hopped from tree to tree in search of nectar filled flowers. She sighed contentedly. What a gorgeous piece of heaven. Pip was lucky to live here.

But if Charlie were to be honest with herself, Pip was also part of the scenery. She'd come to look forward to getting a smile from the woman whom she'd initially thought to be a bitchy recluse. Her laugh was contagious and, by God, the woman was smart, not to mention really cute. Pip was also incredibly patient. And for that Charlie was grateful. She'd always been more of a hands-on learner than book-smart. This experience was right up her alley.

❖

A zombie. That's what Pip felt like: a walking, brain-dead zombie. Between her kangaroo joey and the new animals in care, sleep had been short, disjointed, and severely lacking on the whole. Over the past two weeks both she and Charlie had been on several call-outs with new animals, which was fairly typical for this time of year, but it meant she'd had little opportunity to catnap during the day and get some much needed shut-eye catch-up time.

To top it off, her sugar levels the last two days were starting to fluctuate more than she would have liked. The pump alarm had gone off a couple of times because of air bubbles and kinked cannulas. All she could put it down to was exhaustion. Maybe she hadn't been careful enough when refilling the pump and putting in a fresh cannula and line, which was unusual for her meticulous nature, but not impossible given her current circumstances.

She sighed and hung up the phone, noting a doctor's appointment in her diary to discuss how she was progressing with the new pump. Up until the last week, it had been going relatively well. But she was genuinely puzzled as to why things had been less than ideal the past few days. She gazed out the window at Charlie hanging freshly laundered joey pillow slips on the clothes line. Even Charlie had been looking tired the last few days. Maybe she should suggest they each take a night about at feeding time for the joeys so at least one of them could get a decent night's sleep.

Pip stood up, yawned, and stretched. The feed bottles were due to be sterilized before the next feed and her notes needed updating. If she didn't keep moving she feared she might start sleepwalking.

She'd just picked up the last of the bottles when her phone rang. It was Jodi from the vet surgery. Another reason for her sleep deprivation had involved a week of two hourly feeds for a four-month old koala joey. He should have still been in the pouch, but had been taken into care after the mother had to be euthanized due to her extensive injuries received as a result of a dog attack. The little joey had several bite wounds of its own and in the last forty-eight hours had succumbed to both the stress and the beginnings of infection. She and Charlie had driven it to the vet's and Jodi had placed it on an overnight drip.

Pip looked down at her phone. Jodi's number flashed as it continued to vibrate in her hand. She took a deep breath before answering. "Hey, Jodes. Please tell me you have some good news." Her heart sank when Jodi paused before answering. They'd had lots of conversations like this in the past. Pip knew in her heart that you couldn't save them all. She was no stranger to death or electing the green dream to end an animal's suffering, but Jodi's words tumbled across her tired mind, only to fall heavy, like a rock, deep inside her. Jodi had stayed with the joey through the night but the infection had been too great and the tiny body lost its gallant fight just over an hour ago. Pip thanked her and hung up.

The fight left her too. Her knees weakened and she slid to the floor, her back against the cupboard. She rested her head down on her bent knees, closed her eyes, and let the tears flow, too tired to even try to hold them back.

"Pip? Pip, what's wrong? What's the matter?"

Pip started. She hadn't heard Charlie come in, and here she was, kneeling beside her on the floor, her arm wrapped around her shoulders.

"Wha? Oh, sorry. No, I'm fine. Fine. Sorry." When she struggled to get up, Charlie helped her to her feet. To cover her embarrassment she scrubbed her hand across her wet face.

"You sure? You're crying."

"It's nothing. Really."

"It's something."

Annoyed at herself, Pip pushed away from the sink and began to rearrange the now clean bottles. "I just got a phone call from Jodi. The little koala didn't make it. It died a short while ago."

"Oh, Pip. I'm so sorry." Charlie walked forward and opened her arms to put around her. But Pip managed to sidestep the embrace as she made her way over to the computer.

"It happens." Her reply came out a little more gruffly than she had intended.

Pip tried to pull up the koala joey's file to enter the last and final update but she was having trouble focusing. "Goddammit." She punched the keys and opened another folder. "Where the hell is the file?" The more she grumbled and fussed, the less success she had. A warm pair of hands on her shoulders broke through her mumbles.

"I've made us a cup of tea. Take a break and come join me on the couch for a minute." Pip felt the room spin as Charlie slowly rotated the chair until she faced the couch. Two mugs sat on the coffee table, the steam rising hypnotically. She stood and allowed herself to be guided across the room.

As she drained the last of the tea from her mug, Charlie gently took it from her hand. Pip watched on, her weariness throwing up a veiled sense of being disjointed from her surroundings.

The mug slid easily from her fingers. "You make a nice cup of tea."

"I'm glad you liked it."

Pips eyes were heavy. Her blinking was slow and laboured. "How's the tawnies today?"

"They're fine. I think they'll be ready for release tomorrow."

"Nice. Maybe we could make a night of it and let last week's possums go too. They're more than ready. An' pick up some take-away in town, to celebrate. Do you like Chinese?"

"I love Chinese."

"Good. Good. Then that's what we'll do." Pip closed her eyes just as an errant tear escaped to run freely down her cheek. Charlie wrapped her arms around her and pulled her down to her shoulder.

"I'm fine."

"I know you are." Charlie's voice buzzed in her ear as Pip lay against her chest.

"Little buggers just break your heart sometimes," she mumbled.

❖

She didn't remember falling asleep, but the vibrating phone at her hip woke her from a wonderful dream. She was reluctant to open her eyes and let reality take hold. The dream arms felt so warm and nice wrapped around her. It had been so long since she had felt the body heat of another woman, moulded snuggly against the length of her back. She wanted to hang on to the dream for just a little bit longer before it faded away.

Another vibrating buzz at her hip poked at her consciousness to wake and lose the last vestiges of the dream's warm hand that had wrapped across her front, to nestle low against her stomach. Her lips quirked in a half smile as she found her own fingers to be entwined with her dream's hand. It felt so real. She shivered when the fingers underneath her hand twitched against her stomach.

They twitched again.

Her eyes snapped open. The fingers felt so real because they were. They belonged to Charlie who lay spooned behind her on the couch, her arms wrapped securely around her, snugging her in close against her body.

Shit.

Her phone vibrated again.

"Are you gonna answer that or let it go to MessageBank?" Charlie's sleepy voice grumbled in her ear.

She looked reflexively at the phone. It was Terese. Her heart pounded in her ears. Pushing Charlie's hand away she sat bolt upright. "It's Terese. I have to take it." Adrenaline propelled her out of the prep room and into the house, where she finally came to rest on the edge of her bed. "Terese, hi." She scrubbed at her face. Her hand shook. She reached out and unclipped the lolly jar she kept by her bed. She snagged a jersey caramel and popped it into her mouth. She allowed the burst of flavour and warmth of the sugar rush to flow. She popped another one in and chewed quickly in agitation.

"What? Sorry?" She swallowed the mushed-up sweetness. "No. We're fine. And busy. Charlie's been great." She contemplated a third when Terese's words caught her full attention. "You want to come out? Why?" She clipped the lid shut. "But Charlie's doing great. Ask her yourself if you don't believe me." She screwed up the bedcover in her hand. "I'm fine." She gritted her teeth just a little on the last word. "And I am *not* crabby." She looked down at the scrunched-up cover and attempted to smooth it down. "You know you're always welcome, Terese. I…" She closed her eyes and listened to Terese explain the protocols. "Fine." She was too tired to resist. "Just text me the details when you know." She stood up and looked out the window in time to see Charlie carrying fresh water bowls over to the aviaries. "Yep. Love you too. See you." She disconnected and put the phone back on her hip.

She paced the room. What the hell just happened? In the space of an—she checked her watch—hour, in the space of an *hour* she had lost the plot, fallen asleep, and woken up tangled in the arms of someone whom she was supposed to be caring for, mentoring, supervising.

It was wrong. On so many levels. Her heart pounded. Damn if it didn't feel good though to have the warmth of another's touch along the length of her body. Good. But wrong. At what point had she fallen asleep, and Charlie too, and when did she entangle her fingers with Charlie's long tapered ones and pull her in close? What the heck was that all about?

The alarm on her pump went off. Her cannula was kinked again. "Bastard." She stomped off to the bathroom to replace it and recharge the line. The stomping felt justified. She hated to admit it, but Terese was right. No sleep, weird stuff going on, crappy levels, and a pain in the arse pump…She was crabby.

Chapter Eight

Charlie had all the feeding done except for Pip's joey before Pip returned. Although she was nearly dead on her feet, she pushed on and did the chores that the two of them normally shared. Charlie knew Pip was no less tired than she, but she was concerned with Pip's health. She'd heard the alarms go off on the pump more than once, and although Pip had assured her it was under control, it still gave her cause to be concerned.

"You've been busy. You should've waited. I would've helped." Pip stood in the doorway while Charlie finished washing the bowls she'd taken from the cages.

"Can't deviate too far from schedules. My Aussie mentor taught me that." Charlie smiled at her. "I didn't do it all. You still have to feed Emmy. I've got her milk ready for you."

"Thanks." Pip walked a bit unsteadily to the tiny joey's stand.

Charlie came to her quickly and took her elbow. "Listen, you just sit down and I'll bring everything to you."

"Don't fuss. I'm not a bloody invalid. I'm just tired," Pip said, but gave in and sat down heavily onto the couch, as a yawn punctuated her grumble.

Charlie set the joey pouch onto Pip's lap and placed a mug containing hot water and a milk bottle on the table next to Pip. She returned to the sink and the remaining dirty bowls and waited until Pip got the finicky joey suckling before bringing up the phone call.

"How is Terese?"

Pip sighed. "She's good. She's planning on a trip up to check on you."

Charlie spun around on one foot. "Check on me? Why? Didn't you tell her we're doing fine?"

Pip flipped the teat off the now empty bottle and let the joey mouth it. Charlie now knew this acted as a kind of pacifier, or dummy, as Pip called it. After a feed it seemed to relax the joeys.

"Terese says it's protocol to check up on our international guests."

"How many of us are there?"

Pip rolled her eyes. "One."

"Oh, for God's sake. You would think Terese would let it slide given how well she knows you."

"Hardly. She'll be up in the next day or two. I guaran-*bloody*-tee it."

"Well, she can see for herself how much I've learned."

"I think she mainly wants to see how we're getting along." Pip kept her attention on the joey.

Charlie didn't reply. When the phone had woken them earlier and she'd found herself wrapped around Pip, no one could've been more surprised than she. When she'd recovered from the shock, she found she missed the warmth of Pip's body when she got up. It'd felt nice. Comforting, really. Holding onto Pip while she'd slept seemed surprisingly natural. Admittedly, she'd really enjoyed the closeness they'd developed over the past couple weeks.

Initially, Charlie had been attracted to Pip's mind—and totally her Australian accent. Eventually, as she got to know her, Pip's personality drew her. But this new development of being attracted to her physically was unexpected. She had no idea if Pip felt the same. If she had to guess, and based on how fast Pip had escaped her arms, she thought no. And that was okay. Her stay in Australia was only temporary. It would only complicate things if their relationship evolved into something more serious. So she'd have to cope with whatever attraction she had on her own. Besides, she still had Kim to contend with.

Charlie looked at her watch. "Crap. I've got to run. I'm Skyping with Kim tonight."

"Tonight's the night, eh? D-Day."

Over the course of the past week, Charlie had told Pip about Kim's confession. It had actually been Pip's idea for Charlie to initiate the contact and set up a Skype session to talk it over.

"Yep. It's a lay your cards on the table kind of night. I'm not sure either of us can move forward until we do. We'll still need to see each other because of the dogs, I'm sure. But I think the getting-back-together boat has well and truly sailed."

"Good for you." Pip waved her away. "Go on then. I've got this."

"You sure?"

"Yep. Good as gold. See you in the morning."

Charlie took the pouch holding Squeak off the frame. As she passed the couch, she grasped Pip's shoulder and said, "If you need anything—"

"I won't. But thanks. Now go on, get going. You've got stuff to sort and loose ends to tie off."

An hour later, Charlie sat at the desk and waited for the laptop to boot up. She'd fed Squeak, showered, and ate a quick dinner of scrambled eggs. Normally she would've gotten dressed in a tank top and boxer shorts in preparation for bed. But not tonight. She didn't want anything she said to be mistaken for indecision, or her appearance to be construed as sexy, and therefore a come-on to Kim. So she wore cargo shorts and a polo with the Cody WRS insignia embroidered on the left side.

It was seven o'clock. Charlie blew a heavy sigh and launched Skype. Kim was already online, so she dialled. Kim picked up the call after two rings and her face appeared on the screen. Charlie hadn't yet enabled video chat. She wasn't sure how she'd feel about seeing Kim. She was pleasantly pleased to feel absolutely nothing.

"Hi, babe! Where's your gorgeous face?" Kim leaned in towards her screen, as if that would enable her to see Charlie.

Charlie finally pressed the button.

"Ah, there's my gorgeous woman. How've you been? You look tired."

Charlie looked out the window that faced Pip's house. Although she couldn't see the structure through the thick vegetation, she felt content in knowing it was there. She gathered her composure and looked back at the screen.

Charlie smiled wanly. "I'm fine. I've just been really busy."

"Ah, it's great to hear your voice. Although you haven't picked up the Aussie accent yet."

"I don't expect to. I won't be here long enough." Charlie smiled inwardly. She had found herself using some Aussie terms, but she sure wasn't going to try them out on Kim.

"You signed up for a year? Any chance you'll be coming home sooner?" Kim smiled expectantly.

"Yes, a year. And no, I'll stay until my term is complete. Look, Kim, let's cut to the chase."

"Okay." Kim leaned back in her chair and crossed her arms. Her body posture intimated she thought she was going to control the direction of the conversation. "Chaz, I'm really sorry about how things went down."

Charlie clicked a pen nervously. She was unsure of how and where the next part of the conversation needed to go.

"I made a huge mistake. We were made to be together. We're soul mates. I know that now."

Charlie flexed her hands hidden in her lap and laughed, knowing there was an edge to it. She drew in a slow, steady breath and spoke in a carefully controlled tone of voice.

"We were good together…for a time. But that time has passed. You did make a mistake. We both made mistakes. And now you want to be forgiven. It took me a long time to get over what you did and how you did it. I don't want to come home to you. I just can't do it. I've had to learn to move on."

"Baby, please."

Charlie held up her hand. "I'm not your baby any more. You need to do what's best for you. I'm not it. I think it's best you give up on me and go your way."

"If you would just—"

"Goodbye, Kim. When I get home you can come visit the pups. But that's all you can expect. I'll see you when I see you."

"I will—"

Charlie disconnected the call before Kim could finish. She'd said what she wanted Kim to hear. All that she could hope was for Kim to move on, because she already had.

❖

There'd been an elephant in the room the entire day. A big unspoken entity hovering on the fringes of everything they did. Neither of them spoke of the couch incident or Terese's pending visit. As they worked throughout the day in the vegetable garden, cleaning out pens, or collecting food, from time to time Pip looked up from what she had been doing, only to find Charlie studying her.

Over afternoon tea Pip brought out a plastic tub and placed it on the kitchen dining table.

Charlie pointed at the container, one eyebrow raised in question.

"I thought you might like to pick out something for this evening." Pip wiggled her eyebrows up and down suggestively and laughed at Charlie's wide-eyed surprised expression. "They're torches and headlamps. For tonight."

"Oh."

Pip chuckled at Charlie's obvious relief. "I've got a set in the car for night rescues or releases. I figured you might like to pick out a set for yourself."

"Cool." Pip watched on as Charlie sorted through them and selected two. She adjusted the straps of a headlamp and put it on. "How's that?"

"Perfect. You look like a natural." Pip liked the way Charlie laughed softly. She slid a wrapped package across the tabletop.

"What's this?"

"Open it."

Pip watched on as Charlie meticulously undid the wrapping to reveal a black pouch, complete with a belt loop. With a nod of encouragement, Charlie opened the pouch and pulled out what looked like a folded up cane.

"I like to use a tree branch when I want to help put birds up high into the tree, or to coerce an animal down to a place that's easier to catch them. But sometimes, I can't find anything suitable, so I kind of came up with a handmade extendable version."

"You made this?"

Pip's cheeks burned in self-consciousness as Charlie unfolded the device, locking the joints into place with each length released. She shrugged. "I still prefer a branch, but sometimes it comes in handy. I thought you might like one yourself. Maybe you can try it out tonight."

Charlie stood up and tested the stick's reach and stability as she manoeuvred it around a door frame and a light fitting on the ceiling. She twisted her wrist and turned the leather handle. She started to laugh.

Pip frowned. "What's so funny?"

"Must come in handy, I expect, when you want to dust and remove cobwebs from up high."

Pip shook her head as she stood and cleared their afternoon tea dishes from the table. "A short joke. You're hilarious, Gigantor. Just for that, you can drive tonight."

Charlie brought the stick around and unhooked the truck keys that had been hanging up on the key rack, deftly reeling them in until they were snug in her hand.

Pip couldn't help but giggle at Charlie's playfulness as she rinsed the dishes in the sink. Finished, she turned around to find Charlie standing behind her, the stick folded and back in its pouch, attached to Charlie's belt.

Charlie lightly tapped the pouch at her hip. "Thank you. You're very sweet."

Pip held her breath as Charlie leaned in and kissed her on the cheek. Faces bare inches apart, she felt Charlie's breath brush across her skin as they held each other's gaze. Her voice came out as a whisper. "You're welcome."

Air rushed back into her lungs as Charlie stepped back. She fought for equilibrium, to return back to safer ground. "What say we feed the joeys right on five and then we can head straight on in and release the birds. It should be just on dusk by the time we get there."

"I've got the addresses they were picked up from back at the cabin—I'll bring them up when I come back."

"Sounds like we're all set then. I'll see you back here when you're finished with Squeak. Oh, and make sure you wear long pants and boots."

Pip looked on as Charlie started to walk out the door, only to stop and turn back to face her with a huge grin on her face. "I'm really looking forward to tonight."

"Me too." She waved Charlie goodbye with a smile that was genuine. She had felt the excitement building up inside her all day. She loved release days, but something about this one felt just that little bit extra special because she was sharing it with someone. Charlie. Having worked largely alone for so many years, the thought of having someone tail her all the time had rankled, big time, when Terese had first put her on the spot. Now she found herself looking forward to sharing all sorts of things with Charlie, from feed times, to chores, to the ultimate experience of a successful release.

Pip squatted down and stroked behind Chilli's ear. "I guess old dogs *can* learn new tricks, huh, Chill? Just don't tell Terese I said that."

Chilli's tail slapped against her leg as they headed back inside.

❖

Charlie closed the cabin door behind her at twenty after five. Squeak had fed well, cleaned up quickly, and was now fast asleep in the sack strapped on her back. She'd thought about leaving the joey behind in the cabin, but wasn't sure what time she'd get back after they'd released the frogmouths and possums. Pip had promised a celebratory bottle of wine upon their return and she wasn't about to pass on that. She not only was celebrating the successful rehabilitation of the animals, but also her release from Kim. A sigh left her lips. Had she done the right thing with Kim?

On one hand she felt confident in how she'd handled Kim. Yes, her anxiety attacks had lessened. Her sleep was more often interrupted by Squeak's feeding schedule than insomnia. But then, hadn't she worked herself to exhaustion in the States so she'd simply drop into bed and hope her brain would leave her alone? Hadn't she relied on the sedative power of whisky to calm the apprehension and yearning for Kim? Australia, the work, and God, yes, Pip, all were beginning to teach her to thrive. She hated the saying *Life is good* because for so long it hadn't been for her. But now, maybe she could not only convince herself but also finally begin to allow herself to believe it.

The sun had dipped to the level of the treeline. The friarbirds and currawongs started their evening chorus. Her chest was light and she automatically picked up her pace. She felt like her insides were vibrating with the excitement.

The pouch containing the stick thumped against her thigh with each stride, reminding her of Pip's thoughtful gift. She'd definitely put it to good use when she got home.

She counted the weeks since her arrival and was surprised when her mental tally came up with seven and a half weeks. Where had the time gone? In some ways it seemed like she'd just arrived. She had so much to learn. Yet she'd already experienced so much. Pip was now more than a mentor. She was a close friend and could be so much more. Charlie stopped short in her tracks, stunned. Where on earth had that thought come from? A fluttery feeling swirled in her belly. No. She couldn't do that to Pip. She was absolutely *not* going to let Pip be a rebound lover. No way. She loved her too much for that. What was going on with her? Love? *That* kind of love was not in the equation. Was it? Charlie shook her head to clear it and focused on what the evening had in store.

Pip had already moved the possums into their release cage by the time Charlie got there and was loading them into the back of her truck.

"I figured you wouldn't mind if I handled the possums." Pip winked at Charlie.

"Aw, you're so kind. Smart-ass. I just need a little more time to get used to them." Charlie playfully bumped Pip with her shoulder. "You should come to the States sometime. I'll let you play with a wolverine to see how you like it."

Pip shrugged. "Okay. Deal. But tonight you're in charge of the tawny frogmouths. There's a travel box in front of each of their cages for you to put them in."

"Now those I can handle."

Charlie shoved her hands into leather gloves and walked to the first cage. "Hey, buddy, you ready to head back into the woods tonight?" She unlatched the door and opened it enough to put an arm in. The frogmouth blinked at her and then poised its body like a slanted tree branch. "Come on. I can still see you." She shoved the door wider and then gently grasped the bird around its body. The frogmouth hissed and clapped its beak, but settled quickly when she put it in the box. The second frogmouth kept its eyes on her but didn't struggle as Charlie put it in a box as well. She checked to make sure both hasps were secure, and then lifted both by the topside handles.

"All good?" Pip said over her shoulder as she opened the truck door for Chilli.

"These guys are easy compared to some of the raptors I've handled." Charlie slid the two boxes onto the bed of the truck. She lifted the tailgate and closed it. "Do we need anything else?"

"Just some mozzie spray. So we don't get carried away by the buggers." Pip ducked back into the prep room. When she returned, Charlie was already in the driver's seat.

"Did you go to the right side yet?"

Charlie laughed. "Hell no. Wouldn't want to change anything."

Pip slid into the passenger side and looked at the release notes. "Okay. The possies go to Gulmarrad, Froggy Frank goes to Townsend, and Froggy Frieda goes to Iluka. What should we do first?"

"Well, since we need to hang the possum box in a tree, I'd rather do that while we still have a bit of daylight. So Gulmarrad first?"

Pip nodded. "Perfect." Pip offered up a triumphant wave forward. "Lead on Macduff."

Although the sun had set by the time they arrived at the release destination, it was still light enough to pick an appropriate tree in which to put the possum box.

Charlie backed the truck as close as possible to the selected red gum tree.

"Here's fine," Pip said as she craned her neck and looked up the tree. "You should be able to attach the box high enough from there."

Charlie crossed her arms over her chest. "Me? I don't think so."

"You're taller than I am. You'll be able to reach farther." Pip crossed her arms as well.

"You're lighter than I am. You won't come crashing through the top of the cab."

"Wouldn't happen. I had it reinforced for that very reason. Besides you're the newbie. You need to learn how to do it."

"I'll watch from the ground." Charlie leaned against the side of the truck.

"The roof can hold both our weights. How about we both go up?"

Charlie considered it for a moment. "Well, since it's getting darker by the minute, I guess we better do something."

Pip brightened. "And you can hold a torch for me."

Charlie coughed in surprise. "You do know that has another meaning, don't you?" Charlie felt heat crawl up her neck. It wasn't a torch she was holding, although it did have some semblance to a match.

"Huh?" Pip put the tailgate down and climbed up. She lifted the box with the possums inside onto the roof.

"It means that someone will wait until the time is right to be in a relationship with someone. You know. Hold out."

"Oh." Charlie could just make out a blush rising up Pip's neck. "All I meant was you could show me the light. The *flash*light."

Charlie burst out laughing. "Sweet, I think you've seen a lot more light than what you're letting on."

Pip shook her head and rolled her eyes as she gave Charlie a hand up onto the truck roof. "Okay. Let's see if this tree will work." She pushed aside the foliage, leaned in, and effectively disappeared from the waist up.

Charlie watched her shuffle from foot to foot and chuckled. Pip had no idea how cute her butt looked as it wiggled back and forth.

Charlie wondered how she'd never really noticed how attractive Pip was from the back.

"Charlie!" Pip stuck her hand out.

"What? Oh. Sorry." Charlie handed her the torch.

"Not that. The possum box."

"Oh. Sorry."

Pip backed out and looked her. "Bloody hell. What are you doing?"

A tingle swept up the back of Charlie's neck and across her face. She looked at Pip guiltily. "Sorry. I was a bit...distracted." Her eyes tracked back to Pip's rear end and quickly back up to meet her eyes.

"Well, quit looking at my arse and just be ready to hand me the possums when I ask for them." Pip disappeared again.

Charlie widened her eyes in surprise. How'd Pip know? She tightened her grip on the possum box. Her cheeks burned. Pip had to have been joking. Charlie ran over Pip's words again and grimaced at her tone of voice—she didn't sound like she was amused at all.

"Possums!"

Acting on a couple second delay, Charlie lifted the box and set the handle in Pip's open hand.

A few minutes later, Pip reappeared. "Okay. Go an' have a look at how I've hung the box. Shame there wasn't enough room in there for both of us, otherwise you could've watched."

Charlie ducked in, turned the flashlight on, and followed the tree trunk up with the light until she saw the box. Pip had rested it on a larger branch and secured it on the limb above with the wire that was nailed onto the back of the box. Charlie saw two eyes peeking out from the box. "Take good care of your joey, Miss Possie."

Charlie stepped back and turned around just in time to see where Pip's gaze was: on her butt. "Quit looking at *my* ass. We've got more work to do."

Pip smiled mischievously but said nothing as she sat down and slid off the roof and onto the tailgate.

"Will the possums make that their permanent home?" Charlie said a few minutes later as she navigated the truck off the dirt road out of the national forest.

"Depends really. Possums usually have a couple of hangouts or dreys. As we've got no idea of the exact coordinates of her original territory, she might stay there for a bit and get adjusted, feed up, and then head off back closer to where she came from. Then again, she might like her new digs and decide to stay too. Depends on what competition is around. It's hard to tell what they'll do."

Townsend was a short drive from Gulmarrad. Pip flipped through the paperwork and checked the surroundings. "Turn down this road. It's a shortcut to where we're headed."

Charlie signalled and made a left turn. She flicked the high beams on and shifted into a higher gear.

"I'd be care—" Pip started to say.

Without warning, a kangaroo leapt out in front of the truck. Charlie swerved, slammed on the brakes, forgetting to put the clutch in, and stalled the truck. "Holy hell. That was close."

The kangaroo continued hopping down the middle of the road as if he had the right of way.

Charlie realized her arm was pressed against Pip's chest. "Oh, sorry." She pulled it away, but not before she looked down and chuckled. Pip's hand was firmly holding on to her thigh. "I guess we all have our own forms of seat belt."

Pip removed it quickly. "Sorry."

"Personally I think my way is much more effective. I automatically do that when I have dogs riding with me." Charlie turned the key and restarted the truck.

Pip held her hands up in a defensive position, a crooked smile flashing across her face. "Mm. I am so not gonna go there."

"Turn right here, and then pull over," Pip said a few minutes later.

Charlie did as told and shut the truck off. Except for the ping of the engine, there was no sound. Charlie stared in awe out the windshield.

"Oh, my," Charlie whispered.

The sky was ablaze with stars. The Milky Way painted a huge swath of white through the middle of the sky. The moon was barely a crescent in the west.

"See over there?" Pip pointed to the south. "That's the Southern Cross."

"Wow," Charlie said again. "What an amazing sky. I've never seen anything like it."

"Really? Why's that? I thought your view of the sky in the mountains would be similar. You know, no pollution or competing lights from big towns and stuff."

"No. I have no idea why, but this sky is so much more brilliant. Could be the humidity I suppose."

Charlie unlatched her seat belt and let it retract. She couldn't take her eyes off the sky.

"You ready?"

Taking a deep excited breath, Charlie nodded. This was what she had been waiting for. This was what it was all about. She looked across at Pip and knew, by the huge smile on her face, that she felt the same.

"Let's do this." Pip opened her door and got out.

Charlie followed suit and met her at the back of the truck.

"You're up, Charlie. This one's yours. Time to set your bird free." Pip lowered the tailgate and sat down.

Charlie drew the box to her. She hoisted herself into a standing position on the tailgate, lifted the box, and set it on the roof of the truck. She opened the latch and stood back.

The frogmouth blinked its huge eyes and stared out at the space beyond. It hopped off its perch inside the box and onto the roof of the truck. It swirled its head back and forth, cocked its head and seemed to listen for a moment. It finally crouched, sprang up, and flew off on silent wings.

Charlie couldn't stop smiling, nor could she stop the tears. "They're so beautiful."

"That they are." Pip stood up and put the release box into the truck. "One more to go."

The second frogmouth was released in Iluka about an hour later. The bird didn't pause as long as the first one. It was more than ready. As soon as Charlie opened the box, it launched itself into the air and flew off.

Charlie joined Pip on the ground. "That was uneventful. And I didn't get to use my stick."

Pip threw her arm around Charlie's shoulders. "Don't worry. There'll be plenty others. You ready to head home and celebrate?"

"You bet." Charlie raced to get in the truck. Too late, she once again found herself on the passenger's side. "Dammit!" But she couldn't help but smile when she heard Pip's laughter.

❖

"Do you want a fork or chopsticks?" Pip was mid-serve of their meals while Charlie poured their wine.

"I'll have both."

Pip couldn't help but get swept along with Charlie's mirth. She knew she was an absolute chopstick tragic, and having had a rare two glasses of wine already, knew that reputation would well and truly remain intact. It had been nice though, just relaxing and recalling the highlights of each of the animals that had been released just hours before.

"It's funny. If I close my eyes I can still smell Froggy Freida." Charlie took a sip of wine.

Pip laughed openly. "Tawnies have a real distinct smell when they are nervous or upset. And as you discovered, once smelled, it can never be unsmelled."

"Ain't that the truth?" Charlie raised her glass and sipped a toast in acknowledgement.

"Oh screwbugger that." Pip threw aside her chopsticks and picked up a fork. "I'm throwing more food on the floor than in my mouth."

Charlie snagged a stray piece from the table next to Pip's plate and deftly popped it into her mouth. "And you pea'd on the table."

Pip smiled around a mouthful, waving her fork mid-air expressively. "Yep. That's me. No table manners at all. Can't take me anywhere."

Pip expected Charlie to play along but was surprised when Charlie's expression turned serious instead.

"Do you ever get lonely—out here, on your own?"

Pip pushed her food around on her plate. "No."

"Never?"

Pip put her fork down and picked up her wine glass. "Never's a big word."

"All right. Sometimes then?"

Pip shrugged.

"Well, what do you do when, you know, you get physically lonely?"

"I work hard. It passes."

"At what?"

Pip got up and cleared their plates away. "Lots of things. The garden mostly."

Pip turned around in time to see Charlie snort and choke on a mouthful of wine. She went to Charlie's side and patted her on the back until her breath returned enough for the choking to become laughter.

Pip narrowed her eyes and took a step back. "What's so funny?"

Charlie dabbed at the tears gathering in her eyes. "Nothing."

Pip glared at her, hands on hips, and waited, albeit impatiently, for Charlie to share. Pip couldn't help but notice how Charlie struggled to keep a straight face.

"I was just thinking. You have a really huge garden."

Pip blinked at her. It took her a moment to understand. She *did* have an extraordinarily large garden. She raised her eyebrows as she finally got Charlie's point and a snigger crept out in recognition. "Well, some days it takes longer to pass than others."

The wine slopped out of Charlie's glass as she brought her knees up, her body rocking with laughter. Unable to maintain her strait-laced facade any longer, Pip flopped down onto the lounge beside her and laughed until she had to bend over double to catch her breath.

As the laughter faded, Pip laid her head back against the lounge with a smile still lingering on her lips. "I have a feeling that when I get up tomorrow and look at the garden I am going to blush like a beetroot. I never realized—there's nothing very subtle about it. In fact, it's rather a bloody big tell, isn't it?"

Charlie snorted in agreement. "Would make for a funny television series though, wouldn't it? *The Randy Gardener.*"

Pip turned and tucked her feet up under her bottom to face Charlie. She stuck her tongue out at her. "What about you?"

"What about me?" Charlie looked past her.

"Do you have a big garden at home?"

"Heh. Hardly."

"Do you miss her? Kim."

"Do I miss her?" Charlie leaned forward and topped up both their glasses. "No. And yes."

Pip let her gather her thoughts.

"I miss what we had. The sharing and the intimacy, the closeness of it all. After the break-up, it was hard initially. I had to relearn a whole lot of things, not the least of which was I had to rediscover myself, who I was, who I'd become, and where I needed to go from that point."

"Would you go back?"

Charlie shook her head. "To Kim? No."

"What happens then when you go back to the States?"

Charlie cocked her head. "I don't really know. I guess I'll go back to work. For a while anyway. Maybe look for a transfer somewhere. A clean break. A new start. But then again, maybe by the time I get back from Australia…" Charlie shrugged. "I don't know. Coming here has been a good thing. It's been the break I needed. I'm learning how to live again. I'd forgotten how to do that there for a while." Charlie reached out and entwined her fingers with Pip's.

The heat of Charlie's hand permeated hers, travelled up her arm and across her chest, and suffused her with a wash of warmth.

"You helped me do that. You and Squeak. To feel without hurting. To laugh. To look forward to every day."

Pip squeezed her hand lightly. "Nah. You did all that yourself. I just chucked some cute things in your way to get your attention."

"Well, it worked. You got my attention."

Pip looked down at their joined hands. "I reckon I owed you one anyway."

"Why's that?"

Pip went to pull her hand away only to stop as Charlie's thumb stroked the back of her hand, dissolving all thoughts of creating distance.

"Why do you owe me?"

"Because." Her voice faltered with nervousness at the disclosure. She cleared her throat in an effort to wrestle back some bravado and control. "Because you called me on my diabetes. And you didn't make a big deal out of it." She bit her bottom lip self-consciously. "You didn't look at me any differently because of it."

"Isn't that what you want?"

Pip closed her eyes and nodded. "More than you can imagine." A sniffle escaped her. She opened her eyes, withdrew her hand, and scrubbed across her face. "Bugger it. Sorry. It's the wine. Too much D and M. Tonight is about celebrating. Ignore me."

Charlie held the bottle up to the light. "There's just a bit left. Want to go halves?"

Pip put her hand over her glass. "No, thanks. I've gone over my limit already."

"Is that a bad thing?"

"No. But I'm gonna have to fiddle around a bit to balance it all out. No big deal—just a pain in the bum is all." As timing would have it, Pip's pump vibrated. She lifted her shirt and saw that her levels were a little on the low side. "Will you excuse me a minute?"

Charlie's hand intercepted her movement forward. "Can you show me?"

Shock reverberated throughout her body. She froze.

Charlie must have guessed at her level of discomfort. She broke the moment to stand, take the glass from her hand, and walk it over to the sink, giving her some much needed space to think. "Not necessarily tonight. But sometime, when you feel it might be okay."

Pip smiled briefly at her. "I'll be back in a minute." It didn't take long to test her levels. She snagged a couple of lollies from the bedroom before returning to Charlie who had stacked the dishwasher with their dishes.

"There's a couple of phone messages on the machine. The light's flashing."

"Oh, right, thanks."

She crossed the room and pressed the replay button. The first message was from Terese saying she was flying in to Coffs Harbour to meet with a couple of the local rescue group coordinators and that she would see them late the following day. Pip and Charlie looked at each other and shared eye rolls and conspiratorial grins at the news of the impending visit. The second message was from the doctor's surgery asking if she could ring them back when she got the message. "I'll ring them in the morning. Too late now."

Charlie yawned. "Mm. It's getting late. Squeak and I had better take off. Tomorrow's another big day no doubt."

Pip followed her to the door. "No doubt."

On the threshold of the door, Charlie stopped and turned to face her. Pip had no time to stop herself from physically colliding into Charlie's taller frame. She took a step back only to find her back against the door frame. Charlie followed her. They were so close their breaths intermingled. Pip watched, entranced, as Charlie's tongue darted briefly from between her lips, the moisture catching the overhead light.

"Thank you." Charlie's voice held the slightest tremble. "For tonight. For everything." With the smallest of movements, Charlie stepped forward. Their lips met.

Pip marvelled at Charlie's softness and warmth, her lips holding just a hint of the evening's wine painted on the surface. As unconscious as breathing Pip found her hands encircling Charlie's body, one around her waist, the other slightly higher to rest along Charlie's ribs as Charlie's tongue sought and asked for entry. A humming noise from deep in Pip's throat signalled her permission, which Charlie responded to.

Pip's head swam and she was extremely grateful for the door frame, once a barrier, now effectively her saviour as it held her up. She found herself ignorant of almost everything except Charlie's lips on hers, dancing, tasting, seeking, teasing.

Just as Pip found herself short of breath, the kiss lightened and finally eased off. Charlie leaned back a little to look at her intently. Pip's heart pounded in her chest and butterflies skittered from her toes up and down her legs, to lodge in her belly, leaving a trail of excited nerve endings in its wake.

Charlie caressed Pip's cheekbone with her thumb. "And for the record, you don't owe me anything. I think it's more like we're even."

With a last gentle kiss, Charlie stepped back, turned, and walked into the dark, leaving Pip leaning heavily against the door frame, still trying to catch her breath and still the rapid beat of her heart.

❖

Charlie waited for the bed to stop spinning as she lay on top of the sheets. Every time she closed her eyes, the gyroscope that was her picked up speed, and she worried she'd be flung off the bed from the centrifugal force. She snorted at the scientific reference, but it made her head hurt so the humour was lost.

She barely remembered the walk home other than having to step over the python that had stretched across the path. She was more than a little convinced the snake was a product of the wine anyway. It was probably a log. At least that's what she kept telling herself.

What a lovely evening with Pip, though. The stories and laughter they shared were some of the best times she'd had in a while. No, it'd been a long time. A very long time.

Charlie sighed.

The spinning slowed to the point where she dared to close her eyes. She replayed some of the conversations with Pip. She was an amazing woman, hands down. It hurt her heart that people had been so cruel to her because of her illness.

The ticker tape in her head wound down to when she'd been about to leave. She'd only intended to kiss Pip on the cheek. But the combination of wine, the closeness they'd shared, and...Okay, now she was going to have to admit it. She was insanely attracted to Pip. She'd spent months wanting to only be left alone and to be alone. This couldn't be a rebound relationship, could it? No. Pip had brought out a part of her that she hadn't recognized until now. Faith and confidence in her own influence and ability in her personal life had been absent since her dad had died. Professionally, she had no issues with her job in the States. She was comfortable there. Having to become acquainted with and learn the ins and outs of a foreign land, however, had put personal and professional inadequacies on par with each other. Both as low as one could get.

Pip made her rise to the challenges of the work they did. She encouraged her to learn and love what she was doing. But would she have the courage to commit to loving a woman again? That was the part Charlie wasn't sure of. Hell, she didn't even know how Pip felt about her. *I'm sure I shocked the living hell right out of her when I kissed her.*

She could blame it on the wine, sure. But she couldn't deny she was falling for an awfully cute Aussie with the sexiest accent ever. She just wasn't sure what the morning would bring and what Pip would say, if anything. So like the fate of all the animals they rescued, what Pip did with the love she had to offer was all to be determined.

Chapter Nine

Even behind closed eyes Pip's world seemed to tilt and swirl. She was uncomfortably hot and tossed her head restlessly from side to side. She threw the blanket off, the cooler air a comparative blessing as it brushed against her soaked cotton singlet and bed shorts. A rivulet of sweat ran through her damp hair, over her scalp, and past her ear.

Tired. So tired. She struggled to put a string of coherent thoughts together.

The bed seemed to move, causing her world to tilt violently again. She kept her eyes shut. Noise. Loud noise. Barking. Chilli. Toenails scraped against the soft flesh of her forearm. More barking. Loud. In her face. She felt a hard tug at the waist of her bed shorts. Chilli seemed to be trying to get her out of bed. She rolled to the side and landed heavily on the floor on all fours. A grunt escaped her lips.

Even through her foggy brain, she knew her levels had become dangerously low while she had slept. She reached up and felt clumsily along the bedside table for her lolly jar. But her hand missed in its attempt to grasp it and only succeeded in knocking it to the floor to shatter into pieces.

Pip lolled her head in defeat. She crawled towards the end of the bed, only vaguely aware that a piece of the broken glass jar had sliced her hand, leaving a crimson trail behind her. With what felt like a gargantuan effort, she pulled herself to her feet.

Chilli danced and barked in front of her.

She swayed unsteadily. "Trying."

Chilli barked louder, the sound bouncing off the walls of the room.

She moved drunkenly on leaden feet down the hallway, sliding her bloodied hand along the wall. Her sole mission was to reach the gel tubes she kept in the fridge and a fruit juice popper. She tottered at the edge of the kitchen, having lost the security of the wall as she weaved closer to the island bench.

Chilli ran back and forth between her and the fridge. Her barks echoed off the high ceilings. Chilli darted past her. Pip tried to turn her head to see where the dog was. The momentum of turning her head made the world swim blurrily before her eyes. She reached out in an attempt to steady herself on the nearby kitchen island but her hand grasped at air and she fell. Her forehead caught the edge of the fridge door and finally the cool of the floor against her cheek.

❖

It was a great dream. Charlie was on the beach. The bright sun against the water made her squint. A person waved as they walked towards her. Charlie could barely make out a woman's face in the glare of the sun. She waved back. As the woman drew closer, Charlie smiled when she recognized her familiar stride. She called out a hello and was surprised to hear the woman bark. Confused, she waved again only to hear more barking. Charlie frowned and started at the oddness of it all. The edges of the dream faded and dissipated. But the barking continued. She rolled over onto her side and cuddled up to her pillow. Stupid dream.

The barking continued.

Charlie opened her eyes and looked at the time. It was nearing five a.m. The barking was getting louder and closer.

"Why on earth would—?"

The barks came from outside and were now accompanied by frantic scratching on her front door.

"Chilli!"

In a single motion Charlie flung the covers off, leapt out of bed, and opened the door to find Chilli frantically barking and pacing.

"Chilli, what is it, girl? Is it Pip?"

Chilli barked boisterously at the sound of her owner's name.

"Hang on." Charlie threw on a pair of shorts and a T-shirt, and slipped her feet into her sandals. She was halfway out the door when she turned back to grab Squeak, her mobile, and the handheld radio.

Chilli whined in seeming desperation and panted loudly.

"I'm coming, girl. Let's go."

She hadn't remembered the torch but didn't want to waste time going back to get it. She ran after Chilli, the dog's pale coat guiding her along the pathway in the predawn darkness.

Squeak's bag bounced up and down against her back as she ran. She figured it wouldn't be too dissimilar to bouncing through the bush in a mother's pouch, all tucked up safe inside.

Charlie pressed the radio button as she ran. "Pip, can you hear me? Come in." Hoping above all hope that Pip would pick up and answer on the other end. But the fact that Chilli had come to find her quickly quenched any false hopes she harboured.

"Pip? Come on, babe. Pick up for me."

Chilli whined in front of her. There was only silence on the other end. Her heart rate picked up another notch with increasing worry.

It only took a few minutes to get from the cabin to the main house but it felt like a small slice of eternity as she ran up the ramp and through the back door.

The house was dark, but she could just make out a beeping noise coming from the kitchen. She scrabbled for the switch on the wall and lit the room up. Pip was face down between the kitchen island and the fridge. She rushed over and knelt down next to her. She saw a brief flash of blood on her hand, but nothing too dramatic. Pip's pump's light was flashing with alternating alarm sounds. Pip's clothes were soaked in sweat. Her hair was slick and damp. She rolled her over. Pip had a lump high up on her forehead, just beginning to colour up into a bruise. Her face was pale, her breathing shallow. Charlie felt for Pip's pulse. It was racing. She could barely keep count of it. Pip's breath had a distinct odour to it, not unlike pure alcohol or acetone. She racked her brain through her first-aid training and knew Pip was having a hypo.

Charlie picked up her phone and automatically started to dial 911, only to disconnect the call. She was in Australia now. What was their emergency number? "Fuck!" She didn't have time to look it up on the internet. Charlie scanned the room for inspiration and finally saw Terese's business card on the fridge. She dialled the number and waited until a groggy voice answered.

"Terese, it's me, Charlie. Pip's having a diabetic episode and I need to call an ambulance, but I don't know Australia's emergency number. What is it?" She heard how high, loud, and tense her voice was, but she didn't care. She just needed the damn number. Terese gave her the number. She didn't even bother to say goodbye. She hung up and dialled 000 and gave all the details she could to the operator. But she knew she had at least a half hour wait before help arrived. Her insides quivered with adrenaline and the frustration of not being able to do anything.

She damn near jumped out of her skin when the house phone rang. She hustled to her feet and pulled it off the counter before returning to Pip's side. It was Terese. She told her about Pip's emergency hypo kit and where to find it in the bathroom. Charlie quickly retrieved the red container and listened as Terese walked her through how to prepare it. After giving Pip the glucagon injection, she rolled Pip's unresponsive body onto the side and lay down behind her. Charlie spooned her body around Pip's unconscious form. She wrapped her hand around to rest between Pip's breasts, where she could feel every heartbeat and count each of her breaths until help arrived.

Chilli lay alongside Pip's front, resting a paw on top of Pip's limp hand. She whined and laid her muzzle down on Pip's forearm.

Charlie lifted her hand briefly from Pip's chest and stroked Chilli's head. "I know, girl. Help's coming."

Chilli's sad eyes nearly broke her heart.

❖

The gentle touch of a hand on Charlie's shoulder roused her from a sound sleep. She lifted her head, opened her heavy lidded eyes, and blinked hard. It took her a few moments to recall where she was, but she was quickly reminded by the regular beep of a heart monitor. She stared blankly at Pip's hand resting in her upturned palm.

"Charlie."

"Huh?" Charlie looked behind her. "Terese." She started to get up, but Terese firmed the grip on her shoulder.

"Stay put, pet. I can see you're knackered. You've more than earned a kip."

"I don't remember falling asleep." Charlie followed Terese's gaze to Pip, who lay unconscious, looking small in the hospital bed. "I don't know what happened, Terese." Tears welled in her eyes. Charlie blinked them back.

"The pump failed." Terese stepped closer and drew soothing circles on Charlie's back with her hand. "Apparently a recall was issued. Only Pip didn't get the message."

"How do you know all this?"

"I stopped at Pip's house before coming here and intercepted a phone call from her doctor. A replacement is being mailed out today. With a bit of luck it should arrive tomorrow."

Charlie blew a hard sigh. "That's a relief."

"It is. But it also means that when Pip wakes up, and they stabilize her blood sugar levels, she'll still have to stay in here for monitoring over the next twenty-four hours at least. And hopefully the pump will be here by then. But I'll give you a heads-up. She'll more than likely tell everyone to get nicked no matter how crook she feels."

"She'll be pretty pissed if she has to stay a moment longer than what she deems necessary. Especially if she thinks we're missing call-outs." Charlie glanced at the clock and gasped. "Jesus! It's nearly noon. I've got to get back and feed." She started to her feet, but once again Terese kept her from rising.

"Stay still. While I was at the house I checked the records and fed everybody. They'll be right for another few hours." Terese smiled. "From the looks of it, you and Pip are getting on quite well."

Charlie self-consciously let go of Pip's hand. Her own was numb from being in one position for so long, so she shook it out to get some feeling back into it. "She's come to mean a lot to me."

"Does Pip feel the same?" Terese sat down on the edge of the hospital bed.

Charlie snorted. "Your guess is as good as mine." She looked sheepishly at Terese. "I'd hope she would. But I just don't know."

Neither spoke for several minutes. The beep of the heart monitor counted the seconds. The intravenous drip flowed silently into Pip's veins. Charlie watched the steady rise and fall of Pip's chest as she breathed.

"How long do you think until she wakes up?" Charlie stroked Pip's hand.

"I'd say it depends on Pip." Terese stood up and shook Pip's foot. "You can't play possum forever, Pip." She turned her attention to Charlie. "Do you want something to eat? I can go down to the cafeteria and grab something for both of us."

Charlie smiled appreciatively. "That'd be great. Thanks."

Several minutes passed. Charlie rested her head on her arm, still holding Pip's hand. She squeezed it gently. "Okay, sweetheart. You can wake up any time now. You're worrying the hell out of me."

Charlie started when she received a reciprocated, albeit weak, clasp of her hand. "Pip?" She looked up into Pip's squinted eyes. "Hey. How're you feeling?"

Pip closed her eyes. Charlie thought she might've gone back to sleep.

"Ratshit." Pip's voice was low and hoarse. "Bloody headache."

❖

Pip hated the aftereffects of a severe hypo. When asked to describe it once, the closest she could offer was to think of your worst hangover headache. And double it. Only then could someone be close to understanding the misery she knew she was in for over the next twenty-four hours. Her stomach roiled from the glucagon injection Charlie had given her and she was struggling to keep down the fruit and yoghurt the nurse had given her earlier.

Terese stuck her head in the doorway just as a nurse was leaving the room with a basin and washcloth. “Hey, kiddo. How you doing?”

“Crap.”

“Ah. Fresh sheets and gown. Guess that means hospital food didn’t agree with you, huh?”

“Meh.” Pip shut her eyes against the steady pounding in her head. She knew Terese was familiar with her reactions to a serious episode. Pip heard her close the curtains. Even behind her eyelids, the dark relief was tangible. “Thank you.”

“You’re welcome.”

The squeak of rubber-soled shoes announced the nurse’s re-entry. She placed a fresh replacement bowl of fruit and yoghurt on her tray side table and looked at her. In full understanding of the nurse’s look, Pip nodded, knowing the importance of consuming carbohydrates to replenish her liver glycogen stores and to prevent a secondary hypo from occurring. Seemingly satisfied, the nurse sought out Pip’s hand and took a blood sugar reading from the tip of Pip’s ring finger. They had been going through this routine every second hour and had it down to a fine wordless art. Sometimes, when she was trying to blot the world out with the blanket over her face, Pip simply stuck her hand out from under the sheet and withdrew it when the nurse had finished seeking her bloody sacrifice.

Pip looked expectantly at her, waiting for the reading.

“Just a shade under four. Three point nine. We’re getting there.”

Pip tolerated the insulin injection from the nurse in silence.

“See you in two hours. Good luck with your lunch.” The nurse tapped the bowl to highlight its significance.

Pip waved her out.

Terese chuckled softly. “Looks like you got a subtle one.”

“Mm.” Pip yawned and blinked back the resulting tears. “Thanks for coming so quick, and for feeding everyone.”

“No problems. It was a bit like old times. I quite enjoyed it.”

"Charlie told me about the pump." Pip rubbed at her eyes. "Where is she?"

"I sent her home after you fell asleep again. She looked pretty wiped. And I don't think having the life scared out of her helped matters either."

Pip picked at the taped edges covering her IV cannula on the back of her wrist. A frown marred her features as a thousand thoughts warred back and forth in her mind. Well, that was that then. "No doubt she's at home packing up. Can't say I blame her. She didn't sign on for this shit."

"Stop it." Terese's hand intercepted her fingers. "She's fine. She just had a fright is all."

"I s'pose she'll be going back with you?"

"What? No. At least, not as far as I know. She hasn't said anything of the sort, and I certainly haven't suggested anything."

Pip didn't feel overly convinced. "Not exactly what she signed up for though, is it? Being a nursemaid wasn't mentioned in the brochure, I'm sure."

Terese sat on the bed, put her arm around Pip's shoulders, and gave her a light squeeze. "I'd forgotten how much fun you are after a turn." She kissed her on the forehead and rested her chin on top of Pip's head. "Charlie's fine. Like I said, she just got a fright is all. Because she cares for you, you idiot." Terese relinquished her grip and turned until she sat facing her.

Pip drew her knees up to her chest. She couldn't look at Terese.

"What are you thinking?"

Pip shrugged.

"Don't give me that bullshit."

Pip rested her forehead on her knees and closed her eyes. "I don't want her to go."

"Who said she was going?"

Her head wasn't up to having this conversation.

"Pip?"

She felt Terese's hand on her arm. She shook her head.

"What are you afraid of?" Terese's voice was low and soft.

"Protocol."

A surprised bark of laughter escaped Terese, causing Pip to look up, confused by Terese's odd response.

Terese covered her mouth. "Oh, darl. I'm sorry. You caught me by surprise. Never thought I'd hear you say that."

Pip scrunched her nose up in wry acknowledgement of the ironic truth of it.

"Do you like her?"

Pip sighed. "It's hard not to. She's a nice person."

"Do you have feelings for her? Do you want more?"

"I'm trying not to." She scrunched up the bed sheets in her hands. "It's frickin' hard. I mean…I *can't*."

"Protocol."

"Yes." She raised her head and looked directly at Terese. "We both know she'd have to go." She made a conscious effort to unclench her fists, release the sheets, and smooth the bedding out in an attempt to regain some semblance of control. "I can't compromise her study and all the effort and money that's gone into her coming to Australia."

"How about you let me worry about protocol?"

"I'm her *host* for Christ's sakes, Terese."

"Technically speaking, I am her host. You are her mentor."

"Doesn't matter. It's still wrong."

Terese stood up, patted Pip on the forearm affectionately, and winked at her. "If there's one thing my darling Derek taught me, is that life is for living. Grab hold of it. Celebrate it. Embrace it, my friend. And all that comes with it. Cause you just never know what's around the corner." With a small melancholy smile on her face, Terese kissed her cheek and left.

❖

Charlie parked the truck beneath a tree in the hospital parking lot the next morning. Chilli sat in the front seat at the moment because two duffel bags, filled with various types of clothing, took up the back seat.

She ruffled the fur on Chilli's neck. "I'll be back in a bit with Pip. So you keep the truck safe."

At the mention of Pip's name, Chilli brightened and wagged her tail.

She'd gotten up early as usual to feed, but when she arrived at the prep room, Terese had already cleaned and fed everyone. Even Squeak, who'd been staying with Terese, to free Charlie up to go back and forth to the hospital. Despite her worries about Pip, Charlie felt somewhat naked without the little joey attached to her back in her makeshift pouch.

Charlie slid the envelope Terese had given her into her pocket. She had been given strict orders not to open it until she saw Pip. Terese hadn't given her any clue what it contained. She'd merely told her to pack a bag and then had put one in the truck for Pip, before handing her the envelope marked with *Pip & Charlie* on the front.

Charlie took a series of deep breaths to calm the hordes of butterflies fluttering in her chest and stomach as the elevator began its ascent to Pip's floor. *Pip.* Although she'd visited her every day for hours, she missed the ease with which they worked together, the close camaraderie they'd developed. She missed being with Pip in an environment that wasn't sterile and tile floored, that didn't smell like antiseptic. And she wanted to explore beyond the kiss they'd shared. But would Pip want to? They had some talking to do, if only Pip would open up about what she was feeling. What happened after that, well, both of them had to be happy with it.

The elevator chimed, signalling its arrival. The doors slid open. Charlie paused for a moment while the other four people exited. She stepped out, rubbed sweaty hands on her shorts, and turned right, towards Pip's room.

Charlie hesitated and leaned against the doorway when she saw Pip sitting on the edge of the bed. Pip swung her legs back and forth, bracing herself with her arms, and hung her head. Everything about her body language said she was anxious to leave. White tape covered the IV sites on her arms and her clothes appeared to hang looser on her. Like it or not, Pip was going to have to allow Charlie to take care of her.

Pip must have sensed Charlie standing there. She lifted her head and gazed right into Charlie's eyes. The smile she gave Charlie somewhat masked the dark circles under her eyes and the residual fatigue on her face.

"Hey," Charlie said softly as she walked in.

"Hey, yourself." Pip's eyes remained locked on Charlie's. "Boy, are you a sight for sore eyes. Never thought I'd be so grateful to be rescued by a Yank."

Charlie pointed over her shoulder. "I suppose I could go looking for an Aussie to help you out, but I'm not sure I'd find anyone who'd liberate the likes of you."

"Ha. Fair enough. Guess I'm stuck with you then, hey?"

Charlie took Pip's hand in hers. "Guess you are. Is the new pump working okay?"

"Yep. I've been given the green light. Everything is holding steady. The nurses have finally promised to leave me alone and the doc has signed me out."

"Good." Charlie loosened her hand to let go of Pip's. Pip held on a bit longer before releasing her. "Before we head out"—Charlie slid the envelope from her pocket—"Terese made me promise not to open this until we were together."

"What's that?"

"Danged if I know, but I get the feeling she's up to something." Charlie slid her finger under the flap and tore the envelope open. Inside was a folded note.

My dearest pain in the neck, Pip, & Charlie,

You've both been through a lot these past few days and I think you have a lot of catching up to do. Pip, you know what I mean when I say don't fret about the rest ;)

I'm shouting you to a three-day stay in Angourie, at the Rainforest Resort. I want you both to rest and relax—and don't worry about home. I'll hold the fort down. And before you ask, I've checked with the management and because Chilli is an assistance dog, she's welcome there too. Both of you, have fun, and don't show your faces back here until checkout time, hear me?

All my love to you both, T

Charlie looked at Pip and said, "Do you know what she's up to?"

"Buggered if I know. Can we just get out of here?"

"Absolutely. There's someone down in the car that really wants to see you."

Pip beamed. "Chilli. Poor girl. That's the longest we've ever been apart. Is she okay?"

"She is. We kept her busy. And she didn't mind sleeping with me every night either."

"Guess she did all right then. Lucky girl." Pip averted her eyes and slid off the bed.

Charlie shrugged a tangle of thoughts aside that there was any double meaning behind Pip's comment.

As soon as they got within sight of the truck, Chilli hung her front end out of the window and yipped excitedly. Her tail was a constant blur behind her wiggling butt.

Charlie stood back and watched Pip reunite with her beloved dog. A prickle started behind her eyes and she blinked back the burn of tears. She knew exactly how both of them felt and a tinge of jealousy rose. She missed her Labs terribly. If there was one thing that called to her from home, it was the urge to see them again.

Pip let Chilli out of the truck so she could release some extra energy born of excitement to see her. Charlie took that opportunity to move the duffels from the back seat and into the bed of the truck. She leaned against the driver's door and waited patiently for the two to finish their reunion. Charlie knew Chilli would stick to Pip's side like glue even more so than usual. She didn't blame her one bit.

The forty minutes it took to get to Angourie, just outside of Yamba, were spent in conversation as Charlie caught her up on all the animals they had in care.

The resort, true to its name, was located within rainforest habitat. After checking in, Charlie parked the truck and they followed a path lined with flowering shrubs to their designated villa. They opened the door to their spacious accommodations and walked into the lounge room. This in turn led to a dining area and a fully equipped kitchen. The rooms were stylishly decorated with modern furniture and accented with photos of birds and local landscapes. A sliding glass door off the kitchen led to a lovely porch fenced for privacy. A luxurious two-person spa bubbled and churned invitingly. Rainforest vegetation surrounded it on all three sides. In addition to an outdoor daybed, a table and chairs sat tucked under an overhang. Access to the pool was from the lounge room. Two couches, shaded by a huge umbrella, sat just outside. The pool was pristinely blue.

"Wow," Charlie said, turning in a circle to take it all in.

"You got that right." Pip set her duffel down and slid the door open to the pool area. Chilli followed her out.

Charlie hefted her own bag and entered the bedroom. "Oh, boy. What are we going to do about this?"

"About what?" Pip peered around her. "Oh."

They both stared at the only bed in the entire villa.

"Pip, I think we need to talk."

❖

"You take the bed, I'll take the sofa." Pip tossed her duffel on the lounge and stood with her arms crossed over her chest.

"You just got out of hospital, for Pete's sake. You are *not* sleeping on the sofa." Charlie threw hers on the lounge as well and stood defiantly with her hands on her hips.

"Well, then, we'll take it in turns and flip for it on the last night."

Charlie looked like she was going to protest but stopped and threw her hands up in the air. "Fine. Whatever."

Pip picked her bag up and put it next to the lounge. Chilli pranced up and down. Pip sensed that she was picking up on the escalating tension in the room. She also felt the need to do something to dissipate the rising energy. Unfortunately, there were no animals or call-outs to distract her from Charlie's nearness. She spied a tourist guide on the coffee table and picked it up.

"The brochure says there's a waterfall about a forty minute walk from here. Want to pack a picnic lunch and go exploring?"

"Is that wise? I mean…" Charlie waved her hand vaguely up and down at Pip.

"I'm fine. Good as gold and back to normal. No. Big. Deal."

"You could have died."

Pip didn't miss the wobble in Charlie's voice. She walked over, took Charlie's hand, and guided her to sit next to her on the couch. Her thumb brushed back and forth over the back of Charlie's hand as she held it in her lap. She felt Charlie's hand trembling through the light touch of her fingers. She gentled her voice. "But I didn't. I had you and Chilli to help me. And now I'm fine."

"But what if we hadn't been there?" Charlie's lower lip quivered.

"Shh." Pip cupped Charlie's chin and cheek. "But you were." She leaned in and kissed Charlie on the lips. It was natural. Soft, warm, fleeting. "Thank you." As their lips parted, Pip wasn't ready to lose contact. She closed her eyes and leaned her forehead against Charlie's. Pip marvelled at the simple comfort of the moment.

Chilli whined softly and nudged her muzzle between them. They both opened their eyes and smiled. Pip easily read recognition in Charlie's eyes of the enormity of what could have happened, but fortunately didn't. How lucky was she to be sitting here with Charlie and a certain impatient canine?

Pip chuckled and ran her fingers through Chilli's coat. "Okay, girl. In a minute." She raised Charlie's knuckles to her lips and brushed them with a brief kiss. "Let's pack some lunch and head off."

It didn't take long to gather some food and get changed into some comfortable hiking gear. With their backpacks loaded, they headed off in search of the picturesque picnic spot. The walk didn't disappoint as they traversed a well-worn path amidst the trees and cool overhead rainforest canopy. Charlie spied dozens of birds and Pip was able to point out various markings on trees that identified the territorial marks of possums and gliders. Although the tree canopy kept the heat of the sun at bay, the humidity was building with the increase in daytime temperature. By the time they arrived at the falls and the pristine pool of water underneath it, their shirts were soaked with sweat. They dumped their bags and sat on the grassy verge of the pool and wordlessly downed a bottle of cool drinking water each.

Pip was relieved that the tension between them had slowly begun to release as they walked, talked, and compared animal scats or bird sightings. They laughed over Chilli's childlike joy and exuberance as she trotted ahead of them. It was almost like life was getting back to normal as they shared and bounced thoughts and notes off each other.

Chilli ran to the water's edge, spun around, and looked at them expectantly. She loped back and sat directly in front of Pip. Her tail swished happily against the grass. She let out an excited woof and briefly looked over her shoulder to the water and back to her again. Pip threw her head back and laughed. "Sure. Go on then." Chilli jumped up, ran over to the pool's edge, and threw herself into the water with an almighty splash. The look of pure joy on her face was infectious.

With a huge grin on her face, Pip turned to Charlie who was also smiling and laughing at Chilli paddling around in circles and snapping at the watery surface. "You up for it?" Pip unfurled a blanket from one of the backpacks and laid it out atop the grassy carpet.

"What?"

Pip nodded in Chilli's direction. "A swim. It'd be a great way to cool off."

"I didn't bring a swimsuit."

"Me either." Pip jumped up. "Come on." She waved for Charlie to join her.

"But what about your pump?"

"It's all right, I'll just unplug it."

"But won't that—?"

"No. It's fine. I can take it off from time to time. In fact, it's quite liberating. It's nice to feel normal and unattached for a while." Pip unhooked her line, checked the pump's settings, and placed everything in a ziplock bag in her backpack.

"Last one in's a rotten egg." She dropped her clothes into a pile on the blanket, trotted over to the water, and waded in up to her waist. She turned to see Charlie watching her. With a wave of encouragement, Pip turned and duck dived into the cool clear water.

The peace and embrace of the water freed the last of her tension as she breaststroked her way underwater, watching as lazy bubbles rose and tumbled over each other on their way up to the surface.

A flash of white caught her eye as Charlie dove in and swam towards her. Pip curled her legs up underneath her and dog-paddled mid-water, appreciating Charlie's long, lean body as she stroked easily through the aquamarine water. Her need for air broke the spell and she allowed her body to chase the bubbles and carry her upward.

She broke the surface and looked around. Charlie was still underwater. A brief movement around her waist warned her a second before Charlie surfaced and stood before her.

"What a fabulous idea. This is wonderful!" Charlie beamed.

A shiver ran through her body at Charlie's nearness. The water gleamed off her bare shoulders and caught the sunlight. Words deserted her. "Mm."

Charlie came so close that Pip felt the water warm between them. Barely an inch separated them.

Charlie reached out and stroked Pip's upper arm, her face serious. "You sure you're okay?"

"Definitely." Pip heard the huskiness in her own voice.

"Great."

Pip barely had time to register the change in Charlie's expression, from concern to total grinning idiotic joy, as Charlie's hands topped her shoulders and dunked her under the water. Even immersed, Pip heard Charlie laughing.

The challenge had been laid and they swam, chased, and dunked each other for a good twenty minutes. Chilli dog-paddled around them in circles, barking in shared fun.

Pleasantly weary, Pip called first surrender and glided back to shore. Emerging from the water, the liquid slaked off her body as she walked over to her backpack and pulled out a body chamois. She wrapped it around the ends of her hair and squeezed the water out. She was still holding the towel when warm hands enveloped hers.

"Let me." Charlie's voice purred behind her left ear as Pip's fingers slowly relinquished their grip on the towel. She lowered her hands to rest at her sides and closed her eyes. The warmth of the sun and Charlie's steady hands guiding the towel across her shoulders made her hum softly. Her heartbeat tripped and beat a little faster as Charlie eased the wrap down her back, then swept it around her hips and buttocks and back up the midline. Pip sensed a change in the air around her when she felt Charlie step around and face her. A single fingertip trailed down the length of her neck. A hint of a gasp escaped Pip's lips as Charlie swept the cloth along the curve of first one breast, then the other. Her tongue darted out to lick suddenly dry lips as the trail of the towel changed course. It slid down her centre, whispered across her pubic line, only to retrace its path back up, between breasts that burned for more.

Their breasts and hips met. Pip barely managed a moan before further sound was swallowed by the hot lips on hers. The damp cool of Charlie's body contrasted starkly against her own suddenly hot skin. Pip melded her body into Charlie's, desperately wanting more contact. She was rewarded when an answering groan came from deep in Charlie's throat as she slid her hands around to rest low on Charlie's waist. Pip pulled her in tighter against her core.

Pip coaxed Charlie back to the blanket and lowered her down. Kneeling beside Charlie's prostate form she mapped lines, curved surfaces, and circled the landmarks of Charlie's torso with her fingers, equally delighted and fascinated to watch as goosebumps rose and fell with the simple act of her exploratory navigation. Charlie's nipples rose invitingly until their call could no longer be denied. Pip leaned down, hesitated, her mouth bare millimetres from its goal. "Fuck protocol." She smiled as Charlie arched eagerly to meet her lips, and her murmured utterance was lost as she drew Charlie's nipple into her mouth.

Pip lowered herself atop the length of Charlie's body and disengaged her mouth briefly to gasp as Charlie's thigh slipped between her own and rose to press against her sensitive centre. She mirrored Charlie's actions with her own thigh and teased, alternating pressure and rhythm to match Charlie's heightened breaths. She hummed in satisfaction as she felt her thigh grow wet with Charlie's slickness. Her fingers seemingly knew their way home as they crept lower, and she was rewarded with a whimper as she explored soft, slick folds.

Pip pushed up onto an elbow and concentrated on discovering what gave Charlie pleasure. To find what made her breathe faster, grind deeper, writhe and moan with each of her touches, and to enjoy the flush of desire that rose up Charlie's body with each new lesson learned.

Charlie sat up, roughly capturing Pip's mouth in a searing kiss before releasing her lips to slide her mouth and tongue downward to torture her breasts. Pip threw her head back and ground her hips against Charlie's thigh, her own wetness coating them both. It seemed Charlie was as keen as she was to learn and please.

Breathless, Charlie released Pip's breast and pushed her hips harder against each of Pip's thrusts. "More."

Pip was happy to obey. She paused her fingers at Charlie's opening only briefly before she pressed forward and Charlie took her deep inside.

"Oh God. There. Yes. There."

Bodies striving only to give and receive the ultimate pleasure, they rocked and slid into each other, pushing higher, harder, faster. A cry came from deep inside her chest as Pip felt the energy rise from her toes, shake her limbs, and finally coalesce deep within, blossoming out to consume her chest and the lengths of her limbs. As the wash of pulsing spasms rang out, she felt Charlie tighten around her fingers, arch up into her arms, and release with a cry before falling back down, boneless against the blanket. Charlie lay with her eyes closed, her mouth open as she panted and groaned.

Pip lay down alongside Charlie's length, her fingers still nestled safe inside Charlie. Her head lay against Charlie's chest, her own mouth open with exerted breaths. She kissed Charlie's chest before putting her head down again and closing her eyes, giving in to the lassitude that was stealing over her.

Pip felt the buzzing in her ear as Charlie purred with pleasure. Pip hummed softly when Charlie jerked with sensitivity as she slowly withdrew her fingers.

Pip closed her eyes as Charlie's long fingers stroked through her hair.

"Guess we won't be needing the sofa tonight."

Pip chuckled. "Guess not."

❖

"Will you show me?" Charlie pointed at Pip's pump.

Pip hesitated.

"Please," Charlie said quickly. She rubbed her forearms, knowing she was probably overthinking the possibility Pip would have a repeat incident. But she didn't want to take any chances.

Pip nodded and retrieved her pump. She showed Charlie how to prepare a new site for the cannula and allowed her to use the disposable injecting device that inserted it into her skin. Next Pip talked her through priming the line to get the air bubbles out, connecting the pump, tubing, and cannula all together, and setting the device to resume.

Charlie brushed the backs of her knuckles against the smooth soft planes of Pip's abdomen whose surface was marred by several small bruises from previous injections. "Does it hurt?"

Pip shrugged. "Not so much. You just get used to it, I suppose." Charlie trailed her fingers back and forth, enjoying the mesmerizing feel of warm skin against them.

Pip intercepted her fingers and lifted them for a kiss. Charlie's toes tingled with the simplest touch of Pip's lips. She caressed the plump tender surface of them.

Startled when Pip nipped her thumb, she quickly withdrew her hand and giggled. "I think we need to get you some lunch."

"Couldn't help myself." Pip leaned over and kissed her, her tongue lingering briefly on her upper lip.

"Mm. You're forgiven."

Pip retrieved a small black case from her backpack and proceeded to test her blood sugar levels while Charlie set out their picnic lunch.

"Everything okay?"

Pip packed away the case, stood up, and walked over behind Charlie to plant a kiss on the top of her head. "Perfect."

Charlie leaned her head back to receive Pip's lips in another lingering kiss. When they pulled apart, their eyes met and held. Pip brushed her fingertips against Charlie's cheek. They both smiled.

Chapter Ten

"We should probably head back, hey?"

Charlie lay with her eyes closed and the comforting weight of Pip's head on her belly. "I suppose." She reached down blindly and ruffled Pip's hair.

"I don't know about you, but I've donated more than my share of blood to these bloody mozzies." Charlie heard a loud slap as Pip did away with one of the pesky insects. "Damned things."

"Okay." Charlie sat up. "But only if you promise to stay close to me."

"Wouldn't dream of venturing more than a metre from you." Pip got to her feet and brushed off the back of her shorts. She offered a hand to Charlie and helped her up.

Charlie rewarded her by pulling Pip in close and brushed her lips with a soft kiss.

"You can pash me any time you like."

Charlie raised an eyebrow in question. "Pash?"

"This." Pip draped her arms over Charlie's shoulders, stood on her tiptoes, and kissed her softly. She slid her tongue over Charlie's upper lip, inviting hers to dance.

"Mm, I like this pashing of which you speak." Charlie smiled against Pip's lips.

"I know, me too. And if I recall, despite my slightly alcohol-infused self the other night, you're the one who started it." Pip folded the blanket and stashed it into her backpack. "Ready?"

Charlie held out her hand and smiled when Pip linked their fingers together.

The walk back was peaceful. Chilli panted quietly as she ambled next to Pip. A magpie chortled and was answered by another. Small blue and black birds, which Charlie now knew as fairy wrens, chased each other back and forth across the trail in front of them. Every once in a while a breeze brought the scent of gardenias and ocean.

By the time they reached the villa, their water bottles were empty. The refrigerator provided fresh cold water and they eagerly quenched their thirst.

"Did you pack some cossies?" Pip rummaged through her duffel.

"Some what?"

"A costume." Pip dangled a swimsuit in front of Charlie. "*This* is a costume. We also call them swimmers."

"God, you Aussies have so many weird words. Yes, I did bring my swimsuit. I knew what you were talking about at the waterfall." Charlie looked past Pip at the completely unoccupied pool. "Fancy another swim do you?"

"Nah. I'd just as soon stay out of the chlorine and save swim time for a return to the waterfall. I feel the need for some vitamin D though. Do you fancy soaking up some rays?"

"Of course."

After changing into their swimsuits and refilling the water bottles, Charlie prepared a plate of cheese and crackers for a snack, while Pip arranged the chairs on the sun filled porch. Charlie was concerned that Pip had expended a lot of energy over the past few hours. She was bound and determined to help Pip keep her levels stable.

"Mm, yum. Nothing better than cheese and biccies." Pip shoved one into her mouth and chewed slowly.

"Crackers."

"Biscuits. People'd look at you weird if you ask for a cracker. They'd more than likely think you were a few loaves short of a dozen." Pip tapped the side of her head. "Y'know, a little less in the head."

"Whatever." Charlie shook her head. She looked at Pip, who lay splayed out with her eyes closed and a smile on her face. She was gorgeous. Her colour was finally back and she looked healthy again. Charlie admired Pip's splendid physique. The swimmers left little to be imagined, but she knew well what was under them anyway.

She sighed contentedly. Not only was she sexually sated, for the moment anyway, but her body was hyperaware of Pip. A euphoria she hadn't experienced in, well, a really long time embraced her like an aura.

Pip had been so gentle during their lovemaking. Every touch, no matter where on her body, was compassionate, loving, and filled with affection. But although Pip's actions spoke volumes, she'd not actually put words to how she felt about her.

Charlie was compelled to talk to Pip about it. "Pip?"

"Hmm?"

"Can I tell you something?"

Pip visibly stiffened and swallowed audibly, but didn't make a move to look her way. "I guess."

Charlie took a deep breath and hoped she could convey how she felt without fucking it up.

"When I got together with Kim, I thought she was the one. The woman I would spend the rest of my life with. It worked for a while, and then she seemed to stop listening to me. I eventually realized we had very little to say to each other. Our differences had become too great. We were spinning in different circles. I guess, thinking back now, if she hadn't left first, I probably would have eventually. My salvation was the time I got to spend alone in the field and of course with my dogs."

Charlie waved vaguely with one hand. "Our sex life was pretty good through it all, actually and—"

Pip turned her head and squinted at Charlie. "Really? After the lovely afternoon we just had? I hope you're not trying to compare me with her."

Charlie shook her head quickly. "No. Not at all. Sweetheart, please hear me out." She sat up and swivelled around to face Pip.

Pip nodded but didn't look happy.

"When our relationship ended, my body shut down. My libido was nonexistent, even when I tried…tending my garden to relieve some stress."

A hint of a smile crossed Pip's face, but she remained silent.

"I found I bored myself to bits and eventually gave up. You, you brought me back to life. And that was even before what we shared today. I had to heal emotionally and mentally before my body could respond. I have you to thank for that initial healing. For the past month or so, I've realized that I'm falling for you. I don't know if that's good or bad, right or wrong. But I needed to tell you. I have no idea what came over me when I kissed you that night. I just…needed to. When you kissed me back, I was so happy. When you made love to me today, holy shit. My body finally woke up and listened to my heart." Charlie hung her head. "This isn't any rebound. This is real."

Pip lifted Charlie's head with a finger under her chin. She kissed her softly.

Charlie pulled back from Pip's kiss and held her with a steady gaze. "Pip. I need to know how you feel."

❖

How do I feel? Oh, crap. Confused. Wonderful. Scared. The enormity of the simple question caused a cramp in her chest. Pip absently rubbed at it. She bit her lower lip and tried sorting through it all enough to put into some semblance of words.

"I see." Charlie stood up, her back rigid. "It's all right. You don't have to explain."

Pip jumped up, stood in front of her, and waved her hands in a halting motion. "No. Stop. Wait. Please, sit back down. I just need a minute." Pip guided Charlie back to sit and share her lounge. She kept hold of Charlie's hand, hoping that her body would convey better than any clumsy line that came out of her gob how she felt about Charlie.

She looked off into the distance and tried to calm her thoughts. She finally brought her focus back and tried to meet Charlie's eyes.

But Charlie's gaze was seemingly on a far away place. She had to get Charlie to come back. To her. A half smile escaped her control. "You know, if you asked me about animal poo, euthanasia, weather patterns, maybe even religion, I reckon I could waffle on for ages." Pip scrunched her nose up with the admission. "I'm way out of practice with the one-on-one personal stuff." Pip couldn't help but notice that Charlie's posture was still stiff as a board. She needed to try harder. *Be honest*, she thought. Charlie had just spilled her guts and was sitting next to her exposed and vulnerable and here she was feeling like a complete chickenshit in comparison. *Just tell her.* She took a deep breath. "I'm terrified."

Charlie's head swung around. Her expression was so raw it tore at Pip's heart. She lifted Charlie's hand and held it to her chest so she could feel how hard her heart beat inside. "And I'm excited, and happy, and confused as all get out." She desperately wanted to get up and pace around to help gather her thoughts but Charlie's grip held her firmly in place. "I haven't been with anyone for quite a while now. Well, you know that, vis-a-vis the garden." Pip was mildly relieved to see a small smile flash briefly in Charlie's eyes. "Yeah, well, anyway. You arrived. And everything changed. To have company, *good* company…took me by surprise actually. I thought you were going to be a huge pain in the bum. But I found myself looking forward to every day and spending time with you. Sharing things with you and learning from you. I haven't felt that in a long time."

The tree vista surrounding their unit lent her both peace and strength. "By showing you things, I unlocked doors within myself that I had closed off. I found myself being more and more drawn to you. I was conscious of holding myself back, trying not to touch you. Watching what I said. And the more I felt for you, the more terrified I became."

"Why?"

"Because you came all the way out here, to Australia. That's a huge thing to do. I didn't want to cross the line and be inappropriate and wreck everything, for you, the program, and the organization. I was terrified you wouldn't be able to stay, that you would go if I let my guard down and let you know how I felt."

"How do you feel?" Charlie's voice was low and husky.

She felt tears well in her eyes. But she held them at bay as the words finally tore themselves free of the prison she had locked them down within. "I think I'm falling in love with you, Yank. I can't help it. God knows I've tried, but I can't."

"Oh, sweetheart."

Pip shook her head. Her voice was a tortured whisper. "I don't know what to do."

Charlie pulled her close and wrapped her arms around her.

"I've crossed the line, Charlie. But so help me God, I don't think I can go back to just being friends."

❖

"Baby, you haven't wrecked a thing. Why would you say such a thing?"

"*Mmmff.*"

"Huh? Oh." Charlie loosened her arms. "Sorry. That's what you get for being so short."

Pip pulled her head back from between Charlie's breasts. "It's okay. I didn't mind it. Except for the fact that I couldn't talk. Or breathe." She turned her head and rested it against one of Charlie's breasts. "Mm. That's better."

Charlie kissed the top of Pip's head. "Good. I'm glad you're comfortable. Now want to tell me why you think you're the world's worst wrecking ball?"

Pip sighed heavily. "In a word, protocol."

"What the frig does that have to do with anything?" Charlie leaned back to try to get a look at Pip's face, but Pip followed her chest back like her head was Velcroed to it.

"Don't move. I kinda like it here." Pip paused long enough to fluff Charlie's breast like a pillow and then put her head back down, humming in seeming satisfaction.

Charlie rolled her eyes. "Are you ready to talk now?"

"I'm pretty sure that falling for you isn't part of the company plan or recommended standards of operating procedure. In fact,

I'd hazard a guess that what we're doing is a definite no-no. We're talking international relations and sponsorship, money, politics, rules. I dunno exactly what the rules are for this, but I reckon I've probably broken all of them and compromised you into the bargain by allowing myself to succumb to your magnificent womanly charm."

"Listen here. You have in no way taken advantage of me. I kissed you first, remember? Would any of this have happened if I hadn't made the first move?"

"Possibly." Pip snorted softly from her breast pillow. "Probably."

Charlie laughed. "Good answer."

"Honestly? I don't know. Maybe not for a while. Like maybe not until you were nearly ready to go back to the States." Pip pulled in and then slowly released a deep breath.

"Don't you think waiting that long would have made things more difficult and even more convoluted?" Charlie rubbed Pip's back. "Look, you're not alone in this. We'll figure out how to make it work."

"Terese more or less gave me the green light. Said I should leave worrying about the business stuff to her."

Charlie gasped. "Are you saying Terese knew you had the hots for me before I did? That's low, Pip. Really low." She snorted and said, "But I guess that comes natural for you."

Pip groaned and laughed.

"What'd Terese say she was going to do?"

"She didn't. All she said was to hurry up and have my way with you and she'd take care of the rest."

"She didn't!"

Pip laughed openly. "No. She said to do what I needed to do."

"And did you?"

Pip nuzzled Charlie's cleavage. "Yes. But I think I need to do it again." She stood up, held out her hand for Charlie to take, and led her into the bedroom.

❖

"You need to eat something." Charlie shook Pip's shoulder. Pip lay on top of Charlie. Her even breathing told Charlie she was in an after-sex doze.

"I just—"

"No. Don't even say that."

Pip giggled and pushed up onto her elbows. "You're right. I do. What's the time?"

"It's after six. Dinnertime. How about I make us a salad while you test?" Charlie instantly missed the connection of their bodies when Pip rolled off her.

"Sounds good. Then Chilli needs a walk. Might be tricky though."

"Why? She needs to go out."

Pip shot her a grin. "Because I'm not sure my legs will work."

Charlie chuckled. "I'm glad she's *your* dog."

❖

Pip snaked her arms around Charlie's middle and pressed her body close as Charlie put two slices of beetroot on top of the bed of lettuce, capsicum, tomato, and cucumber. "Everything okay?"

"Good, considering."

"Considering you've had more anaerobic exercise today than you've had in, what, since your last garden visit?"

"Yep."

Pip released her and poured two glasses of water while Charlie took the plates to the table.

"It's weird not having any beasties to feed and care for, isn't it?" Charlie returned to the kitchen for a couple of forks.

"Very weird. I don't remember the last time I—oh, no, hang on, I do. It's been about two years." Pip took a seat next to Charlie.

"Can I take a stab that it was another hypo as opposed to an actual holiday?"

Pip sighed. "Eh, sort of."

"That's good, isn't it? What happened that put you over the edge last time?" Charlie speared a forkful of lettuce.

"There was a hazard burn at Bosche Water Hole near Brooms Head. Parks and Wildlife called WREN because there was a herd of eight brumbies that got trapped. While they were busy with the horses, my job was to make sure all the coastal emus escaped."

"How in the world did you do that?"

"Parks has a helicopter and they radioed in where they saw them. I had to go get them and lead them to safety."

"Wasn't that sort of like herding cats?"

Pip flicked her eyebrows up and chewed her mouthful. "The funny thing about emus is that they're curious to a fault. I took a lid off one of my boxes and waved it back and forth over my head. Once one saw it, they all came running. At me. So I had to run like hell to keep in front of them."

"Let me guess. You didn't take anything in with you."

Pip shrugged. "I did, but I was too busy running to eat. I got them out though."

Charlie shook her head. "What happened?"

"Well, let's just say that after a big day, having run a long way, I got tired, and maybe a little bit slow, and I got run over by a few of the birds. When I didn't meet up at the rendezvous spot, they sent someone from the chopper down on a rope and hauled me up. I woke up in the hospital with a few bruises in the shape of their feet on my back and bum."

"They ran you over?"

Pip grunted. "Bloody ungrateful oversized budgies."

Despite eating a healthy dinner, and Pip's assurances that her levels were fine, Charlie was concerned about how tired she looked. When they returned from a short walk with Chilli, Pip showered, and afterwards Charlie strongly suggested they go to bed. To sleep. Much to Pip's chagrin.

Charlie lay awake long after Pip fell asleep in her arms. She smiled at the ceiling. She felt so at ease with the world. How long had it been since she'd felt so safe and whole? Too long. She'd learned to be on her own and now felt secure with her decisions. Pip however had wanted to live like a hermit. But at what expense before Charlie had ever shown up? Had Pip also experienced the paralysing mental and emotional anguish like Charlie had when Kim left her? Before, when her status as a single woman had been thrown at her like a wet rag, she couldn't cope, had lost faith in herself, and in life in general. But since she and Pip had gotten together, hours of battling anxiety attacks now felt like a distant memory. Confidence built from hard work and new-found love had finally given her back her fortitude and verve for life.

Where would they go now? Despite missing her dogs, Charlie's heart sank at the thought of having to go back to the States. Her current visa allowed her to be in Australia for one year. One year only. If Pip would have her, if they were in agreement to pursue a future together, she was going to have to look to immigration for a solution. She recalled Pip mentioning Terese's involvement. Could she help? Maybe work with immigration on her behalf? Charlie sighed. She still had eight months to go. Surely something could get resolved by then. In the meantime, she was going to enjoy Australia and being with her Pip.

❖

Pip deftly carried the tray of coffee and breakfast into the bedroom, and climbed onto the bed where Charlie was sitting upright, naked, with pillows stacked behind her. Pip shuffled back and sat into the vee of Charlie's legs. The feel of Charlie's breasts against her bare back as she leaned back and craned her neck to accept a kiss was exquisite. She'd been honest with Charlie in the small hours of the night when they had woken, talked, and explored each other's bodies anew. Being single for all those years had been no hardship, once she got used to it. But waking up next to a person she cared for and sharing intimate exchanges was unsurpassable, leaving celibacy and singlehood for dead.

As Pip poured a coffee, Charlie's hand snaked around her waist to rest low against her stomach. She tweaked the elastic of her sleep shorts.

"Does this make you half dressed, or half naked?" Charlie licked the length of Pip's ear.

Pip chuckled as she handed over the coffee. "Six of one, half a dozen of the other."

"Mm. Thanks. How come?"

"Gotta clip the pump to something, and I'm not really into nipple clamps."

Charlie coughed and choked on a mouthful of coffee. "Ah. Yes. Fair point."

Pip opened up the paper that had been delivered under their door and was amused as Charlie read over her shoulder. Their companionship was so easy and comfortable she almost jumped when Charlie leaned over and pointed at an advertisement. "Hey, look. Whale watching tours. Fancy catching one of those tomorrow, before we head on back home?"

"Sure. Haven't been on one of them for years. Weather should be perfect too." Pip handed Charlie a slice of buttered toast.

"Well, if the weather turns we could do a bit more exploring of the rainforest, and the beach is only a short walk away. Or we could drive into town and look for a nice café somewhere overlooking the water. Nothing too strenuous." Charlie winked suggestively. "I'm pacing myself."

Pip couldn't help but laugh. "Is that right?"

Charlie took her coffee cup from her and put the breakfast tray beside her on the floor. Charlie slid down the bed and pulled Pip with her.

"Oh, yeah. I'm in it for the long haul. Been a long time since I had someone wonderful between my sheets. Got me some makin' up time to do."

Pip giggled around Charlie's kisses. "Far be it from me to stand in your way."

"I was kind of hoping you'd say that."

Pip found herself rolling as Charlie manoeuvred herself to be topmost. She closed her eyes and lost herself in Charlie who seemed to be taking delight in mapping every square millimetre of her body with her warm lips. Tomorrow. The whales could wait until tomorrow.

❖

With no whale tour boats available, Pip and Charlie meandered along the marina hand in hand marvelling at the types of boats moored and debating about the money needed to own one of the impressive seafaring vessels.

Pip pointed off to the right with her chin. "I think that might be more in my line of affordability." An old unloved fishing trawler sat up on wooden stilts in dry dock. *For Sale* had been spray-painted crudely against the splayed base of the wooden rudder.

"Oh, how sad. It breaks my heart to see her all scarred and peeling and unloved like that." Charlie frowned.

"I know. But doesn't part of you burn inside and want to take it home, and fix it up, and restore her back to her glory days?"

"I'm thinking that old lady of the sea could tell you a few tales."

"And eat all your money. She needs a lot of work."

"It'd be fun though, wouldn't it?"

Pip sighed. "It would."

They ambled on by after a last long look at the boat and watched a pelican circle overhead. Pip stole a sideward glance. She loved how the breeze played with Charlie's curls, lifting them from her forehead. Her fingers twitched with the memory of their softness. She swallowed with the sudden lump of nervousness in her throat.

"So, how do we do this"—she gestured between the both of them with her hand—"when we get back?"

"What do you mean exactly?"

"Us. Where do I drop you off? At the cabin or at the house?"

Pip noticed Charlie nibbling at her bottom lip. "Terese'll be there still, right?"

"Uh-huh."

"And she more or less gave us her blessing?"

"Mm."

"Well then…how about we all have a talk over lunch, and if she's still okay with it, then maybe I could stay up at the house with you?"

Pip didn't miss Charlie's nervousness. She raised Charlie's hand to her lips and brushed her fingers with a gentle kiss. "I think that sounds like a splendid idea." By Charlie's beaming smile, she silently congratulated herself for saying the right thing.

"I guess that's settled then."

"I reckon it is." Pip smiled, having passed the small but nerve-racking test.

"Do we need to pick up any groceries while we're in town?"

"Um, we should probably top up on—" Pip stopped mid-sentence as Charlie's phone rang. They stopped walking and disengaged hands while Charlie dug around in her pocket for the noisy device.

"Hello?" Charlie winked at her. "Oh, hi, Terese."

Pip looked at her questioningly. Why was Terese ringing Charlie? Charlie just shrugged at her.

"Um, soonish. We were just thinking of getting some groceries before heading home. Why?"

Pip watched as a frown crawled over Charlie's previously smiling features. "A visitor?"

Charlie turned half away from Pip towards the water as she listened to Terese. "We can be there in about an hour." She turned back to Pip for silent confirmation and Pip nodded. "Okay. We'll see you soon then, I guess. Bye."

Pip hovered uncertainly at Charlie's side. "What was that all about?"

"I'm not sure. Terese just asked if we could head on home. There's someone asking to see me."

"Who?"

"She didn't say. She just thought I might like to get on home sooner rather than later."

They turned and made their way back to the truck. Pip hesitated at the driver's door. "You don't think they know about us already, do you?"

"How could they?"

Pip opened and shut her mouth, not really having an answer. "I don't know." A hollow lump formed deep in the pit of her stomach. She stepped inside the vehicle and drove the short distance to the supermarket where they quickly grabbed some necessities, fresh fruit, and vegetables, and continued on home.

The trip was largely silent but was bolstered by their linked hands across the console.

As Pip turned into the driveway she smiled softly and turned to see a matching expression on Charlie's face. "Are you looking forward to seeing Squeak as much as I am to seeing Emmy?"

"I sure am." Charlie laughed softly. "I can't believe how much I have missed the sleep deprivation, and the midnight feeds and farts."

Pip pulled up next to the house and cut the engine. They stepped out and walked around to the back, each grabbing a couple of grocery bags. Pip bumped Charlie playfully with her hip. "Sounds like you're hooked, Yank."

Charlie shouldered her playfully back and gifted her with a beaming smile full of warmth and humour. "I reckon I might just be at that."

"Ahem." Still with smiles plastered across their faces they turned to see Terese standing there.

A woman stepped out from behind Terese with arms thrown wide open.

"Hey, baby. *Surprise*!"

Chapter Eleven

A sudden coldness hit Charlie to the core and her mouth fell open when she saw Kim. Every muscle in her body quickly tensed. She raised her hand to ward Kim off as she approached.

"Kim, what are you doing here?" Charlie felt Pip move slightly away from her when she said Kim's name. Terese shot her an apologetic look.

"You know Australia has always been on my bucket list. What better time to come Down Under than when my partner is here."

"Kim, I'm not—"

Kim offered her hand to Pip. "You must be Pip. Terese told me you've been mentoring Charlie."

Pip shuffled the grocery bag to her other arm and shook Kim's hand. "I'm not so much mentoring her any more."

Kim raised an eyebrow. "Does that mean she's done here?"

"No. She's not." Pip glanced at Charlie. "It's all about experience now."

Up until now, Chilli had remained quiet, but Charlie didn't miss the low throaty growl. She reached down and put her hand on Chilli's head, silently agreeing with the dog. Despite what Kim thought, she had no business being here.

"I see." Kim seemed to dismiss Pip and Terese in an instant. "I hear you have a cabin in the woods. It's been a long day. What say we go there?" She threw an arm around Charlie's shoulders and pulled her close. "We have a lot of catching up to do."

Charlie looked helplessly at Pip. There was nothing she could do about Kim's unexpected arrival. But as much as she wasn't looking forward to it, she knew they had to talk.

Pip stepped forward and took the groceries from Charlie. "Go ahead," she said without expression. "Terese and I can handle the feeds today."

Charlie tried to read Pip's eyes. But they'd become bleak and impassive. The muscles in her jaw tightened as she clenched her teeth. Charlie wanted to reassure Pip that nothing between them had changed and she nearly cried when she saw how Pip's shoulders slumped in seeming defeat.

"I'll be back first thing in the morning."

"Take all the time you need." Pip handed Terese the two bags of groceries. "I'll just get my things and you can take the ute."

No one spoke while Pip retrieved her duffel, slapped her thigh, and went into the house, followed by Chilli and Terese.

Charlie's heart hurt when the door closed, putting a sturdy wall between her and Pip. She hated seeing Pip walk away from her. She wanted nothing more than to run into the house and into Pip's arms.

"That was nice of your boss to give you the day off and offer you more time off if you wanted. Why don't you take her up on that and take a few days to show me around?"

Charlie walked out of the arm that'd snaked around her waist. She put her hands on her hips and glared at Kim. "Kim, I came here to work. And that means taking care of injured and sick wildlife. Not carting you around and showing you the sights."

Kim put her hands up in surrender. "Okay, okay. Let's go to your cabin. We're both tired and not in the best position to think straight."

Charlie wordlessly walked to the ute and got in, not bothering to wait for Kim to grab her suitcase and follow. The back of the ute gave up a low thud that echoed in the bed as the baggage was thrown in. Kim showed up at the driver's side of the ute and Charlie pointed to her left side with her thumb.

Kim rounded the front of the ute and got in. "That's kind of a pain in the ass, isn't it?"

"What?" *Having you here?* Charlie turned the key and started the diesel.

"Having the steering wheel on the wrong side."

"It's not the wrong side, Kim. All old British colonies have cars built like this."

"Well, it sure doesn't make any sense to me."

Charlie swallowed her growing irritation. "It's because in the past, almost everybody travelled on the left side because it was the most sensible for feudal, violent societies. Since most people are right-handed, swordsmen preferred to keep to the left in order to have their right arm nearer to their enemy and their scabbard further from him."

Kim snorted. "I don't see too many people walking around with swords these days. It still seems silly to me."

Charlie rolled her eyes.

All too soon, they arrived at the cabin. Charlie set the hand brake and turned the engine off. When she opened the door, the always-present birdsong was absent. The wind had picked up and the tops of the canopies swayed. Nature reflected her mood perfectly.

"What a cool place, babe. I'm surprised your boss doesn't live here instead. I know I would."

While Kim oohed and aahed over the interior of the cabin, Charlie unpacked her duffel and put everything away.

Charlie'd had enough of trying to justify everything. In the past, she had, without a thought, defended anything Kim had issues with. Now she remained silent.

Kim's suitcase plunked onto the bed and broke Charlie's thoughts.

"Have room in the dresser for my clothes?" Kim sat on the bed and bounced as if trying it out. "This is nice."

"I'm not sure that's such a good idea given that you probably won't be staying here very long."

"I've only just got here. Be reasonable, Charlie. I'm hardly going to get on a plane and leave tomorrow. We've got things we need to sort out and that's not going to happen overnight. We need a bit of time."

"Okay, fine. But in the next little while I suggest you get on your phone and look at flights home."

Kim grinned at her. "My phone doesn't work here. Same as yours probably didn't either, did it?"

Charlie suddenly felt stupid. Of course her phone wouldn't work. She'd had to get a new SIM card for her phone. "Fine. Then you can either use mine or get on the computer and make new arrangements."

"Can we talk? I'm not about to give up on us."

"You already did, remember?" Charlie remained standing and crossed her arms over her chest.

"Yes, and I admitted it was a huge mistake." Kim stood up and put a hand on each of Charlie's shoulders. "I've just come fifteen thousand miles to be with you. But I can see you're uncomfortable. How about we just relax a bit?"

Charlie stared at her. As much as she wanted Kim out of her cabin, out of Australia, and permanently out of her life, she had to admit, she *was* tired. The sleepless nights with Pip had taken their toll. God, she missed Pip. But right now she needed some rest to get her wits about her so she could somehow get Kim back on a plane bound for the US.

❖

Pip carried her bag of clothes straight through to the bedroom and tossed it onto the bed. She stood transfixed as the bed bounced with the heavy assault. The temptation not to unpack and to run away was overwhelming. A hollow, dull ache cramped inside her chest. She shook her head. She didn't want to think about Charlie and Kim now. She couldn't. It was too close. Too raw. She strode out to the kitchen just as Terese hefted the shopping bags up onto the kitchen bench.

"I'm sorry, I didn't have time to warn you. It was all rather sudden and unexpected."

Pip gathered up the food items as Terese unpacked them, and moved robot-like between the fridge and the pantry, putting things away. "Not your fault."

"Did Charlie say anything to indicate she might have been coming?"

"You saw her face. What do you think?"

"Mm." Terese turned her back and leaned against the bench with folded arms. "How was the resort?"

"Lovely. Thank you."

"What did you two get up to while you were away?"

"We swam. Slept. Went for walks. Did some touristy stuff at the marina."

"And did anything…happen?"

Pip walked over to her and planted a soft kiss on Terese's cheek. "I got the rest I needed, thank you. But I'm back now and there's work to be done." She looked at her watch. "I've got time for a quick run to go and get some more leaves for the koalas. So if you'll excuse me"—she picked up the quad runner keys—"I'll be back in time for the evening feed."

She slapped her thigh. "Come on, Chill." She turned on her heel and made her escape. She didn't want to talk about the last three days at Angourie, and she sure as hell didn't want to dissect what it meant now that Kim had turned up.

She lifted Chilli into her special handmade seat on the back of the bike, and attached the leaf trailer with the pole saw and clippers. The engine roared to life and she headed off down to the property's back bush blocks where she had taken Charlie all those weeks ago to teach her which were the best trees and leaves to pick for the koalas.

Charlie. Tears stung her eyes as images flashed in her mind. Charlie on the beach looking in wonderment at the squeaky sand, laughing as she dunked her in the water at the waterfall, or smiling in the sun, their hands and fingers linked across the two sun lounges they sunbathed on, and making love. It'd been a long time since she'd given herself as freely as she had with Charlie. If ever.

She'd told Charlie she didn't think she could go back to just being friends. She swiped at an errant tear. She never thought she'd have to test that theory quite so damn soon.

❖

Charlie reviewed the animal records to see if Terese had noted any changes. She'd tossed her phone to Kim as she sat down to the computer. She shook her head and rubbed her brow with one hand. She had no idea how long Kim would stay. She could only hope that it wouldn't be for long.

She yearned to talk to Pip, but knew she wouldn't have any privacy in this small dwelling. She could only guess how Pip felt after spending the last two days together, finally admitting their feelings, and exploring new possibilities. Only to have Kim show up. Would Pip now doubt the sincerity of how she felt? She was furious for freezing up when Kim revealed herself. She should've asked Terese to drive Kim to a motel. They could still talk things out, but then Pip and she could have moved forward with building on what had developed in Angourie in private.

Charlie's frustration continued to mount. Her mind went blank. She mentally ordered herself to calm down and relax. Kim would be leaving soon. She desperately needed to reconnect with Pip, but couldn't see how that could ever happen while Kim was still here. The shock and sadness in Pip's eyes when Kim revealed herself still haunted her.

"I've got good news and bad news." Kim stood behind Charlie and placed the phone next to the computer.

Charlie flinched as if she'd been touched. She rubbed the back of her neck and avoided Kim's eyes. "What did you find out?"

"Well, here's the thing. While I was on hold, I got to thinking. I came all this way so we could talk and hopefully mend our relationship. But I'm not stupid and I can feel the resistance radiating off you."

Charlie spun around in her chair and got up. "For fuck's sake, Kim. Quit telling me what I feel. What did you find out?"

"If you'll let me continue. Then there's the jet lag because of the time difference. So you'll be happy to know I'll respect your wishes and go home early."

Charlie pinched the bridge of her nose and squeezed her eyes tightly. God, she hated when Kim dragged stuff out. "Would you please answer me?" She felt a headache coming on. Aspirin wouldn't even touch it. Some of Pip's scotch would do the trick.

"Don't be mad. A flight out within the next two days would cost me an arm and a leg. So I'll be leaving Monday."

Charlie shook her head. "That's four days." Her body flushed hot and her heart tried to beat itself out of her chest. Feeling suddenly trapped, she moved past Kim and flung the back door open. The fresh air cooled her overheated skin. She sucked in deep gulps to calm herself. A boobook owl called in the distance with its classic *boo-book* song. A willie wagtail chirped beneath the cabin, probably from the nest a pair had built. A gentle breeze brought the musky scent of the bush with it.

"I'll make a deal with you though," Kim said from the doorway.

Charlie clenched the railing until her fingers hurt. "What?"

"If you'll agree to talk about *us*, and at least try to see that we're good for each other—"

"You've already proved we're not."

"I already admitted I made a big mistake. I just want us to try to talk to each other on the same level again, see if there's the possibility of another go. If not, then I'll make arrangements to leave you alone and spend my remaining time up the coast somewhere near the airport."

Charlie didn't want this conversation. She just wanted the tension to end. She so wanted to tell Kim to get stuffed and go away. She almost giggled at the absurdity—she'd incorporated one of Pip's favourite phrases in her deliberations—but considering the seriousness of the situation she needed to rally her thoughts into some sort of order. She turned around and leaned against the railing, arms crossed over her chest. "You left me. I had to learn to move on. I did. And now I'm here. That took, what, about one point two seconds?" There was no disguising the heaviness and sadness she heard in her own voice.

"Baby, please. Think about it. All I'm asking for is a day, maybe two, depending on how our conversation goes. I know you have work to do, so I don't at all envision we'll have hours and hours to talk. I'd love to experience some of what you do here, as well as see some of the wildlife you work with."

"It seems strange to hear you say that given you were never interested before."

Kim rolled her eyes. "Different country, different animals. Come on. Please. I'm trying. Please say yes."

Charlie weighed the options. Kim said four days. That was certain. But would she be able to cope having Kim and Pip in such close proximity? Her head and heart were torn. She didn't want to be cruel to Kim. She knew what it felt like to have her heart and world ripped out from under her. But she didn't want to risk hurting Pip either. Moreover, would she be able to work with Pip without causing suspicions that there was much more between them than mentor and mentee? Hold on. What would it matter if Kim found out she had feelings for Pip? She sighed. No. Kim had a jealous side and Charlie had seen it first-hand. Kim might lash out and report them both, outing Pip to WREN in the process. From what she could see, she didn't have much of a choice. She felt powerless. There was no way she'd risk Pip's job or reputation within WREN. She gave Kim a small nod.

Kim closed her eyes and put her palms together in a prayer motion. "Thank you, sweetheart. I promise you, I won't get in your way."

"Mm," Charlie mumbled.

"I know. I showed up unexpectedly. But after we Skyped, I got desperate. I needed to see you. I—"

"Look, Kim, I'm tired. I have to get up early and go to work. I'm not expecting Pip to pick up my share of the work."

"Terese is there. Why can't she help?"

"Because this isn't Terese's job or responsibility. She's leaving for Sydney tomorrow."

"Then why—"

Charlie shook her head. "It's just the way it is. I'm going to bed. I'll help you set up the couch. It's a pull-out. I'll get you some sheets and a blanket."

Thankfully, Kim didn't object to the sleeping arrangements. Charlie just didn't have the energy to argue any more.

❖

Kim was still asleep when Charlie woke the next morning. She quickly got dressed, but waited to put her boots on until she was safely outside the door. Afraid the diesel would wake Kim, she opted to walk to Pip's house. She needed to have some alone time with Pip before Kim showed up.

The air was already heavy and humid, and the sun wasn't even up yet. It was going to be a hot one today. Charlie swatted at a mosquito that buzzed near her ear. She'd have to put on some repellent before heading down to feed the animals.

King parrots swooped through the trees and called out their presence to one another. Lorikeets and gallahs squawked as they flew overhead. The farther she walked, the lighter her mood got. She loved the mornings and the familiarity of the environment in which she lived.

She was just about to open the door to the prep room when she heard Pip's voice. "Kim is here, Terese. They have history, even though the recent part wasn't the best. Besides, you've seen her. She's drop-dead gorgeous, stylish, with legs that go on forever. She's all the things I'm not. Christ. How can I compete with that?"

"Don't be ridiculous, darl."

A cupboard slammed. "Ridiculous? Did you not *see* Kim?"

Terese said something too quiet for Charlie to hear. Several moments passed. Apparently the discussion was over. She took a deep breath and went in.

"Good morning." Charlie smiled in an attempt to lighten the gloomy mood she knew she was walking in on.

Terese got up and gave her a hug. "Tread lightly. She's a bit fragile today," she whispered into Charlie's ear. She released Charlie and smiled. "If you're good here, I'll get my things together and make tracks on home. It's going to be a long hot drive today."

"No worries. I'm ready to get back at it." Charlie looked past Terese at Pip, who had yet to acknowledge her.

Terese mouthed, "Be patient. She'll be right."

Charlie nodded. "Have the roos been fed yet?"

"No." Pip lifted the kettle and poured hot water into two mugs. She set a bottle of milk into each to warm.

Terese squeezed Charlie's arm twice and walked out.

Charlie approached Pip and rubbed her back. "How're you feeling today?"

"Where's your other half?"

"I left her sleeping so I could spend some time with you. And she's not my other half."

Pip lifted Emmy out of her pouch and spoke quietly to the joey. "How's my girl this morning? Did you miss your mum? I think you've grown since I've been away."

Charlie's heart fell at Pip's cold shoulder. She blinked back the tears that threatened. Squeak needed tending to and was the perfect diversion.

Squeak moved her nose up and down and flapped her ears.

"Hungry, little one?" Charlie retrieved a cotton pillowcase from a shelf and turned it inside out. She'd learned early on that seams and cotton threads could cause trouble with joey nails. She lifted Squeak from the wet pouch by the tail, held the dry one in the other hand, and let Squeak tumble into the new sack head first, as she naturally would into her mother's pouch in the wild. "Okay, let's give you some brekkie."

Charlie sat down next to Pip. Once Squeak took the teat into her mouth and had begun suckling, Charlie said, "Terese did a wonderful job with these two."

"Terese is an old hand at this."

"Who're you calling old?" Terese said as she appeared in the doorway.

Pip smiled at Terese. The first one she'd seen, Charlie noted. "You of course, Nanna. Ready to hit the road, I take it?"

"Yes, yes. If you find anything of mine, just stash it somewhere. I'll get it the next time I'm up."

Pip put Emmy back in the hanging pouch. She quickly washed her hands before hugging Terese. "I owe you one. Again."

"No, you don't. Besides, I had a ball. It was nice to dust the rust off and get my hands dirty again." Terese released Pip and sat next to Charlie. "You're doing a great job up here. With the animals, and trouble over there." She wrapped an arm around Charlie's shoulders and gave her a sideways squeeze. "I'll be in touch. I have some research to do when I get home."

"Let us know when you get there. And thanks for all your help." Charlie leaned into Terese briefly.

"Will do. If I don't leave now, I may have to stop for the night somewhere and play the pokies." Terese laughed heartily.

Pip walked Terese out while Charlie started cleaning up. By the time Pip returned, she'd finished and began mixing the lori-wet food for the lorikeets.

"Terese get off okay?"

"Yep."

Charlie turned to Pip and put a hand on each shoulder. "Sweetheart, please tell me you're okay, that we're okay."

Pip's eyes seemed vacant. She shrugged and said, "I don't know. Are we?" Her voice was toneless.

"Sweet, nothing has changed. Kim—"

As if on cue, there was knock on the door. "Charlie? Are you in there?"

Charlie dropped her hands from Pip as if touching her burned. She couldn't help but hear Pip's long, low sigh and see the droop in her shoulders. "We need to talk," Charlie said quietly just before Kim swung the door open.

"I'll go do the koalas." Pip averted her eyes and brushed past Kim without a word.

Kim watched Pip leave. "I wish you would've woken me. I could have kept you company."

Charlie shrugged. "The animals are on a set schedule and can't wait." She gathered the food and water bowls for the lorikeets. Her arms, like her heart, felt burdened and heavy. "You said you want to see. Let's go."

Charlie's head spun. She wanted to go after Pip, pull her into her arms and hold her, and be held in return. A painful lump formed in her throat. How did this get so screwed up? She needed to sort her and Kim out. Tonight. Even if it did mean subjecting herself to renewed anxiety and revisiting her feelings. But she couldn't move forward with Pip until she and Kim had come to a much needed final resolution. And she wanted, more than anything, to be with Pip.

Kim followed her outside to where the birdcages sat. When the housed lorikeets and rosellas saw Charlie coming, they squawked and screeched as they flew wildly about the aviary.

"Holy moly, they're loud." Kim covered her ears.

Charlie rolled her eyes. As soon as she slid the food bowls into the aviary, the birds quieted and began to feed, chirping contentedly.

"I don't suppose you can teach them to be quiet." Kim peered into the cage and wrinkled her nose.

"They're wild, Kim. We don't teach them anything unless they're young. Then our job is to make sure they know how to fend for themselves before we release them."

"So what's the matter with them? They look fine to me."

Charlie sighed. She didn't have the energy to explain the care it took to get the birds to this stage: the multiple daily feedings, splinting broken wings and legs, subjecting themselves to finger bites, and traipsing around looking for native flowers for the food the birds needed to transition to.

"Let's just say they're all coming along fine and should be able to be released soon."

They walked over to another aviary housing four magpies. Charlie chuckled to herself. If Kim thought the lorikeets were loud, that was nothing.

"Hi, guys, I'll be right back to feed you." Charlie pointed to an area of the aviary blocked from the birds' view. "Can I get you to stand over there so they can't see you?"

"Why?" Kim put her face to the cage wire and peered in. The birds panicked and all flew wildly, slamming themselves against the walls of their cage. Their terrified squawking was deafening.

"Goddamn it! Kim. *Please.* Just do as I say. They don't know you. You're scaring them. I need you to move back." Charlie moved in front of Kim to shield the birds. "Hey, hey. It's okay. Settle down." At Charlie's voice, the birds seemed to relax and landed on their perches. They began their *feed me* scream once again. Charlie glared at Kim. "Don't move. If they do that again, they could severely hurt themselves." She stormed off to get their container of food out of the refrigerator. "Idiot," she mumbled. "We didn't work this hard to have you scare the crap out of them so bad they'd break their necks."

Charlie was pleased to see Kim hadn't budged an inch when she returned with the magpie meat. "Thank you."

Charlie unhooked the door and backed in through the shade cloth. "Okay, guys, here we go." She scattered some pieces of meat on the shelf for two of the birds that were getting used to feeding themselves. She had to feed the other two by picking up morsels with a pair of tweezers and inserting it into their gaping mouths. When the birds had eaten their fill, it was once again quiet but for a few satisfied chortles.

"They're pretty demanding, aren't they?"

"Only when they're hungry. Wild ones drive their poor parents crazy. They follow them around and pester for food constantly. At least we can easily fill these guys up. For a little while anyway."

Kim smiled at her. "I love seeing you interact with these animals. It's like they all think you're their mom."

"In some instances, Pip and I are. Come on. I just have to feed the doves."

"What cage are they in?" Kim said from behind her as they walked towards the prep room.

"They're in a basket at the moment."

"Oh. Right."

Kim sat on the lounge while Charlie added warm water to the neo-care mix. She put two syringes and a crop needle into a mug of warm water. Once the mixture reached the consistency she wanted, she filled the syringes and attached the needle to one of them.

Two baby doves peeped and flapped their tiny wings when Charlie opened the lid on the basket. She carefully lifted one out, held it against her chest, and secured its head between two fingers. Then she gently inserted the needle with its bulbous end into its crop and slowly depressed the syringe. She repeated the process with the second, replaced the paper in the bottom of the basket, and closed the lid.

"That's all you have to do with them?"

"At this age, yes. Eventually they'll learn how to eat seed from the ground."

Kim shook her head. "Amazing."

Suddenly the door swung open and Pip rushed in.

"What's up?" Charlie recognized the look on Pip's face.

"Just got a call for an urgent rescue. A female eastern grey got hit by a car. Sounds bad. She may need to be euthanized. I'll need your help. I've already brought the ute up."

"Sure."

"Kim, you're welcome to come, but feel free to sit this one out if you want."

"No. I'm good. I want to see what you guys do."

Pip retrieved the .22 calibre from the locked cabinet. "Okay, but this could get ugly."

Kim nodded in acknowledgement.

"Come on. I'll explain on the way."

Charlie grabbed her rescue bag and followed Pip out. Kim had to share the back seat with Chilli, who kept a guarded eye on her.

"Where?"

"Harwood Island. Apparently the roo dragged herself back into the paddock from where she came. Remember the big buck in the back paddocks?"

"I'm not likely to forget him any time soon."

"Well, I know the buck in this mob. He's bigger and a helluva lot more cantankerous. He has a file. He's attacked before. National Parks have been keeping a close eye on him."

"Oh, brother."

"Kangaroos aren't that dangerous are they?" Kim leaned forward between the front seats.

Charlie turned in her seat. "Very. They can kill a person very easily. The bucks mostly attack women and children. Somehow they know those people are more defenceless."

"Um, Charlie."

"Yeah."

"We're women."

"Good of you to notice."

The rest of the drive was made in silence. Charlie felt confident she and Pip could handle this situation, though it was the most dangerous she'd experienced thus far.

Once they reached the outskirts of town, it wasn't hard to locate the mob. It was a big one consisting of about thirty kangaroos. The buck stood about ten feet away from the injured female who lay on her side, pouch bulging with a joey inside.

"Sweet Jesus. I'm not going in there with that thing." Kim crossed her arms and remained buckled into her seat.

Pip looked at Charlie and shot her a half grin. "You don't have to. Your job will be to drive us to the hospital if he has a go at us."

"What?" Kim's voice was squeakier than Charlie had ever heard it. She nearly burst out laughing but for the seriousness of the situation.

"Just stay here, and whatever you do, make sure Chilli doesn't jump out. Can you do that?"

Kim's face had grown ashen, but she nodded quickly.

Pip inserted a clip of bullets into the gun and handed a shield to Charlie. "Ready?"

"Yep." Charlie licked away the beads of sweat that had already formed on her upper lip. Her job was to watch the buck while Pip assessed the female and, using the Perspex shield, create a safe space for them both. She felt a trickle of sweat run over her scalp and down her neck.

The sun glared sharply into her eyes and waves of heat rose off the ground. Charlie's shirt was soaked before they crawled over the paddock's barbed-wire fence. She glanced Pip's way. Her jaw was set and her eyes focused. Her colour was good and her walk steady. She hoped Pip had eaten a good breakfast. She'd probably need it for this.

As soon as they were on the opposite side of the fence, they were in the buck's territory. He watched them with suspicious eyes as they approached. He tipped his head up to sniff and stomped a hind leg. His harem fled in all directions as Pip and Charlie encroached closer. He puffed out his chest and stood his ground.

"Be ready. He looks pretty toey. He's the wildcard and'll be more unpredictable than others." Pip rested the gun in the crook of her elbow, looking relaxed, but Charlie knew every muscle in her body was at the ready.

Chilli barked and whined nervously from the truck. Charlie hoped Kim could quiet her. They were too close to the six-foot tall, heavily muscled kangaroo to take their focus away from him. Pip was right. This one was immense.

Charlie moved closer to Pip and held her shield in front to make them appear bigger than him. She put a hand on Pip's hip, but allowed Pip plenty of room to hoist the rifle if need be.

The buck gave no warning signals. He just grunted and charged them. Charlie heard Kim's scream just before she was knocked off her feet by the buck's powerful shoulder, into Pip who careened off her, before crashing to the ground. She worked to regain her breath as she hurriedly curled into a fetal position to protect her stomach. She managed to slide the shield across her body just as a massive blow tore it from her grasp. She groaned as a second blow from a hind leg connected with her kidney area. It seemed like minutes before a shot rang out. The buck fell next to her. His head hit the ground with a loud thud. His now sightless eyes stared at her as his lifeblood drained out of the wound below his ears. He shuddered once and was still.

Pip's arms were around her instantly. "Charlie, are you okay? Are you hurt? Talk to me, love."

Charlie rolled over and took some deep breaths. Her back hurt like hell. "It's okay. I'm good, I think. Help me up?"

Pip helped her to her feet.

"Charlie! Oh my God, Charlie!" Kim rushed up and took her into her arms. "Are you okay?" She glowered at Pip. "Why didn't you shoot sooner? He could've killed her!"

"Kim, it's okay." Despite the pain, Charlie eased away from Kim. "Just stay here. We've got to take care of the injured roo."

Another shot rang out as Pip euthanized the injured female.

"You killed her too? Couldn't you save her?" Kim was frantic and accusing.

Pip flicked the safety as she set the rifle down and quietly took two latex gloves from her pocket. Charlie picked the pouch up from where she'd dropped it and joined Pip, followed closely by Kim.

"Kim, when an adult suffers an injury as serious as this, more often than not, we have to euthanize them. This is a critical injury and adult kangaroos don't deal well with stress at all. Trust me when I say that what Pip did is much more humane than having them suffer from capture myopathy or to leave them to have a slow, lingering, painful death."

Pip reached into the dead kangaroo's pouch and, after a few moments, gently removed a furred joey. Charlie swiftly wiped the rescue bag lining inside the dead mother's pouch to get the scent on it. The joey wiggled in Pip's hands but quieted as soon as she slid it into the dark pouch Charlie held open for her.

Charlie suddenly noticed the bloodied scratches on Pip's arms and neck. "Are you okay, Pip?"

"Yeah. All good. Let's get this little one home."

Chapter Twelve

Despite Charlie's objections on the way home, Pip insisted she go back to the cabin and rest. By the time they arrived, Charlie was forced to agree with her. Getting out of the ute to walk the few steps to her cabin hurt like hell. Every muscle in her body objected to each little movement.

Charlie saw the concern in Pip's eyes, even as Kim helped her to the front door. She wished she could say something to reassure her.

"I'll check on you later." Pip stepped closer. She looked like she was going to touch Charlie. Her heart felt like it was shrinking when Pip merely walked to the driver's side and got in. The last thing she said before putting the truck into reverse was that she'd feed everyone tonight and maybe she'd see her in the morning.

Charlie decided the dull ache in her heart was more severe than the stabbing pain in her back. She knew for sure she'd be sporting some colourful bruises thanks to that buck.

Kim helped her onto the bed and propped the pillows behind her. One thing Kim *was* good at was nursing. Aspirin and a glass of water appeared on her bed stand within minutes. She downed the pills and tried to convince her sore muscles to relax. She closed her eyes and tried to doze.

"I'm not so sure you should continue to work here, babe."

Charlie sighed. "Please don't call me that."

"Sorry. Habit, I guess."

"I'm staying for the remainder of my tour. So don't get any bright ideas about trying to convince me to cut short my stay here."

"Just a thought. It's just that I never thought it would be so dangerous."

"Any wild animal can be unpredictable, whether here or at home. Sometimes things just happen. I never really told you about those incidents." Charlie thought back to the last few years of their relationship. Conversations had been stilted and eventually stalled to almost nothing. In the end there were lots of things she'd stopped sharing with Kim.

"You could've talked to me about it." Kim set the desk chair next to the bed.

"I tried to early on. Until I realized you weren't really listening and changed the subject. I guess after a time I just stopped."

"That was years ago."

Charlie shrugged. "Just like the time you said you wanted to learn the different birds and their calls?"

"Why'd you stop teaching me?"

Charlie opened her eyes and looked at Kim incredulously. "You honestly don't remember the time I asked you to identify a bird call and you said, *I don't really care what the hell it is*?" Charlie tried to tamp down the anxiety rising in her chest as they discussed the past and more memories surfaced.

"I'm sorry."

"Doesn't matter any more. I stopped doing a lot of things because you didn't seem to care or want to know. I don't think you recognize it's a huge part of my life."

"Well, some of us were busy taking care of business. Someone had to care about paying bills and all the household stuff."

"God, you have such a selective memory when it suits you. I can't believe you don't remember telling me that you'd take care of all that because of my workload."

"I promise it would be different if you come back to me."

"Kim, you're making promises out of desperation. You know as well as I do that things would eventually go back to being the same."

"No, Charlie. Please don't do this. I'm still in love with you. I've come to realize that you're the love of my life."

Charlie swallowed hard. How easy would it be to say yes, return to the familiar, to stop some of the anxiety, to halt the whispers back in Wyoming? Kim had made her happy at one time. But with the passing of years, things began to change. And although neither wanted to admit it at the time, they'd drifted apart. It seemed their tenuous strings of sadness and loneliness were among the few things they still had left in common. Partners were supposed to share a kind of warmth, a familiarity outside of others. She had thought a lot about this. Love had been there in the beginning. And she had loved Kim with her entire being. But what she'd mistaken for love had turned into mere tolerance. A lump grew in her throat with the remembered loss.

Her body flushed hot in response to her racing heart. Her chest tightened and she grew dizzy from the accelerated breathing. Her stomach churned and she worried she might vomit.

"Charlie? Are you okay? Did that kangaroo hurt you more than you're letting on?"

Charlie tried in vain to find some moisture in her mouth. "No, Kim. Can you pass me the water please?" She held the glass in both hands. The water rippled inside the vessel despite her efforts to control the shaking.

"What's going on? You don't look okay to me."

Charlie took a deep steadying breath. "It's okay. Just give me a minute. It'll pass."

"You mean you've had this before?"

Charlie nodded sadly. "I've been having these anxiety attacks for the last couple of years."

Kim stared at her. Her eyes grew glassy as they filled with tears. "I—? Oh, sweetheart. I'm so sorry." She put her head in her hands and sobbed. "I'm so, so sorry."

Charlie reached over and tapped Kim's knee. When she looked up, Charlie motioned for her to lie beside her. The least she could do was comfort her. Hopefully Kim had finally come to the realization that their relationship had run its course, that they could never be together again. She steadied her breathing and worked through the anxiety attack.

❖

It was dark when Charlie woke. Kim still lay beside her, an arm draped casually over Charlie's stomach. Oddly, it didn't bother her. Kim had muttered she was sorry over and over again until she finally stopped crying. Her deep breathing had confirmed she'd fallen asleep shortly thereafter and Charlie didn't have the heart to wake her.

When she woke again, it was grey outside and Kim was starting to rouse as well.

"Good morning. I'm sorry I fell asleep in your bed." Kim sniffed and blinked hard.

Charlie smiled. "It's okay. It was a pretty emotional night for both of us."

"Are you feeling okay now?" Kim leaned up on an elbow.

"I haven't really moved enough to see how I feel."

Kim tapped Charlie's temple. "I meant the anxiety I caused last night. You weren't always that acute, were you?"

"I probably bordered on it for a lot of years. But after you left I suffered months of anxiety and panic attacks. It was horrible. I found a good therapist who really helped. I think I finally have it under control though."

"Until I brought it out again."

Charlie snorted. "Yeah, well." She pushed herself up in a half sitting position and winced. The muscles in her back went into spasm and pain radiated down her leg.

"Maybe you should stay in bed and rest." Kim handed her two aspirin and a glass of water.

After she'd downed them, Charlie propped herself up on her elbows. "I think it'd be best to get up and stretch a bit. Knots will form if I don't and it'll be even more painful."

"Charlie, you were attacked by a fucking huge kangaroo."

Charlie waved her concern away. "No worse than getting run over by a moose calf."

"God, you're so damned stubborn."

"Yep. That's me. I have work to do. I can't leave Pip to do it all herself."

"Didn't she do it alone before you got here?"

Charlie stood up and held on to the wall to steady herself. "Yes, she did. But she won't while I'm here. This isn't open for discussion."

"Suit yourself." Kim stood up and went into the bathroom.

"Hey, no fair. That's where I was headed." Charlie shuffled across the room.

Kim came out just as Charlie got to the doorway. "All done." She gave her a smirk. "I'll make us some coffee."

"Thanks."

The enticing aroma of the hot brew drew Charlie out of the shower. She'd stood under the hot water for a few minutes, hoping to loosen up her seized muscles and maybe help dispel some of the bruising that had started to turn a sickly deep purple.

She felt mildly better as she sat down and feasted her eyes on scrambled eggs, toast, and, of course, coffee. "You didn't have to do this. But thanks."

Kim sat down across from her. "Just thought I'd help out and do the cooking for you today. Since it'll be the last time, anyway."

Charlie stopped her fork halfway to her mouth and stared at Kim. "Sorry?"

"I've thought a lot about it, all last night. You were right. We've both changed and getting back together wouldn't fix that. We're too different now. But I'd still like to be friends, if that's all right." Kim rubbed her brow in a seemingly nervous gesture.

Charlie reached across the table and squeezed Kim's hand. "I'd like that."

"So I thought I'd get out of your hair tomorrow. But since you're insisting on going to work today, can I at least help you out some? If you tell me what to do, I'll try not to mess things up too bad."

"That would be lovely. As a matter of fact, I think we'll be releasing a couple of herons today. Would you like to tag along?"

Kim nodded and smiled brightly. "Thank you, Charlie."

Charlie shrugged nonchalantly and grinned.

The hike down to the house took a little longer than usual, but by the time they got there, Charlie's back had loosened up and she felt much better. She'd pointed out several types of birds to Kim and even a goanna that surprised them when it crossed their path.

A lot of things had been mended between Kim and herself. They spent much of the walk bringing up funny things that'd happened during their years together. So many, that Charlie's stomach hurt from laughing about the last story Kim had reminded her of—when one of the dogs had been sprayed by a skunk and come into the house. The odour had been so strong neither of them could identify it or knew it came from the dog. They'd decided the sewerage had backed up someplace and piled the dogs into the car to investigate. It was only then that they discovered the true culprit.

Charlie still had the giggles and Kim was smiling brightly when they walked into the prep room. Pip looked up from feeding the new joey. She didn't look happy at all.

❖

It'd been a long night. Pip hadn't slept much, her mind unable to settle. If she wasn't looking after the new joey, then she was thinking about Charlie. And Kim. Images forever burned mockingly into her brain. Kim running, crying and holding Charlie in her arms, screaming at her for endangering her lover. Kim's arms wrapped protectively around Charlie as she helped her into the cabin. Arms that should have been hers.

She'd gone over and over the incident in her mind ad nauseam. Charlie could have been severely hurt. And it was her fault. Damn that bastard of a buck. If he had just stayed away, none of this would have happened.

She'd gotten up early and written up a preliminary report of the events. She would need Charlie to read it over and countersign the document before submitting it to the authorities. Her actions had been extreme and she needed to account for them. She had already put together several pieces of pictorial evidence, but she would also need to document and photograph Charlie's injuries, and add them to the report. Her stomach churned again. Every time she closed her eyes and tried to rest, she saw the buck hit Charlie. Saw, in detailed slow motion, Charlie fly through the air, Charlie go down and get hit once, twice by the powerful hind legs, and saw the buck prepare for a third assault.

The rescue, although difficult, had been undertaken with all due caution under the circumstances and utilizing standard procedures. Pip knew that under any other occasion she and Charlie could have done what they had needed to do and walked away safely, except for the rogue male. Chances were they would not experience another incident like that for years, if ever, but it had happened and Pip took full responsibility for all that unfolded. Charlie was hurt because of her actions. Her decisions. Her head pounded. She took a deep, pained breath and swallowed against the thickness in her throat.

She rocked the restless joey in her arms. It had begun to begrudgingly take to the teat with the two a.m. hydrating feed and she was pleased at how the new little one had begun to take to the milk formula. It had a small cut and graze below its left ear and some bruising appearing on its left thigh, indicating how it must have lain in the pouch when the mother was struck by the car. It would need careful monitoring for shock over the coming forty-eight hours. There were no obvious sign of internal bleeding or broken bones, but she left a message with Jodi nevertheless. She would take the joey in to the vet later in the morning to get a full assessment to add to the report and the joey's records.

Laughter from the doorway made her start. The joey picked up on her surprise and spat the teat out. Pip scowled in irritation. The joey tossed its head from side to side, refusing the teat, alarmed by the suddenness of voices and laughter.

Pip looked up in time to see Charlie holding the door open for Kim. Her hand rested low along Kim's waist as she ushered her inside. Pip's scowl deepened.

Both of their faces were flushed, their eyes bright, and they wore matching grins about some private joke. To see them so happy together felt like pouring salt and lemon juice into an open wound, doing nothing to improve her mood or outlook on the day. Pip swallowed her irritation.

"You look better than last time I saw you. You're obviously feeling better."

Pip couldn't help but notice the smile slide from Charlie's face. Part of her felt bad for her brusqueness, but part of her felt somewhat vindicated.

"I do. Thank you. A bit stiff and sore in places, but I'll live."

Seemingly oblivious to the growing tension in the room, Kim giggled. "I'd like to think some credit should be given to the excellent nursing care."

Pip quirked an eyebrow. "Indeed. So it would seem." She stood, and with her back to Charlie and Kim, placed the joey into a hanging pouch. "There's a folder next to the computer. It contains a write-up of yesterday's events. I need you to read it over and see if you feel that it's an accurate account of what happened." Pip opened up a drawer and retrieved a small digital camera and placed it on the bench next to the folder. "I'll also need to document your injuries." She tapped the camera lightly to indicate she needed pictures. "Perhaps Kim can help you."

She wanted to leave the room. To get away from them both. She turned to go but was stopped by a warm hand on her forearm. Soft fingers trailed down alongside a long deep scratch on the inside of her arm. Charlie stood so close to her that she could smell the soft essence of her shampoo.

"And what about your injuries?" Charlie's voice was soft, low. Goosebumps followed like the Pied Piper in the wake of Charlie's travelling fingertip.

"Don't have any." Her voice came out gruffer than she intended.

Charlie's eyes drifted to the red scratches on her neck, which she'd gotten when she bounced off Charlie and into a pile of downed branches just to the side of the injured doe in the field.

"I beg to differ."

"They are simple scratches. Nothing more, nothing less. Yours, on the other hand, are potentially more serious and need documenting. It's also further evidence to add to the buck's file."

"It's all a bit dramatic isn't it? I mean, there's no real harm done in the end."

Pip narrowed her eyes. "Perhaps this will help you understand the seriousness of your near miss yesterday. And how dangerous this buck was." Pip turned and retrieved the Perspex shield from behind the door, laying it on the table for both to see. A series of three deep diagonal scars were deeply scored across the shield's surface. "If you hadn't had this, you would definitely be in hospital. Probably in a very bad way. Marks like this—his aim was to disable you. To disembowel you." Pip saw the colour drain from both of their faces as the seriousness of the attack sank in. "Now, perhaps, you can appreciate the need to document your injuries. I'll leave you to look over the report and for Kim to do the honours. Feel free to make whatever changes you feel necessary."

Charlie nodded once, a solemn expression set across her features in full understanding.

"I thought you might like to just do some light duties this morning, given yesterday. I've left the birds for you and I thought you might like to show Kim the koalas and get her to help you change their branches and freshen their water."

Pip turned and picked up the ute keys from the bench top. "I'm going to make a quick run into town and get Jodi to give this little fella the once over." She hefted the new joey's pouch from the stand. "Do you need anything from the shops while I'm there?"

"No, thank you. We're good."

"All right. If you think of anything, send me a text. C'mon Chilli." She clicked her fingers and the Labrador joined her as they headed out the door.

❖

"So you took down the Harwood Horror?" Jodi's deft fingers probed the joey's tiny body, looking for swellings, deformities, or anything unusual.

"Sorry?" Distracted, Pip only half heard the question.

"The Harwood Horror. 'Bout time something was done about him. He was a nasty one that one. Last month I had a farmer bring one of his dogs in. Damn thing shredded it. Nothing I could do. The farmer had to go to hospital and get stiches too where the thing had a go at him when he tried to get his dog. And that's not the first account I have heard about him either."

"Yep. He had a rapidly growing rap sheet. Still, I hated doing it, but he didn't leave us much choice."

"Well, at least he leaves a strong legacy behind. This little bloke looks healthy enough, apart from the contusions and bruising. But you know the drill, keep an eye on him. He feeding okay?"

"Mm."

"How's Charlie?"

"Huh?" The abrupt subject change caught Pip off guard.

"Charlie. She okay? She's not with you today."

"She's at home, taking it easy." Jodi stared at her. "The buck banged her up a bit yesterday."

The vet gently placed the joey back into the pouch and secured the top. Her hands rested on top of the bag, effectively stalling Pip. "You got ten minutes?"

Pip shrugged. She was in no hurry to get home. "Sure."

"Good. Come join me out the back. I'm dying for a cuppa. You go on through and put the jug on and I'll let the girls know where I am."

Pip nodded and made her way out the back to the tea room.

Jodi returned as Pip set two steaming mugs on the table. Jodi snickered. "I had this stashed safely away. Seems as good a time as any to crack it open." She opened up a container of homemade banana and walnut bread, and cut them each a piece.

Pip picked at the edges.

"So fill and spill, Pipsqueak."

"Pardon?"

"Take a decent bit of the cake so as not to offend me, then tell me what's got you so scattered this morning."

"Sorry. Cake's lovely." She took a bite and chewed slowly.

"You've euthanized animals before. So I feel pretty confident that's not what's rattling your cage."

Pip stared into her tea. "It was unfortunate, but it had to be done."

"Exactly. So what is it? Is it Charlie? Is she not working out?"

"No. She's good. Great, in fact."

"Then what is it?"

Pip took a deep breath. "Her girlfriend—*ex*-girlfriend—from the States has turned up."

"Oh?"

"I think she wants to get back together."

"And that's a bad thing because…?"

Pip just looked at Jodi.

"Oh, dear. You've gone and fallen for her, haven't you?"

Pip rubbed the side of her temple to try to ease the pounding that refused to go away.

"Have you had a chance to talk to her? Since the ex turned up?"

"Not really. No point."

"Why not?"

"Let's just say they looked pretty damn cosy together this morning. I suspect the *ex* prefix is about to disappear from her title. And maybe that's not a bad thing. Especially after yesterday. I got distracted and things turned pear-shaped. And Charlie paid the price. I can't let that happen again. I won't."

"Bugger."

Pip blew out an exasperated breath as she ran fingers through her hair. "Mm."

"Damn, Pip. I am truly sorry. I was kind of hoping you two would hook up."

"Well, we did. For five minutes. But I guess it's not meant to be is all."

Jodi reached out across the table and squeezed her hand. "Stings, don't it?"

Pip scrunched her nose up in an effort to ward off tears that threatened to spring forth. What an understatement. "Yeah. Does a bit."

"Well, if you need a break, give me a whistle. I could probably offer her a couple of weeks' work here if you thought it might help you both."

"Thanks, Jodes. I'll mention it to her and see what she says."

A vet nurse stuck her head around the corner and waved to get Jodi's attention. She acknowledged her, stood up, and walked around the table where she enveloped Pip in a much-needed hug. "Sorry, love, need to go. You know where I am if you need me."

"I do. And thanks."

"Call me and let me know how you get on."

As Jodi left the room, Pip finished up her tea, rinsed their dishes, and left them to dry on the sink. Her heart still felt heavy, but talking with Jodi had helped her make up her mind about what she needed to do.

As she drove home she thought more on Jodi's offer. It might be the best thing for both of them if Charlie was open to the idea. It would afford them both a break—one that they would need if they were going to stand any chance of seeing the year out as just work colleagues.

❖

"Holy shit, Charlie!" Kim said when Charlie lifted her shirt up. "Wait until you see the bruising. Christ." Kim snapped a few photos from different angles to take advantage of the best light.

Charlie took the camera from her and pressed the review button. The first photo was of her and Pip standing next to a perch on which a powerful owl sat before they'd set it free. The smiles each of them wore told a story of what good friends they'd become. She pushed through several others, each showing two happy women and the successful tales of rehabilitated wild animals. How she yearned for them to be together again. *Alone.*

She gasped when the first photo of her back slid into view. She took a deep breath and let it out slowly. The bruises were a multitude of hues, colours that normally should not be on someone's skin. There were garish purple splotches, roughly the size of a fist, while others were a sickening shade of greenish-yellow. These were further evidence of how close she'd come to being seriously injured. Pip had saved her life. "Damn. Those are ugly."

"What was ugly was seeing that kangaroo attack you."

"We were both very lucky."

"I'll say. Good thing I had hold of that dog. She was bound and determined to get to you guys."

"Chilli is pretty protective of Pip."

"Is she a service dog?"

Charlie looked up from the camera. "Why would you think that?"

Kim shrugged. "I'm assuming that's an insulin unit under her shirt. Am I wrong?"

Charlie sighed. "No, you're right. I guess she's had diabetes most of her life. Poor thing. Chilli lets her know when her sugar is off."

Kim met Charlie's eyes. "You two have gotten to be pretty close, haven't you?"

You have no idea. "Hard not to, doing what we do. There's a lot of emotion in caring for these animals and trying to make the best decisions for them. We have to support each other."

"Is she gay?"

Charlie scowled and rolled her eyes. "What the hell does that have to do with anything?"

Kim shrugged. "Just asking. A sexy voice like that will turn my head in a heartbeat."

A worm of jealousy squirmed around in Charlie's chest. She mentally shook it off. Pip was hers. Well, she had been. She wasn't sure what they were at the moment. Pip's moods and her inclination to make herself scarce concerned her. She well and truly acted like she wanted nothing to do with Charlie. Pip probably felt the same way about Kim.

Charlie ignored Kim's comment, put the camera on the shelf, and picked up the report Pip had prepared. Pip had perfectly detailed the incident down to the smallest point. Charlie indicated her approval on a sticky note and tacked it onto the report.

"Okay. That's done. Ready to get to it?"

"Please. I can't wait to see the koalas."

Charlie laughed. "The two we have are pretty tame. Because of the injuries they had, they can't be released. But you wouldn't want to mess with a wild one."

Kim clutched at her heart. "Aw, hell. You're ruining all my preconceived ideas about these animals. First the kangaroo and now the koala? The ones I see on Facebook are all cute and cuddly."

"They can be very vicious. People aren't being truthful when they say they aren't. But then again, most people haven't been face-to-face with an irate koala."

"I can't believe they'd be that bad."

Charlie took the magpie food out of the refrigerator and they walked out the door. "Hmm. The guy at the feed store where Pip get's Chilli's dog food had a run-in with one last week. Apparently Ken was out with his mates and had set up camp. They went fishing, and when they came back, they saw a koala at the base of a tree next to their tent. Normally the koalas are up in a tree munching eucalyptus or sleeping, which is what they do most of the time. But this one started chasing Ken, and trust me, they can run fast. It grunted and growled the whole time it was running. His mates kidded that they didn't know who was making the most noise, him or the koala."

"Jesus."

"Well, you know what they say: *Everything wants to kill you in Australia*."

"And you came here willingly?"

"So did you."

"Touché." They shared a chuckle.

Charlie fed the birds, and she was pleased to see Kim keep a distance they were comfortable with. When she finished with the doves, they headed to the koala enclosure.

"Gosh. This pen is so small." Kim leaned over the four-foot high wooden barricade, topped with three feet of wire. The pen itself measured twenty feet square.

"We have a couple of other pens of various sizes, but we moved them into this recuperative one while we rebuild the stands and shelters. When they're sick or injured, they don't need a lot of space. They need food, water, and shelter. If they have those, they're content to sleep up to twenty-two hours a day."

"A day?"

"Yep." Kim handed a bundle of eucalypt branches to Charlie who'd gone inside the enclosure. "They need more sleep than most animals because gum tree leaves contain toxins and are very low in nutrition and high in fibre. So they take a large amount of energy to digest. Sleeping is nature's way for the koala to conserve energy."

Kim raised her head and sniffed. "Is that them I smell, or their food?"

"They smell a little like cough drops, don't they? The males give off a stronger, more musky odour because of their scent glands. But these two girls smell lovely, don't you, sweethearts?" Charlie pulled the branches stripped of their leaves out of the PVC tubes attached to the four wooden poles. She poured some water into each and placed the fresh leaved branches into them. Charlie lifted a koala from her perch and checked her eyes. "This one's name is Alinta, which means flame. Pip rescued her from a brush fire. She didn't get burned, but she's had chronic eye problems ever since."

"What's the other one's name?"

Charlie hoisted Alinta back up so she could eat. She picked up the other koala who had crawled down to the ground and was pawing at her leg. "This one's Lucille. She's a real love. She got hit by a car and has a bit of residual brain damage. That's why she's a little wobbly."

"Poor thing. I'm surprised Pip didn't have to euthanize her."

"She's one very lucky girl. She was carrying a joey when she got hit. Pip knew it was best if the joey stayed in his mom's pouch, so she took a chance. Both survived and Pip eventually released the joey. Pip kept Lucille here to see if she'd recover. You can see she's never quite gotten back to a hundred per cent, and as such she can't be released back into the wild. But she's happy and safe here and makes a great surrogate mom to any orphan joeys that come in." Charlie carried Lucille to where Kim stood. "Give me your hand." Kim did as asked and Charlie placed Kim's palm against Lucille's pouch. "Feel the lump?" Kim nodded. "One night after a storm, a tree fell over and crossed into her pen. A male came in and bred with her. That's her new joey. When it's old enough, it'll get released just like the others."

"Aw, how cool." Kim leaned over and kissed Charlie's cheek. "Thank you."

Charlie smiled at Kim. She caught movement over Kim's shoulder and saw Pip spin around and head back towards the prep room. *Shit, shit, shit.* There was no doubt in Charlie's mind that Pip had seen Kim kiss her. *Shit, shit, shit.*

"I have to talk to Pip for a minute." She put Lucille on a branch and gave her one last pat. "Stay here if you want. Sometimes the joey pokes his little head out of the pouch while she's eating."

"I'd love to see that. You know where I'll be." Kim smiled at her before focusing her attention on the koalas.

Charlie trotted up to the prep room and went in, fully expecting to see Pip. But she wasn't there. So she hurried out and knocked once on the house door and went in.

Pip had her back turned to her. She stood at the kitchen bench cutting up fruit. She didn't acknowledge Charlie's presence.

"Hey, sweetheart."

Pip glanced over her shoulder and then at the door. "Are you talking to me?"

Charlie rolled her eyes. "Of course I'm talking to you. I don't call everybody sweetheart."

"Where's Kim?"

"Down by the koalas. I told her I needed to talk to you."

"Yep. So talk."

Charlie ignored the iciness in Pip's voice. She wrapped an arm around Pip's waist and squeezed her close. "I miss you."

"Did you take pictures of your back and read the report?"

"Yes. All good." Charlie gently grasped Pip's arm and rolled it over so she could examine her wounds. "How are these?"

"Fine." Pip shook her arm out of Charlie's grasp.

"Your levels staying good?"

"Yep."

Charlie scrunched up her face. She released Pip, looked at the ceiling, and took a deep breath, trying to remain calm. This wasn't the Pip she knew and loved. Hell, Pip had treated her better when they'd first met. She threw her hands up in frustration. "I have no idea what's going on here. Or what I'm supposed to say."

Pip stopped chopping and purposefully laid the knife on the bench. She put her hands, palms down, on either side of the chopping block and took a step back. She leaned forward slightly but still refused to meet Charlie's eyes.

"You don't have to say anything."

"Then how are we supposed to work together, Pip? We can't exactly co-exist in silence for the rest of the time I'm here." She scraped a hand across her face as if to wipe away the deep hurt she felt.

Pip shrugged. "I think now would be a good time to experience something else."

"What's that supposed to mean?" Charlie felt flush with fear. Was Pip ending her tour here? Alluding to a return to the States?

"You've done a lot of different things here."

"Christ, Pip, will you just get to the point?" Charlie nervously clicked her fingernails against the bench.

"While I was at Jodi's, she offered for you to have a couple weeks of working there so you could experience the clinical aspect."

"What? I see what she does when we bring an animal in." Charlie moved back slightly and increased her personal space.

"We're not the only ones who bring wildlife to that hospital. There are things you'll never see here. My advice is to take advantage of her generous offer."

"But how will I get there and back? I can't leave you without a vehicle." She stared at Pip with her mouth open. She couldn't believe Pip wanted to send her away.

Pip had yet to look Charlie's way. "There's a fully furnished apartment upstairs. It's normally used for visiting vets and vet students. It's going to be vacant for a few months, so you can stay there. You and Kim, for as long as she's here."

Charlie had completely forgotten about Kim. She'd have to come with her. Great. One more thing to solidify in Pip's overactive mind that they'd reconciled.

"Pip, Kim and I—"

Pip put her hand up. "It's okay. I know it's sudden, but you may as well strike while the iron is hot. Why don't you get your stuff together and I'll take you over this afternoon."

"But who is going to help you with all the work? And look after you?"

"I'm not a child. And I am perfectly capable of managing. Everything."

Charlie looked at her in amazement. She'd effectively been dismissed. "Okay," she said quietly. "If that's what you want."

"I do."

Charlie felt numb as she walked out the door on weak legs. She sighed dejectedly.

"Hey," Kim said as she rounded the corner of the house.

Charlie shot her a half-hearted smile.

"You okay?"

She took a deep breath and nodded. She had to keep up appearances for Kim. "Actually Pip just sprung something on me and I'm a little surprised."

"Oh. Okay."

"Come on. I'll explain on the way to the cabin."

Chapter Thirteen

The ride to Yamba was largely quiet. Every once in a while Kim asked a question about something she'd seen, and Charlie or Pip would answer her. But Charlie felt the chasm widen and deepen between her and Pip; there was no interactive conversation between the two of them. But there was nothing she could do about it. Pip had made it clear she didn't want or need her, neither emotionally nor physically.

Jodi came out of the clinic dressed in scrubs.

"Hey. You just caught me. I'm between surgeries."

"Special delivery for you, Jodes." Pip walked to the back of the truck and opened the cabin and lifted the bags out.

Charlie tried to catch Pip's eye, but was unsuccessful.

"Hey there, Charlie. Come on, I'll show you the apartment. It's not much but it's liveable. You must be Kim. Pleased to meet you."

"Same here. Thanks for letting me shack up with Charlie for a few days."

Charlie cringed inwardly.

"No worries."

Charlie followed Jodi towards the back of the clinic with Kim in tow.

"I'll be right back." Jodi jogged back to the ute, said something to Pip, smiled at her, and returned. "Okay, this way."

Jodi led the way to a back door that looked like the clinic's rear entrance. There were no windows and no trees. Charlie already missed the seclusion of the bush and openness of the cabin, the trees, and the birdsong.

But, Charlie discovered, not all was as it seemed. Jodi unlocked the door and after passing another door, took them up a flight of stairs to a balcony. It looked out over a well-maintained park. A refreshing breeze brought the fishy, tangy scent of the ocean with it as it lifted Charlie's hair.

"Is that the ocean?" Kim shaded her eyes with a hand.

"Sure is. It's only a ten-minute walk from here to the beaches. There are shops just down the road too." Jodi unlocked yet another door. "This is where you'll be staying."

Charlie walked into the apartment and was yet again surprised to see windows looking out in three directions. While not lavishly furnished, the room was bright and exuded comfort, although it was less of an apartment and more like a large motel room with a kitchen and bathroom hidden in a corner.

The alarm on Jodi's watch sounded. "My next surgery is ready to go. Make yourself at home. There's food in the cupboards and fridge. Charlie, I'll see you at eight tomorrow morning?"

"Sure. I'll be there." Charlie smiled at Jodi's cheery face and upbeat personality. She couldn't be mad at her for doing Pip a favour.

"Okay. See you when I see you." Jodi hurried out the door and quickly returned again. "I forgot to give you these." She handed Charlie two keys. "This one is for this place and the other unlocks the outside door and the other door we passed on the way in. It leads into the kennel area of the clinic." She winked and scurried out.

Charlie put her duffel next to the queen-sized bed and sighed. Kim would have to sleep with her, as the only other seating was a lounge chair that was definitely not something anybody but a small child could sleep on.

"Don't worry. I won't try anything. We're only using it to sleep on, right?"

Charlie rubbed her forehead. Pip was probably well aware of the accommodations up here. One more nail in the coffin of…whatever they had. At this point Charlie couldn't begin to describe it.

❖

Pip lasted all of ten minutes before she had to pull the truck off the road. Her vision was severely impeded by the tears that threatened to drown her. She put her head on the steering wheel and let them fall, breathing through her mouth when her nose blocked up.

Chilli whined softly from the back seat.

Pip straightened and leaned her head back onto the headrest. She closed her eyes and blindly gave Chilli, who was leaning forward with her nose shoved into Pip's neck, a one-armed hug and kissed her on the top of her head. "It's okay, bub. I'm okay. Just give me a minute."

Pip was warmed by Chilli's affections as the dog left her muzzle resting on her shoulder. The comfort of her companion, her one true constant in life, soothed her frayed heart just a little. "Guess you're never too old to get your heart broken, huh, Chill?"

She had tried to sound neutral in the car, responding to questions asked as the group made their way to Yamba, but it was a struggle. An enormous effort was required to squeeze out social niceties and pleasantries, when every time Kim opened her mouth it was like a tiny needle puncturing her insides. Kim's comment to Jodi about shacking up with Charlie had been the tipping point. She had waved goodbye and walked back to the car. She needed to get out of there, to get home before her crumbling facade broke.

As her hand grasped the ute's door handle, Jodi had caught up to her and rested her own hand over hers, effectively stopping her getaway. "You okay, Pipsqueak?"

"Not really. But I'll live."

"That you will, my friend, that you will. I'll look after her y'know."

Pip's gaze had dropped to her boots as she nodded. "I know. I wouldn't ask anyone else."

"I'll call you later tonight—make sure you're okay."

"I'll be fine."

"I know. But I'll call you anyway."

She'd made a conscious effort not to look back at Charlie and pointed the vehicle on home. Staring at the road, she desperately tried to shut out her imagination, knowing intimately the layout of the apartment, having stayed there before on critical overnight cases with Jodi, acutely aware that there was only one small couch and one bed. She swallowed. If she concentrated really, really hard, she could almost shut out Charlie's hurt eyes that stared back at her when she had left.

❖

"I'm going to the beach today," Kim announced over breakfast the next morning.

"You may as well. There'll be nothing for you to do here while I'm at work." Charlie sipped her coffee. "There are plenty of little café's along the main street if you don't want to come back here for lunch."

"Cool. Thanks." Kim held a piece of toast over her plate. "I can tell this wasn't part of the initial plan when you came here."

Charlie set her coffee down and folded her hands in front of her. "No. It wasn't. But I've spent some time thinking about it. Australian wildlife is unique and I'm sure I'll learn a lot from Jodi." She looked at her watch. "Oh, I have to go. Don't want to be late on my first day." She got up and patted Kim on the shoulder. "Don't forget to block out. The sun is very intense here."

"Yes, Mother."

"And wear your sunglasses."

"Yes, Mother."

"And if you need—"

"Just go. I'll be fine." Kim stood up and pushed her towards the door.

"You have the key?"

Kim laughed and pointed. "Go."

Charlie smiled. As she descended the stairs, she called back, "Stay out of trouble!"

"Go!"

Charlie let herself in through the door Jodi had indicated. She recognized the room as she'd been in here before. Kennels of all sizes lined the walls. Most were empty but for a couple of dogs that'd probably had to spend the night after their surgeries the day before.

"Good morning," a vet nurse Charlie knew as Cole greeted her from the doorway. "I know you've been here before, but Jodi wants me to show you where everything is before she gets here."

"Okay."

Cole proceeded to show her where drugs and fluids were stored, the equipment room, and finally gave her a detailed tour of the surgery.

"It looks a lot different when you work here."

"Most people are so focused on their pet when they come in, they don't notice anything else."

"Guilty as charged."

Cole sniffed the air. "Jodi is here. She's the only one who can get a decent cuppa out of that damned machine. Want one?"

"Love one. Thanks."

Cole led the way into the reception room where the coffee machine was. Jodi was already taking a sip from her mug.

"G'morning, Charlie. Fancy a cuppa with me?"

"Sure." Charlie took the mug Cole poured for her and joined Jodi in her office.

"Have a seat." Jodi sat down next to her. "Did you and Kim settle in okay last night?"

"Yes, thank you. Kim is thrilled we're so close to the beach. She'll probably go back to the States with a nicer tan than me."

"When's she heading out?"

"Monday."

"That soon?"

Charlie nodded. Although she really liked Jodi, she was Pip's friend first and foremost. So she wasn't sure how much she could confide in her. "Yes, she's got commitments at home."

"You okay?"

Charlie looked down into her lap and nodded. She blinked back the tears that burned behind her eyes and instantly hated herself for getting emotional. "Just tired I guess."

"Mm. Having a visitor will do that." Before Charlie could respond, Jodi said, "So, Cole showed you around. Ready to get your hands dirty?"

"I'm not a certified vet nurse, so I'm not sure what I can do to help you." Charlie envisioned herself cleaning kennels and the examination rooms.

"You'll be fine. You just can't dispense drugs or do any surgeries." Jodi smiled at her. "If you could, I'd be out of a job."

Charlie nodded and sipped her coffee.

"First and foremost, since you're my in-house expert on wildlife, I'll want you to be in the room with me whenever a native animal comes in."

"I'd hardly call myself an expert."

"From what Pip's told me, I understand you work with wildlife back home?"

"Yes."

"Well, mate, I'd venture to guess you have more experience than a lot of the wildlife rescuers in the area."

"Okay. What else?"

"Cole will work with you in the mornings to feed, water, and medicate the animals we have in care. During office hours, you can shadow me in the exam rooms and lend a hand if I need it. Other than that, if you're into it, you can observe during surgeries. How's that sound?"

"I can do all that. Sounds good."

"Excellent. You may find it's much more exciting here than at Pipsqueak's." Jodi laughed. "I'm just kidding. I know you travelled here to work with our native wildlife. Many of the principles I use on pets are the same. Although I have to be careful with what drugs I use and how I use them. I see a lot of little kangaroos here, and they show up with a multitude of problems that need treating. Y'know, after your stint here, you might find yourself going back to Ashby and teaching Pip a thing or two." Jodi winked at her.

"I hardly think that."

"Well, we'll see, won't we? Ready to start the day?"

"Ready when you are."

❖

Charlie spent the majority of her time watching and listening. She was mentally and physically tired when Jodi told her she could knock off at five. She went upstairs with visions of the day reeling through her head.

Kim surprised her with dinner already on the table.

"I didn't think you were going to cook for me any more." Charlie grinned at her.

"I wasn't, but I found this wine that will go really good with spaghetti."

"Spaghetti? Good Lord, Kim, it's got to be about twenty-eight and a hundred per cent humidity outside and you're cooking something hot?"

"Shush. Sit down and see what you think." Kim placed a steaming plate in front of her and then poured white wine into a glass and handed it to her. "Taste it. It's a sweet moscato."

"That hardly goes with pasta."

"Taste."

Charlie took a sip and had to agree it was a nice wine. One of the best she'd had in Australia. "Nice."

"How was your day?"

Charlie tipped her head to one side and smiled.

"What?"

"I was just thinking about how funny this is. We never talked this much when we were together. We never asked about each other's day."

"Huh. You're right. It's weird that we had to break up in order to feel comfortable with each other again."

"I like this friendship stuff."

"Yeah. Me too. So tell me, how was your first day?"

Charlie shrugged. "Just like most first days on a job. Watch and listen and memorize. It was good though. Jodi is fun to watch, both with people and the animals. She's got a great way with them."

"Is she gay?"

Charlie nearly choked on the bigger sip of wine she took. "You are incorrigible. Not every good-looking woman with short hair is a lesbian. To answer your question, I have no idea."

"Just wondering."

"How was your day at the beach? I see you got some colour." Charlie twirled her fork in the pasta.

"Beautiful. They're so clean. And the sand squeaks under your feet!"

Charlie laughed. "I know. I thought that was so cool the first time Pip took me to the beach." She sighed. She missed Pip. She couldn't deny what her heart wanted.

❖

Jodi had rung, as promised. It was a quick phone call. After all, what was there to say? After a brief conversation and some background information for Jodi on Charlie's skill sets and interests, Pip thanked her very much for calling and hung up. She poured herself a glass of wine and took it outside and sat on the edge of the verandah. Her legs swung loosely over the sides and Chilli lay silently beside her. It was quiet. Too quiet. It was funny how she had always treasured the night—the frogs calling out to each other, microbats squeaking as they chased insects, possums and gliders chattering away, birds singing their goodnight songs—there was never silence in the bush as the creatures of the day bid farewell and those of the night awoke and went about their business, but it held a magic auditory aura that always soothed her soul. But not tonight. The stars seemed less bright, the songs of the creatures tinny and disjointed. It had been a hard day and she felt raw and exhausted.

Squeak had been restless with her evening meal, taking a few sips, only to stop and chew the teat, and moments later spit it out.

It was a game of patience. Pip would put the bottle down to rewarm, dampen a cotton swab with warm water, and gently soothe the joey by smoothing it rhythmically over the joey's jawline and brows, not dissimilar to a mother's cleaning actions. It only took a few minutes for the joey to settle enough so that Pip could resume feeding the somewhat calmer infant.

Squeak missed Charlie, plain and simple. So did Pip. Although Squeak tolerated Pip feeding her, her main caregiver was gone. Normally she would have insisted Charlie take the joey with her, but it had seemed easier to leave her here in an environment she was familiar with and where the food was at the ready.

Charlie. Pip sighed. She knew it would only take a few days for Squeak to settle back down. Tired, she closed her eyes momentarily while the regular suck and pull of the teat reassured her the joey was feeding contentedly. She feared it would take her much longer to get used to Charlie's absence. Sending Charlie off to Jodi's had been hard but not as hard as if Charlie had stayed and gotten hurt again because Pip had been too involved, too distracted. Falling in love with Charlie had spun her head out, but seeing her with Kim, all smiles and laughter, left her feeling hollow. She needed the space. She needed time to think. And she couldn't do that with Charlie and Kim around.

Despite going to bed early in an attempt to sneak in some much needed sleep before the next feed rounds, she couldn't settle. She finally gave up trying to sleep at about one a.m. and came out to sit with the joeys, catching an occasional doze on the lounge in the prep room. Squeak wasn't the only one pining.

❖

The next morning when Charlie let herself into the clinic, she noticed an empty bag of fluids hanging outside one of the bottom kennels with the tubing leading inside. A brown and white dog lay on its side with its eyes open. At first Charlie thought her dead, but on closer inspection realized there was a slight rise and fall of her rib cage. Both its hind leg and stomach sported long incisions.

"You poor thing. When did you come in?"

The dog looked at her without moving a muscle. It was then that Charlie noticed the empty water bowl in the corner.

"Are you thirsty, girl?" She quietly opened the door and removed the bowl. The dog didn't appear to have the strength to move and Charlie wondered if she was on death's door. She left the door unlatched, walked over to the sink, rinsed the bowl out, and added some fresh. When she turned around, she gasped in surprise. Somehow the dog had managed to get up and follow her with the IV line trailing behind her.

She crouched down with the bowl and allowed the dog to drink her fill as she gently stroked her head.

"Come on, baby girl. Let's put you in a clean cage so you can rest." She pulled a blanket from a pile stacked near the washing machine and dryer and spread it inside the kennel adjacent to the one the dog was in originally. The dog stayed by her side the entire time. Charlie tapped the blanket to encourage the dog to enter the kennel, which she did, and reattached the IV line and bag to the new cage's door. The dog carefully dropped onto her side, looking exhausted for her efforts.

Charlie moved the spayed cats from their cages and gave them clean litter. Since they had water and food bowls already in them, she felt comfortable replacing them with fresh. She'd just finished cleaning the three cages when Cole walked in.

"Good morning." Cole looked around. "You've been busy." When she saw Charlie had moved the dog into a different cage, she frowned. "You be careful of that kelpie. She's a nasty bitch. There are only a couple dogs in this practice that hate Jodi, and Abby is one of them. I can't believe she let you pick her up. Probably because she's half dead."

Charlie crouched down next to the kelpie. The dog looked warily at Cole. Charlie couldn't miss the tense body posture and low growl. "I didn't have to touch her at all. She came out by herself and went into the other kennel willingly. What happened to her?"

"She got hit by a car last night. I got called in to assist with the surgery. Jodi pinned her hind leg and then discovered the dog had a lacerated liver so she repaired that too. We weren't sure if she'd make it through the night or not. Amazing."

"Wow."

"Kelpies are a tough breed. They'll get nailed by a cow's hind foot and keep on working like nothing's happened. Then later the owner will discover a nasty cut or even a break." Cole looked around and smiled. "You're going to spoil me."

"You can make it up to me by brewing me a cup of coffee."

"Deal."

Jodi was just as surprised as Cole that the kelpie had bonded with her. So it became Charlie's job to tend to her. Whenever Abby had to be examined, Charlie would put a soft muzzle on the dog and hug her close to her body. That seemed to make Abby calmer and more accepting of having Jodi touch her.

The days passed quickly. Charlie looked forward to not only learning from Jodi, but also watching Abby heal. In the mornings, if there wasn't another dog kennelled at ground level, she'd let Abby out to walk around the room while she worked. Thankfully, this all helped keep her mind off Pip. Somewhat.

Sunday morning, after Charlie had fed and cleaned Abby's kennel, she turned the light out and went upstairs. The practice was closed and Abby was the only patient in care. She had the rest of the day free.

Charlie found Kim packing her suitcase. "What time is your flight tomorrow?"

"Eight o'clock. I thought we could hang out until noonish and then I'll take the bus to the Gold Coast and get a room for the night. I can get an airport shuttle from there. Customs is a bitch. I have to get to the airport three hours before my plane takes off." Kim shook her head and put her passport and flight details into her backpack.

"I know. Good thing you have a direct flight. So what do you want to do this morning? We've got"—Charlie checked her watch—"four hours."

Kim shot her a grin. "You can't guess?"

Charlie laughed. "The beach?"

"Yep."

❖

Pip had no sooner finished feeding the last joey breakfast when the phone rang. An old man's dog had found a sugar glider caught in a barbed-wire fence. She took down the address and gathered the necessary things for the rescue. The caller only lived twenty minutes down the road, which Pip was grateful for. She wanted to be home when a load of river sand she had ordered for the koala pens turned up mid-morning.

The old man showed Pip where the glider was and then disappeared briefly to put his dog in the shed so it wouldn't disturb her work or further stress the glider. Pip draped a soft cloth over its head to help keep it quiet and still. She took a deep breath and took her time to figure out the best way to untangle it without inflicting more damage in the process. The job would have been so much easier if Charlie had been there to help. She decided that the safest option would be to cut the section of fence that the glider was caught in and take the whole lot home. She asked the owner if she could cut the fence, and he agreed. Pip retrieved some tie wire from the truck, a pair of pliers, a bag, and a towel. Using the tie wire she bridged the area each side of where the glider was caught. When she was satisfied that the join would take the tension of the fence once she cut the line, she wrapped the glider's body in a towel and handed the wire cutters to the old man while she cradled the body of the possum ready to support its release. With two quick snips, the tiny bundle came away, and she wrapped it into a bag. She carried the body back to her truck and placed it into a carry cage next to a hot water bottle she had prepared before leaving home.

Pip helped the old man fix his fence and was soon on her way back home.

In the safety and light of the prep room she took the glider out of the bag, keeping the little one's head covered to minimize stress, and checked its body over thoroughly. It was a juvenile male. There were two puncture wounds on one of its thigh muscles, and although tricky, they might heal. But her heart sank when she assessed its gliding membranes. The membrane on its left arm had been torn in half in the worst possible way. The tear would never heal and the glider would never be able return to the wild. She had no choice but to euthanize it.

When she finished, she buried the tiny body in the garden and potted a red flowering iron bark tree seedling next to where it now lay. Pip had confessed to Charlie light-heartedly how she got to have such a big garden. What she hadn't told her was that every time she lost an animal in care, it was buried with a plant that was meaningful to the animal's species either as a food source plant or shelter, so that its legacy might live on to support other animals of its kind.

❖

The apartment seemed stark and lonely when Charlie returned from the bus station and saying goodbye to Kim. She'd been a great distraction from the confusion and hurt she felt about Pip. Not surprisingly, she hadn't heard a word from Pip. Not a *How's it going* or *Just checking in*, or even an update on how Squeak was doing. Nothing.

Kim had told her she'd check in on the dogs, and when Charlie got home, they'd hang out. As friends. Now, as she stood at the window looking out at the ocean, she kind of wished she hadn't been in such a hurry for Kim to go home. But who would've known she'd end up working for a veterinarian for two weeks? More, how could she have ever thought that after their time in Angourie, her relationship with Pip would so quickly convert from loving and warm to stony and cold?

She went to bed early that night and wrapped her arms around herself. Surprisingly, she fell asleep and didn't wake until early the next morning. Since she had time, as it was only six a.m., Charlie took a long shower, ate breakfast, and drank her coffee on the balcony. A flock of pelicans circled high overhead, while on the ground below, a pair of lapwing plovers screamed and carried on while trying to keep track of the three youngsters running around in different directions in search of food. A kookaburra called in the distance. Charlie smiled as another must have joined it and they began laughing together.

For the first time in days, her heart beat steadily and her mind was at ease. Although she missed Kim's company, she didn't feel as alone this morning. Maybe Abby had something to do with it. The kelpie was progressing well, which helped boost her own mental fortitude.

Charlie finished her coffee, got dressed, and went downstairs to begin her day. After she finished cleaning kennels and letting Abby out into the grass for a brief spell, Charlie joined Jodi for another cup of coffee.

"Where's Cole this morning?"

Jodi's eyes had a curious glint in them. "She texted saying she'd be a little late."

"Okay. Is there anything you need me to do for her?"

"As a matter of fact, yes. You can help me get set up for surgery."

The tools Jodi had her lay out on the surgical tray were identical to the ones Charlie had cleaned after Abby's surgery. With one exception. The steel rods Jodi requested for pinning a bone were much smaller.

"What's coming in? A Chihuahua?"

Jodi looked up from the anaesthesia machine and grinned. "You'll see."

"Tease."

"I've been called worse."

Charlie laughed. "No doubt by Pip."

"How'd you guess?"

"You forget how well I know her."

"Mm."

"Have you heard from her at all?" Charlie attached the clippers to the extension cord and laid them on the surgery table.

"She called last night to see how you were doing. And she had a couple of questions about echidnas."

"Oh. Okay." Charlie turned to hide her disappointment that Pip hadn't called her directly.

"Can I get some help out here?" Cole called from the reception room.

"Why don't you go see what she's got? I'll finish up here and be right out." Jodi pulled a pair of leather gloves from one of the drawers.

Charlie looked at her with raised eyebrows.

Jodi waved her away. "Go. Don't keep Cole waiting. She gets grumpy if she has to wait."

When Charlie rounded the corner, she stopped short. Cole stood in the waiting room holding the base of a bundle wrapped in a blanket against her chest. Whatever it was, it was big.

"What the hell do you have?" Charlie approached Cole and carefully lifted the blanket up from the bottom. What she saw were Cole's gloved hands strongly gripping two huge taloned feet. She looked up quickly and smiled at Cole. "You have a raptor?"

"A wedge-tailed eagle to be exact. It got hit by a car in front of me as I was coming to work."

"Was it feeding on a roo or something?" Charlie knew wedgies were susceptible to crashes with cars because they often gorged themselves to the point where they were so heavy they couldn't take flight fast enough to get out of the way.

"Exactly. Let's get it into the exam room so you and Jodi can look at it." Charlie took over Cole's hold on the bird's legs as Cole transitioned the bundle into Charlie's arms. "You can deal with it. I'm not a big fan of birds. Especially ones that want to take a hunk out of me."

Charlie carried the eagle into the surgery room. "You knew she was bringing in an eagle, didn't you?" Charlie playfully frowned at Jodi.

"Thought we'd surprise you." Jodi held the blanketed eagle while Charlie donned the leather gloves. Then together, they carefully unwrapped the eagle.

The eagle immediately started screaming and struggled to bite one of them with its sharp beak. Charlie put a surgical towel around its head and secured it with a tourniquet, careful not to tighten it excessively, effecting a temporary hood. The bird quieted abruptly.

Jodi shook her head. "See? That's why I needed you here." She proceeded to gently examine the eagle, starting with its legs.

"Good here." She palpated upward, feeling along its ribs, sternum, and keel. From there she checked first one wing, then the other, returning to the right wing. "Hmm. I'll need to get an X-ray to confirm it, but I'm pretty sure he has a fractured ulna."

"I guess if he was going to break anything, the forearm is the easiest to repair." Charlie held the taloned feet together to further calm the bird. "And the fact that he's a juvenile is in his favour too. See how light brown he is? The darker the bird, the older it is."

"He's lost a few flight feathers, but those'll grow back in due course. Okay. Cole, help me get some pictures and let's see what we can do for Charlie's big bird. In the meantime, Charlie, will you please see if you can reschedule clients for the morning? I don't want this eagle to have to wait any longer than necessary."

It was late morning before the eagle was placed in a darkened kennel so the effects of the anaesthesia could wear off without it further injuring itself. Charlie had watched enthralled as Jodi had painstakingly placed a pin in the eagle's wing. This was the first time she'd seen such a magnificent specimen of a wedgie up close. Up until now, binoculars had been her best friend when looking at one in flight high in the sky.

"If your bird wakes up without incident, then you'll have your work cut out for you. You'll be taking him back to Pip's with you, week after next."

Charlie looked up from scrubbing the surgical forceps and pliers Jodi had used during surgery. "You're sure you don't want Pip to take him sooner?"

"Why? You're here. It'll be one less for her to take care of, and something for you to pamper while you're here. We have a large aviary out the back that we can fix up over the next couple of days."

"There's not much I can do for him while he's in a cage."

"No, but he has to eat."

"True enough."

Charlie waited until after office hours to check on the eagle. In the dim light she could see it perched on a block of wood. It watched her with sharp eyes but remained calm. It held its right wing a little lower than the other, which was normal for a bird with this injury.

Satisfied, Charlie returned to the kennel and took Abby out one more time before shutting the lights off for the night.

❖

Pip's sweat-soaked shirt stuck to her back and shoulders as she hoisted a fresh cut stringy bark tree branch onto the new hardwood Y frame she had put together earlier in the morning in one of the koala pens. She balanced precariously on the ladder, one leg locked around the frame for added balance, as she reached around into her back pocket for her wire cutters. With a last twist of her wrist to tighten the wire binding, she secured the branch into place and stepped down on shaky legs.

Chilli pawed her leg and uttered a throaty huff.

"I know, I know. I just wanted to get it up before stopping to take a break." She pulled over a backpack and sat heavily down onto the grass under the shade of the half-finished new koala shelter and pulled out a bowl, two bottles of water, and a container. After pouring water into the bowl for Chilli, she lifted the container lid, pulled out a handful of dried fruit and nuts, and shoved them inelegantly into her mouth. She offered a dried apricot piece to Chilli, whose tail wagged in acceptance. The canine's mouth stretched in a grin between audible chews of delight. She watched as ants busied themselves making high-sided mounds around their nest holes on the ground. "The ants are busy. Looks like we're in for some rain, Chilli-bub." Chilli's tail wagged.

She'd been up since four. Pip figured if she couldn't sleep, she might as well work. Maybe at the end of the day she would be too tired to stay awake, to think. Break over, she packed away the food and drink, and went off to get more material.

Secured by rope and pins, she hauled the logs into the pen. The hard physical work felt good. Cathartic almost. She had been less than pleasant to Charlie after Kim's surprise arrival. The shame stung almost as bad as the sweat falling into her eyes. Charlie had said she and Kim were over after the Skype call. Pip grunted as she dropped the new log and rope into place on the ground. Images of

Kim with her arm around Charlie's waist, kissing her in the koala pen, mocked her with visual snapshot stills of a couple at ease with each other, clearly illustrating that their relationship was far from over.

In the kitchen, Charlie had called her sweetheart and told her she missed her before she'd left—before Pip had sent her away. Her heart and mind warred back and forth with conflicting information. Pip knew she couldn't be both mentor and lover to Charlie. She just had to tough it out and do her best to move past it if she and Charlie stood any hope of seeing the rest of her year out as colleagues. And the best way for her to do that was to have Charlie be with Kim, and away from her and the distractions of the interlude of an exotic romantic wildlife adventure.

She squinted into the mid-morning sun, looking at how much more work she had to do. The sand had arrived and sat in two large piles off to the side. She would spread that out last, after the stands and roofs had been secured. If Charlie were here, they would've had the pen largely finished in a couple of days. They'd become a smooth team, each seeming to know what the other one wanted before she had an opportunity to voice it. She shoved another piece of fruit into her mouth and chewed thoughtfully. But Charlie wasn't here. She had pushed her away. Pushed her back into Kim's arms.

Charlie had said she wanted to take care of her. She didn't need taking care of. Pip grabbed up the rope and tied off another log and set to drag it across the pen. Gritting her teeth with determination she felt the strain across her shoulders and back, fuelled with the perverse need to prove to her American colleague that she could not only manage, but do so in spades and have several projects finished by the time she came back.

If she came back. Pip paused mid-task. Charlie would come back, wouldn't she?

❖

The next morning, Charlie found the eagle pacing and turning on the wood. It seemed agitated and she knew it was more than likely hungry. She put some frozen mice in a pan of warm water to defrost while she went in search of a large pair of forceps and leather gloves.

After donning the gloves, she slowly opened the cage door. “Easy, big fella,” she said in a soft voice. She put one hand in. The eagle spread its wings, glared down at her hand, and opened its mouth. Having handled eagles in the past, Charlie knew she’d have to be careful not to move fast and send it into a panic. She carefully stroked his powerful chest before lowering her hand to where his legs met his body. Charlie widened her eyes in surprise when the bird stepped up onto her wrist, first with one foot, then the other. Everything around Charlie disappeared. Her heart raced with adrenaline and euphoria. It’d been too long since she’d worked with an eagle.

Careful not to alarm the bird, she opened the cage door wider and eased her arm out. The bird tightened its talons and balanced on its human perch. Charlie turned to where she’d placed the now-thawed mice. She grasped one with the forceps and held it to the eagle’s sharp beak. But the bird showed no interest.

“You’ve probably never had this on your menu.” Charlie removed the wooden block from the cage and placed it on the table. She urged the bird to step off her arm and onto the wood, which it seemed willing enough to do. “Okay. Let’s try it this way.” She slid the glove off, and coming from behind the bird’s head, gingerly placed her thumb and index finger on either side of the bird’s beak. She then pulled upward to open its mouth. She lifted the forceps and mouse, and judiciously inserted it into the bird’s gape. She let go and watched the bird’s reaction.

The eagle snapped its beak open and closed, once, twice, and then swallowed the mouse. Charlie breathed a sigh of relief. “It’s always touch and go with you big birds. If you keep eating, and unless you screw your wing up somehow, I think you’re going to be flying the high skies in a few months, big guy.”

She fed the eagle three more mice. When she held the fourth in front of him to see, he swiftly grabbed it out of her grasp and swallowed, earning a wide smile from her.

"I'll give you some more later. I have some other patients to look after right now. Although none nearly as majestic as you."

The eagle cocked its head as if listening to her and acted as if he already knew the routine when he stepped onto Charlie's gloved arm and rode back to his cage.

Charlie couldn't wait to tell Jodi and Cole, and eventually show them how easily the eagle took to being handled.

She was humming when both women came into the office. She'd fed and cleaned Abby's kennel, the only one occupied at the moment, and tried her hand at making coffee.

"Somebody's been flat out this morning." Jodi poured coffee for herself and Cole.

Charlie couldn't contain her excitement. "The wedgie is doing great. He ate four mice this morning."

"Force-fed or willingly?" Jodi sat down next to Charlie while Cole busied herself listening to voicemail.

"Three forced, but then he took the fourth by himself."

"Excellent."

"I'll feed him again this afternoon. You'll have to come watch."

"Righto. I'd like to see how his wing is holding up with the pins anyway."

The morning went fast. They'd had to overbook because of yesterday's events. But the clinic worked like a well-oiled machine. One o'clock found the last client of the morning waving goodbye with his border collie in tow.

"We've got about twenty minutes before the next appointment. Let's go check on your bird." Jodi washed her hands and changed her scrub top, which had remnants of the morning's appointments smeared on it.

Charlie repeated the same motions as earlier with the eagle, with the same results. That is, until the eagle saw Jodi. He glared at Jodi, screamed, and spread his wings over Charlie's head.

"Hey, hey. Easy, big guy." Charlie looked to Jodi who stood in the doorway. "I have no idea what set him off."

"He's mantling you. It seems he's claimed you as his. Which is very interesting. His wing looks good from here, by the way. I'm not going to distress him further by coming closer."

"Good idea. I'll let you know if I notice anything we should be concerned about."

"Bewdy." Jodi turned to go, and as soon as she was out of sight, the eagle calmed. He folded his wings and ruffled his feathers back into place.

"You're a silly bird. Jodi wouldn't hurt you. She's the one who fixed you up." A light bulb suddenly went off in Charlie's head. Jodi was also the last person he saw before Charlie had hooded him. Maybe, just maybe…

From that moment on, every time Jodi or Cole came into the back kennelling area, the eagle screamed a warning. But as soon as he heard Charlie's voice or saw her, he chirped like a fledgling asking for food.

Charlie took to putting a note on the door, warning them when she had the eagle out of his cage. She also decided to make a hood for him. He was going to be with her for a while, and since he'd taken ownership of her, it'd be safer for all if he couldn't see. A raptor's visual stimulus and input was very high and he could initially be a danger to others as well as himself. He was still a wild animal.

So she walked into town and bought a pair of large leather gloves. She spent the next few nights after work pulling the seams out, fashioning and sewing it into a hood for him.

She wished then that she'd thought to bring the hoods she used with raptors in the States. "Oh, well. I probably wouldn't have anything big enough for you, mister," she said, as she fitted it over his head. She made a few adjustments and cut a larger beak area, but then it was finished.

The eagle still screamed when he heard the others, but Jodi was now able to examine him without incident. If she remembered not to say anything until afterwards.

❖

"You really have a gift," Jodi said to Charlie one afternoon after she'd put the eagle back in his cage. "Animals seem to gravitate to you. I've seen it with both domestic and native animals that come in. No wonder you and Pip get on so well."

Charlie shrugged. "I wouldn't so much call it a gift." She went to the refrigerator and got their lunch bags out.

"What would you call it?" Jodi unwrapped a Vegemite sandwich and took a healthy bite.

"I guess I just know how to read animals. You can thank my dad. I learned a lot from him."

"Does he live in Wyoming too?"

Charlie shook her head and frowned. "No. He died some years ago. Mom lives in Maine."

"If I remember correctly, Wyoming and Maine are really far apart."

"Mm. I don't get to see her that often. Although now that Kim and I are—" She shrugged. "Anyway. I should be able to see her more often now."

"Good. My oldies live in Sydney. I try and get down there every month or so, but it depends on how busy it gets here."

A breeze flowed through the window, bringing with it the smell of impending rain.

"I better get Abby outside before it starts raining."

"Good idea. We're supposed to get some storms over the next few days."

Chapter Fourteen

Pip stepped out of the shower and towelled herself dry. But no sooner had she finished than a fine sheen of moisture covered her body. She sighed in annoyance. Chilli lay on the cool bathroom tiles. "How it's not raining, I'll never know. This humidity is just crap, hey, bub?"

Chilli's tail swished in response.

"I wish it would just hurry up and bloody rain already. I'm sick to death of being sticky. Ugh."

It had been a long, hot, sleepless night with little respite from the day's heat and humidity. She gave herself a second quick wipe over before deciding that undergarments and a T-shirt would be the best and coolest option. With no one else around, she was hardly going to offend anyone's sensibilities. She padded out of the bathroom on bare feet, towelling her hair dry as best as the conditions would allow. She threw herself down onto the couch. Weather like this, she didn't feel much inclined to do anything at all.

The phone rang.

Chilli looked up at her as if to say, *Are you going to get that?*

Pip smirked at her. "It's all right. Don't get up, dog. I'll manage."

Chilli snuffled and put her head back down onto the cool floor and seemed to slip into a light doze.

"Hello? Oh, hi, Pat." Pat Jenkins, an octogenarian, lived down the road on a small plot of land. She had a handful of chickens and some house cows for milk. Pip joked that her good friend would be buried in her gumboots. "Yes, I saw the weather forecast. Looks like we're in for a bit of rain." Pip wiped her damp forehead and looked up at the clock on the wall. "I can be there in half an hour if you like." Pat wanted a hand moving her livestock to higher ground, just in case. "By the time you've got the billy boiled, I'll be knocking on your front door."

Pip looked at her watch. She had a few hours before the joeys needed their midday feed and could help her friend out easily enough. "Righto then. See you soon. Cheerio."

Pip hung up and looked at Chilli who gazed at her with one eye open. "Come on then. If I have to get my pants on, then you have to open both eyes." Chilli sneezed at her but didn't move. "Don't look at me like that. We both know Pat will sneak you a piece of cake under the table."

Chilli barked, stood up, and stretched. She ambled over to the door, sat, and looked back over her shoulder at her. Pip chuckled. "I know, I know. Pants."

Within minutes Pip, with Chilli on the back seat, pulled up at Pat's front door on her quad runner. The ageless woman decked out in a floral sundress, apron tied around her waist, and the famous gumboots adorning her feet greeted her with a frown. "Bessie's not keen on coming off the river flat paddock, stubborn old fool."

"Not a problem, Pat. Chilli and I will rouse her up. You want them all up on the hill?"

"Yes, please, love."

"Good-oh. Be back soon." Pip drove the quad runner down to the paddocks parallel to the river frontage and found Pat's milkers, including the old jersey, Bessie. A rumble sounded overhead. She looked up to see thunderheads building. They were dark and fat, and rolling in fast. With a chorus of encouraging barks, Pip and Chilli trotted the cows through several paddocks up onto the higher ground where there was plenty of feed, and where they were guaranteed to keep their hooves dry.

Back in the farmhouse, they caught up over a pot of tea. Pip laughed. "Pat, enough. You'll make her fat."

Pip shook her head at her friend's attempted look of innocence.

"I don't know what you're talking about." Chilli burped from under the table and Pip quirked one eyebrow up at her old neighbour.

Pat sniffed. "She likes my carrot cake."

"You spoil her."

"Eh. At my age I think I've earned the prerogative."

"True enough."

"Where's your American friend?"

"She's working in town for a couple of weeks and a friend is putting her up while she's there."

"Oh. She'll be back though, won't she?"

Pip was saved from answering the question as a loud clap of thunder made them both jump.

Pat drained the tea from her cup. "That's come in quick. Sounded like it was over the house. You and pup here should get on home before you get a wet tail."

Pip watched indulgently as Pat's hand disappeared under the table. She knew Chilli got another piece of cake as Pip heard her lips smacking together. "*Pat.*"

The old lady stood up and patted Pip on the shoulder. "Don't worry, dear. I saved enough for you to take home." She presented Pip with a Tupperware container, the still warm cake tucked securely inside. "Thank you again. Now go on, scoot, the pair of you."

Pip gave her a quick kiss on the cheek. "Let me know when you want them brought back down again and I'll come give you a hand."

With a quick wave, Pip and Chilli headed back. They pulled up into the shed just as the first big fat heavy drops of rain began to fall.

❖

The lights in the kennel area flickered just before another crack of thunder shook the building. Charlie wiped the sweat from her brow and wished for a cool breeze. The clinic's air conditioning couldn't keep up with the heavy humidity and high temps. Her shirt stuck to her and her hair was damp. She leaned against the sink, drained a glass of water, and refilled it. She drank her fill and then poured the remainder down the drain.

She turned towards the sound of heavy rain on the window. Lightning slashed across the sky and a moment later another rumble of thunder rolled overhead. The sky seemed to twist in turmoil.

"Looks nasty out there," Cole said as she put the soiled surgical towels into the washing machine.

"Doesn't it? I'm hoping the rain will drop the temperature some. And we could sure use it. Everything is so dry." Charlie opened the back door in hopes of catching a breeze.

"Sure is. This is a dangerous time of year because of bush fires and, oddly enough, floods."

"Really? Does it flood here a lot?"

"Not here in Yamba. We're too close to the ocean. But those along the Clarence have had a few nasty floods in the past couple years. Two thousand nine was a bad one and in twenty thirteen, we had three."

"Phew. How much rain has to fall before we go into flood?"

Cole leaned against the dryer and put her hand on her hip. "I'm not sure, actually. But it could rain like crazy down here and we'll just get a little localized flooding. It depends on how much rain falls up in the catchment area. If they get a lot up there, we're totally screwed. I wouldn't worry though."

Charlie looked out the window again. "Looks like it might be letting up some. I'm going to get Abby outside as soon as it stops."

"Good idea. Oh, hey, Jodi said Abby can go home tomorrow."

Charlie's heart sank a little. Abby had become her morning shadow and she'd grown quite attached to her, and, she thought, vice versa. "That's terrific. Her owner must be so pleased."

"Considering we all thought she was going to die, yeah, he sure is. How's Big Bird?"

The mere mention of the eagle brought a smile to Charlie's face. "He's good. Jodi thinks he'll rehab well, even with that small pin in his wing."

"That's cool. Well, I better get the rest of the surgery cleaned up in case we lose power." Cole winced as the lights flickered again.

Charlie watched it rain for a while longer, and then gave up thinking Abby would get her walk. The rain pounded down and bounced up from the deeply dry ground.

She fed the eagle a few more mice to tide him over until the morning, and climbed the stairs to the apartment.

Rain seemed to blow in from all sides of the balcony and she hurried to insert the key and unlock the door. Nevertheless, her clothes were even more saturated when she walked in.

The pounding of the rain sounded like coins hitting the colour bond roof above her. Charlie watched outside the window as she prised her shirt and shorts off. She dropped them in a heap, transfixed by the weather. The sky beyond was roiling grey. The clouds tossed and turned in a wind that seemed to be growing stronger by the minute.

The steady beat on the roof lulled Charlie into a meditative state. She felt at peace with the world. She wasn't sure if it was because of the eagle entering her life, or maybe that she and Kim had sorted things out and would remain friends when she went back to Wyoming. She vowed to herself that when she returned to Pip's, she'd be okay. They could be friends. At least that's what they'd have to be in order to be able to work together for the remainder of her stay. She nodded to herself to confirm it and a weight slid off her shoulders. It *would* all be okay.

The heat had pretty much killed her appetite for anything other than a banana sandwich. So she prepared her meal, put it into the refrigerator to get cold, and then stepped into a cool shower. Sleep came easily to her that night. She didn't have a worry in the world any more.

❖

"I'll take as many bags as you can spare, Henry," Pip yelled into the phone in order to be heard over the torrential rain. "Yep, I know others will want some. Whatever you can manage. Thanks, mate. I'll have Jodi pick them up for me." Pip hung up and hit Jodi's number on speed dial.

It had been another sleepless night as the rain pelted down. Pip brought as many of the animals up into the pens and cages on the upslope of the property as she could manage on her own. She'd carried up extra fuel for the generator, which she had on standby if the power went out. At two a.m. she'd dug drainage ditches in one of the koala pens and used the koala sand to fill a couple dozen sandbags she kept stored in the shed. At dawn she'd tipped out four hundred millimetres of overnight rain from the gauge and it didn't look like it was letting up any time soon. She'd been monitoring the rainfall upstream in the catchment areas. They'd had a similar amount over the past forty-eight hours and it was now headed downstream. Pip chewed the inside of her lip. A tributary creek ran through the property, down near the cabin, past the paddocks where the teenage joeys were, and eventually out into the Clarence River.

At seven she drove to the river. It was rising rapidly and so was her creek. She needed more sandbags.

"Jodes, I need a favour." She figured she'd be cut off before lunchtime at the rate it was going. "Can you swing past Henry's and pick me up some more sandbags? He's got a pile waiting for me." Pip nodded. "The water levels are rising pretty fast and I need more bags for the cabin." As she listened to Jodi she grabbed some fruit and snack bars from the countertop and threw them into her backpack. "I'll meet you at the bridge. All the ferries have stopped. It's too dangerous. I can be there in twenty minutes. Thanks." Pip hung up and grabbed some water bottles. She stacked a handful of dry towels by the door for when she returned.

Grabbing the keys to her ute, she and Chilli dashed through the rain and into the safety of the truck's cabin. Almost instantly the insides of the windows fogged up. She put the demister on, turned the wiper blades on full speed, and headed out to meet Jodi. Even with the frenetic swiping pace of the blades, Pip needed to travel cautiously. Her visibility was challenged by the heavy rain. Rising condensation levels inside the cabin conspired to turn the glass into a frosted panorama, further obscuring her view.

"Shit!" She jammed the brakes. The truck aquaplaned several feet before coming to a halt. An echidna was trapped on a roadside fence. The force of the rushing roadside drainage water pinned it in the Ringlock mesh. She hit her hazard lights and turned to look at Chilli. "Stay." She flung open the car door and was immediately hit in the face by a wall of rain. She groaned out loud as she launched herself forward towards the roadside drainage ditch. With water up to her mid-thighs, she stumbled from the force. She waded to the fence line near the trapped spiny creature. Dipping her hand under the water, she located its soft belly, cupped her hand around its torso, and liberated it from the fence. Clutching it to her chest, she pushed through the water until she got to the edge of the ditch. She clawed her way up and back to the roadside. She placed the echidna in a plastic tub, then put it in the back seat with Chilli and got back in the car. She was soaked to the skin. Water ran off her hair and into her eyes.

Pip put the ute into gear and continued on until she pulled up at the bridge meeting point where Jodi was already waiting. She retrieved the container with the echidna and, squinting into the rain, walked over to where she could make out Jodi's bright yellow raincoat. Jodi was already bent over pulling out tied bundles of hessian sandbags from the back of her car.

"Fancy meeting you here." Pip grinned at the absurdity of it all. The raincoated figure straightened and she found herself looking not into Jodi's face, but up into Charlie's hazel eyes.

"Fancy indeed."

Pip's grin faded. She stood and stared, her mind blank with the shock of seeing Charlie so close, so unexpectedly. She faltered.

Charlie nodded at the box in her hands. "Who's your friend?"

Pip started before remembering the echidna. "I brought Jodi an exchange. For the bags."

"Seems a fair trade." Rain ran off both their faces.

"Sorry. I thought you were Jodi."

"It's okay. I overheard the phone call and offered to come out and help. If that's okay."

Pip found herself lost for words. She nodded.

Jodi stuck her head out the car window. "You two right to go? I have to get back to the surgery."

Charlie lifted the box from Pip's fingers. "I'll just give this to Jodi, shall I?"

"Yes. Please. It was stuck in a fence half submerged. I think he took in some water. He might need monitoring for a day or so."

Charlie smiled at her and Pip couldn't help but offer her a tentative smile in return as she let go of her charge and picked up the bags.

Pip swiped the water from her hair and got back into the truck. Jodi was already backing up to turn around and head back to Yamba. She met Charlie's eyes through the window and her heart ached. Chilli wagged her tail when she saw Charlie, and whined when Jodi drove away.

"I know just how you feel, bub."

Pip blinked through the droplets on her eyelashes and shook her head. Part of her had been so happy to see Charlie again, while the other part was heavy, weighted down with the memory that everything had changed and that she was back with Kim.

The splintered crash of a floating tree smacking into one of the bridge pylons as it rushed downriver reminded her that introspection could wait. She needed to get these sandbags home, filled, and into place.

❖

Charlie stared out her window. The force of the rain was so incredible, she was only looking at water running down the glass.

She was surprised at how her heart had banged against her chest when her eyes met Pip's. Her stomach fluttered and then a feeling of emptiness overcame her. She missed Pip.

"It's getting worse." Jodi carefully drove around a huge puddle in the road. "I haven't seen it this bad for years."

Charlie grunted and sighed.

"What's up?"

"Huh?" Charlie looked at her. "Nothing. Just worried about Pip, I guess."

"I've been meaning to ask. Did Kim make it home okay?"

The sudden change of subject yanked Charlie out of her pout. "I guess so. I only got a quick email from her a few days ago."

"You can tell me to butt out if you want. Are things okay with you two?"

"Kim and me? Yeah. We'll always be friends."

Jodi turned and stared at Charlie, then swerved hard. She braked to a stop on a safer part of the road. "Wait. You and Kim aren't together?"

"No. We were. But we're better off friends than lovers."

Jodi slapped the steering wheel and laughed.

"What?"

Jodi shook her head. "Does Pip know any of this?"

"She should, although I never had a chance to tell her."

"Can I ask you something?"

Charlie raised her eyebrows and shrugged. "I guess."

"Do you have feelings for Pip?"

Charlie sighed loudly and nodded slightly.

Jodi smiled and pulled back onto the road. "When we get back to the clinic, I want you to go upstairs and pack your bags."

"What? Why?"

"Because, mate, you need to take your eagle and be with Pip. It's going to get hairy out there and I don't want her to have to handle all that by herself. And while you're getting your stuff together, Cole and I are going to make some phone calls and cancel everything for the rest of the day, except for emergencies. The roads are getting too bad for people to be out on them anyway."

"Jodi, I can't ask you to drive me all the way back to Ashby."

"You don't have to. But I'm going to anyhow." Jodi patted the dashboard of the old Land Rover. "This ol' girl has gotten me through worse. Plus, that's what four-wheel drive is for." She shot Charlie a mischievous grin. "I'm not letting anything as simple as a little storm keep you two apart any longer." Jodi giggled and bounced in her seat like a little girl. The truck lost traction and they nearly went off the road. "Heh. Whoops, sorry. I got a bit excited there. Steady up, old girl, we've got a few more miles to go before the day is over."

❖

It was slow going but Pip managed two runs of thirty sandbags down to the cabin. On the return trip with the quad runner, the wheels gouged deep, wet, muddy furrows into the ground. She desperately wanted to do a bigger run but knew she risked bogging the bike and the trailer if she did. The rain beat a steady monotonous cacophony against her broad-brimmed straw hat. It wasn't waterproof and she was soaked underneath, but it afforded her some protection in keeping the rain from her eyes so she could see to drive. She fumbled into the pocket of her raincoat and pulled out a banana and ate it on the way. She'd left Chilli back up at the house. She didn't want the dog anywhere near the swollen creek waters or run the risk in the blinding rain of not seeing her with the quad runner and accidently running over her. The canine wasn't happy about being left behind. For Pip it was a simple relief to have one less thing to worry about for the moment.

She pulled the quad runner next to the pile of sand in the koala pen and turned the engine off. For what seemed like the millionth time, she picked up a bag and placed it into a homemade frame she'd designed. Using the shovel, she began the rhythmic dig and fill movements to fill the new bag. With the sand close to the top she dropped the shovel and tied the bag closed. She lifted it free of the frame and straightened, hefting the weighty bag up into her arms. As she turned towards the trailer, Charlie appeared in front of her, bright in Jodi's sunny yellow raincoat, a tentative half smile on her face, arms extended, ready to accept the heavy bundle.

"I figured you might like a hand."

Pip felt her heart pound against her chest wall. She didn't know if she wanted to laugh or cry. She tipped her straw hat up and down and water cascaded off the edge. She gratefully accepted Charlie's offer and transferred the bag into Charlie's waiting arms. "I would. Thank you."

A broad grin stole across Charlie's face and Pip couldn't help but smile back at her. She'd missed their teamwork. And their easy friendship. Charlie might be off limits as a lover, but it was nice to be working together again. Her heart lifted and her arms felt stronger. In far less time than it had taken her previously, another trailer load was on its way down to the cabin with Charlie riding shotgun in the trailer on top of the bags.

Pip assessed the rising water levels. "Let's leave this lot here and quickly go and get another run while we can still get it across. We can stack it all up at next load." She had to yell over the top of the rain splatter's staccato beats resonating off their coats and hats.

"Got it." They worked in a line. Charlie lifted from the trailer and handed to Pip, who stacked the bags on the ground nearest the cabin's pole foundations. They went back and filled another thirty bags.

Charlie held aloft ten empty bags. "That's the last of them. Should we fill these as well and sneak them on the load?" Pip gave her the thumbs-up signal and made some more room on the trailer to evenly distribute the additional load.

As Pip loaded the last bags, Charlie held up a hand. "Gimme a minute." Pip watched Charlie run back up to the house. She turned and stretched her tired back. She'd been going for hours, non-stop, and knew she would feel every load of sand she'd hoisted later on when she eventually rested. That's when she'd start to stiffen up.

She couldn't help but smile as Charlie ran back down, a grin on her face, a plastic bag swinging off one hand. She pulled up slightly out of breath, her cheeks pink with the effort, and handed Pip the bag. "Here. I'll drive." Charlie jumped on the bike seat and kicked the engine over. "Hop on already."

Pip scrambled up and sat in Chilli's seat behind her and opened the bag. She discovered two sandwiches and choc chip biscuits. Lucky for Pip the rain was the perfect camouflage as tears pricked her eyes and escaped down her cheeks at Charlie's thoughtfulness. Pip reached under Charlie's arm, offering her a biscuit, and smiled when warm fingers wrapped around hers and the snack. Charlie threw her a wink before turning back to concentrate on the trail down to the cabin, sneaking in bites as she went. With a quick pause to shove their sandwiches in, Pip looked at the marker she had placed on her first run. The water had already risen two thirds of the way up it. It was lucky this was the last run. Pip didn't feel confident they would have gotten another load over before it became too risky.

They offloaded the bags, and while Pip stacked them around the cabin's stilt foundations she got Charlie to quickly run the quad runner back across the water to the top side of the creek. She didn't want to risk it getting bogged and the water washing it away before they could get it out. Her feet slid out from under her. She fell to her knees in the mud for the umpteenth time as she dumped another bag into place. To her left Charlie was just as muddy and having trouble keeping her traction as well.

They used the last ten bags to fortify a part of the stonewall bank which oozed water. They were soaked. Pip's hat had disintegrated. She gave up and threw it aside. They were both spattered in mud from head to toe. "Thanks for coming out to help me. I really appreciate it."

"You're very welcome." Charlie manoeuvred a bag into place.

"When we're finished here you better head on up to the house and give Jodi and Kim a ring to come and pick you up before the road gets cut off."

"What?" Charlie yelled over a roll of thunder.

"You need to ring Kim to come and pick you up before we get cut off and you get stuck here."

"Kim. Why?"

"Because she'll be worried about you."

❖

Charlie dismissed Pip's suggestion with a wave. It wasn't the time or place to discuss Kim. "We'll talk later. Right now, since you've got my help, let's do whatever you normally do during one of these storms."

"But the road—"

Charlie put her hands on her hips. "To hell with the damned road. I'm staying. You're not doing this alone, Pip." She swiped at the stream of water rolling down her face. "And don't get any ideas about calling Jodi to come pick me up. She won't."

"She would if I asked her."

Charlie laughed. "Trust me, she wouldn't." She shook her head. "It's too dangerous for anybody to be out in this. You should know better than anyone. So let's just do what we need to do." Charlie grabbed the last sandbag and placed it with purpose.

Pip stared at her for a few moments. "Okay. Let's head back to the quad and up to the house for a bit so we can feed the babies. We've done all we can here. If you need anything from the cabin, you'd best get it now. You're going to have to stay at the house until this is over."

"I took all my stuff with me when you sent me to Yamba." Charlie didn't know what came over her, but she couldn't resist the little dig.

"Fair enough." They reached the quad and Pip got on. "I think we have time for showers before we have to feed the joeys. Squeak will be happy to see you. She missed you."

Charlie smiled. "I missed the little urchin too." *And you.*

Chilli met them at the door with happy yips and a tail that wouldn't stop.

"If you don't mind me showering first, I'll whip up some lunch for us while you're getting cleaned up." Pip pulled two huge towels out of the linen cupboard. "You can at least get out of those clothes and wrap yourself up in one of these in the meantime."

"Thanks." Charlie waited until Pip disappeared into the bathroom before rolling her wet, muddy clothes off. She washed her face and hands in the kitchen sink to get a slight reprieve from her feeling of grunginess.

When Charlie finally emerged from her shower, she looked at the empty table in confusion. "Um, I don't want to seem picky or anything, but…food?"

Pip chuckled. "I put it in an esky for us to take next door. It's later than I thought so we can eat in the prep room." She started out the door with Chilli on her heel.

"Pip, you should probably let me go in there first." Charlie tried to get to the prep room door ahead of her, but too late.

Big Bird sat on a makeshift perch in the middle of the room. He screamed and waved his wings as soon as he caught sight of Pip. Charlie had trained him to respect a tether on his leg so that she could safely leave him anywhere. But not knowing how long she'd be outside helping, Charlie had taken his hood off.

"Eff me," Pip said in surprise. "Where'd that come from?"

Chilli lowered herself to the floor and combat crawled under the table.

Charlie scooted in front of Pip and quickly covered Big Bird's head with his hood. The bird fell silent and folded his wings. The only sound was the heavy pounding of rain on the roof.

"He came into the clinic last week with a broken wing. He's kinda attached to me."

Pip raised her eyebrows and cocked her head. "I'll say."

"I didn't know where else to put him when I got here."

"Here is as safe a place as any for the time being, as long as he doesn't carry on like that all the time. It's stressful on the joeys. We can rig him up something in the shed next to the house. There's nobody in there at the minute, since we released the possums."

Charlie shook her head. "He's pretty good when he has his hood on, and perfectly quiet when it's only him and me, or just him."

"He's a beauty for sure. We'll give him his own castle soon."

Squeak greeted Charlie with little clicking noises when she opened the joey's pouch and lifted her out. "Hello, my little darling."

Squeak rocked and fidgeted to be fed. She shook her head and flapped her ears. It was the most animated Charlie had ever seen her.

"Told you, she missed you. I had trouble feeding her at first, but she eventually took the teat and ate."

After Charlie fed Squeak, she cleaned up while Pip fed the other two joeys. She felt the need for small talk if only to break some of the remaining tension. "How's the new one going?"

"Harwood Harry? He's good. The bruising he had has all but disappeared and he's actually started to put weight on at a regular rate."

Charlie opened the esky and lifted out a container of soup and another of salad.

"The soup is chicken noodle. I had leftover meat so there's grilled chook in the salad too."

Charlie chuckled. "You've been busy." While the soup heated in the microwave she pulled the lid off the salad and was delighted to see lots of raw vegetables including carrots, cucumber, and spinach. Pip had topped it off with sunflower seeds, dried cranberries, and avocado. Her stomach growled in anticipation.

"It's good comfort food." Pip looked up and must have realized the implication. "For when the weather is crappy." She got up, put Emmy back in her bag, and came to the table.

Thunder rumbled deeply overhead. Charlie didn't think it possible, but it seemed the rain started to hit the roof even harder. It was so loud, neither of them tried to talk above it.

The sound of rushing water made them both look up at the same time. Chilli whined nervously from under the table. She hadn't moved since they'd come in.

"Uh-oh. That's not good." Pip rose to her feet.

A crash sounded from outside. The lights went out, leaving them in pitch black.

Chapter Fifteen

Pip felt along the walls until she came to the cupboard she was after and opened it. She blindly wrapped her fingers around the torches she kept there, grabbed them both, and turned them on, handing one over to Charlie. "I'll kick the Genie into gear."

She went to the laundry and started the generator. It could run for several hours before it needed refuelling. The lights came back up and she turned the torch off and put it in her pocket.

She stuck her head through the prep room doorway. "Stay here. I'll just take a look around and see what's going on. Hang on to Chilli for me." She saw Charlie open her mouth to protest. "Please." She turned and left before Charlie had a chance to get a word out.

Threading her arms through her raincoat sleeves as she ran out the door, she ploughed her way through the curtain of rain to where she thought the sound of rushing water was coming from. It confused her. She couldn't work out why the water would be coming from such a direction. What she saw took her breath away.

Several large trees had fallen near the cabin's upright supports. Two of the supports were broken and another one dangerously compromised. The fallen trees and the single large tree running through the building's centre were effectively the only things holding the front of it up. The cabin had a somewhat drunken lean to it. The sound of water was due to the fallen trees, having created a dam effect on the distended creek. The raging water was now tearing a new diverted pathway straight through the koala pen currently housing her two residents, and down into the teenage joeys' paddocks. She spun on her heel and ran back to the house. She and Charlie needed to get everyone moved to higher ground or they'd be trapped and would be washed away.

"Charlie! Charlie! Get your boots on!"

Charlie stuck her head out the door just as Pip ran up the ramp and straight into the prep room, leaving a trail of water behind her on the floor. She grabbed two koala crates and lined them with towels while Charlie sat on the floor and laced up her boots. "Trees have come down and the water has been redirected. It's flooding the koala pen and the teenage joeys' yards. We have to move them. *Now*."

"Shit." Charlie put her coat on and grabbed the second crate. "Right behind you."

They raced down to the koala pen. The water had completely obliterated one of the pen walls. They ran straight through to the shelter. A foot of water swirled at its base. After a bit of quiet consoling, Lucille crawled into Charlie's arms easily enough. Pip had to monkey up one of the poles to get to Alinta. With limited eyesight, the noise was distressing the koala and she had climbed to the highest point of the shelter. Pip murmured to her as she inched ever closer. Despite the urgency, she talked nonsense to Alinta for several minutes until she was calm enough to allow Pip to manoeuvre her off the pole and onto her shoulder. Pip sucked in a quick breath as Alinta's sharp claws pierced through her coat and T-shirt, and into her skin.

Pip was pleased to see Charlie was able to put Lucille into the crate and secure the lid. Charlie squatted down and opened up her raincoat, spreading it over the crate in an attempt to try to keep the worst of the rain from wetting the small, terrified beast.

"You need a hand getting down?" Charlie squinted at her as water ran into her eyes.

"No. All good. Can you open up Alinta's crate for me, please?"

Pip shinnied down the pole, still murmuring to Alinta. She bent over until her face was mere inches off the top of the crate. Pip felt every ounce of the koala's weight in the claws she had embedded into her. Charlie stepped close and carefully disengaged the koala's claws from her skin and helped her ease Alinta down in to the crate.

"Up to the prep room?"

Pip nodded. Despite the seriousness of the situation she couldn't help but think of all the animals they were collecting and grinned wryly. "Yep. Gonna be a regular Noah's bloody ark soon."

"Ha!" Charlie lined the crates up side by side. "Don't you need to have two of everything?" She took the front handles of both crates and left Pip to grab the handles at the backs. Together they ferried the animal boxes up to the house.

Pip groaned. "Dear God. Don't say that out loud. I don't want to be responsible for the smell and the massive clean-up afterwards if we get two of everything."

Charlie laughed. "I don't know how Noah did it. All that poop lying about. The smell. Standing in it. Hey! I wonder if Noah was taller when he finished with the ark. Maybe you could—"

"Don't even *think* it, Stretch. Just shut up and keep lugging these babies. Smart-arse." Pip couldn't help but laugh with Charlie. They were in the middle of a flood, and laughing together again. It felt good.

They set the koalas off to one side in the room. Pip made sure the lids were secure. "We'll put some leaves in with them later, when things calm down a bit. But they'll be right for the minute."

Charlie brushed at the wet hair hanging in her eyes. "The joeys next?"

"Yep."

"Do you have a plan in mind?"

"It's too wet for the quad runner. We're never going to catch them. Not without hurting them and us, so we're just going to have to herd them on foot. We'll open up some gates so they can make their way up here to the house and close off the gates closer to the water so they don't go back down until it's safe."

"Do we take anything?"

Pip chewed her lip as she thought for a moment. "Some rope and the torches."

Charlie looked around the room. Pip wondered what she was thinking. "What about if we tear up these rags and tie them along the length of the rope? We could stretch the rope out between us. It might just help us in herding them up. Create a kind of visual wall."

Pip grabbed the rags on the bench and handed them to Charlie. She reactively kissed Charlie on the cheek and grinned. "Brilliant plan." They set to tearing up the rags and tying them along its lengths at spaced intervals. It only took a few minutes. Pip looped the finished rope up and slung it over her shoulder. "Ready?"

Charlie threw her a half grin, half grimace. "And to think I was just starting to dry out. Come on, let's do this."

They trotted down to the pen, propping gates open as they went. The bottom half of the paddock was already submerged and swelling as the volume of water continued to build. The water's force swept trees and branches along with it. Pip pointed to the edge of the waterline.

"Let's start here and work our way up. Just be careful of the trees and stuff coming down the waterline." Pip had to yell to be heard above the sound of the water, which slapped and boiled as it ate its way along the new causeway.

Charlie gave her a thumbs-up and grabbed one end of the rope. She proceeded to walk and stretch the line from Pip, who went in the opposite direction. They started in the far corner nearest the waterline and slowly edged up towards the mob. They shined and waved their brightly lit torches and catcalled to encourage the teenage joeys to move uphill to safety and away from them and the water. All was going to plan until the youngest of the joeys panicked and broke ranks. In pure fear it changed direction and bolted for the far corner, back towards Charlie and the waterline.

Pip watched as Charlie anticipated where the joey was headed. She dropped the rope line and ran with arms outstretched to try to herd it back away from the water, and towards the fence line leading up to the rest of the mob. But the terrified joey wasn't convinced and it jumped into the water, with Charlie in hot pursuit.

Pip finished herding the rest of the joeys past the gate line and loosely latched it shut. They seemed content to wait and she ran back down.

Charlie had managed to grab the joey by the tail and was dragging it out backwards through the water. She turned and, despite it's struggling, steered the roo back to face the mob. She was almost out of the water when a tree hurtled down from off the rocks and straight for her.

Without hesitation, Pip ran towards Charlie, yelling, trying to warn her of the tree. But it was obvious Charlie couldn't hear her over the hiss and boil of the tumultuous water. With barely twenty feet between them, Charlie looked up at her just as the tree hit her from the side and lifted her off her feet. For a small second of time Charlie was airborne. A look of astonishment etched on her face for just an instant before she fell back and disappeared under the swirling surface of the water.

"Charlie! *Charlie!*" Pip screamed until she thought her throat would bleed. She ran alongside the waterline. She caught flickers of Charlie's torch and flashes of the bright yellow raincoat tumbling and twisting in the water.

She ran until she thought her lungs would burst. Charlie's head finally broke the surface in front of a large tree that lay across part of the creek. Pip gasped in relief. Charlie's coat snagged on one of its branches and she jerked to a sudden halt. The rage of water buffeted her body as it desperately tried to rip her off the hook and reclaim her.

"Hold on, I'm coming. Hold on, Charlie." Pip sobbed and gathered loops of the rope over her shoulder as she ran towards the log. She ran headlong into the water, fighting to keep upright until she crashed against the base of the log. She climbed up and crawled along its length until she was level with Charlie.

"Charlie! Charlie, are you all right?"

"Wha?" Charlie was barely conscious. A cut high up on her hairline bled profusely down the side of her face.

Pip grabbed under her arms and tried to pull her free. But the force of the water had her wedged in tight against one of the upper branches. She needed to secure Charlie so that if the branch gave way she wouldn't be swept further down the river.

Pip looked frantically about. A large branch from an old stringy bark gum rooted strongly on dryer ground hung over the newly created waterway. She followed the branch with her eyes. It was right above them. She sat up and removed one of her boots and tied it to the opposite end of the rope to use as a weight. She swung the rope back and forth several times and released it in an upward motion, trying to hook the line on the overhead branch. It missed and fell into the water. She retrieved the line and started again. Several more attempts failed miserably before she succeeded. The line dangled off the sturdy overhang. She tied one end off around Charlie's waist and proceeded to use the tree and her weight to lift Charlie up and free of the downed log. At first there was little movement, but bit by bit, her teeth gritted, her arms and shoulders straining until she thought they would burst, Charlie's body began to sway in the water, the liquid fingers reluctant to release her. With a guttural scream, Pip clenched her jaw, wrapped the rope tighter around her wrists and hands, and pulled with everything she had. The rope bit into her skin. The pain gave her strength. Half of Charlie's body came free of the water and bobbed in mid-air. The rushing water made Charlie's bottom half dance around like a macabre puppet in the current.

She couldn't loosen her grip on the rope and risk dropping Charlie back into the water. Securing the line against her waist, Pip walked back over the log until she found an anchor point and tied Charlie off. She scrambled back along the length of the log and slipped into the water beside Charlie, using her body to shield Charlie from other debris coming down with the rapids. She threaded her fingers into Charlie's coat, barely registering her torn hands and wrists, red and raw from the rope burns. She wrapped her arms and legs around Charlie and looked about to see what other options they had.

Secure for the minute, Pip dropped her head onto Charlie's chest. A sob escaped her lips as she wept in temporary relief. She pulled Charlie's inert body closer.

Charlie coughed and groaned.

Pip's head snapped up. "Oh, sweetheart. You're okay. It's okay. I've got you." She released Charlie's jacket and stroked her face. "Open your eyes for me, love. I need you to wake up for me."

Something big smacked into her right hip and buttock. She grunted in pain. "C'mon love. I need your help here." Charlie's head lolled and one eye cracked open to blink, glassy and unseeing. Pip tapped her on the cheek lightly. "Charlie. Open your eyes. We need to get out of here and I need you awake. C'mon, sweet."

With a groan and shake of her head, Charlie gifted her with a two-eyed bleary look. "What happened?"

Pip's heart swelled and she couldn't help but smile through her tears. "We got a bit wet, love."

❖

Charlie tried to make sense of what had happened. Pip's voice sounded far off in a tunnel, yet she was comforted by her tone and the arms wrapped around her. She blinked hard and after a few moments she was able to focus. Mud smeared Pip's face, broken only by clean tracks coming from the corners of her eyes.

"Are you okay?" Charlie reached up and wiped Pip's cheek with her thumb.

"Yes," Pip said, sobbing and laughing with relief at the same time. "Most importantly, are you okay?"

Charlie looked around her. "I think so. Why are we sitting in the middle of the creek?"

Pip laughed and shook her head. "I'll explain later over a hot cup of tea. Do you think you can walk?"

"I'm not sure. Give me a minute and I'll try."

Pip looked upstream over her shoulder and suddenly stiffened. "Charlie, you need to try! Quickly!"

"Why? I don't think I can yet."

Pip put her hands under Charlie's arms and pulled. "Come on. It's not safe. We need to move. *Now*." She quickly fumbled with the knotted rope around Charlie's waist.

Charlie peered in the direction she'd seen Pip look, but couldn't see anything but a few brown branches seemingly fighting the water, but heading straight for them. Her eyes grew wide. Branches didn't move like that. "Oh my God. Are those—?" Charlie pushed up on her feet, which only tightened the knots Pip was pulling at.

"Don't say it. Please don't say it. I know what they are." The knots finally loosened and Pip turned Charlie around. "Go, go, go, fuck, fuck, fuck."

Charlie tried to scramble onto the log she'd been leaning against. Her body was heavy from her drenched clothes, her feet leaden from water-filled boots. "I can't."

Pip put both her hands on Charlie's butt cheeks and pushed. Hard.

Charlie nearly plunged into the water on the other side, but managed a death grip on a branch sticking high in the air. "Pip, come on!" She leaned down and grabbed Pip's collar and yanked with all her might.

The two deadly brown snakes slapped against the log and tried to get purchase enough to get on.

Pip screamed and scooted as close to Charlie as she could get.

Charlie held on as Pip nearly climbed on top of her.

One of the snakes managed to get a third of its body onto the log. Charlie and Pip screamed together. They had nowhere to go.

The second snake curled around the first and the two struggled to get out of the rushing water. But the weight of both proved too much. They suddenly lost their grip and the water claimed them. They were gone in an instant.

Charlie looked at Pip for reassurance, which quickly turned to amusement. Pip's face had gone ashen and her eyes were as big as saucer plates. "Are you okay?"

"No," Pip squeaked.

Charlie started to laugh and then confined it to a series of snorts by biting her lip.

"Are you seriously laughing?" Pip's voice was still high.

Charlie doubled over and laughed. She felt Pip's hand on her back and started to cry. She forced herself to stop because her head hurt like hell. Blood from the cut mixed with water and ran into her mouth. She spat twice, stood upright on weak legs, and put her arms around Pip. "Let's get out of here."

❖

The trek back to the house was slow and arduous. The pelting rain and slick mud made each step difficult. They were both physically and emotionally drained. Neither had the energy for another shower, so for the time being they simply stripped their wet gear off and donned heavy robes.

Each nursed a cup of hot tea and rested side by side on the couch.

"Christ, my head hurts." Charlie closed her eyes and leaned her head back. She gingerly fingered the wound dressing Pip had put on her.

"You've probably got a concussion. Let me see your eyes."

Charlie carefully twisted her neck to look at her. Pip's eyes were bright and glossy which made Charlie smile.

Pip skimmed her fingers over Charlie's jawline and looked from one eye to the next. "They look equal, but I wouldn't rule it out. You clobbered your head pretty hard."

"Can I ask you something?" Charlie bit her lip to keep from laughing.

"Mm."

"Which were you more scared of? Losing me or those god-awful snakes?"

"You, of course." Pip paused. "But those bloody things were a close second." Pip shivered.

Charlie patted Pip's leg. "You know when the python came into the cabin?"

"Won't forget that soon." Pip chuckled.

"You know I was scared witless. But you. I remember thinking that you were the bravest soul I'd ever met." Charlie frowned. "And now…"

"Nuh-uh. I'm not afraid of much. Except snakes. They scare the bejesus out of me." Pip snorted softly. "Terese wanted me to take the snake course. Thought it might help me deal with the fear. But I told her, unless you can claim underwear, I'm not doing it. I'm too reactive. I'd spend the whole time shitting myself."

Charlie giggled. "The python didn't seem to scare you."

"Well, I wasn't about to show a weakness to someone I'd just met *and* someone I was supposed to mentor. And pythons aren't venomous. They can chew on ya, but you won't die from it."

"Uh-huh. My brave little mentor."

"Shoosh."

Pip was silent for a while and Charlie began to think she'd fallen asleep. She fidgeted deeper in the couch, put her head on Pip's shoulder, and sighed contentedly.

"I guess you should really call Kim before we lose service."

Charlie sat up quick. Too quick. She blinked back the pounding in her head and stared at Pip. "What is it with you wanting me to call Kim? Christ, she's not even in the country, let alone having anything to do with what's going on here. And frankly, it doesn't matter."

"But you two—"

Charlie put her fingers against Pip's lips to stop her speaking further.

"Kim and I had a long talk. We were good together for a lot of years. But then we weren't. It's all sorted now. We'll always be good friends. But that's the extent of it."

Pip took Charlie's hand from her mouth, but didn't release it. "I don't understand. I saw you guys kissing by the koala pen."

Charlie shook Pip's hand. "What you saw and what you *think* you saw are two totally different things. Kim merely kissed me on the cheek to thank me for showing her all the animals. If you hadn't walked away so quickly, you would have seen that I never kissed her back. That's why I came after you. I figured you were thinking we had resolved our issues. But you sent me to Yamba. I didn't think you wanted me any more."

Pip shook her head. "That's not true. After the kangaroo incident I realized I couldn't be both your mentor and your lover. I couldn't keep you from getting hurt, and then I saw you two laughing, and touching each other…and the koala thing. It was kind of the last piece. I wanted you to be happy. And I wanted you to be safe. I figured you two were getting back together and that you'd be better off doing that away from here. Away from me."

Charlie raised Pip's hand to her mouth and kissed her knuckles. "I hope you realize now how silly that was."

Pip leaned forward until their foreheads touched. "I'm so sorry. I thought I'd lost you to her. And, well, when I saw you two together, so happy…it was like rubbing salt into a fresh wound."

"Which wouldn't have happened if you had let me explain. I love you, Pip. That hasn't changed. In fact, since you've now saved my life, I love you more."

"Twice."

"Twice what?"

"I saved your life. Twice."

Charlie rolled her eyes. "Yeah. Whatever. Just shut up and kiss me."

Chapter Sixteen

Pip poked Charlie for a third time. "Wake up sleepyhead."

Charlie grumbled and burrowed in deeper against Pip's chest.

"C'mon, Charlie. You need to answer some questions."

"Don't want to."

"I know, but the doctor said I have to keep waking you every hour and checking on you for a bit because of the bump on your head. Come on, sweet, just for a minute, then you can go back to sleep."

"Okay, okay. My name's Charlie Dickerson, I live in Wyoming, when I am not swimming in flooded, snake-infested creeks here in Australia, giving myself a headache. I love you, now can I go back to sleep please?"

Pip laughed softly as Charlie mumbled some more before she closed her eyes and wriggled even further down into her robe. They'd been doing this routine over the past several hours, and much to Pip's relief, Charlie's awareness had improved to the point where she thought she was as good as back to normal, if a little sleep deprived and grumpy. "Hang on and I'll get you some paracetamol for your headache."

Charlie grumbled some more but let Pip get out from underneath her to retrieve the pain relief. Pip grimaced as she stood up and limped into the kitchen. At a quick assessment, about the only things that didn't hurt were her hair and teeth. She figured after Charlie had the tablets it would be safe to let her sleep and she could take a shower, grab something to eat, and maybe catch some shut-eye herself.

Charlie gratefully swallowed the tablets and put her head back down onto the pillows almost as soon as she had finished swallowing. Pip kissed her on the head and made her way to the bathroom.

She turned on the shower taps and let the robe drop to the floor. Stepping in, she began to relax as the warm fingers of water coursed all over her body. She put her hands on the shower wall and leaned against them, closing her eyes for just a moment.

A gasp from the doorway gave her a start. Her eyes flew open and she turned around to see Charlie, a look of horror on her face.

"Jesus, Pip." Charlie stepped into the shower and turned her around. Fingertips whispered across both shoulders and down the length of her back. Charlie's hand stopped to rest on Pip's hip. "Baby, you are black and blue, and purple, and red. Christ. What the hell did you do?"

Pip gave a dismissive half shrug. "Not much."

"Don't give me that. And your hip. Holy hell."

"Mm." Pip had caught sight of her back briefly as she stepped past the mirror on her way into the shower. She knew she was a colourful sight, with her right hip and bottom cheek the most dramatic of all the bruises from whatever the big thing was that hit her when she first jumped in next to Charlie. "I think it was a tree. In the creek."

"When?" Charlie took the soap from the holder and carefully lathered her shoulders, her fingers tentatively circling the puncture marks from Alinta.

Pip swayed slightly. The water and Charlie's hands were putting her sleep-deprived body very quickly into a drowsy state.

"When did you get hit?" Charlie whispered in her ear.

"After I jumped into the water next to you." Pip hummed as Charlie's fingers massaged her scalp as she washed her hair.

"So you were my very own human airbag."

Pip chuckled and moaned gratefully as Charlie rinsed her hair clean of the grime and suds. "Terese always tells me I'm full of hot air. Guess it came in handy."

Pip reciprocated and washed Charlie, being particularly mindful of the cut on her scalp. "You got yourself a nice bump on your head. How's it feel?"

Charlie scrunched her nose briefly. "Just more of a dull ache now. I think those tablets you gave me have finally kicked in."

Pip wrapped Charlie in her arms and let the water flow over them both for a few minutes. She yawned. "How about we hop out and finish that lunch I promised you earlier?" In answer Charlie's stomach rumbled and Pip patted it lovingly. "The jury's spoken, it seems."

Wrapped in a towel, Charlie sat on the edge of the bath while Pip gently applied a new dressing to her cut head. "Remind me to beat myself up more often."

Pip took half a step back, frowned, and looked down into Charlie's smiling face. "Sorry? Come again?"

"Is it an Australian tradition to nurse someone back to health naked? Your medicine is delightfully distracting if it is." Pip giggled as Charlie placed a kiss followed by a light nip between her breasts.

With a last smooth of the tape, Pip tapped Charlie on the nose to signal she was done. "Idiot. Get dressed already, Yank." She softened her comments with a warm kiss to Charlie's lips.

As Charlie dressed, Pip took a blood sugar reading. She calculated a dose and drew it up into a syringe.

"What are you doing?"

Pip took a moment to breathe. For pretty much as long as she could remember, her life had been dictated by her diabetes and other people's reactions to it. Here she was, feeling open and comfortable in front of Charlie. If she had any doubts at all about their relationship, this certainly erased them. She felt at peace and completely… normal. She smiled at the realization. It seemed there had been more than one watershed moment during this flood event. "I'm giving myself a dose of insulin." She pinched a piece of skin on her abdomen and injected the clear liquid.

"Where's your pump?" Charlie trailed her fingers over the bruise where the pump's line had been connected.

"I lost it somewhere. In the creek." Pip vaguely remembered feeling the line tear uncomfortably away when she first jumped into the water and never gave it another thought until now.

"But what's gonna happen? We're cut off. You need another one. Who can we call?"

Pip heard the rising tone of alarm in Charlie's voice. She placed the needle in the sharps container and reached out and drew Charlie into an embrace. "It's okay. I'll just go back to manual injections until a replacement arrives."

"But what if something goes wrong?"

"It won't."

"But it might. What then?"

"Then I've got Chilli." Pip placed her hands either side of Charlie's face. "And I've got you." Pip leaned in and sealed her affirmation of the ultimate trust with a lingering kiss. She sighed contentedly as Charlie wrapped her arms around her and drew her in close. Warm lips met warm lips to dance together in a long awaited kiss.

❖

Although the rain let up significantly the next day, it remained overcast, with heavy clouds threatening more. Water continued to flow downhill from the Clarence River catchment area, causing the creek to rise another two feet before stabilizing three days later.

Pip and Charlie spent the time they were housebound recovering and caring for the animals. The first day it didn't rain, they set about building a makeshift enclosure for the koalas from a couple of trees that had been thrown to the side by the rushing creek. Charlie still nursed a headache, so at Pip's insistence, she wore ear protection from the sound of the chainsaw and allowed Pip to do a lot of the heavy lifting.

"The girls will be so happy to get out of those crates." Charlie handed Pip a bunch of new eucalypt branches, which she carried up a ladder positioned under the shelter.

"I know. They've been amazingly good. That was a good idea to put the front ends of their crates together." Pip secured the feeding tubes on the koalas' shelter post and arranged the new leaves and branches in the tubes.

Charlie smiled. "I figured having Lucille close enough to touch and smell would help Alinta not feel so insecure." Charlie poured fresh water into bowls on the ground.

Pip climbed down and placed a kiss on Charlie's cheek. "I know that having you close helps me." She wrapped an arm around Charlie's waist and pulled her close. "Let's put the girls in their new home."

They carried the two crates in the same fashion they'd done just a few days earlier. Only this time there wasn't a rush to get them out of the storm. The koalas fidgeted inside, making their trek arduous because Charlie and Pip had to keep compensating for the shifting weight.

"You'd think they knew where they're going." Charlie grunted as she adjusted her grip.

"I think they're excited to be out in the fresh air." Charlie felt a tug on the crates behind her. "Hey, Stretch, don't walk so fast. My legs are half the length of yours."

Lucille grunted from inside her crate. It was a low-pitched sound that Charlie had never heard before.

"Is Lucille all right? I've never heard her make that sound." Charlie glanced under her left arm.

Pip chuckled. "You wouldn't have. It's a mating call. She's just letting the local male know she's back in residence. Koalas have an extra pair of vocal cords outside of the larynx. It's where the oral and nasal cavities connect. That's how they can make such low-pitched calls."

Charlie laughed.

"What's so funny?"

"Based on those high-pitched squeals on the log the other day, I guess I won't hear anything like that from you." Charlie laughed again at her own joke.

"Oh, you're so funny. If I remember correctly, you did some screaming yourself."

"Loud, yes. High pitched, no. I can't make my voice go that high."

Pip snorted, which made Charlie chuckle all the more.

They set the crates down next to the enclosure. Charlie unscrewed the bolts holding the top of Lucille's crate while Pip hopped over the enclosure wall. Lucille blinked at her and then raised her arms. This ask to be picked up always made Charlie smile adoringly at the koala. She knew it was a rare gift on offer and appreciated it even more. Charlie picked Lucille up under the arms and handed her to Pip, who settled her on a branch. Happy, Lucille grabbed onto a eucalyptus branch and started stripping the leaves off. Charlie murmured quietly to Alinta while she opened her crate the same way so the koala would stay calm as she passed her across to Pip.

Pip joined Charlie and they stood watching the koalas feed.

"It seems weird not to be getting rescue calls, doesn't it?" Charlie rubbed Pip's back.

"Enjoy the peace and quiet, love. Trust me, it'll start with a vengeance again as soon as we get phone service back and people can get back on the roads."

Charlie looked around at the mud and grooves the water had made. "We've a lot of work to do getting the cages back to where they can safely house animals." She spied the cabin through the trees. No more damage had been done, but it still sported a lean from the broken supports. "What are you going to do about the cabin?"

Pip looked in the cabin's direction. She let out a deep sigh and frowned. "I don't exactly know right now. One thing's for sure though, I don't want anyone to stay in it at the moment."

"Does that mean I'll have to keep shacking up with you at the house?"

"You okay with that?"

Charlie grinned. "Absolutely."

They introduced Big Bird to his perch in the shed later that afternoon. The dimensions were suitable for his current stage of recovery. Pip had a bigger, taller raptor-suited aviary that Charlie could transfer him to where he could fly and regain his strength and fitness when the time was right.

"While you feed him, I'll start feeding the joeys. I'll leave Squeak for you."

Charlie swirled the frozen mice in warm water. "Okay. I won't be long."

Once Pip had walked a safe distance away, Charlie slipped the hood off the eagle's head. He yawned once and stretched his wings as if he'd just woken. He immediately spotted his meal and chirped, demanding to be fed.

"Hold on. It's coming, it's coming."

"So is Christmas," a voice said from outside.

Charlie poked her head around the corner and smiled brightly. "Terese!" She put the forceps down, rushed to Terese, and wrapped her in a big hug. "What the heck are you doing here?"

"The way the weathermen in Sydney were talking, it sounded like you had yourselves a mini Armageddon here. From what I've seen, they weren't too far off. Anyway, when I couldn't get in touch with either of you, I got progressively more worried."

"You didn't have to come all this way. The phones will be back soon."

"Well, what I need to talk to you about couldn't wait. So I called Pip's friend, Jodi, to see if she'd heard anything from here, which she hadn't. So then we both got unstrung."

"Are the roads open? We haven't had a chance to go out and see. We've had some things to deal with here."

"Not for the most part. But, bloody hell, I don't think there's much Jodi's truck can't get through. She's a bit of a nutter behind the wheel." Terese peered at the bandage on Charlie's head. "You can tell me later all about what happened to put that bandage on your head."

"It's a story." Charlie rolled her eyes.

"I'm sure it is." Terese looked around. "Pip?"

"She's good. In the prep room feeding the joeys. Go on up. I'll just be a minute."

Terese gave Charlie another hug and turned to go.

"You said you have something to talk to me about?"

"Now that I'm here, and I know you're both safe, we can talk about it over dinner."

After they'd eaten dinner and the dishes were washed and in the drainer, they each nursed a glass of wine while sitting on the lounge. Pip had brought out the big brandy glasses so they wouldn't have to move often for refills.

Charlie and Pip took turns regaling Terese with accounts of the storm. When they finally sobered, more from their laughter than the effects of the wine, Terese set her glass down and rummaged around in the overnight bag she'd brought.

She pulled out several pairs of lacy underwear, much to Charlie's and Pip's amusement, and a bra. "Aha! There it is. I knew I packed it by the important stuff." She stood up and handed an envelope to Charlie.

"What's this?" Charlie set her glass down on the floor next to her.

"Open it up."

Pip leaned closer as Charlie slid her thumb under the envelope flap. She removed an official looking piece of paper with the Australian Department of Immigration insignia on it.

Charlie looked at Terese with raised eyebrows. "This has your signature on it."

"Yes, it does. I pulled some strings and got your visa adjusted. So instead of a twelve month stay, it's twenty-four."

"Oh, my."

Terese put her finger up. "But…and isn't there always a but? Probably more a pain in the arse than anything."

"Terese!" Pip and Charlie said at the same time.

"Yes?" She looked at her finger and seemed to finally remember what she was going to say. "Oh. Yes, sorry. But if you want to stay any longer than that, you have to submit a formal application to Immigration."

Charlie looked at Pip and pulled her into a tight bear hug. Her heart was nearly bursting. "Babe. I can stay. If you'll have me."

"Charlie, I—"

Pip was interrupted by the sound of her pager going off. "Service is back on." She touched a button and the screen lit up. "Uh-oh. Immediate urgent rescue." She flashed Charlie a grin, which Charlie mirrored. "Terese, we gotta run."

About the Authors

Mardi Alexander:

Mardi lives on a farm high up on the mountain tablelands of the Great Dividing Range in New South Wales along with her partner, a myriad of cats and dogs, and prerequisite farm animals. Her greatest frustration remains that neither she nor anyone else has been able to create the perfect water pump that never breaks down.

When not working full time, Mardi is also a firefighter, firefighting instructor, and a member of a local wildlife rescue service looking after orphaned, sick, and injured native Australian animals.

A finalist in the Golden Crown Literary Awards with her debut book *Twice Lucky*, Mardi delights in sharing the richness of Australian culture and heritage in her works.

Laurie Eichler:

Laurie Eichler holds a degree in natural resources conservation and outdoor recreation. She has worked with animals (wild and domesticated) her entire life, including several years spent in the veterinary field and equine industry at training and breeding facilities in New York, Pennsylvania, and Michigan.

She is an avid outdoor enthusiast, whose activities include horseback riding, hiking, kayaking, bird-watching, photography, and one of her favorite pastimes, walking with her pack of canines.

Now a permanent resident of Australia, she is involved in rescuing and rehabilitating native Australian wildlife in northern coastal New South Wales. She's still looking for that first cattle-mustering experience in the Outback.

Books Available from Bold Strokes Books

A Lamentation of Swans by Valerie Bronwen. Ariel Montgomery returns to Sea Oats to try to save her broken marriage but soon finds herself also fighting to save her own life and catch a murderer. (978-1-62639-828-3)

Freedom to Love by Ronica Black. What happens when the woman who spent her lifetime worrying about caring for her family, finally finds the freedom to love without borders? (978-1-63555-001-6)

House of Fate by Barbara Ann Wright. Two women must throw off the lives they've known as a guardian and an assassin and save two rival houses before their secrets tear the galaxy apart. (978-1-62639-780-4)

Planning for Love by Erin Dutton. Could true love be the one thing that wedding coordinator Faith McKenna didn't plan for? (978-1-62639-954-9)

Sidebar by Carsen Taite. Judge Camille Avery and her clerk, attorney West Fallon, agree on little except their mutual attraction, but can their relationship and their careers survive a headline-grabbing case? (978-1-62639-752-1)

Sweet Boy and Wild One by T. L. Hayes. When Rachel Cole meets soulful singer Bobby Layton at an open mic, she is immediately in thrall. What she soon discovers will rock her world in ways she never imagined. (978-1-62639-963-1)

To Be Determined by Mardi Alexander and Laurie Eichler. Charlie Dickerson escapes her life in the US to rescue Australian wildlife with Pip Atkins, but can they save each other? (978-1-62639-946-4)

True Colors by Yolanda Wallace. Blogger Robby Rawlins plans to use First Daughter Taylor Crenshaw to get ahead, but she never planned on falling in love with her in the process. (978-1-62639-927-3)

Unexpected by Jenny Frame. When Dale McGuire falls for Rebecca Harper, the mother of the son she never knew she had, will Rebecca's troubled past stop them from making the family they both truly crave? (978-1-62639-942-6)

Canvas for Love by Charlotte Greene. When ghosts from Amelia's past threaten to undermine their relationship, Chloé must navigate the greatest romance of her life without losing sight of who she is. (978-1-62639-944-0)

Heart Stop by Radclyffe. Two women, one with a damaged body, the other a damaged spirit, challenge each other to dare to live again. (978-1-62639-899-3)

Repercussions by Jessica L. Webb. Someone planted information in Edie Black's brain and now they want it back, but with the protection of shy former soldier Skye Kenny, Edie has a chance at life and love. (978-1-62639-925-9)

Spark by Catherine Friend. Jamie's life is turned upside down when her consciousness travels back to 1560 and lands in the body of one of Queen Elizabeth I's ladies-in-waiting…or has she totally lost her grip on reality? (978-1-62639-930-3)

Taking Sides by Kathleen Knowles. When passion and politics collide, can love survive? (978-1-62639-876-4)

Thorns of the Past by Gun Brooke. Former cop Darcy Flynn's heart broke when her career on the force ended in disgrace, but perhaps saving Sabrina Hawk's life will mend it in more ways than one. (978-1-62639-857-3)

You Make Me Tremble by Karis Walsh. Seismologist Casey Radnor comes to the San Juan Islands to study an earthquake but finds her heart shaken by passion when she meets animal rescuer Iris Mallery. (978-1-62639-901-3)

Complications by MJ Williamz. Two women battle for the heart of one. (978-1-62639-769-9)

Crossing the Wide Forever by Missouri Vaun. As Cody Walsh and Lillie Ellis face the perils of the untamed West, they discover that love's uncharted frontier isn't for the weak in spirit or the faint of heart. (978-1-62639-851-1)

Fake It Till You Make It by M. Ullrich. Lies will lead to trouble, but can they lead to love? (978-1-62639-923-5)

Girls Next Door by Sandy Lowe and Stacia Seaman eds.. Best-selling romance authors tell it from the heart—sexy, romantic stories of falling for the girls next door. (978-1-62639-916-7)

Pursuit by Jackie D. The pursuit of the most dangerous terrorist in America will crack the lines of friendship and love, and not everyone will make it out under the weight of duty and service. (978-1-62639-903-7)

Shameless by Brit Ryder. Confident Emery Pearson knows exactly what she's looking for in a no-strings-attached hookup, but can a spontaneous interlude open her heart to more? (978-1-63555-006-1)

The Practitioner by Ronica Black. Sometimes love comes calling whether you're ready for it or not. (978-1-62639-948-8)

Unlikely Match by Fiona Riley. When an ambitious PR exec and her super-rich coding geek-girl client fall in love, they learn that giving something up may be the only way to have everything. (978-1-62639-891-7)

Where Love Leads by Erin McKenzie. A high school counselor and the mom of her new student bond in support of the troubled girl, never expecting deeper feelings to emerge, testing the boundaries of their relationship. (978-1-62639-991-4)

Forsaken Trust by Meredith Doench. When four women are murdered, Agent Luce Hansen must regain trust in her most valuable investigative tool—herself—to catch the killer. (978-1-62639-737-8)

Her Best Friend's Sister by Meghan O'Brien. For fifteen years, Claire Barker has nursed a massive crush on her best friend's older sister. What happens when all her wildest fantasies come true? (978-1-62639-861-0)

Letter of the Law by Carsen Taite. Will federal prosecutor Bianca Cruz take a chance at love with horse breeder Jade Vargas, whose dark family ties threaten everything Bianca has worked to protect—including her child? (978-1-62639-750-7)

New Life by Jan Gayle. Trigena and Karrie are having a baby, but the stress of becoming a mother and the impact on their relationship might be too much for Trigena. (978-1-62639-878-8)

Royal Rebel by Jenny Frame. Charity director Lennox King sees through the party girl image Princess Roza has cultivated, but will Lennox's past indiscretions and Roza's responsibilities make their love impossible? (978-1-62639-893-1)

Unbroken by Donna K. Ford. When Kayla and Jackie, two women with every reason to reject Happy Ever After, fall in love, will they have the courage to overcome their pasts and rewrite their stories? (978-1-62639-921-1)

Where the Light Glows by Dena Blake. Mel Thomas doesn't realize just how unhappy she is in her marriage until she meets Izzy Calabrese. Will she have the courage to overcome her insecurities and follow her heart? (978-1-62639-958-7)

Escape in Time by Robyn Nyx. Working in the past is hell on your future. (978-1-62639-855-9)

Forget-Me-Not by Kris Bryant. Is love worth walking away from the only life you've ever dreamed of? (978-1-62639-865-8)

Highland Fling by Anna Larner. On vacation in the Scottish Highlands, Eve Eddison falls for the enigmatic forestry officer Moira Burns, despite Eve's best friend's campaign to convince her that Moira will break her heart. (978-1-62639-853-5)

Phoenix Rising by Rebecca Harwell. As Storm's Quarry faces invasion from a powerful neighbor, a mysterious newcomer with powers equal to Nadya's challenges everything she believes about herself and her future. (978-1-62639-913-6)

Soul Survivor by I. Beacham. Sam and Joey have given up on hope, but when fate brings them together it gives them a chance to change each other's life and make dreams come true. (978-1-62639-882-5)

Strawberry Summer by Melissa Brayden. When Margaret Beringer's first love Courtney Carrington returns to their small town, she must grapple with their troubled past and fight the temptation for a very delicious future. (978-1-62639-867-2)

The Girl on the Edge of Summer by J.M. Redmann. Micky Knight accepts two cases, but neither is the easy investigation it appears. The past is never past—and young girls lead complicated, even dangerous lives. (978-1-62639-687-6)

Unknown Horizons by CJ Birch. The moment Lieutenant Alison Ash steps aboard the Persephone, she knows her life will never be the same. (978-1-62639-938-9)